the love fragments

The Love Fragments

Eleni Cay

Chapter 1

'Happy birthday to my beautiful fiancée!' Mark clinked his champagne glass against mine.

He had real champagne, mine was alcohol-free. Still, I felt the blush of red in my face. Our small living room was packed. My friends and colleagues sang, 'Happy birthday to Katie.' Mark and mum sang, 'Happy birthday to Kitty.'

Rooster barked with excitement, his large tail bashing against the wooden floor, his front paws like helicopter skids ready to take off.

Mum carried a giant strawberry cake from the kitchen, all twenty-eight candles of the same size and precisely positioned in the icing on top, burning a small, well-controlled flame.

'Use the bread knife when you cut it. I pre-cut it into twenty slices. See the lines here?'

'Thanks, mum.'

'Happy birthday, Katie,' Lana said as she put a small parcel on the table next to the cake. She sounded suspiciously serious. 'Very proud of you, girl. Three and half years ago you thought you would never walk again. Fast forward to today and you've got a doctorate! Fuck off, Multiple Sclerosis!'

I smiled. I stopped cutting the cake and opened the package. Lana had given me a vibrator. The whole room laughed, except mum. Mark poured me another glass of the bubbly water. 'Ha-ha, a good one, Lana! Dr Kuznetsov and I will try it tonight!'

Lana raised her eyebrows, snatched the pink vibrator from Rooster's mouth and thrusted it into my hands. 'It's for YOU! Scan the QR code, you get access to free videos. It's pretty cool.'

I stared at the vibrator, then picked up the cake knife. The buzzer rang.

Mark answered the door, 'Is that you, Jackie?' Mark stared at a tall blond girl.

'Jackie!' I ran towards her, eagerly abandoning Lana's gift in the living room. 'I barely recognized you!' I gave Jackie a clumsy hug, avoiding her breasts and other fake areas.

'Couldn't get a slot at Timothy's today, so had to do the make-up and hair myself. Took me hours! Sorry I'm late. What did I miss?' She looked so different with the green contact lenses and new hair extensions. But the wobbly walk with her fifteen-centimetre-high stilettos reassured me it was my old good friend Jackie.

'Just cutting the cake. Come in!' I walked her down the short hall from our front room to the lounge. The sparkling dress draped her perfect figure.

'You don't have more guests? Is this some kind of unplugged elopement? I need something bigger for my Insta story!'

'It's all my uni friends, come. I'll introduce you.'

Jackie reluctantly entered the room, picked up one of the canapés, removed the salmon, discarded the bread, devoured the four caper berries. 'I am starving!'

I poured her some mineral water. She took out her stainless steel straw, sipped a bit, reapplied her lipstick, then took a selfie with a cake slice that she didn't touch.

'Everyone looks so nerdy!' Jackie commented loudly enough for my PhD supervisor to turn his head.

'Professor Nicholson, my friend Jackie,' I said, nervously stepping in-between the two. 'Jackie Fox. She is my childhood friend. She works for … for a social media company.'

'Hi, I'm an influencer,' Jackie bowed slightly towards Professor Nicholson.

His mouth dropped half-open, he licked his lips.

Jackie stepped back a little. Professor Nicholson piously folded his hands, but his eyes looked right at the butterfly tattoo in the middle of Jackie's wide-open cleavage.

'Jackie and I went to nursery together,' I threw into the silence but it was met with Professor Nicholson's fart.

Jackie screwed up her face in disgust, controlling herself enough to say, 'Will go say hi to your mum.' She scooted off to the kitchen.

I stayed with Professor Nicholson, thanking him again for the reference letter he wrote for me, both of us pretending we didn't smell the fart.

'Jackie! Sweetheart! What a look!' Mum and Jackie didn't need to be loud for the whole room to stare at them. Jackie was in her element with the glittery, golden dress and red stilettos. She used hashtag #Boring and put a starfish sticker on her Instagram story.

'Is it just heavy make-up or did she get implants?' Lana whispered to me. 'Can't see any scars by her ears but she's way too tall to see close.'

'Just some fillers, I think,' I whispered back. 'Who would like some cake? Last piece left!' I courageously waded through the mini crowd, but it was only Rooster who heard me.

'Shush, Rooster, shush!' Mark put his hand on Rooster's mouth, took a spoon that looked like it had already been used and gobbled down another piece of cake. He leaned to me and whispered: 'When we have kids, there'll be no make-up. And no social media. Deal, Kitty Kat?' he checked that Jackie was still with mum and added in a louder voice. 'I want my kids filter-free.' Rooster licked Mark's plate clean, Mark put another slice of cake on it.

'Surely one is enough, Mark?' Mum asked, then turned away from Mark and looked at the last piece of cake that I was trying to cut into two parts. She placed her hand on top of mine, 'You have to slice it into even triangles!' she pushed the knife in, still holding my hand, her multiple rings leaving ditches in my skin.

'Just do it yourself, mum.' I pulled my hand away.

'Excuse me?' Mum looked offended.

I quickly added, 'I need to get changed. You know, this mesh fabric is not breathable.' I pointed to the sweat stains forming under my arms.

Mum nodded approvingly. 'Yes, you better do that, sweetheart.'

I liked the dress. It was yellow with half sleeves and a long, fifties-style pleated skirt. I walked into our bedroom, switched on the light.

'Ay!' I jumped. I hadn't been expecting anyone in the room.

'Sorry, didn't mean to scare you.' Jackie was sitting on the double bed, sobbing.

'What's wrong, what happened?' I put my hand on Jackie's arm.

'Elliot broke up with me!'

'Oh, I am so sorry, Jack!' I came closer to the bed, sat down on its edge.

'Such a bastard! Now I have to clean my gallery.'

I looked at Jackie's phone and watched her deleting the photos from her Instagram profile, one by one. There were not that many. Fifteen maybe.

'How long have you guys been together?'

'Ten days.'

'Ten days? Come on, Jackie!' I thought it was funny but Jackie was dead serious.

'Ten days is a LONG relationship. You know how long it took me to pick him? And to edit those photos? He had such a big nose. Such a bastard. He did it just to get more attention on his timeline. But revenge is sweet.'

'What are you doing?' I kept watching Jackie's fingers move around the screen, opening and closing the profiles of hundreds of men.

'I am going to date one of his friends now.'

'You know his friends?'

'No, but he has a public profile, and I can see all his followers. He hasn't blocked me yet. Who shall I pick, what do you think?' Jackie scrolled down Elliot's follower list. 'What about this one? Looks like he is working out a lot … look at that tri-pack …'

'Probably just injections,' I pointed out a photo on his time-line from two months ago. There were no signs of him working out then.

Jackie nodded, scrolled to another guy with a naked chest in his profile photo.

'See this one has gym photos from the past five years. And he's into nutrition and living life to its fullest. Let's see who he followed first … Steve Jobs! Okay, good, this one could be a match!' Jackie tapped on Follow, liked twenty past photos of the guy, sent him a private message with a heart emoji.

'Are you sure about this Jackie? What is the point with this kind of dating …'

Jackie ignored me. She held her phone sideways, shook it vehemently when it didn't register her Like.

'You are worth more than this.' I gently tried to pull Jackie towards the birthday party.

'I know! I'm gonna message another two guys, don't you worry. I am worth more than cheap swaps! Get ready, Elliot! Here comes the payback from your trophy girl!'

'Is this some strange couple challenge or what?' I dimmed the lights and opened the window, hoping Jackie would slow down a bit. But she was on a roll, her fingers furrowing the digital field, me passively watching her from the sidelines. She was jubilant when two of the guys she tagged responded. She followed and unfollowed some accounts, wrote disappearing messages, hid her story from a selection of followers. The rules seemed very complicated to me, but Jackie was in full control.

She was confident and excited as she managed the array of options, controlling what selected people could and couldn't see. She sat next to me, but her mind was in a world that uprooted her from the world I knew.

'Jackie, hun, listen. You are wasting your energy. You could channel it into a *real* relationship. Someone who knows you, someone who cares about you.'

'What do you mean? I gave them access to my full profile. They see my history, hobbies, stuff I like.'

'Then choose one guy and talk to him. Meet him. Like do it properly.'

'I won't make an investment until I am sure. You need to have at least four men for a ranking. You can't climb the ladder if the new boyfriend has no one to compete with.'

'Competitions are always toxic, Jackie. Between couples or within couples. Competitions just lead to someone feeling worthless. Constant comparisons with ex-partners, doubts about what the other one has or doesn't have. Thoughts that leave a scar. You need closure.'

I was talking to myself; Jackie was on her self-appointed mission hunting Likes.

Mark and I had both been single when we met. Neither of us felt jealousy when we got together. He knew about my ex, I knew about his, we both ended those previous relationships on friendly terms. We were in the love game for either a joint win or a joint loss, there was no other rule.

'I really don't think there is any league table in this, Jackie, come—'

'Oh come on, don't be like that naïve Johanna from the *Unplugged Show*! Did you watch the latest episode? Where the wife found out that her husband was following hot girls on Instagram and posting comments about their boobs?'

'I never watched the show.'

'Johanna had the couple in her studio. For anti-porn therapy. I mean, what the fuck! Following hot girls on Instagram is not porn! Besides, generic porn doesn't work anymore, everyone wants it personalized. Get closer to the body. Interact with it.' Jackie tapped on Johanna's profile, showed me a profile photo of a kind-looking woman next to a man. 'I hate her double standards! Look at the profile photo! I mean could she not squeeze their dog into that circle too?! 200k followers. She posts every time a new *Unplugged* episode is out. You preach to unplug when plugged in? I can decide that for myself, thank you very much!' Jackie blocked Johanna's account again.

I heard the clinking of cutlery from the living room. Mum probably started serving the vegetable pâté. I knew Jackie wouldn't eat it. I could see she wore slimming pants, the dress clung super-tight on her completely flat belly with no visible belly button. I wasn't sure how to lure her back to the party. She was busily trading her photos with other singletons, fragmenting her heart, improving Instagram's algorithm. The algorithm was intelligent enough to package people into stocks and Jackie delivered fast with high returns – a loyal customer. She would get cross with me if I interrupted her. And who was I to tell her off anyway? Another moralist à la Johanna? Maybe Jackie needed to get hurt to stop herself. Hurt is baked into the love algorithm with purpose: people pay more attention when they are in pain. When they herd together, it doesn't matter whether they send pink hearts or angry emojis to each other. Love and hate run on the same principles. Same psychology, same design, just a different flow of effects.

Jackie changed her profile status to 'In a committed relationship'.

'How long do you expect this to last?' I asked.

'You don't need to specify that for a status change. Everyone expects regular updates.'

'Not everyone, Jackie. Mark and I have been together for five years now. We are in it for good.' I looked at the white bedding set, thought of lying on Mark's chest, his regular breaths, our long Sunday mornings together. 'We have been through tough times. And are still going strong.'

'Mark looks anything but strong to me. Sorry, but he must be like eighteen stone now. And he is so boring sometimes. I mean, hun, I want the best for you. Do you really want to stay with him? Like you have enough money on your own now, don't you?'

'I would not stay with a man for financial security,' I said, trying to hide my irritability, but my blood pressure was rising.

'No, I know. But I mean like you are healthy again, you don't need him to take care of you. You could date anyone now.'

'Jackie, couples don't stay together because they need each other. They stay together because they want to.'

'I get that. But what do you want from him? Like do you guys have good sex? I mean how often? Like he doesn't strike me as particularly attractive to be honest.'

'Why are you so mean?'

'Mean? Me? I just want the best for you. Mark is so behind, spreading ideas from at least a decade ago, he won't ever catch up! I bet he will soon create a podcast or get an electric milk frother!' Jackie laughed, then tapped on my Instagram profile. 'You have 899 followers now. Let's see. Okay, about half of them are men. Your pool of potential matches is pretty high. You can have higher expectations.'

I wasn't sure whether Jackie was kidding or whether the influencer persona had completely devoured her. We sat on top of the white duvet that Mark and I had snuggled under that morning. He had said I looked like sunshine when I put my fifties dress on, but next to Jackie I felt like a rotten yolk.

I got up, opened my homeopathy kit, put a Gelsemium tablet under my tongue. Jackie's eyes were fixated on the screen. I saw how the social media experiment worked, what its theory of change and impact were. What I couldn't understand was why clever people like Jackie succumbed to cheap gratification for someone else's profit.

'You realize that online dating is a testing arena, not the real playground?' I probed.

'Why are you so serious? Of course I know that. Everything is a game. What do you think of this fella?' Jackie enlarged a photo of a Robert Redford-like man for me to see.

'Profile says he is married! Leave him alone, Jackie. He's got kids. Let's go back to the party. Please.'

'This is his wife. She watched my stories for months and then sent me a follow request. I dismissed it. She can boil inside her little family bubble. If people are so insecure in their relationships, why do they stay in them?'

'Jackie, that's really not on. You are encouraging him to cheat.'

'How? We don't have sex.'

'Emotional cheating. Emoji cheating. I don't know what it is called. But it's wrong.'

'Ah, you are so Puritan about everything! I am not cheating. He is not cheating. We are just exploring the market.'

I adjusted the duvet.

She continued. 'It's like viewing a penthouse for sale, you know? Like we know we can't afford it, but boy is it cool to view the kitchen design! Fantasy plays, nothing more.'

'Property is not the same as a person. And how do you know what his intentions are? He could think he can really date you.'

'Him? No way. A plumber following 450 and only 200 follow him back? He is like waaay out. I breadcrumb guys like him. He won't get more than two seconds per day from me, you can be sure of that!'

I wasn't sure of anything. I got a waft of hydrogen sulphide as I stood up from the bed. It could be my dress, it could be from the kitchen.

'He could be a sixty-year-old pervert! It's so easy to lie online.'

'Everyone above sixty is on Heritage.com, hun. The old ones are not building their future. They are rebuilding their past.'

I looked into Jackie's eyes. Maybe she saw beyond the gratification mechanisms. Maybe she knew more about psychology than I did. And maybe the algorithm knew more about love than either of us. Everything looked so pristine on the platform. There were no signs of hurt. Maybe the algorithm created a place where hearts do not get broken but are created anew.

'So what's the future with these married guys? I mean how long do such online flings last?'

Jackie put her phone down. 'It depends on how immune they are. I can tell by their first reply. Some men get high immediately. They love the change. The ones with cracks in their marriage, you know. I breathe life into them. They become better husbands afterwards.' Jackie looked at me as if I was supposed to reward her. 'Some are quite resistant. The hero types, you know. I tell them how lonely I am, you know, the line from Notting Hill that I am super famous but also, "I'm just a girl, standing in front of a boy, asking him to love her." They protect me from nasty comments, pamper me in their superman arms.'

I listened intensively to every word Jackie said. With no screen between us, Jackie leaned towards me: 'Then the wife finds out and has a breakdown to win him back. Or develops cancer or some kind of illness. He sees her in pain, and his superman instinct kicks in. The superman wants to always protect the weak, you know, so he returns to her.' Jackie's pupils had enlarged, indicating how much she was enjoying the situation. 'I make marriages better. Like in an epic way.'

The Gelsemium left a sugary taste in my mouth. I heard screams of joy from next door, signs of a cake-induced bedlam. Jackie's phone beeped, the battery needed charging. She closed down some apps she had running in the background, turned back to me.

'So this secret service in marriage you offer, what do *you* get for it?' I asked. 'What if he does not return to his wife but wants to be with you?'

'You mean, if he becomes obsessed? I had that several times.' Jackie must have sensed that I saw her as a victim rather than beneficiary of the emotion transactions. She held her hand out to me, then propped her chin in her palm. She said confidently, 'I block them on Insta, and if he stalks me on other platforms, I publicly shame him on my timeline. That generates a lot of interaction actually, you know, people want to help. So, don't worry, I am safe.'

'But he could be genuinely interested in you! You are messing with the guy's head!'

'I can't be responsible for anyone's choices. Like don't cheat on your wife if you can't deal with a rejection! Anyway, stalkers usually come from my Tier 4 category.'

'Tier 4? What is that?!'

'Your ignorance is pretty insulting actually.' Jackie crossed her arms and held them under her chest. 'The Tier system is clearly explained on my profile. Tier 1 is face-free photos. Tier 2 are selfies. Tier 3 recorded videos. Tier 4 live videos. I won't send Tier 4 material unless the guys pay in advance.'

It was all too much for me to process. I wished we could go back to a time with no tiers, back to offline dating or at least back to the party in the next room and sample some of the hummus dips. I spent three hours preparing them and haven't had a single one.

Jackie's phone bleeped again, 'Please charge me,' Siri said.

Jackie showed me her feed full of Likes and notifications, but I had had enough of hearing how she was serving her raw emotions to some desperate men.

'Come on, we've talked a lot now. You need some proper food. Reset your system. Calibrate.'

Jackie's Siri picked up on all my keywords, generating a personalized diet plan for Jackie. The phone was flashing with recommendations for recipe box delivery services.

'Ha! That was quite original, thanks!' Jackie thanked Siri for processing my words.

I looked at Jackie. 'Original as a personalized ad sent by Jackie to her love clients?'

'Now it's you who is being mean! Yes, I send my selfies in a bulk email but I do it per Tiers and the system tailors the messages to individual clients.'

I was beginning to see the logic in it all, the levels of services. The closer a follower got to Jackie, the more they needed to pay to get her authentic side. Bespoke content took her more time to produce so it required more investment from her clients.

I was giving all my content to Mark in private messages – until now it had never dawned on me that I could be sending my photos to several guys in parallel and ranking their responses as Jackie did. I had the same tools as Jackie. I didn't need to become an influencer to see what it feels like to be wanted by many men.

'So what would happen if you were just sending photos to guys privately? I mean without posting anything into the gallery that everyone can see?'

'I would get a massive dip in followers. Nothing is more embarrassing.'

'Maybe those who disappear are not worth having anyway? You can't be expected to be posting something every day?'

'It used to be once per day. Now it's something new every five hours. I can schedule the posts … but I tell you it's a lot of pressure. Imagine having 400k followers breathing down your neck all the time. You have just one boss and are all stressed about it. I have four hundred thousand bosses!'

I heard cutlery rattling again. I wondered whether Mark saved the sweet potato strips as a side dish for everyone or whether he had eaten it all by himself.

'Poor you. Come, I bought low-fat bread for you. It's wholemeal. I thought you'd need the wholeness of someone fully caring for you.' I gave Jackie a fake smile and she smiled back but her eyes were serious. The uncertainty of pleasing diverse and multiple men had splintered her. There were thousands of men interested in selected parts of her, but none was ready to love her as she was, in her entirety. I wanted to help her, to see beyond the digital facades that atomised people into trading platforms.

I gently stroke her hand holding the screen. 'My dear. What about a nice selfie with a sunset in the background? Would that work for your followers? Increase your revenue stream?'

Jackie liked the idea, so I finally pulled off the unbreathable dress and put on my hiking clothes.

We returned to the party, but only Mark stood in the room, devouring the remaining dips.

'Where is everyone?' My tone of voice oscillated between semi-horror and semi-relief. 'Has everyone gone home?'

'Well, the star of the show disappeared, so the guests did too.' Mark swallowed an entire mini courgette. 'Your friends said they had work to do, so they left, but Mrs Weight Watcher is in the kitchen.'

'And you are eating everything to wind up mum even more?' I grabbed the last carrot button.

'Yup!' Mark exclaimed, with a dollop of sour cream dip on his fleshy, round cheek.

'Jackie and I are going to watch the sunset from Dragon Hill. Will take Rooster.'

Rooster jumped at the sound of his name, immediately fetched his lead and carried it towards the front door.

'Wait! Girls only? You are leaving me here alone with *her?*' Mark whispered the last bit, pointing towards the kitchen with a breadstick.

'We're gonna take some selfies for my new profile.' Jackie walked up, wobbling in her stilettos.

'I see. Is that a new profile for one of your six persona?' Mark loosened his belt and pulled out his T-shirt to cover it.

'Are you jealous because yours is tiny?' Jackie looked towards Mark's masculine parts, then pulled out her phone. 'My footprint is huge. And for your information, I make £60,000 per month. Think of what you could buy Katie with that money.'

'Luckily, Katie doesn't believe in sugar daddies.' Mark said as he tried to hug me.

I passed by him on my way to the corridor, shouting 'thanks' to mum. Rooster was getting impatient and began barking, so I quickly put on my old jacket and my new birthday scarf.

'Nice scarf!' Jackie scrolled the scarf fabric in her fingers. 'By the way, your boyfriend has still not grasped the principle of the personal data economy!'

'He has successfully managed to avoid it but they will get him eventually.' I forcefully smiled.

'I will eventually get what?' Mark misheard me. 'Could you explain, Dr Kuznetsov?'

'The splintering of personalities into data points. You share little data, Jackie a lot. You miss out on interactions, Jackie monetises them. Anyway …'

Rooster barked again, I grabbed the lead, wet with his saliva. Jackie took the lift, even though we lived on the first floor.

'Will be back before eight. Need to take my medication a bit earlier today. Love you!' I loudly shut the door, almost catching Rooster's tail and my scarf.

Chapter 2

I CAME HOME LATE. MARK was sitting on the sofa, his eyes fixated on the football match.

'Hi Mark! … Mark! Hello?!'

Mark couldn't hear me with the loud TV on.

'Can you lower the sound?'

'What?' he shouted.

'Well, precisely!' I lowered the volume with the settings on my app. 'Was it okay with mum?'

'She left minutes after you.' Mark grabbed his phone, put the volume app again. 'She didn't finish all the dishes,' he shouted.

'And you didn't bother either.' I sighed and poured some fresh water into Rooster's bowl.

'I didn't bother? I … I … BOTHERED to entertain your bullying mother. I bothered to entertain all your fucking weird nerd friends. I bothered to prepare the party and everything. And this is your thank you?'

'Stop swearing! You are drunk.'

'I don't get drunk after a couple of beers. Is that what your plastic Barbie friend told you? She totally corrupts you! I'm not your slave!'

'Would you stop being so rude about my friends?! And thanks for being so kind on my birthday! You could have asked whether I had a good time at Dragon Hill. Instead you just shout at me!' I slammed the kitchen door.

Mum had stacked up the clean plates on the table, probably having recognized that they did not belong to our cupboards.

I began counting them, praying none was broken and I could return them to the neighbour tomorrow.

My phone bleeped. It was an alert from my bank, prefaced with a birthday wish. My account was in debit, and they would debit thirty pounds per day until I had the account in credit again. I sighed. 'The rich get richer by making the poor poorer … Calm down, Katharina, you need to be calm to keep your MS under control,' I whispered to myself quietly.

'Goaaaal! Yes, yes, yes!' Mark celebrated in the next room. I sighed again. Could he not clean up even once? Not even on my birthday? I began counting the plates again but could not stop thinking that instead of wallowing on the sofa, Mark could play some football himself and be getting into better shape. I began from zero again, trying to stop thinking like my mum.

I sat down to check my emails, but I couldn't focus. I went on Facebook, mindlessly scrolled down my timeline, wondering how different mine must be from Jackie's. My timeline was full of posts about new MS symptoms and coping strategies. Jackie was getting kissing emojis from potential lovers.

I logged out and clicked on 'new' to set up a new account. I scrolled through my photos looking for some semi-naked shots. I, too, could be rolling in a red stream of heart emoticons. Mark would have no idea, and maybe it would make our relationship better. I wouldn't need to meet those guys, just chat with them, just get some compliments that I didn't get from Mark. A bit of thrill to brighten my day, a bit of a high to keep me going.

Rooster ruffed, his nose pointing towards his empty bowl.

'Ah, sorry sweetheart!'

Poor soul, I had completely forgotten to feed him. I gave him a half cup more than usual, compensating for my self-absorption.

I returned to the kitchen table, reopened my laptop, logged into the University Centre's intranet page. I skimmed the News and Community messages, clicked on Data Stories. I would be working with those stories from Monday onwards. Real, data-driven stories about well-being and prevention for people with Multiple Personality Disorder. Our Centre has been specializing in MPD since 2022.

I clicked on the first video. A fifteen-year-old girl was talking to the researcher's camera. 'That's me,' she said in a high-pitched voice. 'That's still me,' she said in a deeper voice. 'That's still me,' she said, putting on a brown wig. 'Still me,' she said putting on a moustache and pulling off the wig. 'Still me,' she said tying a tie into a knot. 'All me,' she said, showing the researcher her multiple Instagram accounts. I shivered at the last scene and pressed pause. What if Jackie had MPD? What if she was one of the thousands who need our Centre's help? The diagnostic tools were not precise enough yet. I shouldn't be guessing from just a few symptoms. Jackie might not feel the different personalities; she might just be acting them out on her online accounts. She might be still okay inside. I pressed play.

'Don't ask me who I am! Don't ask me to verify myself!' The girl in the video screamed as she was taken by police from the health-card ID scanning station.

I stopped the video again, watching as Rooster happily munched his meal. I looked at the girl's blurred face on my screen. I so wanted her to be happy. I so wanted to solve the riddle of MPD. To find out about the triggers, the prevention tools.

Mark slowly opened the kitchen door. Rooster was lying on the floor, Mark sat down next to him and petted him.

'I am sorry, Kitty. It was the booze.'

'Well, don't drink then.'

Rooster raised his head, his belly still on the cold kitchen tiles.

'I'm training for when we go out.'

'You don't have to drink when we go out. None of my friends expect you to drink. I don't expect that either. You know I hate the macho culture.'

'Yeah, you and your leftist feminist ... sorry, I mean, I know you and your friends don't drink ... much ... But my friends do. And I want to hang out with them.' Mark saw my raised eyebrow. 'They are good people. They helped me get my job. You wanted me to get a new job, remember!?'

'So, you have to drink to afford our mortgage?' We both laughed. Mark hugged me. 'What are you up to?' Mark glanced at my open laptop.

'Getting ready for work tomorrow. MPD stuff.' I smiled. I was excited about my new job. I could make the world a better place.

'What was MPD again?' Mark asked as he opened the fridge and served himself a big portion of the remaining vegetable pâté.

I clicked on the definition on our Centre's page and read it aloud to Mark, 'The multiple personality disorder is a mental disorder characterised by an individual's identification with more than three different persona. MPD sufferers do not have any sense of coherent or integrated self. The causes are unknown but extant studies show that children with higher propensity for role play have a higher likelihood for social media self-performances. We also know that the occurrence rates are higher in the Smooth Revolution generation, who grew up with periods of enforced isolation and unregulated personal data economy.'

'Interesting! So hanging out with Jackie is part of your job, right?' Mark finished the pâté, putting his plate inside the sink.

'NO. Jackie is my friend. Your ignorant questions can actually hurt people, Mark.'

'Sorry, sorry. You need to diagnose her first, right?'

'No, I don't. For your information, I have a clear line between my private and professional self.'

'Gosh you are sexy when you speak so seriously! Do you scientists get a high when you find out about something? Like when you know something others don't know?' Mark began to play tug-of-war with Rooster, putting his hand inside Rooster's mouth.

I closed the laptop, put it aside. Mark closed Rooster's mouth, put him on the floor, then opened the kitchen cupboard, emptied a tube of sweeties into his mouth. I stood up, Mark came to give me a quick kiss on the cheek.

'I was just kidding. I know you do serious stuff. I think it's cool what you do … but Jackie I mean seriously she is—'

'Not everyone can manage their choices. That's why some people need help.' I jumped into Mark's sentence but didn't stop him getting a chocolate bar. I sighed, said aloud, 'Some people just don't bother.'

'I *choose* not to bother.' Mark grinned, revealing chocolate on his front teeth. 'I'm just me, all the time. Online, offline. Mostly offline.' He grinned again. 'Blissful ignorance.' Mark caressed his belly. He grabbed another chocolate bar. The bar was the same colour and size as his phone.

'It's not about all or nothing, Mark. You can regulate what you do … online and offline … see here.' I showed my screen to Mark. 'You treat your online stuff as separate from offline and then you wonder why your personalized recommendations are so off-target. If you were more mindful of your movements, you'd get better results. Seriously Mark, don't laugh! You spend hours searching for what I get in seconds.'

'Ah, excuse me, Dr Know-It-All! Even though my apps are a mess, I am still loveable!' Mark moved to pinch me but I withdrew my arm just seconds ahead.

'You have like a hundred apps on about thirty different pages on your phone!'

'Yup! Successfully defeating the idea of smart and speedy use. Won't let the money guys control me!'

'But then it takes you ages to flick through multiple screens!

And you panic when you get an alert that you got a new message because you don't know where to find it.'

Mark held his phone with the screen tilted towards me. He accidently retweeted a Tweet, quickly undid it, Liked it instead. He put the phone down, wiped the sweat from his forehead. He spotted the unfinished pack of biscuits on the table and pulled two out. He saw my look and quickly hid them behind his back.

'Come on, Mark, are you five or what? It's not like I am your teacher scolding you! If you want to drown in your self-soothing bucket, I will not get you back to land. Besides we talked so many times about removing snacks from the kitchen. If you can't handle temptations, remove them. It's that simple,' I said quietly to myself. 'Democracy never works for people with low self-regulation.'

Mark didn't say anything, placed the two biscuits on the table in front of my laptop. I looked into his eyes, they were so similar to Rooster's. Was I really in love with this man?

'Will take a shower.' At least I had that – the shower. I had missed it so much during MS relapses. The shower drops had stabbed me, and there was no gentle touch then. Now, in remission, the drops were the warm hands rocking me to sleep. I tilted my head to drink the water running directly from the showerhead, letting the whole stream run through my core. I let the warm water comfort me, hug me all over, massage my head, caress my arms, cascade over my thighs. I could be crying, I could be bleeding, I could be shouting, the water just ran, and ran, its reliable rhythm soothing all my pains.

I switched off the shower, could hear Mark snoring through the door. I sat on the bathroom's hard tiles, crying quietly. I looked at myself in the mirror, thought of the cheap novellas with women having their breakdown moments on the bathroom floor, wiped my tears, and resolutely got up.

I quietly opened the bedroom door. Mark's snore was loud and regular. Good. I didn't need to put on the lubricating gel. I could put on my favourite body cream and just tuck under the duvet. As I snuggled next to him, he let out a loud snore. My noise cancelling app did not work, I wished I could mute Mark with a single button. I put on my headset with the sea-soothing sounds, closed my eyes.

A neighbour slammed the entrance door. Rooster began barking, louder than Mark's snore.

'Shush, Rooster!' Mark said two seconds after Rooster stopped. 'We will need to have him on the balcony when we have a baby. He could wake her up.' Mark muttered and extended his arm towards my breasts. I could barely breathe when he climbed on top of me. He got very sweaty too, I had to take another shower and change the bedsheets afterwards. When I came back to the bedroom, Mark was rooted in the deep unconsciousness of his non-lucid dreams again. I was counting sheep, desperately trying to fall asleep. I was too excited about the prospect of meeting my new colleagues the following day. I wished to expand my thinking to new horizons. The only expansion Mark wished for was having a baby.

I counted 1,023 sheep, then went to take another shower. The water ran over my face. I was not crying. I held onto the rectangular enclosure of the shower cubicle feeling like a small white-handed Gibbon in a zoo of extinct dreams. I was growling and screaming with the water in my mouth. Mark didn't hear any of that.

Chapter 3

Mum: Your father cheated on me, and I am filing for divorce.

I re-read the message.

I re-read it again.

I stared at the message for a good ten minutes, then walked out of the meeting room and rang mum up. Her voice was agitated. 'Marie told me.'

'Who is Marie?'

'My friend, Marie? You met her at the garden centre last September. She works for the infection tracking people. She saw that Dad and that girl, or shall I say some Mrs Bower, had spent lots of time together. And had often been geographically close to each other.'

'What? The infection-detection app is supposed to be completely private!'

'Yes, Marie was dismissed.'

'I am so sorry, mum.'

Mum began crying, she was too distressed to talk more, I hung up. I was furious with dad. After such a long marriage, was it worth it to destroy our family? And I was furious with Marie. Her job was to detect deadly viruses, not the love virus. I looked Mrs Bower up online. She worked for the local bakery.

'So average looking!' I said to Lana.

Lana was my new colleague. We shared the office at the end of the Centre's long corridor.

'True! And what a naïve cow that Marie. Like why would you ruin two people's lives AND lose your job? Some people are so obsessed with telling the truth that they forget the consequences. What does your dad's new catch look like?' Lana bowed over to see Mrs Bower's profile photo.

'Ehm, yeah, I guess.' I couldn't process what mum had told me. It sounded like a romcom, not my parents' love story. 'I thought they would be married, you know, forever.'

'Well, that's naïve, too.' A spider scuttled across Lana's desk, but she showed it no mercy, killing it with her fist and scrapping off the blood with a sticky note.

'Men should just tie their dicks into knots! My parents divorced when I was a baby. Two months old, I think. Mum has remarried three times since.'

Lana walked towards the window with a duck-style gait. She had a symmetric face, large breasts and wide hips. She was thin but when she walked she looked heavy as if each step was supposed to shape the world.

'I thought that my mum and dad were happy together … I mean I never saw them argue much. Dad was working all the time, mum was keeping the house in order. I never thought they would separate.'

'Marriage has never been beneficial for women. It's time to destroy that institution for good!' Lana said as she raised her arm in protest, revealing a colourful rainbow tattoo on her arm.

I pulled my little diary from my purse. I always carried it with me. I crossed out the title *Today's Symptoms*. I wrote:

Marriage. Marriage is an old institution with strange rules. People swear in front of witnesses to follow the boundaries established by their predecessors. When they cross the borders, the institution punishes them.

Lana stood by her desk, fiddling with the table that was supposed to be adjustable, watching me. 'People are very loyal to institutions but institutions are not loyal to individuals. Remember that. It will serve you well in this job.'

I nodded. I closed my diary and reopened Mrs Bower's profile. 'I don't get it. Like, what does Dad see in her? She is ugly. A fat baker! Mum said it has been going on for three years! Three years lying to our faces!'

'Maybe he needed time to figure out his strategy. You know, keep your mum quiet in the cushiony-lie. Maybe your mum was too weak. If she collapsed, everyone would attribute it to him, so he was protecting everyone. Some men are like that. Hunters-protectors. Primitives.'

'Mum will never forgive him.' I was suddenly queasy. I knew mum would not forgive him. Three years was a long time. Three years of lies. Maybe dad had been texting 'Little Mrs Baker' when we were on family holiday in Turkey. Or maybe when we had been sitting at the table for Christmas dinner. How could he do that? *My* dad. My hero. Now a cheap figurine who needed someone to cook and look after him.

I googled random family therapy sites. One site stated: 'Most cheaters are not self-aware enough to understand that their actions cause ineradicable pain.' I looked towards Lana, she finally finished adjusting the table. The vintage #MeToo bumper sticker fell off the noticeboard above her desk. She picked it up. I returned to Mrs Bower's profile.

'Look at her, look how fat she is! She only has seven LinkedIn connections! Her profile says she's been working in the same bakery for twenty-three years. What a boring life. What does dad see in her? I don't get it. Look at my mum. She is a hundred times prettier!'

Lana reluctantly came closer and looked at the two photos on my screen.

'She looks very similar to your mum, to be honest …' Lana said as she served herself some coffee. '… which … makes sense.' Lana added some sugar into her cup.

'It doesn't make sense to me at all!'

'She looks similar to your mum. That's why your mum is asking for divorce. That's why your dad is not going to apologize. It wasn't a fling. It was a real thing.'

'What??'

'You know, the same type. People fall for the same types. Unconsciously. Your mum will find a fella who is similar to your dad, you'll see.'

I had no desire to see that. I wanted to pretend that Dad had never cheated. I wanted my parents to be still together. I didn't want to hear the narrative Lana was sketching. She poured some coffee into my cup. I said thank you even though I disliked instant coffee.

'Mum does not deserve this.' I sipped the black coffee, my throat constricting at the bitterness but I swallowed. I looked towards the office window. Some shouting noise filtered in from outside. I got up and checked that the window was closed. I looked at the football stadium next to our Centre's main building. Men were shouting at each other as they were kicking the ball around. Bright lights shone on the pitch, glinting off the tall wire fence. There were no lights, no tall fences around the ballet school next door. I wrote in my diary:

The differences in how men and women release energy are visible everywhere. An unfair urban and biological design.

'You write every thought down? I guess that's what makes you a good scientist, right? I do that sometimes too. Like when I see the patterns, the bigger themes. It's fucking amazing how predictable these things are. Your mum can see your dad didn't get an upgrade and feels even more hurt because his choice degrades her. She might go out to find a loser to return the wrong. That will unleash your dad's revenge. Maybe he will have a kid with this Mrs Bower. A little Katie, ha-ha-ha.'

'Dad is sixty-five.' My words froze Lana's laughter. She moved to my desk to give me more coffee. I pulled my mug away.

'Look, it's between your mum and him and that woman. Don't put yourself between them, okay? There'll be lots of toxic resentment until they fully separate. I've seen it many times. Don't let them drag you into it. A new sibling is a good thing.'

'I don't think dad will father more children, honestly.'

'Clint Eastwood had a daughter when he was sixty-six. You never know.' Lana winked, but I was staring at the screen, searching all of the social media channels for Mrs Bower.

'Look, she has a son! And grandchildren! Two! No, three! Three grandchildren!' I was furiously tapping on the grandchildren's private accounts.

'Of course she has kids. Did you expect her to be virgin at sixty or what? Look, girl, you need to pull yourself together. Men do this to women, okay? And women do this to men. Cheating happens in every relationship that lasts longer than one Christmas. It will happen at some point to you and your fella too. So take it as a lesson and relax. And work on a Plan B for your marriage. What's your Plan B by the way?'

'Mark and I are not married.' Lana gave me a surprised look so I explained: 'We were engaged but I had an MS relapse a week before the wedding … so we had to cancel. The insurance only gave us half of the money back. It was so embarrassing … I mean … very embarrassing. For us and the guests and everyone involved. I don't want to talk about it.'

'I see. But you still need a Plan B! Who do you fancy besides Mark? Is it a her or a him?' Lana insisted on an answer.

I was wiggling around in discomfort, pounding on the virtual keys as if it was an old desktop keyboard. Lana propelled herself on the office chair to the window. I thought she would open the window and fly off into space. Our whole conversation was so surreal to me that nothing would surprise me.

'I have no Plan B. Mark and I don't need a Plan B,' I said, sitting straight in my office chair, trying to keep my feet on the ground, pushing against the chair's rolling wheels.

'Don't be so sure of that, Girl! Crushes are always serendipitous. But change of topic. Have you booked your hotel for the conference?'

'No, not yet.'

'You wanna share a room? Double occupancy is way cheaper than two single rooms. New York is ridiculously expensive …'

'That's a good point. Okay then.' I managed to think of something other than dad's affair for half an hour while I booked the hotel and flights with Lana. The conference was the biggest event in the academic year with all top scholars attending. The Centre was happy to cover all the travel costs because the acceptance rate for submitted papers was only 8 per cent. I only got a slot for showing a poster, but I could present it in person, which counted more than a virtual presentation. The tough peer review process strengthened the credibility of my work.

'Next year you'll be automatically selected as a reviewer. Your name is part of the system now,' Lana said. I smiled but then she added: 'Part of a system that determines promotions. Salaries and dinner lists.'

I worked overtime but felt guilty that I did not make as much progress on the paper as I was supposed to. Mum rang me as soon as I finished work.

'You mustn't tell anyone that I told you about it.'

'Mum, people will find out eventually. You said Marie was already sacked, so what's the point of keeping it secret?'

'Your father doesn't want to sell the house. He wants to get it valued at a lower price so that he pays out less. He's accusing me of exploiting your feelings against him.'

'Come on, mum, I am not ten anymore. I have your side of the story and dad will tell me his version.'

'There are no two sides here, you understand? He lied! Lied and lied and lied! He destroyed everything we ever had together,' mum sobbed loudly. I waited a while, then she continued. 'He damaged our reputations, he divided our family!'

I stopped the video and put mum on audio only. I couldn't watch her exhausted face, her tears disappearing into her deepening wrinkles, the ever-expanding bags under her eyes. The nice moments she and dad had lived together for over twenty years seemed completely submerged, her face drenched with angry bitterness. Dad called me three times while I was talking with mum, then sent a message to call him back. I reluctantly scrolled down the list of my previously dialled numbers. Dad's was right after Jackie's.

'I know your mother told you what happened. I would be happy to explain if you want to listen.'

'I don't want to hear anything, Dad. I want you two to sort this out and leave me in peace.'

'Kitty, listen.'

Kitty?! Did dad just call me Kitty? Is he suddenly using my nickname to shortcut his way to the lost intimacy between us?

'I'm not Kitty to you,' I hissed.

'Okay, Katie then. This is hard, you know. For everyone.'

I didn't reply.

'I'm just asking you to not listen to everything people say. It's easy to throw dirt at others. I sacrificed a lot for this family.'

'Go on then, tell me your story, Dad.'

A loud truck passed in front of me, so I didn't hear what he said. 'What?'

'I said maybe we can meet and talk when things calm down a bit.'

'Yeah, let's do that, preferably in the local bakery!'

Dad went quiet, then picked up where he left off. 'Look, I don't know what lies your mother and her friends are spreading but AS YOU KNOW, your mother and I had problems for many years BEFORE this happened.'

I could hear dad's anger reverberate through his words. He had high blood pressure and was at a high risk of a heart attack, but I was furious and this was news to me. I didn't know mum and dad 'had problems'. I knew they argued from time to time but isn't that normal? Was it a reason for adultery if they disagreed sometimes? Was it a reason for divorce if mum still counted in Russian roubles and wore that *ushanka* hat in winter even though dad hated it and told her to be more respectful of the British culture?

'I must go now, Dad. Speak later.' Dad finally hung up. I neared the park close to our flat. Two girls jogged by, neither of them wearing a sports bra, their boobs bouncing anywhere but where they were supposed to be.

A duck shat right in front of me, the shiny emerald on his neck distracted me and I stepped in it. I did not bother cleaning it off in the grass. I cast a look over the park. Mark stood in the middle of a puddle, Rooster was enthusiastically circling him, splashing mud all over his jeans, and barking for the whole neighbourhood. I staggered towards Mark, leaving dirty footsteps on the uneven path. Rooster was enthusiastically bringing a stick to Mark, who was ignoring him and typing on his phone. I sent Mark a Snap, he looked up.

'Kitty Kat! Rooster, look who is here, look who is here!'

Rooster turbo-charged towards me. I stepped aside but he left my coat full of muddy prints. I sighed. There was too much stuff to fix and save around me, I suddenly felt too weak to go home with Mark. I hankered after a nice warm croissant with a cup of coffee and some retro music in the background.

We went inside and Mark left his dirty shoes in the corridor. I cleaned Rooster and threw my muddy coat in the washing machine.

'Could you at least not sit on the sofa in your muddy jeans, please?' I walked into the lounge, where Mark sat watching TV.

'You want to return the sofa to the store or what? It's out of guarantee now, Kitty. We can actually use it, you know?'

'I want it to last. I want things to last. I …' I dissolved into tears. I was annoyed with myself that the small argument made me cry, and that annoyance made me cry even more.

'Why are you bugging me about this?' Mark asked, pulling off his jeans in the middle of the room.

'I want it to last. I want things to last …'

'Come here, Katie Kat. What happened?' Mark understood that it was more than the sofa that I was crying about.

'My parents … my parents are getting a divorce.'

'What? I'm so sorry.' Mark pulled me to his chest, gave me a warm hug, caressed my hair. I sobbed even more. 'Kitty, don't think of your parents. They are them, and we are us, okay?'

'But there are no guarantees! Do you think that affairs are inevitable? That all relationships are like that? When it comes, will it destroy us?'

My voice sounded like a ship's loud horn, Mark's like a calm harbour. 'Why are you asking that?'

I pulled away from Mark's chest. 'When I ask you if you want toast, you don't question why am I asking about toast. Can you not just answer?! I hate it when you question my questions!'

'But you asked like five questions in one. Which one do you want me to answer?' Mark cuddled me back to his chest, 'Come here little baby, you need some *cafuné*.' He ran his fingers through my hair. His chest and arms were warm, his cheeks were still a bit cold from outside. The smell of mud reminded me of the grass we laid on when we were in Portugal and talked about untranslatable words.

'Just for Kitty …' Mark had whispered, '*Cafuné* …'

The untranslatable word sounded like beautiful music. I caressed Mark's hand on top of my hair.

'Mark,' I slowly took my hand off. I swallowed two times before formulating my question. I asked slowly. 'How long did it take you to accept that your parents had died? Was it the funeral? Or when you saw the photos from the accident? Do you mind me asking that?'

Mark looked at the ceiling. 'I don't remember. But Kitty, you haven't lost your mum and dad. Life will be different. But they are still here. They didn't die. In fact, in fact, when they both remarry, you get a new set of parents. That's pretty cool, like two for the price of one!'

'You know I'm not into the *two for one* offers …'

'Come on.' Mark squeezed me tighter. 'Stop sulking. It's gonna be all right. They will work it out. You still have me. Your good old Mark. Your everything.' He tickled me under my arms. We laughed and it felt good. Yes, I still had Mark. He was the missing sibling I never had. The stable parent figure. The carer when I had an attack. The loving boyfriend. Could one human take on so many identities?

'What are you thinking about?'

I didn't want to tell Mark my thoughts. They were dark and brooding. I looked up, noticed a cable hanging from the ceiling. It looked so ugly, so out of place. 'Nothing in particular. Was that cable always like that?'

Mark nodded. 'Yup. Always been like that.'

'Tech should be invisible by now. With all the wireless we have, we shouldn't have to see any of this. It is so old school!' I vigorously rubbed the mud stain on the sofa with my wet tissue. 'And so much right into your face! I want tech to be more like the Finish have it. Like hidden in a birch tree, you know, easy on the eye.'

'Agree.' Mark stopped me from rubbing the stain. 'Tech should be more feminine.'

'You mean feminine as in hide the hard work and look perfect?' Mark didn't get my pun, he bubbled. 'But schools should take it slowly. Like not jump on the bandwagon and replace all old with new. I want my kids to learn proper handwriting and know how all the analogue stuff works. Technology can wait till they are older.'

He did it again. On every possible occasion, Mark deviated our conversation to baby-turf. On one hand he was saying he was proud of me working in academia, on the other hand he wanted me to spend a year changing nappies.

'You can't have it both ways, you know. You can't expect tech innovation if you don't let children tinker with it early on. Bad design can actually spur innovation.' I threw in.

'So how many kids do you want?'

I loudly flapped my hands. Could he not see the double standards? 'People think that kids are losing out with multimedia but it is just an evolved type of literacy. That's what we need to teach children in schools today!'

'I would like two or three.'

I got up from the sofa, didn't say anything.

'Fancy some pizza?' Mark didn't wait for my answer, walked into the kitchen, put the oven on, and squeezed three pizzas in. A quarter of one was for me, the bit with pineapple on. I went to our bedroom and put on my white cotton pants and a few drops of vanilla essence on my wrist. After switching off the lights, I folded myself into the north-facing windowsill. Rooster wanted to sit next to me but I pushed him away. People get excited when they see animals in windows: they give them names and create Facebook pages for them.

I looked outside. The darkness gently poured over the city. I watched how the lampposts perforated the black cover. Rooster put his front paws on the windowsill, nuzzling my legs. I gave in and let him sit next to me. The city was all dark now, no one outside could see us. We viewed the spectacle in front of us, the city skyline switching on its evening filters as the minutes progressed.

The clock tower transformed from an ugly steel construction to a romantic minaret. Behind thousands and thousands of white windows, human souls were revealing their layers to each other. With its cryptic algorithm, life was braiding their layers into new love stories.

'Pizza is ready!' Mark peeked through the crack in the door. 'Don't forget about your basic body needs with all that mind-fulness stuff! Oh, you are not meditating?'

I climbed down from the window. 'Need to download a new app. The fake Buddhist girl spoilt it for me, you know. But I had my quiet moment, so we can eat now.'

Rooster, understanding the word 'eat', jumped all the way to the kitchen.

'Mindfulness is a lifestyle, not a scheduled task!' Mark parroted my favourite sentence. He fed Rooster a slice of his peperoni pizza, then switched on the TV while drinking a beer. I didn't want to have pudding, my indulgence was a warm shower. I headed to the bathroom right after we finished eating. I was grateful for the en suite, away from the smell of pizza, and Mark's loud munching and knife scraping on the plate. If I used the coconut shower gel, our bedroom would smell sweet again. I undressed, throwing my clothes into a big pile, and was about to step into tub when Mark burst in.

'You scared me!'

He hugged me from behind and kissed my neck. 'Oh, I love to see your little apricots jumping!' Mark cupped my naked breasts.

'I thought they were melons? That's quite a downgrade?' I attempted a smile, gently pulled Mark's hand away but he lifted me up and carried me towards the bedroom.

'GIANT melons! And raspberry lips! I want to eat everything on display here!' Mark sucked the knuckles of my fingers. 'Nom nom nom, my blueberries!'

'Help, help, I am being attacked by a grizzly bear!'

Mark came in less than ten minutes. He collapsed on the bed next to me. 'That was good!' He stood up and bowed, holding up the condom, like a hunter with his prey. He stared at it for a while. The fluid was not the usual milky colour but transparent, as if tears.

'You wish you could finish in me?' I whispered.

'It's okay. That time will come.'

I propped myself up on my elbows, 'You mean what we have now is some kind of waiting time for the happy times later?'

'Here we go again … just forget it, Kitt. Forget what I said. Enjoy the NOW.' Mark fell asleep, content, the condom still in his hand, the sweat from underneath him soaking into the sheets on my half of the bed. I returned to the shower. I felt hollow and thirsty. The dullness inside me was shapeless, the absence of a baby formed a silence I could no longer hold. I almost wished that Mark was unfaithful to me. That would be a spiky feeling, a feeling that I could name and perhaps do something about.

The drops were sliding down my skin, I heard Rooster's scratching on the bathroom door. I stopped the shower, patted him on my way from the bathroom. I glanced at sleeping Mark. I had no butterflies in my stomach, I even had no fear of losing him. My passion for Mark had flittered from me like a tree branch torn off by the wind. I was unable to pick it up and turn it into a magic stick for Rooster to catch.

Chapter 4

'Is it okay to have Rooster on my knees?'

'Sure!' Jackie said half towards me, half towards the car navigation system. I rolled down the window and Rooster immediately stuck his head out, his tongue drooling and his ears flapping in the wind. I stroked his back, smiling. The last time Jackie drove me was from home to the hospital. I had been using my wheelchair, imprisoned at home and reliant on others to take me to places. Jackie would pick me up and we'd go to the hospital but also to a café or a park. She was documenting every trip for her IG stories, but I didn't mind. She spent hours composing, curating and archiving her small vignettes. I neither lost nor gained anything by being the protagonist. I was glad that my disability could enable something positive for her.

'The airport is advising passengers to arrive later because of queues.' I was reading the alert from my watch. 'Shall we stop by Dragon Hill?' I asked Jackie, checking the virus levels there. 'It's on the way and Google says it's green right now.'

Jackie parked in the disabled car park of the White Horse pub at the bottom of the hill.

'Let's go up!' Jackie walked towards the rails with binoculars. Rooster charged right behind her, pulling me so hard I almost fell over. Jackie positioned herself by the rails, gazing at the magenta-tinted sunlight flowing down the valley. Jackie's silhouette cast a pencil-like shadow on the gravel. Her real hair waved in the wind, her fake hair stuck firmly to her scalp. She released a mini drone to take photos of the scenery, simultaneously uploading them to her story feed.

I soaked in the silence. I let Rooster off-lead and he chased some floating leaves. The wind courted the air with gentle vibrato, with Jackie's drone buzzing above us now and then.

'Look at this shot, amazing hey?' Jackie turned the camera to me. Her stunning Barbie smile was illuminated by the fading sunlight colours. Even I looked fairly attractive with an overhead shot. Jackie added the hashtag #Sunset to her photos and posted them all in a quick sequence.

'The beast needs feeding all the time, right?' I attempted to distract her.

'With fame comes responsibility.' Jackie was glued to her screen, watching the Likes coming in.

'Agree. So you did not tag Elliot this time but the brands you are ambassador for, right?'

Jackie briefly looked up, saying, 'I tag both. Gotta keep the base warm while adding new followers. I need at least 2,000 more new followers to replace the dip after Elliot.'

'But there is no upper limit Jackie, you understand? You get 2,000 more, then you will want another 2,000 more and more and more. There is no upper limit. The population grows and people develop new profiles. It works on the principle of more is better. That is the capitalist trap.'

'That's what makes it so exciting.'

'No, Jackie. That's why you are drowning in it. You cannot get empathy or anything humane at this scale.'

'You're just jealous. Admit it. You're jealous because when you post a picture, you get thirty Likes. And when I post the exact same picture, I get thirty thousand Likes within an hour.'

'My dear, I know who the thirty Likes are from. People I care about. You get thirty thousand from a mass that dehumanizes you.'

'You have no idea how the algorithm works. It highlights Likes from powerful people. Like the other day I got a Like from Greta. She liked my post about smartcars. The size of her following is triple mine. Can you imagine? Her Like boosted my account for the day. I sent her some Bitcoins in return. You're not part of the community, so don't judge it, okay? Quite frankly, you and Mark are the only, the ONLY people I know who have below a thousand followers.'

'That's because we are the only ones outside your bubble, Jackie. For me, you are the only one who has two hundred thousand followers.'

'Ha! So we're each other's wild cards?'

'Match made in heaven.'

We both laughed.

I played with Rooster on the grass for a bit while Jackie finished her story. Rooster jumped randomly, fetched a stick, dropped it, brought me another one, ran away with it, then came back after a while. He had no clear pattern in his play – it wasn't about A-B transactions, digits, or dots and lines. The only constant was an abstract inconsistency. Maybe that's why he was such a happy dog.

'When you got Rooster, did you think it would help during the lockdown?' Jackie asked while responding to one of the comments on her story.

'No, Mark and I have always wanted a dog.'

'So that Mark moves out of the kitchen?'

'He does NOT live in the kitchen! In fact, if you would like to know, I was the one who practically lived in the kitchen. Mark worked from the bedroom, sitting on the bed while I had access to the big table. And kettle and snacks.'

'He probably hid all his snacks in the pillowcase. Come on Katie, lockdown was the golden age for dogs, not couples. You have reached the five-year anniversary – it's time to move on. What do you think of this guy?' Jackie pulled up a profile of a man with a friendly smile. 'CEO from Intel, based in Brazil. He's bold but hey, it means he has a stressful relationship behind him. So he will get you what you want. You are not demanding anyway.'

'He is a complete stranger to me!'

'Exactly! You need to get out of your bubble! Otherwise you'd just date friends of your friends!'

'At least I'd know that they are decent people!'

'You mean all equally bland. You need to spice it up a bit, girl!'

'Speaking of spicy food, you haven't eaten anything for hours. Let's get something at the airport, shall we? There is a nice café in Departures.'

'Can't eat there. I am ambassador for Alfonso's this week.'

We got back in the car and I looked at Jackie's thin arms, her slim fingers clenching onto the flamingo-coloured steering wheel of her Cabriolet. The car was too glamorous for the shabby road. Jackie turned back onto the road towards the airport.

'New York, New Yoooork!' Jackie turned up the volume by raising her eyebrows. Sinatra was inaudible with Jackie's singing. 'You made it, my friend! You are a successful professor now!'

'Me? I'm just a giving a poster presentation. But I love my new job. Postdocs are hard to get these days. And it's a good project. The multiple personality disorder project is the biggest one in Britain. I'll be working with the top experts in the field. It's super exciting!'

'Very proud of you. You have to stop underselling yourself,' Jackie said.

I clenched my bag, excited. This trip to New York is my first long-haul journey after the long isolation during my last MS relapse. Jackie dropped me at Departures, her Cabriolet tyres screeching as she parked. Several faces turned our way. Lana enthusiastically waved from the airport entrance. I caught her eyes fixated on Jackie's back window.

'You didn't tell me you two were friends!'

The look on Lana's face was angry.

'I didn't know you follow Jackie on Instagram!' I defended myself.

'Everyone follows Jackie Mulligman!'

Lana looked at me as if I was her older sibling who hid a hot friend from her. I wanted to defend myself, but we needed to check in. Luckily, the virus checks didn't last as long as we thought, so we had an hour before take-off. Lana and I decided to wait in the lounge dedicated to our health category. Only about twenty people waited there. Four glass walls enclosed the completely quiet lounge. Lana was fiddling with her facemask. I did my olfactory test and logged the data in the app. Boarding started, people started moving. Priority passengers – those with the best health insurance – walked through the air bridge first. When walking to my seat in the back, I recognised some military personnel and celebrities, I gave them a nod.

'You know, transport vehicles have been designed to seal the hierarchies between people,' I said to Lana, but she did not hear me, shuffling her way towards the window seat.

'Can we swap seats? I always work best on planes.' Lana asked, putting a refreshing mint into her mouth. All her essentials were inside one small suitcase, with miniature toiletries, books and electronics. She was clearly a frequent traveller. *Travelling must be more enjoyable that way*, I thought, wondering if miniatures were the secret to Lana's mobility. When I was thinner, I was certainly more mobile. I was much thinner when I was at the hospital. Back then, Mark had it easier when he had to lift me or push my wheelchair.

I let Lana scoot past me. 'Thanks, Kate, appreciate it. My creative juices run wild when I am airborne.'

'No problem. I actually prefer the aisle. I need to use the bathroom every hour or so.' I unwrapped the free, synthetic plane blanket. 'But actually, it's not being airborne that inspires you, it's the lack of oxygen. When you climb mountains, you get the same creativity rush. Have you never noticed?'

'I'm a city girl, you see … but I agree. What you breathe is bloody important. We inhale so much rubbish every day.'

'Rubbish? Do you have any rubbish, Miss?'

A member of the cabin crew rushed to our seats at the word 'rubbish', shaking a colossal, US-sized rubbish bag. Lana held out a tangerine peel. The crew member took the peel wearing disposable blue gloves, then wrapped the peel in a plastic bag, and then into another plastic bag before she threw into the giant US-sized bin bag.

'Thank you,' she said to Lana loudly and politely.

Lana pouted and rolled her eyes. I saw her doing it before with girls she fancied.

'It was trained politeness not sexual interest. It was just a transaction, Lana, no invitation,' I said, but Lana shushed me.

'Who says I expected anything more? As if there were more to life than transactions!'

Within moments of the last passenger being seated, we heard a high-pitched whine. I felt a shockwave as the plane sped down the runway, it must be a hybrid electric.

Lana continued, her voice loud over the engines, 'We all transact, we are all data, analysing and making profit out of each other. With so many people, we need to organise the mass into some stories.'

'Is that what you will talk about at the conference?'

We were airborne now, I chewed gum to calibrate my ear pressure.

'Nope. I'll talk about sex.'

'Sex?' I asked 'sex' but because of the take-off noise, it sounded like 'seeeex' in a Kiwi accent, revealing my insular knowledge of Lana's work.

'Everything can be linked to sexual patterns. Even MPD.' Lana bit into an unripe orange as if it was a green apple. The juice splashed onto my jacket, I pulled away in disgust.

'Google built their algorithm on the basic psychology of social proofing. They cracked it! Did you not know? Searches are propelled by curiosity and need. But Google ranks the results hierarchically, based on economic relevance.'

'I can't see how Google's algorithm relates to sex?' I asked without looking at Lana's orange.

'You haven't read my paper? Typical! Cite it but never actually read it!' Lana yawned. 'You'd better come to my presentation then. I'll use your father to illustrate the case. He's a great example of the beginning stage of MPD.' Lana yawned again but I was fully awake, hanging on every word she said.

'My father?!'

'Yeah, your dad is pretty fragmented. Did you not notice? He has one identity as a good father. He had one as a married man. Then he got one identity as a cheater to your mum and lover to that lady. Are your grandparents alive? Then he will be performing his identity of a son with them …'

'What? You seriously want to use him as an example for your theory? That's insane! You have no evidence, you can't just make things up!'

'Come on, what's at stake?' Lana put the rest of the fruit in a bag underneath her seat. She said in a quieter voice, 'You should do some shadow work, girl. Fight your fears, stop being so worried all the time. Scared girls attract psychopaths.'

Lana closed her eyes, mine remained wide open.

Scared girls attract psychopaths. Mark is definitely not a psychopath. And I had done what Lana called 'shadow work' as part of my mindfulness class. I learnt that I feared snakes and swimming in dark water. The screening app identified that I was also scared of the multiple selves disorder. But I was not scared of it since I started researching it. I looked straight ahead, dismissing Lana's presence. I mentally counted the number of passengers on board. There were fifty-six on our deck, together with the cabin crew and the second deck, it was about 130 potential deaths if we had an accident.

I opened Lana's paper on my phone. I skipped the abstract and first two paragraphs of the introduction, and began reading from the middle.

Some desires correspond to societal values, some don't. Aschilton (1998) argues that the desire of finding a partner who is one's opposite corresponds to the societal value of sustaining marriages that lead to reproduction. A relationship between two partners who are each other's opposites creates the productive tension necessary to sustain 'the marital bond in periods requiring self-sacrifice such as raising children' (p. 45). The 'opposites-attract' pattern of relationship is unsustainable in periods of low energy and exhaustion (e.g., illness, job loss, older age) when partners tend to favour compatibility, care and compassion (Brown, 1998; Joules & Fillington, 2023). In high-income populations with high social protection, most children are created with the 'opposites-attract' pattern. Deviation from this pattern leads to the social perception of anarchy. For partners who are in committed but psychologically unsatisfying relationships, deviation implies the requirement for breaking away from their current persona. This process creates conflict that won't be resolved until the old persona fully dies off and both partners accept their new identities. To break the pattern, partners who are perceived as socially stronger need to deviate first (e.g., a successful businessman has an extramarital affair). The deviation act changes the identities of all involved. In the case of heterosexual relationships, women were biologically designed to have a higher negotiating power with bearing children. While perceived as socially weaker, they have a higher internal power and typically use their new identity to advance their social position (the Cinderella model). In our project, we studied …

I stopped reading. Lana's theory sounded too subjective to me, too anecdotal to be of scientific value. It is a well-known phenomenon that when people have casual sex it means they do not believe in social order. So what did she mean about social anarchy? If I had sex with a guy from first class, I would break the pattern of sitting in designated rows and that process would grant me a new identity? She was right that the sexual patterns were mediating new selves but sex with different partners would not generate new identities. Lana had made the classic error of confusing correlation with causation. I wanted to talk to her about it and ask if she studied psychology to analyse her own relationships. But Lana was asleep, I didn't need to check it through the Sleep Verification app, it was obvious from her fully open mouth and badly tilted neck. I tried to sleep too, but the constant bursts of ads and announcements made it impossible. The closer we came to the US, the louder and shorter the sanitising and entertainment interruptions.

***

'Will you pay by scanning your phone or card?' the taxi driver asked as she swapped the sign of Lyft to Uber and quickly pulled away from the curb, avoiding the twenty dollar fee for standing at the airport.

'Card? You still use cards in the US? Even in New York?' Lana acted refreshed after the plane journey, but I barely registered we were sitting on different seats. 'We need a verified receipt.' She smiled towards the taxi driver's rear window.

'Got you! You need to claim it back from the state coffers!' The taxi driver smirked and activated the aircon. 'First time in New York?' Lana began talking but the taxi driver's phone rang, and we listened to her conversations on loudspeaker for the rest of the journey. We found out that our taxi driver was not only giving rides but also coordinating other drivers, delivering for Amazon and managing the after-school schedules of four kids.

'You have four kiddos, hey?' Lana jumped in a short pause between the calls.

'Can't afford NOT to have them. I need someone to take care of me when I can't drive. The state doesn't care.' Her phone rang again.

I felt sorry for the driver. Some decades ago she would have driven us in a horse and carriage, today she was driving us in an old Land Rover. The distance between the driver and passenger has not changed, we were the ones paying her, she was the one serving us. Her skin was darker than mine and that made the pattern even more depressing.

'Hit me with this code and give me a rating! Appreciate if it can be a ten!' the taxi driver spoke as if she had a machine installed in her head. She helped us with the suitcases from the back. We thanked her, gave her ten points. She swapped the sign from Uber back to Lyft and drove off. I found her on Facebook and gave her a Like there too, fully aware that doing that had only perpetuated a corrupt system that generates the feedback greed.

Lana and I checked in our average-priced hotel and went upstairs. I used the stairs, Lana the lift.

'What do you think of the room?' Lana caught my suspicious look.

'It's huge!' I jumped onto the giant double bed. 'You could have a whole class sleep here.'

'Enough space for two, agree.' Lana inspected the bathroom. 'They only gave us one set of towels! And three sets of shampoo! Americans always have problems with maths!'

I plumped the pillow that said 'Katie' and covered myself in the white sateen duvet. What a luxury. It was so nice on the skin and so nice to look at. And all those differently sized pillows! I wished we had such bed linen at home but we wouldn't be able to; there was no storage space in our bedroom. Mark was glad that we were able to fit the king-size bed in without having to take the door off.

'Personalized pillows, nice!' Lana came back to the bedroom and opened the minibar. 'I'm starving!' She opened the instant noodles, mixed them up with some sauces in tiny bottles. 'Hope that's included in the room price.' She ate with her fingers and a wild, barbaric look in her eyes.

'I'm hungry too. Maybe we could find a supermarket?'

'You have to stop being so cheap all the time! This is a business trip! Uni pays for everything. Didn't you get the food advance?' Lana threw the empty plastic cup on the floor.

I was very hungry and her words were eating at my psyche. *Am I really too frugal? Maybe … I have always been sensitive to the number of zeros in my bank account.*

I bent to pick up her dirty cup but Lana stopped me. 'Are you silly? Don't tidy up! You need to leave the room messy in US!'

'What are you talking about?'

'You need to boost the economy. Let the cleaners have a job.'

I said nothing, leaving the room a mess. We stepped into the bright street. The sky was dark blue, no clouds, only scratches of the airplanes' vapour trails. Perhaps it was an effect of a long flight without sleep but everything in New York was loud to me. The cars, the people, the birds. Or perhaps it was the size of the cars, the people, the birds. A house finch that was triple the size of our finches nearly flew into my face, shrieking.

Lana stepped into the street but jumped back after nearly being hit by a cyclist. 'Yeah, mate, right into my face, thank you!' Lana shouted after him.

'Fuck off!' the cyclist shouted back.

'Do New Yorkers care so little about subtlety? Is this place about stark contrasts and numb emotions?' I attempted an intellectual conversation, but Lana followed her navigation app at a staggering speed. I was jogging behind her, almost breathless. There were so many binaries to take in. My head was flipping from left to right like a saloon door. On the left, a tall banker left a trace of mud on the marble floor. A squad of girls immediately cleaned it up. A homeless man was sitting on the famous steps up to Columbia University. He had a misspelled donation request on his sign. How could one cope with such brazen differences? I needed food, lots of fatty food, to cover up the sharp edges of unfairness crying inside me.

'Nothing helps a jet lag more than a nice big steak,' Lana proclaimed, scanning the QR code of our table.

Locals were seated by the front bar, but we sat in the corner, asserting our position as foreigners. An old Roxette song played in the background but the people in the bar weren't listening. They wanted *their* voices to be heard. Passive audience was a foreign concept to Americans.

'They just pretend. Look at that obese couple with the water bottle!' Lana whispered and hacked at her steak. 'Impostors! They buy water in restaurants and devour the fridge at home.' Lana finished her steak, wiped her mouth with the thin napkin. 'Do they think they'll shed some pounds by carrying their water bottles or what? Fake it till you make it?!'

I thought of Mark when Lana said this. Mark did not hide his appetite in restaurants. He would order double portions and several courses if he could afford it. I visualised the fat couple consoling each other with packets of crisps and telly at home, their bellies weltering over rationality. Without sufficient support systems, choices become self-destructing. Mark was part of a corrupt system.

'There should be more restrictions on our choices … although I suppose that time shrinks everyone's appetite,' I said and looked up. 'Time shrinks even big American dreams.' I yawned. I felt rather small in that moment. I was sleepy and weakened with the foreign food in my stomach. I was mentally jotting notes for my diary:

Lana is very pragmatic in the way she tackles difference. Maybe it's because she grew up in Britain, a country that demands a tolerance of south and north. She is able to tolerate the sweet orange juice concentrate on the plane with the sour stake in the bistro. I am not like that. I need a hug, a confirmation that life is worth it. Lana walks in New York streets as if she were selling life to everyone. I like the differences between Lana and me. She had what I called the squirrel mindset. She knew she could throw herself towards a tree branch, eyes wide open, and it would catch her and propel her to another branch. People could mistake her for a rat with a fluffy tail, she didn't care. She trusted her sturdy body, she trusted her hands. I wished I had that confidence in my body.

'Do you want to finish it, mate?' Lana asked as we passed the homeless man in front of the hotel entrance. Lana handed him the doggy bag we got from the bistro. The man grabbed it and tucked it under his coat but continued smoking. Our eyes met. He had the word FATE tattooed on his forehead, and JESUS tattooed on his wrist. He did not fail as a person, and he knew the system did not fail him either.

'Do you think they will introduce doggy bags to our canteen?' I followed Lana in the busy street lounge. 'The lunch portions have got so big. The Centre should do something about it.'

'Maybe for students. The profs will continue with their small portions, no doubt about that! You know how it works … The posh don't need to save food for worse times. They can afford to undereat.' Lana looked knowingly towards the thin tourist entering our hotel lobby. 'US profs are even slimmer, you will see tomorrow.'

'Really? Do profs get paid more in US?'

'Oh yeah, way more. It's the typical "sow collectively, harness individually". US profs have armies of students working for them to push their papers out. Watch out when they invite you to *collaborate*. They say *collaborate* but they mean to work on their agenda. Americans haven't moved from the industrial revolution mindset. They don't even know the difference between socialism and social democracy.'

'Surely in New York they do?' I was still two steps behind Lana even though I was running as fast as I could. 'The local conference organising committee is full of bright people.'

'Just wait for the cocktail reception tomorrow.'

Lana got to bed first, without brushing her teeth. I couldn't fall asleep. I kept on memorizing my conference abstract and checking that Lana was genuinely asleep. I had never presented at an international conference before and I never shared a room with a lesbian. *What if I forget my lines? What if Lana starts undressing me?* I tossed around on the bed for a while, then quietly got up and opened the room window.

Fresh air was in short supply in the middle of New York. I looked outside. The only greenery were the Starbucks and Whole Market logos down Canal Street. I looked up and spotted the full moon. I looked down and saw a big puddle. The water surface reflected the moon's white light. The light flew so slowly and steadily that I mistook it for a fallen skyscraper. The moon was pulling me towards the sky, I almost fell out of the window. A couple passed by the Starbucks. I watched them passionately kissing by the moonlight. They were two random people who fell for each other, at a particular moment in time. Just like me and Mark.

Mark and I overcame many obstacles together and we would survive this little crisis too. Mark's parents died in a car accident when he was young, mine recently divorced. Mark had lost his job when he had burnout. I almost lost my body when I was diagnosed with MS. Mark got a new job and I recovered. Life is brutal and we survive it by holding onto each other. The couple walked away, the man holding the girl around her shoulders.

I looked at Lana, she was snoring quietly. I didn't believe in Lana's philosophy. Love – deeply felt, genuine love – was a gift from the universe. I lay down, put in the earplugs I had taken from the plane. Loud noises filtered in from the street. I was still too jetlagged to fall asleep. My head was banging, my legs aching. I didn't want to take a sleeping pill. I tried tuning into the soothing sounds in my headset but a loud male voice was rising beneath our window. The man talked fast in Italian, occasionally reaching the top tones of a Pavarotti aria. I had a sudden urge to meet the Italian man outside, view the photos on his phone, see whether he too took a selfie by the memorial to send to his loved ones as I did. If I could speak his language I would ask him about his roots, tell him to keep at least one photo just for himself. I put up the volume in my headset, again and again flicked through the photos I had taken from the quick walk with Lana. I sent all thirty-six to Mark, they were delivered but he has not viewed them yet, the app was telling me. He was probably busy at work. The man began singing, the aria smoothed my kaleidoscopic thoughts.

Chapter 5

THE CONFERENCE WELCOME PARTY WAS divided into four sections: one for graduate students, one for assistant professors, one for associate professors, and one for full professors. Lana joined the assistant professors' section that offered fruit nibbles, while I stayed in the graduate students' section with triangular sandwiches, half-ripe tomatoes and discoloured ham slices.

I stood alone by the tables, small circles of three to four people filled the room. A tall guy was cruising between the islands of people; I decided to do the same. I headed towards a girl who had not a circle but a queue around her. She seemed popular by being unavailable – as soon as someone came within her talking distance, she suddenly needed to talk to someone else.

'Excuse me, do you know where the bathroom is?' I asked a lady with a name badge of the same colour as mine, indicating we were both using the 'she' pronoun.

She pointed in an exaggeratedly slow way to my phone as she said, 'It's all clearly marked in the conference app.'

I went to the bathroom but I clearly misunderstood the directions as I ended up in the posh bathroom reserved for the full professors. I hid my badge with my scarf, glancing at the expensive hand lotion and cloth hand towels that were not meant for me to touch. I was about to leave when I passed a beautiful lady washing her hands. I glanced at the name badge pinned to her sleeveless lace blouse. It was the wrong way round in the mirror but I could decipher the letters: Professor Valerie Mukherjee.

Professor Valerie Mukherjee!

I had cited her research at least thirty times in my thesis.

My academic heroine! My intellectual guru is washing her hands next to me!

I waited, watching Professor Mukherjee dry her long, elegant fingers. As she moved to throw the towel in the bin, I plucked up all my courage and burst out, 'I love your work, Professor Mukherjee! I am … I am Katie Kuznetsov. I just graduated. I followed your approach in my PhD. I agree with everything you wrote about personality splintering. I cite you all over my thesis. Your 2010 book is my Bible. I … I … I think your work is excellent.' I saw my blaring-red face in the mirror and felt embarrassed at my declaration, but Professor Mukherjee smiled gracefully and gently touched my shoulder.

'Thank you, that's very kind of you to say. I'm interested to hear more.' She adjusted her blouse and said in a soft voice, 'I need to go now, but come to my dinner party. Tomorrow at 5 p.m. The address is here.' She handed me her business card and quietly closed the bathroom door. I completely squashed the card, then quickly unfolded it, held it up:

335 W 19th St, New York, NY 10011

Professor Mukherjee had invited me to her house! The best professor in the universe invited me to her home! Tomorrow! To her private house! I knew it wouldn't be an ordinary dinner. This was a golden ticket that would open the door and boost my career. I skipped back to the conference room.

'Katie! Where have you been? My presentation starts in five minutes!' Lana hissed at me, then nervously continued counting the number of people in the audience. 'Did you know they stream the whole conference to Times Square?!' She ran a bright red lipstick over her lips, then took a small spray and began spraying the seats closest to the stage.

'What is it?'

'Just some oxytocin,' she explained, then hid the bottle away and said more quietly, 'People are more generous when they have high oxytocin levels. I want a generous audience. Did you not know that hormones influence what people value?'

'Everyone who studies psychology knows that!' I said louder than usual. I did not like how Lana used her psychology knowledge to manipulate others. That was not what psychology was meant for. Her presentation started on time, I sat in the back of the room, surveying the many empty chairs in front of me. It was an embarrassing turnout, even for post-Covid21 audience standards.

'Our next speaker, Dr Lana Fidgely will talk about multiple personality disorder from a feminist-biological perspective. Dr Fidgely's presentation has an intriguing title: "Find sex patterns behind everything!" Dr Fidgely, the floor is yours.'

'Thank you and hello everyone. It is an honour to be here.' Lana cleared her throat – I did not expect her to be nervous. 'I would like to start with the premise that multiple personality disorder started in the Neolithic Revolution, when we turned from hunter-gatherers into agriculturists. The multiple personality virus began propagating at greater speed and reached its peak in today's age of Neo-infosphere.'

Lana's slide deck had some disturbing images from history. A Tweet from the audience got displayed above her presentation screen: 'Listening to Fidgely. Idealising the current era as enlightened. Propagating the myth of a primitive past.' #NotImpressed @fazersuni

Lana did not see the Tweet, she spoke confidently for the rest of the session, her eyes addressing both the camera and the empty chairs. 'In our study with two adult participants we found increased grey-matter volume and this was negatively associated with the participants' marital status. In other words, the MP virus is more active in people who are single. Now why could this be?' Lana clicked over to another slide.

'The reason MP sufferers cannot consolidate their multiple selves is because there is no single dominant identity in them. This is why MP individuals practise polyamory and casual sex. What does this tell us?'

I looked at the five people sitting in front of me: one was answering her emails, one was fiddling with his own presentation, one lady had fallen asleep, and two lads were quietly leaving the room as Lana clicked to the next slide.

'This tells us that the key problem is rooted in biology and that healthy biological function became suppressed in the Neo-infosphere era. From a sexual patterns' perspective, the current era introduced social media dates and robot-stimulated sex. Although these episodes provide some opportunities for experiencing new identities, they do not promote the exchange of bodily fluids. Without such an exchange, there is a hormonal imbalance. People start excreting oxytocin in alternative contexts.'

Another audience Tweet flashed above Lana's presentation screen 'What's new about this?? We all have multiple facets! That's why you never invite all your friends to the same party!' #Old-Theory @fazersuni

'In our recent study, we found higher oxytocin levels in MPD suffers. We suggest this is because of the new identities MPD people experience on a regular basis. Seeing how others engage with their new persona gives MPD patients the dopamine boost they would otherwise get from copulation. In our current study, we will be studying …'

I couldn't listen more, I knew Lana's theory anyway. I slipped out to catch Professor Mukherjee's keynote that was running in parallel in the main auditorium. I crept up and down the rows, unable to find an empty seat. Professor Mukherjee stood on the elevated stage and, unlike Lana, talked in a deep, calm voice. Her slides had no text or numbers, just full-size, full-impact photographs.

'You will hear many theories, but only our theory is fully sci-
entifically proven, backed by years of solid, rigorous research.'
Professor Mukherjee double blinked to move forward her slides. 'I
start from the premise that multiple personality disorder intensifies
in certain situations. The key context that unleashed the multiple
personality pandemic is that of micro-servers and personalized
technologies. Why? Well, if you have read our studies,' Professor
Mukherjee paused to acknowledge the sea of nodding heads and
smiles from junior colleagues, 'you will know that we documented,
step by step, how the GAFA companies abused the psychological
principles of seduction. The historical data support our theory,
too. Indeed, the Smooth Revolution accelerated the global use of
seductive technological design. I have seen young patients in my
clinic whose brains show substantial scarring. This indicates that
full recovery may not occur. Or, if even possible, it will take much
longer with the current treatment options.' Professor Mukherjee
clicked to her final photo, a girl with a mosaic face.

I was sold and so was the rest of the audience, we all queued
at the end of the talk to get Professor Mukherjee's signature into
our copies of her latest book.

I got a personal dedication and beamed with satisfaction all
the way back to the hotel room.

Lana did not. 'You liked it?! Did you hear what she said at
the end? I couldn't believe it when I watched the recording.'
Lana switched on the small lamp by her bedside. She imitated
Valerie's Indian accent, sitting on the bed with her head high,
'The biological theory follows the wrong model. It is not the case
that humans are born with a whole heart.' Lana's imitation of
Valerie's accent was better than a deep fake. 'Humans are born
with broken hearts.' Lana gestured a lot and stressed her syllables.
'MPD sufferers are broken-hearted people. They need our help.
Donate now. PATHETIC!'

'She used the broken heart as a metaphor. …'

'Gold digger! She should be careful with her conspiracy theories!' Lana continued talking in a high-pitched voice, 'She has even infected me with that Indian accent!'

'It's you who is infecting people, Lana. You could get into trouble by propagating that MPD is a virus. And that it is linked to polyamory. You are offending both the MPD and polyamory communities by saying that. They don't need offending, they need help. You should be careful with what you say.'

'I am not offending anyone by stating the evidence.'

'A few small studies don't prove anything.'

'Great, so you are on her side?! You know that Mukherjee paid her way up the ladder? Her husband works on Wall Street. People are scared of the rich. The university promoted her to keep the enemies quiet.'

'I am on neither side. I think MPD develops from a combination of biological and environmental factors. We can't go back to hunter-gatherer family groups, and we can't get rid of personal technologies either. The sweet spot is in combining the two approaches.'

'So why are you picking on my theory?' Lana asked. 'Jealous. You're jealous! Don't you worry, one day it will be you speaking.'

'I am not jealous. And I hate public speaking. I wish I could be as calm and confident as Professor Mukherjee.' I was getting very tired, so I switched off the bedside lamp. Lana and I lay in semi-darkness.

'You just need to practise,' Lana whispered.

'No, I tried. I get really nervous.'

'Stop stressing then. It's not like *you* are on the line! You're presenting a study. They can shoot the study if they don't like it, not you. Besides, there is more to life than work. Why stress about a twenty-minute presentation?'

'I know, it's not rational. Or maybe it is. I … I worry because I leak. You know, my Multiple Sclerosis – my bladder isn't so strong. Especially when I get stressed.'

'Get pads.'

'I don't think that is Professor Mukherjee's secret weapon, you know.'

'She's a professor! She can say what she likes and people will gobble it up. She can be arrogant and nasty and people will call it leadership.'

'But she is kind. She invited me to her dinner party.'

'Did she?' Lana paused, then added, 'Probably to have a junior on the invitee list. Profs need to show they support the lower ranks. There is no such thing as altruism.'

'Yes there is. I hope you get to experience altruism one day.' I turned my back to Lana. I wanted to sleep and not listen to her nasty remarks anymore.

'Hope without critical thinking is naivety. Anyway, sleep tight!' Lana finally switched off her bedside lamp. I heard her switch off her phone, too. I tossed and turned until about 2 a.m., my head buzzing with memories from yesterday and expectations for tomorrow.

I woke up before the breakfast buffet was open, but I was too nervous to eat anyway. Before leaving the room, I checked three times that I had my poster and notes and looked decent.

The poster presentation session was scheduled in a big room. Apart from fifty fellow postdocs, only two people came to see our posters. We all stood there for the two hours of the presentation time, looking at each other and our own posters. I had spent two weeks designing mine.

I consoled myself with the thought of having 'conference presentation' on my CV. That was what counted for promotion, and all fifty postdocs in the room knew it when they took their posters down and tossed them in the recycling bin. I attended a few other presentations, then began preparing for Professor Mukherjee's party.

I applied and reapplied my make-up, wrote some key points I wanted to memorise before leaving. The taxi was late, and the journey long, the price equivalent to a month's grocery shopping for Mark and me. I tried to not think about money and time. I enthusiastically knocked on the door. It swung open with Professor Mukherjee holding the door handle.

I clumsily handed her a bouquet and bottle of wine. Other bouquets already filled the foyer, triple if not four times the size of the one I gave her.

'Thank you for the gifts. Call me Valerie. No photos allowed. Please come in.'

I hoped she couldn't see me blush. I reluctantly entered Professor Mukherjee's mind-blowing penthouse. The main hall led to a 200 square-metre rooftop garden with a stunning view of the Manhattan Financial District and Flatiron Building. Huge floor-to-ceiling windows wrapped the dimly lit rooms, with electronic shades adjusted to the changing daylight. A giant hot tub sat on the terrace, surrounded by cushioned lounge chairs. The terrace had Asian décor fused with Western elegance. The different rooms had different temperatures, and I preferred the semi-cold living room with the fish buffet. I ran my fingers over the luxury wallpaper, catching the little stars it created with its 3D effect.

I had no idea who to talk to or what to say, my impostor syndrome was at its peak. I circulated around the house, holding a half-full wine glass and pretending to feel comfortable. I tried an olive but it was stuffed with cheese so I had to spit it out. I wanted to drink some water but with the first sip I discovered it was gin with tonic. It was hard to say who was an important academic and who was Valerie's personal friend. I wished the guests had labels on the glasses and that people had name badges with number of citations and social impact factors.

After some unsuccessful cruising, I stopped by a lady who stood by the window near the hot tub. She held the plate in front of her breasts. I came a bit closer but not too close in case she started laughing and enlarged the nimbus around her.

'Nice house …' I started but she ignored me. 'Delicious salmon …' The lady turned towards me. 'I am going for the cake now.'

'Can you get me a slice?' Her small, red-painted nails exaggerated her short fingers. She used her whole hand to move the food closer to her mouth, like a puppy with its paw. She managed to text with her left hand though, so she probably didn't have dexterity problems, just a bad upbringing.

I took the plate off her, she said thanks and puffed her attractive chest up. Academics don't have an attractive chest, most men suffer from corona back and most women have sunken shoulders. I concluded she was not an academic and regretted offering to bring her food and continue the conversation.

I walked towards the kitchen where all the cakes and desserts were. There were big windows in the corridor. I glanced at the sky, stretching the entire horizon. I tried to cheer myself up. I smiled at my own face in the window reflection, for a second pretended it was a photo frame and I was part of Professor Mukherjee's family. Frames can accommodate any photo, any face, so why not? But there were no family photos on the walls of Professor Mukherjee's house. It felt strange for a place someone calls home. Perhaps Valerie doesn't need that kind of visual reminder of who matters in her life. The house was nigh on empty, with a few mini statues on the shelves and some abstract paintings on the walls. Mark and I have pictures of us everywhere. We have shelves full of stuff, especially in the kitchen, lots of nuts, muesli bars and snacks bought in bulk. Professor Mukherjee definitely didn't buy anything in bulk. Her huge house with minimal contents epitomised privilege.

I handed the chesty lady her dessert plate topped with a giant piece of a strawberry Pavlova and said, 'The chocolate cakes looked like sushi, so I got us proper cake.'

'Ha-ha, you are funny!' The lady shook with laughter, with the full plate dangerously close to the cashmere cardigan I borrowed from Lana. 'She is funny! Marcia! Marcia, over here!'

A short, elderly lady came towards us. She was wearing an orange dress that blended with the alligator skin on her neck and arms.

'My friend Marcia from Florida!' the chesty lady introduced us. I eyed Marcia to establish whether it was real skin or a leather jacket. She looked so fragile, I was worried that if I shook her hand, the skin would fall off.

'I'm Katherine.' I attempted a semi-smile.

'She is from Britain,' the lady added, as if my passport had a high entertainment value.

'Nice to meet you,' Marcia said in a mind-blowingly loud voice.

Professor Nicholson also had a very loud voice and a tiny, fragile body. He was good for recorded but not for live presentations.

'I think Professor Mukherjee's keynote yesterday was excellent.' I held onto my dessert plate with both hands, looking for a meaningful conversation with Marcia.

'Do you? Everyone knows she fiddled with the numbers. No way you can get that result from so few participants.'

'What do you mean?' I looked into Marcia's eyes.

'Is that Greg Wooks?' Marcia turned towards a tall man whose name I recognized – the publisher of the flagship journal in MPD studies. Marcia did not bother excusing herself and just walked away. I did the same. I went straight to the small garden on the terrace. I tiptoed on the manicured lawn, hoping to balance my thoughts with some nature, but it was a garden to watch, not to walk around. There were no birds or insects: the garden was lifeless with a design copied from retirement homes.

'Valerie, Valerie!'

I turned towards the right corner of the terrace; a group of half-drunk women cheered as Valerie held up her glass. She moved around the terrace, serving champagne into tens of tall, thin glasses.

'Armand de Brignac, my dear friends! Enjoy, courtesy of my late husband, Eric.' Valerie poured some drops of the expensive champagne into my glass too. Her friends by the hot tub were laughing, with their identical porcelain teeth, hiding their small eyes behind sunglasses even though it was 9 p.m. Then they sat down around the hot tub, and turned towards the illuminated side where Valerie stood in her pink sari. The mass of heads and the strong lights merged into one big dollar sign in my eyes.

I booked an Uber back to the hotel. Lana stayed up, waiting for me in her leopard-print pyjamas.

'Sooo … how was the academic party of the year? I bet she has a giant house?'

'Yeah, two floors. Five toilets.'

'Five?! Holy shit!'

'I don't know how she can live like that. The champagne bottle she opened could have paid for somebody's house. Or health insurance. I would never want to live like that.'

'So what's your revolutionary idea then? You want to save the world by washing the feet of orphan lepers?' Lana inspected her nails, began clipping them.

'No, but empathy could do a lot …' I tried to ignore the harsh sound coming from Lana's nail clipper. 'This is a traumatised generation, Lana. We need more empathy for them. We need to listen more to them. We won't figure out the cure for MPD by sitting in our ivory towers and citing each other's papers. These young people, they were damaged twice. By the false illusions of the Smooth and by the lack of support when the revolution evaporated. They need collective support. We need to collaborate with them. Embrace all their persona, say we are witnesses to all their identities, acknowledge them, feel them, deeply, in our own bodies.'

'Jeez you memorised some good lines from that book! But okay, yeah, I get that point. We can support the kids with virtual reality …'

Lana was translating my ideas into wrong targets and I was getting even more frustrated.

'No, not a technological fix. We have had enough of those. I want a new future, a bright future.'

Lana finished clipping her nails and threw the mini clipper into her mini travel bag. She turned to me. 'Look, Miss Philanthropic, there are many who think they can change the world by pushing their religious opinions onto others. What gives you the authority? Live in the real world before you go on your moral rant!'

Lana didn't bother to switch off her phone; the blue light was illuminating the room. I felt we were in our shared office and not in a New York hotel room at 1 a.m. I lay on my back, began texting with Mark, he was probably having breakfast. I had the phone on mute, but Mark texted a word per message and that kind of ping-pong messaging made the phone flash every second, which was annoying not only for me but also for Lana. She got up and asked angrily who I was texting with.

'What do you see in that guy? Like tell me one reason why you are with Mark.'

'The morning hug.'

'What?'

'The morning hug. That's why I am with him.'

'Does he not have horrible morning breath?!'

'No.'

'No one else does that!'

'Precisely. Love is not a commodity, Lana.'

'Are you cross with me?' Lana finally paid attention to what I said.

'Yes. You offended me.' I was surprised how direct I was in describing my emotions. It must have been the American air.

'Sorry, I didn't mean to do that. I was just angry you are in Valerie's camp. MPD is a crisis. We need to be of one mind. You weaken our community by siding with her.'

I wondered whether it was Lana's belonging to the lesbian community that made her so worried about her academic identity.

She was so clever and yet didn't recognise the paradox in her clique mentality. I switched off the phone, it was so tiring to have a conversation when Mark texted one word per message, I told him off several times, he just continued.

'Morning hug …' Lana murmured to herself in disbelief.

I thought of Mark's morning hug. He did have morning breath sometimes but sometimes he did not and I could only smell his CK Men. I loved how he would gently lift the duvet and slip in next to me, embracing me from behind and in that spoon position make me feel safe and his only one. Sometimes we talked about the dreams we had the previous night, sometimes we talked about the dreams we had for the future, sometimes we talked about the birds outside the window. I missed Mark. I longed for lying on his chest, absorbing his air into my lungs. The sudden geographical distance between us created a want I didn't know I harboured.

Chapter 6

THE JOURNEY BACK SEEMED CONSIDERABLY quicker than the journey to New York. Lana didn't sleep, she was keen to chat. I sat next to her and had little room to escape.

'Trust me, divorce is a good thing. It gives people the chance to remake their lives into what they want.'

'Now why would divorce be a good thing …' It was supposed to be a query, but I was too tired to lift my voice into a question.

'Divorce is a good thing when it's timed well. Folks get a unique chance to shift identities. And as we know, identity shifts are far more attractive than marriages.' Lana began searching inside her bag, I thought she would take her laptop out to show me some made-up graphs but she just took out a carrot and began munching it, her face mask tucked under her chin.

'It happens to every couple. Every couple gets into an affair at some point. The question is how the partners respond to it.' Lana had remarkably strong teeth, the carrot was being sliced into equal strips inside her mouth. 'My philosophy has always been transparency. So if you have sex with someone and that someone is seeing someone else, TELL THEM. Like don't be an asshole and hide it, they will find out eventually.'

I didn't like Lana's forthrightness and I didn't like that she was right. Dad did change after the affair. He wore a new aftershave and more sporty clothes than before. He changed his hair and skin and looked younger. He was calling me a different name. Yes, perhaps he did adopt a new persona. One I was not ready to accept. Definitely not so quickly.

'People change, and people *need to* change.' Lana swapped her carrot with a mangetout. 'You don't eat this kind of stuff, right?'

'Not plain like that, thanks.'

'Yeah, so I was saying change is part of the natural cycle. A new partner can turbocharge the process. It's a very old technique. They use it to disrupt religious groups, royals and other brainwashed groups. You introduce a hot girl, and all strict protocols are out the window. Sometimes an affair is enough but the point of a divorce is to go through that public humiliation, you know. The experience of breaking your past identity because you broke the promise you gave in front of your friends.'

I looked towards the window, pulled the blind up a bit to see the clouds, then turned to Lana. 'I guess you are right. I think dad did change. He looks happier, actually.'

'A clear sign he is getting regular and satisfying sex.'

'You could be a bit less direct, you know. This is hard for me.'

'Oh, come on. It's not what I say. You can't accept your dad's new identity. That's hard, I get that.'

'What about my mum? All the pain she's going through at the moment. The doubts she has about all men now. About herself. The feeling that she is not enough. You just—'

'That's another identity change.' Lana cut me short, bit the mangetout into two equal pieces. 'Your mother needs to separate the cause from consequence. Like think about it. Men do not cheat when they are loved by their wives. The consequence is tough but she should not see the consequence as what triggered the mess.'

Lana could see the raging fire inside me, she put her hand on my knee. 'There is no need for drama. Be honest with yourself. Do you want your parents to be happy or do you want them to stick together just because it brings you back to your childhood?'

'My mum was not the cause of my dad's affair,' I said and resolutely pushed Lana's hand away from my knee.

'I didn't say she was the *only* cause! It is always about blended influences. That's basic statistics for you my girl.' Lana put her hand back on my knee. 'Listen. You're going to drive yourself crazy with your Jesus attitude. You are not the Messiah to save this world, okay? There are always different versions of truth. Your mum has hers, your dad has his. They probably had arguments before it happened. They probably slept in separate bedrooms for some weeks. Think of the sequence of events. The timeframe is important, you know. Important if you want some kind of objective truth. Which I think as a daughter you should want. Like don't side with one parent or the other, that's the worst thing you can do.'

Lana moved her hand to my shoulder and began caressing the back of my neck. She came closer to me and whispered into my ear, 'If you buy into your mother's or father's split reality, you will fragment yourself. You cannot help others with MPD if you, yourself, are fragmented.'

I pulled away from her and hit the man sitting next to me on the other side. I excused myself, Lana waved at him, 'Sorry mate.' She stopped eating the rabbit food and put her face mask back on.

'You are the rising star of the department. Be the star in your life, too. Don't let others take over your part,' Lana mulled through her face mask. The cabin crew began the cleaning procedure two hours before landing and I was grateful it interrupted Lana's remarks. I was seriously beginning to think that I needed to report that Lana was hitting on me. She probably thought that all her negative remarks were supposed to excite me but I was not impressed.

'You completely missed the plot! Do you think that life is some kind of Shakespeare drama or what? It's you who should get real, Lana!'

'Ha-ha, no drama, comedy please! Human history needs more comedy!'

'So now you are going to pull some random history data to prove your argument?'

'I don't need affirmation. Men do. That's why they cheat. The divorce rates go up in Movember. Just look it up. Some extra hair and their testosterone kicks in. Women don't do that to other women. We support each other to the top. We don't need sex to cope with the pressure. We have built work environments where—'

I put my hand over Lana's face mask.

'Lana, PLEASE, could we just sit in silence until we land? I am really tired. And what you say isn't relevant for me anyway. My dad was not particularly rich or successful when he cheated on mum.'

Lana slowly moved my hand away from her mouth. 'It's all about perspectives, right?' she said and reluctantly leant back into her seat. 'For a baker he was a good catch. For Mrs Bower seeing a businessman buying a croissant before he heads to the office is enough for a lift.'

I was annoyed with Lana. I was annoyed that she was so direct. I was annoyed that there was some truth in what she was saying and that the truth was hurting me. I dreaded the train journey from the airport with her, another two hours of verbal missiles. I was secretly hoping that Mark would pick me up from the airport but I knew he wouldn't do it without me asking him and I didn't want to ask him – it would be selfish to expect him to take the expensive airport train there and back, only to carry my luggage. I should have packed less, I was cross with myself as I dragged the trolley behind me, silently cursing that the cheap design had wheels that needed a pull force I didn't have. I looked up.

'Mum?! What, what a surprise … I mean how did you know when I was landing? I mean you never come to the airport, are you okay?'

'Of course I am okay! What's wrong with picking up my own daughter after a long journey! How was your big conference, sweetheart?'

I was tired after the journey but mum's behaviour totally woke me up. She has never been interested in my work, or in academia overall. She had cut her hair short and was wearing a coat I hadn't seen before. Lana knowingly winked at me as in 'See, I told you so,' and took the train home on her own.

It was the first time mum drove to the airport, and she struggled to find her way out. At least that hasn't changed – mum was a hopeless driver and had a terrible sense of orientation. 'Shall I ask for directions?' I suggested but mum immediately stopped and asked a lady in the car park. I stared at mum, she asked a stranger in a confident voice I hadn't heard before. Her short hair in lieu of a helmet, her actions forcefully demonstrating some kind of spurious self-esteem to beat the enemy. For a minute I thought I had been kidnapped by the British Army.

The lady pulled her non-transparent mask down, revealing her bad teeth and thick accent, and explained the directions to mum. She explained them slowly two times. She spoke with exaggerated pronunciation and with so much detail that I began wondering whether she thought she was giving mum a free English course. Mum's English was impeccable but even if she tried, she spoke with an accent, revealing her Russian heritage. In contrast, the lady she asked was clearly British born and bred. Her badly cut fringe and dark brown hair above her upper lip were a proud testament of her loyalty to the inner beauty philosophy. She even had a patch of dark hair on her left cheek. But she was kind to us, so by the time she explained that we had to turn left after the bridge, I mentally cut all the unnecessary hair, put some foundation on that uneven skin and some mascara on those short eyelashes. I gave her an imaginary makeover session in exchange for her free course to mum.

The episode was a perfect reminder that I was back in my home country. Mum desperately tried to show she was a UK citizen, too, with long-term settled status. She said 'lovely weather' at least three times. The lady kept on giving us driving directions, as if they were directions for making tea, or another mundane activity that the British elevated to a royal status of seriousness. If mum could have, she would send the lady a thank you card. After about half an hour, mum finally charged to the motorway. It began drizzling but mum kept her giant sunglasses on. She passed all the cars in front of us even though she was above the speed limit and her car was not built for speedy drives.

'It's okay. It's okay. She was just a practice girl, you know. A small, ugly girl for local men to test their moves. I was, I AM …' mum said as she dried the tears running from beneath the sunglasses. 'I am now choosing to leave him. Because I am not going to tolerate lies. Because I am worth more than lies. I am worth more.' Mum passed another car, this time with so much force on the accelerator that the car nearly suffocated. 'Any man in the street can now replace him. It's gone, you know, gone, all the admiration and respect I had for him are gone.'

Mum wasn't holding the wheel with her hands but with her fists – it was not a confident driving style. I braced my hand against the dashboard.

'Mum, don't be so hard on yourself,' I wanted to return some grace back to her arms, I stroked her gently on the right arm closer to me but it was stiff and cold. 'This happens in long marriages. In fact nearly 55 per cent of couples divorce. Men have a bigger pool to choose from, there is always a surplus of attractive women looking for a man. Nature arranged it that way, you know, women carry a baby and men look for partners. It's quite common, really …'

Lana's strategy was the wrong tactic, mum got even more upset and we had to stop for her to calm down and drive me home.

Mark was watching a series when I arrived. He stopped it when he saw me. Rooster was happy to see me too, I almost fell down when he jumped at me.

'Did your mother pick you up?' Mark took the suitcase off me and proudly carried it above his head up all three mini steps necessary to bring it to our bedroom. I nodded.

'Your father called too. What's wrong with your parents?'

'I know …' I threw my jacket and jeans directly into the anti-virus washing basket. 'They are probably trying to reduce the gap between them by stretching me in the middle. I am tired of that.'

'Weird,' Mark said and sat down to continue watching his series.

That offended me. I thought he would ask about my trip, make me dinner, or somehow welcome me home. The kitchen was a complete mess, there were dishes from at least five different meals in the sink, an unfinished breakfast on the table, together with empty beer bottles.

'You could have surprised me with a clean kitchen for once,' I shouted from the sink, pouring some warm water on the dried chicken fat on the plates.

'Have been waiting for my collaborator!' Mark grinned but I didn't find it funny.

'You know it's not a collaboration when one person does everything and the other person just rides for free.'

'Wow, one trip abroad and you come back totally changed. What's wrong, babe?'

'Why should anything be wrong with me? You didn't even ask how my trip was?!'

'I saw everything on your Facebook wall. You texted me two times, wrote you didn't have time, but you had the time to update your profile like every five minutes. I am not sure who you are trying to be, to be honest. Like you put serious conference pictures on your Instagram and some crazy party photos on Facebook. What for? For whom? Who are *you* actually?'

'I'm the lead character in my own show.'

'Yeah, Russian doll!'

That was the most offensive comment Mark had ever said to me. He knew I was extra-sensitive to racism. I slammed the kitchen door. I stayed in the kitchen until late, until Mark switched off the TV. He slept on the sofa, I slept in the bedroom alone. I was too tired to cry. I didn't unpack the magnet I bought for him at the airport. I decided I'd put it on the small fridge door in my shared office with Lana.

Chapter 7

'DID YOU READ THE DEAN'S email?!' Lana stormed into the office, my 'Please don't disturb' sign on the desk clearly had no currency for her.

'Email from the Dean? Today? No.' I quickly synchronised the half-analysed extract with my personal cloud, hoping I hadn't lost any of it after Lana's interruption.

I was analysing the interview data of my study participants, looking for some common themes that could help me establish patterns. I typed:

> My life like a play with many stories to tell but no one sitting in the theatre. Is the lack of an authentic audience the major factor in multiple personality disorder? Or is it loneliness? Or both?

I had ten new cases to examine before Monday's deadline. I nervously looked towards Lana, hoping she would start working and stop disturbing me.

'Katie! Hello! The Dean's email! Did you read it?'

I shook my head, put on my headset, hoping Lana would stop. I logged into my StoryScarper account. All ten cases were teenage girls. They were on the long tail of social media traffic, they were not influencers but ordinary users. I scarped the stories they posted on their various accounts in the last month. I had access to their IP addresses, our study was co-funded by the UK's national Internet provider. I could see the girls were posting under multiple names. I ran hundreds of their photos and texts through the micro-narrative analysis software. As my PhD model predicted, their stories scored similar amount of points in multiple categories. Their online lives did not reflect multiple parts of one personality but multiple personalities without one coherent narrative. These girls were posting photos that were neither about seeking feedback nor about documenting their everyday experiences. These girls did not aspire to be celebrities. They acted out as separate individuals and their online behaviours were a manifestation of an internal self-fragmentation.

'They hired Mukherjee!' Lana waved her hand in front of me, interrupting my intense focus staring at the screen. She shouted over the forest sounds inside my headphones. 'They appointed her as the new Centre director! She is going to move from the US next month.'

'Wow, that's pretty exciting!' I was genuinely thrilled to hear that, took off my headset.

'Exciting?! It's the worst news since Thunberg announced her retirement at thirty-two. We need good women in leadership, not old cows like Valerie!'

'That's so mean, Lana. Professor Mukherjee published some good stuff. She is kind – in contrast to you. And she is not that old.'

'She totally fakes her age! Slathers on moisturisers to mask the wrinkles. Look at her chest and you will see the turkey skin! If you want to fake it, then do it well, otherwise it's just sad to watch, don't you think?!'

'I tend not to look at women's chests, Lana.'

'Well there is nothing to see on Valerie's chest, I can tell you that – just one long flat bone! It protrudes from her breastbone, fits well with her parrot intelligence.' Lana was the only one laughing in the room, I got up to stretch my legs, I lost the thread in my analysis anyway.

'Why are you so jealous of her? And why offend poor parrots? They are smart. You could at least pick another bird.'

'Which one, Kea? You know what Kea birds do? They are loyal. When the male dies, the female starves herself to death. Not like your pundit Valerie splashing her husband's dollars on lavish parties.'

'I heard it was the other way round. I heard that when the female Kea dies, the male starves himself to death. And when the male Kea dies, the female finds someone else. The male dies because he was used to her taking care of him, so when she is gone, he cannot sustain himself without her.'

'Ha! Interesting! Your version sounds more human-like. How is it going with you and Mark by the way? Has he apologized?'

'No, not yet. He likes to take time for things …'

'Men always take more time for things. On purpose. Have you not noticed? At work meetings? A man has the same point as a woman but the man takes triple the time to say it. Just to show he has the power. Because of course, as we learnt from Bourdieu's work back in the 1970s, those who have time have power.'

'Sadly Mark says we don't have much time left if we want to have kids …'

'Kids? Who wants kids? I hope you won't let him push you in the corner. Your work will outlive you, in a way you want. Please don't fall into the trap of getting kids now that you started your career. Honestly! It will set you back five years, at least. You will lose the connections and everything you worked so hard to get!'

I didn't want to lose my place at the academic table, but I also didn't want to end up being a bitter feminist like Lana. Is there not some kind of in-between possible?

'It's sad really, that there is not more support for women. I mean why has gender inequality been going on so long in this country? Why can't we have it as they have it in Scandinavia?'

'It's not about gender. You want to be successful in academia? Then climb on others' backs and leave the weaker behind. Simple evolution. Inequality is INBORN, my dear. Inequality equals vagina.' Lana burped and opened a fizzy drink.

I was seriously considering asking for an office swap, but I was put off by the huge amount of paperwork required.

'The only way to eradicate inequality is a war or a natural catastrophe like an earthquake.'

I stared absentmindedly. I kept on thinking about my argument with Mark. I may have been successful in my academic work, but I was constantly failing in love. Lana was doing reasonably well on both fronts, but my body was rejecting the agenda she was setting forward. I did not believe that emotions were just data points and sex was just an 'exchange of bodily fluids', as she put it in her paper. I was willing to work harder on my relationship with Mark. We had passed the time of romantic ideals and impulse-driven affection. We accepted each other for who we were, we knew each other's childhood traumas, we talked openly and were honest with each other.

'It's time to act, not just sit here and moot ideas,' Lana said, diverting my gaze. 'Come on, the opening of the new lab starts in ten minutes.'

'Oh no! I promised to help with the garden exhibition!' I quickly put my coat on and left the office without waiting for Lana.

I had volunteered to help with the public opening of the new neurological section of our Centre. The exhibition panels were heavy and there were no proper stands to secure them in the ground, so I had to stand next to them to keep them erect and ensure that the pinned list of our Centre's successes didn't get blown away. As I stood there, my mind drifted.

Would Professor Mukherjee bring some fresh air to our Centre? We certainly needed to innovate things. Especially the ways we involved the public in our research. Our marketing team had worked on the exhibition plans for months but the space was devoid of visitors. The same lack of audience engagement online. We had drafted and approved the Tweet about the exhibition in three rounds of emails, but in the end, it was retweeted and liked only once – by our sister research centre.

'It's quite understandable you're disillusioned.'

I jumped at the sudden voice behind the exhibition panel. A man with a big, inviting smile appeared. I smiled back. The man was taller than me but not by much. He wore large black Derby shoes and a tight pink shirt, revealing hard nipples and a gently trained chest. His eyes were calling for righteousness. I got a whiff of cucumber from him, he had probably come straight from the director's welcoming speech and had a canapé on his way here. His visitor name badge was upside down, but he was clearly not bothered about it.

'How ... why do you say that?' I moved slightly away from the poster, so that I balanced on two feet. The man was attractive. Seductive, I'd say. I felt the colour rise in my cheeks.

'Of course, I could be wrong,' he added in the most charming tenor voice, and self-depreciatingly bowed towards the poster I was holding, helping me keep it straight. As he stretched his arm, a whiff of L'eau d'Issey flew towards the back of my nose, calling to mind all the Hugh Grant films I had seen.

'Of course you are right. Of course this is not why I work weekends and nights. To stand in front of a poster that no one reads.' I did not know why I said 'of course' twice, it wasn't a word I usually used.

His face softened. 'I did read it. I think it's great what you do at the lab. Important work. Interesting.'

He emphasised the 'ing' and it sounded like a baby rattle. Sweet and playful.

'Well, that's a first. Most people don't know anything about our Centre.'

He laughed in a gentle staccato like men from Eton do, while looking straight ahead.

'So tell me about yourself.'

I loved how the 'so' softened the brave invitation. 'You want the Instagram version or the non-sanitised version?' I was ready to tell him anything.

'I want both! Can you leave your post? Fancy a walk? I'm Aron, by the way.'

I left the poster leaning against the wall. Aron did not usurp my space as we walked, and he did not deviate from his side of the pavement not even once. He walked a bit like Lana, with his feet turned slightly outwards. But unlike Lana's wobbly duck gait, he walked with an assured zig-zag.

'Sooo … you call this a low-maintenance garden or a customisable garden, doctor?'

I liked the way he teased me as if we were friends from long time ago.

'Can a garden have many identities?' Aron picked up a leaf from the gravel and put it on the grass.

'Well … I haven't thought about it … But I guess that with so many pebbles everywhere one could add some flower pots and turn it into a Mediterranean garden. Or a Japanese garden with some more energy investment. Or a—'

'Yup, or a gravel and rock garden.' He interrupted me. 'But not a cottage, right?'

'Right. No chance at Prospect Cottage here!'

We both smiled. A moment of silence rose between us but it was a moment of good, rewarding silence. No one had an urge to check their phone anytime soon, we just looked intensively at each other, wondering not whether, but *where* we met before. We talked probably an hour but it felt like we talked for days about all sorts of topics. There was so much mutual understanding.

I told him about the work we did at the Centre, about some of the initial findings. Aron was not a scientist but he knew a little about many things, he was the typical hedgehog type. I was the typical fox type, I knew a lot about a few things. He could connect many diverse dots and generalise from them. I could analyse the same thought for hours and hours. He told me that everything he knew was from what he heard from others. Everything I knew was from books and my studies. I was the nerdy academic type who could sit for hours in the library and he was the wild gangster who had no patience for formal studies. We admired each other's differences. If Tinder had been recording our answers on that walk, we would have been a perfect match.

'I'm not sure what it is, but there's something I like about you,' Aron said as he smiled. 'Do you want to meet for a coffee sometime? Or dinner?'

I have never felt as awake as when he asked that. Wings grew on my back and I was ready to take off. 'Yes, definitely.'

We followed each other on Instagram. He had no profile photo, just a name: Aron 007. Six followers and all seemed fake. *Had he set up his account in a hurry? Was he was not interested in social media, but in higher causes, like me?*

Unlike Mark, who got pathetically excited with five Likes for his photo of a beer can, Aron didn't post anything. He used Instagram just for messaging. Talking to him was like reading a *New York Times* article, the thoughts were synthesised, prompting new thoughts in me. He was so different from Mark. He was so different from all the men I had ever met.

Chapter 8

I GOT HOME LATE AND Rooster was desperate for a walk. 'I thought you would walk Rooster since you worked from home today?'

Mark switched off his computer and said in a loud voice, 'Working from home. Emphasis is on the first word my dear: WORKING. I can't be walking a dog while running the Excel sheets.'

'Running them? That's totally the wrong verb for tables! Come on, let's have a proper run, Roosti!'

I jogged alongside Rooster, Mark walked four metres behind us. I was doing small circles to return to him. I thought I was doing him a favour; he thought I was ignoring him.

'The point of a joint walk is that we WALK together. And talk. You hop around me like you've just won the lottery!'

I slowed down, trying to walk alongside Mark. 'I'm just feeling very happy today. What is wrong with that?'

'What's the reason behind the happiness?' Mark asked.

'Professor Mukherjee is joining the lab.' It wasn't a lie – I was genuinely glad she was joining the team, but I couldn't tell him about Aron. I didn't want him to get unnecessarily jealous. *I haven't done anything anyway. I just talked to him and followed him on Instagram.*

'I talked to your dad, by the way. He rang out of the blue, said he just wanted to chat. Quite remarkable how talkative your parents have become since the divorce!'

'I know! Sorry he rang up. Thanks for talking to him.'

'It was quite a good talk. He even invited me for a beer!'

I was equally surprised as Mark, since it was very unusual for my dad to be inviting out anyone, let alone Mark, AND for a beer. I always thought dad only drank whisky. 'Very, very strange. And did you see the email from mum, the one she copied you in?'

'Yeah, I was going to ask you about that. What does she want us to donate money to? And sign a petition? A desalination plant in Russia? Since when is your mum interested in environment? And in water in Russia?!'

'I know … but I signed it. I want to support her. Her self-esteem is so low right now. She is campaigning for others, you know, it's a good sign that she is healing. Just sign it please. I can transfer some money from both of us.'

'Don't worry, I've signed it and sent some Bitcoin already. I just found it very strange.'

'Thanks for doing that, Mark. Did you book the train for Saturday?'

'No, I was waiting for your instructions. We can do it now, actually.' Mark stopped and sat down on a bench, catching his breath while getting his phone out.

'My instructions? It's all straightforward, Mark. We have the date and time, you just need to book it so that we get the early booking discount.'

Mark started typing into the search box: train … early booking discount …

I stopped him and typed the train company directly into the browser. His finger hovered a good minute above the site, then typed on the booking box but instead of using his fingerprint for autofill, he started entering all the information manually. I couldn't watch the slow process, I snatched the phone from his hand, put my finger on the screen and booked the tickets within two seconds.

'So now you know what I'm gonna do next time you ask me to do something,' Mark said, furiously snatching his phone back.

'Well, sorry but I'm all sweaty from the jogging and am getting cold and it is a real pain watching you type so slowly.'

'I was trying—'

Rooster began barking at another dog in the park. I ran to fetch Rooster. We got home and Mark ordered some Chinese. I cleaned Rooster, then fed him before climbing into the shower. I let the water run down my head. I loved the head massage. I didn't want to get out of the shower. I didn't want to face another argument with Mark. I didn't want to sleep next to Mark. I felt as if I was not dating just him, but him together with mum and dad. My relationship with all three was entangled with Jackie and Rooster and our ancient flat in Lavender by the run-down Stratford Station. And with MS and a divorce. It was tangled with my past life that felt like a sore muscle full of knots and kinks. I tried massaging my back with warm water, to untangle the loops. A thought of Aron crossed my mind, releasing all pressure from the muscles, leaving only a delightful, sensuous glow.

As I dried myself I looked into the mirror. Who was I kidding with my princess dreams? How could I be so egoistical? How could I think that I could leave Mark after all we had been through? He didn't deserve it, and I certainly had a bigger agenda than messing up my life because of a sexy guy. I knew nothing of Aron. I could find virtually nothing about him online, and he hadn't even told me why he had come to the lab exhibition. I needed Mark and he needed me, we needed to look after Rooster. I put on moisturiser, the expensive organic one mum got me for Christmas, careful not to use too much so it lasted longer.

'Sorry, Kitty, about earlier,' Mark whispered and pulled me into him, my back on his chest.

'No, I'm sorry, I—'

'Feel this!' Mark rubbed his thigh against my thigh. 'Can you feel, can you feel how soft?'

'Ehm, yeah?'

'I put on the coconut cream, you know how you said my skin is too rough, so I put your cream to soften it. Is it better?'

I didn't have the guts to tell him it was his badly shaved cheeks that I had been commenting on and that the cream was for women, and especially for me. He was trying to please me and I needed to try, too. I didn't object when he started pulling my knickers down. I was dry and not ready but I didn't stop him when he penetrated me from behind. It hurt but I tried to respond to his rhythm. I tried to breathe in shorter bursts, making the sounds I knew would turn him on. I tried to avoid his badly shaved beard stabbing my cheeks. I tried to help him come as soon as possible. He did, eventually, and I quickly put my knickers back on. Mark began snoring, and I curled myself into a tiny ball, hugging my small pillow. I whispered into it that I had just been raped and no one should ever know.

Chapter 9

Is love authentic only at the beginning of relationships? Do all love stories become a well-rehearsed scenario after the first three dates? Is that why the question 'How did you two meet?' is the most exciting question to ask a couple?

I WAS FURIOUSLY JOTTING MY thoughts into my diary.

Are we simply too many people on this planet, with too many connection possibilities, that there is simply no room for originality anymore? When did Mark and I cross the threshold of routines? On which morning did I start switching on the coffee machine without thinking it is my expression of love to him? When did my brain learn the command and automatize it? Did it all start when I placed myself before Mark in my deepest vulnerability? Because caring for me during MS attacks gave Mark the control to hold our relationship together with a set of commands?

My phone alerted me that Jackie was by the door, six seconds earlier than Rooster began barking. I closed my diary and looked around. The kitchen cupboards were sparkling clean, scented with organic rose water. Our yellow table, with lemons in a glass bowl, matched the colours on my T-shirt. Yellow is for hope. Lemons are for perseverance. A thought of Aron cut my mind. I smiled, opened the door to Jackie.

'I can't sleep. I keep thinking of him all the time.'

'What, after ONE conversation? You must text him! Meet him again!'

'I don't know, Jackie. I worry that Mark will find out. I would never cheat on him … but every time I think of Aron, my heart starts bumping! I can't eat or sit still. I just want to dance! You know that feeling?'

'You are in love! You are TOTALLY in love with that guy!' For once Jackie was not on her phone but excited to hear my news. Not for long, though.

'Can I take a snap of your fridge?' she opened our fridge and took a step back to take a shot of all shelves. 'It's for my new campaign. I'm calling it #TF, Transparent Fridge. It's about showing what's inside people's fridges. March is the month of social media transparency, you know. I was at Frank's earlier today. Look at his fridge!'

Jackie showed me a photo of a fridge with nothing but an old broccoli stem, a yellow melon, two bottles of mustard and a half-open yoghurt.

'I mean what the hell is he going to cook with these ingredients?!' Jackie tagged the photo with a confused emoji face.

'Does Frank know that he is part of your Transparent Fridge project? You might wish to consider informing him. Your sharing might have a negative impact on others.' I was choosing my words carefully with Jackie. She was not emotionally stable and I knew that a negative comment could truly upset her.

'I blocked Frank, so he won't see what I am sharing. What do you mean *might have* on others? Just say what you want to say not all this *might* and *could* stuff. You mean I should block Frank's followers too? He only has 200.'

'That wouldn't necessarily be helpful.'

'Ah come on, Dr Wikipedia! No one understands when you talk like that. Do you mean it's fucking useless? Do you mean my project is rubbish?'

I opened my Instagram, typed in #InstaGood. I wanted to show Jackie some landscape photos but scrolling took me down the same rabbit hole Jackie was falling into. Endless image streams of more and more content resembling the gross video of a hot guy that I initially tapped on. I had to purposefully tap on at least twenty random photos that had nothing to do with my interests to reset the algorithm and delete the irrelevant ads. Jackie was part of the uncontrollable personalization push generating revenue for others.

She didn't see how her counting of followers resembled magnates counting dollars rolling in. The more advert money she got, the more she invested into follower campaigns. And the more followers she gained, the more she became the target of trolls. People were interested in stealing her identity and damaging her reputation. At least two fake accounts impersonated her, and more than a dozen must have blocked her. She was not just a brick anymore. Jackie had reached the stage when her digital façade had become a wall. A prison wall locking her out of the external world, online and offline. She was despairingly lonely behind that wall.

I didn't want to think of my friend as an ill person but I was certain she was in stage 1 of MPD. I wished I could talk to someone about it. Not anyone from work – my colleagues would turn Jackie into a study object, a number for our database. I didn't want to talk to Mark about it either – he would think that Jackie was even more crazy than she was. Mum adored Jackie, and she would get unnecessarily worried if I told her. Perhaps I could speak to Aron. I could talk about anything with Aron. I had so many things to talk to him about.

'Come on, text him.' Jackie saw me staring at Aron's empty profile photo.

'I'm not sure. What if he is not single?'

What if Aron was married? Did he have children? How many people would I potentially upset if I got involved with him? Would I damage anyone's reputation, or make someone unhappy? I had so many questions stopping me from pressing Send.

'You're worried whether he is single or not? Hun, you don't want to target single men! Let me show you.' Jackie pulled out her phone, sat down, legs crossed, tossed her hair back. In olden days, a secretary would pull a file from the cabinet. In our time, Jackie went onto the Viral-love.com portal and logged into her dashboard. 'Targeting single men is like employing someone who is unemployed,' Jackie explained. 'You want someone who thinks that you are better than what he currently has and who would leave his current partner for you.' Jackie scrolled down a gallery of male photos and numbers attached to them.

I was taking mental notes. Finding a match was not about filling gaps but about comparison scores, Jackie was saying.

'Basically, you compare previous exes against the new guy's health records from the national database, job history on LinkedIn, and friends' status on Facebook. You want someone with at least one hundred friends actively liking their posts. You know, someone who is liked by his immediate community. Now, watch this! See how the comparison score changes? That's because being followed by a celebrity pushes the Friends status up. So you are lucky that I follow you back. Your score is quite high.' Jackie smiled.

I was trying to process what she was telling me.

'Then you check Ancestry.com scores and his history on Insta. If he's more of a studious type, he will likely have something on Twitter, too. Oh, and the other cool thing with this dashboard is the list of past purchases on Amazon. Buying history has a higher truth-related score, so it's definitely worth checking. But to be honest with you, all the data are pretty accurate. This is a decent company, you know, they hack personal micro-servers, so they get the data directly from individuals. Don't go for the cheap firms that just scrape data from Internet providers, you need authentic data to crack the love algorithm.' Jackie looked away from her screen towards me.

My face must have looked baffled.

'Don't worry, you will get the hang of it, the learning curve isn't steep. Look at this guy, for example. His social score is quite low but the algorithm ranked him higher so I looked him up. And guess what, the guy posted on his timeline that he dreamt that I followed him back. So I did and it went viral, you know a star follows a loser kind of story, so it got me lots of medium-quality new followers. I muted him when he started messaging but the point is: sometimes it's worth following back those with low scores, too.'

What Jackie was explaining disgusted me. What was the purpose of such love scores and games? I preferred not knowing this was the way some people looked for their prospective partners. I thought this data-based matching was the worst example of how people can abuse each other's trust.

'What are you thinking?' Jackie interrupted.

'I am thinking … that that this is the worst example of … of democratic design with stealth meritocracy.'

'Wealth what? You speak so weird! Anyway, hun, one more thing. When checking the scores, you also need to check the local area. Like if a guy lives in a low density area and he is popular in that area, then that decreases the match score. Same if a guy and his partner share many followers between each other. Like more than twenty shared friends should activate alarm bells. Makes sense, doesn't it? Local politicians and guys who co-own businesses with their wives, those guys are hard to get.'

I couldn't hide my puzzlement. Jackie continued guiding me. 'I've created a profile for you, don't worry, and I can help you out with the first match. You can upload Mark's pictures into your exes folder. That releases his data to the market.'

'What? No, stop! I haven't broken up with him! Yet. I mean I don't know whether I will. I need time to process this. I don't want to be part of this platform, delete it, Jackie! Please!'

'Hun, you are part of the platform anyway. Everyone is. This way you can be in control. See, this is how other users can view your profile.'

Jackie searched in the database for my name, clicked on my photo, showed me how my data had been ranked by the algorithm, photos of my face scored according to attractiveness and symmetry, my PhD ranked higher in the intellect category, but my MS data and wheelchair use dragged most scores down and revealed 'potential' matches with a community of men with MS.

I lost my composure and said in agitation, 'I don't want to be part of this.'

'And this is my profile.' Jackie showed me the long list of people who had viewed her profile in the last twenty-four hours. 'You know who is stalking me? Liam Gallifor!' Gallifor was ranked first because of his two million followers. He did not follow Jackie but checked her profile three times in the past week. Jackie clicked on Liam's list of followers. He followed only sixteen accounts and all of them were charity organisations or national bodies.

'So you need to become an institution so that the hot guys follow you?' I was trying to understand how the game worked so that I could delete my data from the platform. 'Do you need a logo to attract Liam?'

'A logo? No! I'm not a company. I'm a BRAND. I don't do free ambassador crap. I only take on paid partnerships with other brands. I want Netflix to pick me for their next celebrity show. I'm pretty close now.'

Jackie clicked on her Revenues tab, showing me colourful graphs and charts with precise revenue growth and detailed breakdowns of individual and group engagement with her campaigns. I was both excited and frustrated by the graphs. Academic graphs were so difficult to interpret that we needed to take weeks of expensive courses to understand them. I was frustrated that such systems were not being used for diagnosing people but for commercial use. The love companies openly stole data. They clearly copied the data collection techniques from researchers and spy agencies. They brazenly used basic psychology principles to make the most money for their coffers.

Jackie relished watching me 'get' it.

'You can choose your own love cookies and benefit from the whole package.' Jackie had probably not eaten the whole day and her breath was really bad. I had to pull my chair back a bit. She began uploading photos she had taken of me to my profile.

It was all so against my motivation, actions and values that I did not bother with careful politeness around Jackie and told her she had a bad breath. She took it okay, thank God. I offered her a banana, she took out her pocket knife, cut it into a slice that was thinner than altar bread and let it linger in her mouth. When Mark eats a banana, he puts the entire fruit inside his mouth and makes jungle sounds. When Jackie eats a banana it becomes an Eucharist liturgy. I finished the rest of the banana, threw the skin into the green bin. My phone bleeped when I closed the bin's lid. It was an alert of increased rat count in the area. I double-checked the lid was sealed.

'Was it the rat alert? I saw a gigantic one on my way here!' Jackie momentarily looked away from the profile photos.

'Yeah, rats are getting bigger and more resilient with each generation.' I looked at the photos Jackie was selecting for my profile. Some were very old.

'Probably because of all the rubbish that we eat.' Jackie spit the banana into a napkin.

'The sad thing is that rats eradicate the birds. We already have the problem of very low numbers of mating birds because of noise pollution.' I was trying to distract Jackie by pointing to the kitchen window. I could see she would soon attempt to throw up. I hadn't realized her bulimia was so severe. 'You know the birds can't find each other in the noisy towns. They spend winters practising their love songs but when they sing, their partners can't hear them. We lost so many nightingales in the past twenty years.' I was talking quickly, frantically flapping my arms, hitting the window screen.

Jackie didn't run to the toilet, she was fixated on the screen. Maybe it was a treatment option I hadn't considered before.

I gently placed my hand on Jackie's shoulder, I asked in a low voice, 'All these men you connect and chat with Jackie, do you ever meet? Like in a pub for example?'

'What for? We can have a pub background on Zoom. We both have sex toys.' Jackie immediately showed me the background options on her screen. 'He can pay for my home delivery. Why would I expose myself to danger? I can switch off the camera or totally log off whenever I want.'

Why are you doing this to yourself? I did not say it aloud. I stood up, looked down at Jackie's small head. She was enthusiastically crafting my profile, but all I wished for was to delete the data, and take her on a trip to Legoland and reset her mind.

'Influencing is good money,' Jackie said proudly and switched to a screen background showing a 3D cot for babies with a Christmas tree and fireplace with burning logs. I could not watch the self-destruction anymore. I left some low-calorie muesli bars next to Jackie, unwrapped one in case Jackie found the packaging difficult, and left the kitchen.

Mark was not at home, the living room was quiet and tidy. Rooster was lying on the sofa on his dedicated mat. He raised his head when he saw me come in.

'Good boy.' I petted him behind his ears. I felt pity for my best friend and indifference towards my long-term boyfriend. I lost trust in my dad, I did not understand my mum. I didn't want to go to the office, I didn't want go to the library, I didn't want to check my phone. I wished I could be elsewhere but did not know where. I didn't want to exist in the world Jackie showed me. I sat down on the sofa next to Rooster. I looked towards the window, I looked at the clouds. The sky looked so indecisive – it could be rainy or sunny in the next half an hour.

I felt a strong urge to speak with someone who would understand me. Someone who would spotlight the path in front of me, cut through the foggy air. My phone bleeped. Lana sent me a photo from our office, a photo of my empty desk, accompanied with Lana's customized heart emoji. Was she hitting on me? I was sure I was not attracted to her. If I were to deviate from my current situation, I would do it for Aron, not her or any other 'match'.

I did deviate once before. Mark knew about it, the short 'affair' in Critten with Dr Andrew. The doctor who misdiagnosed me. The doctor who caused me so much pain. He ghosted me afterwards, and I swore never ever to fall for lust again. I sat with the phone in my hand and in a momentary lapse of weakness, I unblocked Dr Andrew and looked at his latest posts and photos. My fingers trembled as I scrolled through the profile that I had hidden from myself for the past three years. I scrolled faster and faster and I accidently followed him. I immediately unfollowed him, but I Liked the latest photo, my fingers trembling, so I quickly unLiked the photo and quickly blocked him again, hoping he would never register the quick notifications and deletions.

What a stupid idea, Katie! That guy damaged you so much. He abused your vulnerability when you were ill, misdiagnosed you, gave you the wrong medication to earn money. Why would you waste any of your energy on him?! I was cross with myself that

I had done that. I was worth more than that. I had a degree, I was not disabled anymore. I deserved to be loved. I was worthy of an attractive man's attention. I had the right to leave Mark if I wasn't in love with him. Maybe Aron was my next new big love. Maybe he came into my life at the right time, and I should honour his presence and not dismiss it with my fears.

I stood and messaged Aron. He responded immediately. We decided to meet at an Italian restaurant the same evening.

Chapter 10

'THAT JUMPER LOOKS AMAZING ON you,' Aron said as he opened the restaurant door for me. He took off my coat and guided me to the table he pre-booked. He poured me some water that was waiting on the table. He told me to order what I fancied because the evening was on him. It was good that I checked the menu before our meeting, the myriad of choices with the extra options on top of salads and their combinations with mains was overwhelming, I had to work hard to remain focused.

The Italian waitress stood by Aron's side of the table, her glances and lipstick a slash pouring over Aron. 'The daily special is red peppers. They are big and hot. Recommended. Or if you want something really special we have home-made tiramisu.'

But her open flirting was in vain – Aron firmly replied, 'Thanks but my life is sweet enough with my hot date here. We'll order from the menu.'

He ordered oysters for the starter with some bread and dark sauce. He said that oysters tasted best in Uramura in southern Japan. I had never eaten oysters before, and I had never been to Uramura before. Aron told me a story about the Japanese huts on islands, he delivered it with perfect intonation and choice of words. I laughed, I had a great time. Aron opened a bottle of white wine without any hesitation, sliding out the cork with the typical 'pop.' I told him I shouldn't drink too much because of a past health issue, but that one glass was all right.

'I won't drink more either. I need to work on my abs … was in the gym this morning. I don't want all the calories back in a glass.'

He looked stunning but I could not find the words to say that to him. The perfection and competence with which he acted had shrunk my tongue. I was sure that whatever he did, if a nurse, plumber or banker, he was competent at it. *What am I competent at? Writing papers for other postgrads to read?* I felt so small in comparison with all the information and knowledge he possessed.

A family with a toddler was seated next to our table. The baby began screaming as soon as the parents pulled out their phones. The father reluctantly picked up the baby, held his little daughter awkwardly in the air, as if she had a new Covid variant. The baby screamed more, the mother looked equally helpless, tapped her daughter on her back while the father held it up at a distance.

'Why don't they hug the baby?' Aron whispered to me.

I nodded and cut the side vegetables on my plate. *Could his words be more connected to my thoughts?* I wanted to say something that would connect us even more, set down our joint thoughts into the place around us.

'Sometimes I wonder what would happen if people could reproduce like leeks. You know you put a piece into water, like this white end, and it grows on its own. It is independent you know. And strong. Ready to be eaten up.' I half-swallowed the end of my sentence with the leek.

Aron smiled but the baby cried again, so we moved away from the noisy family. Aron and I switched seats, we exchanged smiles. I wanted to switch my job for time with Aron. I wanted to exchange Mark for Aron.

I tried to remain rational for the rest of the evening, but once the thought of leaving Mark entered my mind, I could not think of anything but wedding dresses and baby names. Aron was recounting his military experiences to me. I tried to look formal and not think of undressing him from the uniform and giving him a hot oil massage. I lost control of my thoughts, I could not even categorise Aron into one of the basic Hippocrates' classification types.

'You seem to be thinking,' Aron teased me and placed an untouched prawn from his plate on mine.

'No, I was just, just listening …' I looked at the prawn. I could not sustain Aron's gorgeous eyes on mine.

'Tell me exactly what you're thinking, right now, in this moment,' Aron challenged me with the sweetest couple challenge.

'Nah … well, okay, then. I was thinking about the four seasons, and I was wondering which one you like most.'

Aron smiled. 'All four. I was born during the worst year of global warming, remember, no clear four seasons. I thrive in all conditions.'

I laughed. His eyes, full of small stars, shipped me to another universe. I went to the bathroom, his eyes following me in and out. He paid the bill before I returned to the table, as all gentlemen in romcoms do. Then he helped me put my coat back on, gently adjusted the scarf. Like all good leaders, Aron was both direct and soft. *Could this man one day be my lover? My partner? My husband?*

As soon as we left the restaurant Aron asked, 'This was very nice. May I see you again?'

'Yes, I would love that,' I whispered, screaming YES! inside.

'When is good for you?'

Anytime! Anytime, Aron, anytime! My body was fizzing and my mind deleting any forthcoming deadlines. Aron was my calendar from that evening onwards, my whole life arranged around Aron's agenda.

'Thursday, maybe?'

Aron nodded.

We walked towards the tube entrance, hands brushing against each other. Aron took his coat off, his white shirt shining, an Excalibur in the dark night. He shivered as we passed the river but he would not admit he was cold. All he said was, 'The wind is a bit fresh.'

We came to the tube entrance. The strong neon light reminded me of all the Critten hospital stays. I stepped out of the light, removing its bad filter from my face. Aron did not need to know about my past. I stepped closer towards him, he came a bit closer too and asked, 'How would you feel if I kissed you now?'

My entire body spasmed, Aron leant towards me and we kissed. On the lips. I was flying and sinking into the ground at the same time.

'Good night, beautiful.' He swiftly turned the corner, his grey coat glistening in the dark, his shoes clopping in the distance.

I did not take the tube, I did not walk home, I *swam* through the park. I was stretching my arms towards the sky as if diving into a blue ocean, my arms making the same movements as when swimming a breaststroke, my legs walking instead of kicking the water. I looked weird but I couldn't care less. I used to stretch my arms like this when I was sitting in the wheelchair and swimming pools were closed because of the pandemic. In those days I lived a dim reality and dreamt of better days. But after my evening with Aron, the world flipped. For once, I was living a reality I didn't want to escape.

I quietly unlocked the door. I jumped when I saw Mark in the living room.

'Where have you been? I was worried about you. I texted you and called you three times! Jackie said she can't tell me.'

'I was just out with … with some friends from work.'

'Until nearly 1 a.m.?! You could have texted me!'

I stood there, unable to answer.

Mark continued, 'Rooster has diarrhoea. Don't know what it could be. I rang the vet. He said to give him some potatoes. I think he's better now. His nose is wet again.'

'Roosti!' I threw myself on the floor to caress him, overwhelmed with a wave of guilt. 'My darling! My sweet.' I kissed Rooster on his forehead, touched his dry nose, then changed the water in his water bowl. What would happen to Rooster if I left Mark? We both loved our Roosti. We needed the doggie in both good times and lockdown times.

'See? There are other problems in the world, not just yours. Academia is for narcissists!'

'You think it's narcissistic that I want to pursue my career, Mark?'

'It was a joke.'

'It was not funny. Do you realize what the odds are against me? Family, woman, disabled. You call it narcissistic that I want to find fulfilment?!'

'Sorry, I shouldn't have said that.'

'But there is truth in it, right? You do think that. You think that my career is selfish because I don't want children.'

'Sorry, Kitty, I didn't mean it that way. Come on, let's go to bed, we're both tired.'

I wanted to take Rooster to bed with us but Mark refused. I insisted, it was my subconscious way of preventing Mark from touching me. I should have insisted more, I was telling myself, lying next to Mark, naked.

'I can't, Mark. I am not in the mood, sorry.' I pushed his hand away but he caressed me more and pushed himself closer to me. 'No, Mark, I don't want to. Okay?'

'Why? What's wrong?'

'Nothing is wrong, I just don't feel like it tonight.' I turned my back towards Mark but he didn't stop and started kissing my ear.

'Mark, stop!' I screamed.

Mark sat up, his face shocked.

'Are you in pain? I mean is it your MS?'

I looked at the ceiling, my head a complete whirl after the alcohol and kiss with Aron.

'Yes, I am in pain,' I said quietly.

'Oh, Kitty, I am so sorry. You should have told me. I would have been more careful. Does it hurt when I touch you here?'

Mark carefully placed his hand on my thigh, remembering that was the place where I began losing sensation with my first MS attack.

'No, it doesn't hurt there, it's … it's …' I wanted to explain but tears streamed down my face. I remembered all the pain I suffered through at Critten, how Mark looked after me, then the dream of a beautiful life with Aron and I just cried like a baby, unable to talk. Rooster began whining, so Mark gave in and brought him into bed with us. I caressed his little belly, put his paw on my arm and fell asleep.

Chapter 11

I WOKE UP WITH A very dry mouth. Mark made my favourite green tea in the kitchen before he left for work. I sighed. I didn't want Mark to be doing good things for me. My plan was to break up with him that evening. Or in the morning. But instead, I did the routine thing: I took a picture of the mug full of tea and sent it to him with a heart and thank you emoji. Mark immediately texted back with a smiling emoji. We had been in that kind of situation many times before. We relied on emoji talk after arguments.

I drank half of the tea and opened my Instagram.

A message from Aron: Good morning, princess.

I spilled the tea out of excitement. *Good morning, princess!* It sounded like a refrain from the evening before. I wanted to sing it, I wanted to shout it to the entire city. I couldn't hold it in anymore. I must tell Mark. It was cowardly of me to lie to him yesterday. *I need to tell him the truth.* I did not love him anymore. *No, hang on, Katie, you can't tell him that, it will hurt him! But what else can I tell him? That I don't want children with him? That I met a fantastic guy and I'm totally in love with him?* If I told the truth to Mark, it would destroy him. I don't want to destroy Mark. I want him to be happy. I want both of us happy.

I typed a message, then stopped myself. *I can't break up with Mark with a text message and generic emojis.* Our relationship was worth more than that. But could I tell him the truth face-to-face? I thought of mum and how destroyed she was after she found out about dad's affair. I didn't want to be a liar. I needed to be brave. It didn't need to be very complicated. I would just tell Mark that I didn't want to be with him anymore. No more explanations. I had the right to say 'no.' Why was I so scared? Aron wouldn't be scared. Aron would give me confidence. Aron would guide me through the decision-making. At work. At home. In life. I was clear in my choices. I wanted to be with Aron, so why was I so careful about not hurting Mark? *I was the one who was hurting in the relationship. I was the one who had to clean, tidy up, organise everything. I was the one who always initiated fun things. Mark only ever initiated sex. I was the one who arranged for the new sofa delivery and its assemblage. We could afford the trip to Portugal only because of my university discount. I have had enough. It's time to move on.*

I was no longer feeling sorry for Mark. I had made up my mind. Mark could say what he wanted, but I was leaving him. I decided to tell him that evening.

Mark came home late. That irritated me because I didn't want to sleep at home after breaking up with him. I had arranged for Jackie to pick me up at 6 p.m.

'How are you feeling today, babe?' Mark wanted to hug me but I withdrew. 'Oh, is it that bad? Kitty, we have to tell Miss Peake. You know she said to call her immediately when the symptoms return.'

'No, no, don't call Miss Peake. I don't want you to call her or any nurse. I am fine.'

'You are not fine, Kitty, I can see that. You are trembling, and you can't be touched. You look like you've been crying.' Mark looked up the nurse's number on his phone.

'No, Mark, listen to me. Stop, stop looking for the number. I am not well because I … because I don't want to be in this relationship anymore. I … I think it would be best if we went our separate ways.'

'What? No, NO! No Kitty!'

I stepped back.

Mark furiously shouted. 'No, you did this before. Remember? When you had your first attack. You wanted to break up because you didn't want to hurt me. Now your MS has returned and you want to do the same. You want to protect me again. I know you too well now, Kitty. Come here, Kitty. I love you despite MS. Okay? I will not let it break us. I know you are in pain, and I am here to help you.'

I was speechless. I hadn't expected this. Mark's generous eyes fixated on my tears, I was breaking inside and outside. *Come on Katie, put yourself together!* I looked out the window and saw a white bird flying towards the blue sky. *Was it a dove?* I swallowed. I felt the taste of Aron's lips on mine, his hand brushing against my shoulder as he held the coat for me.

'I can't be with you, Mark.'

'Kitty, don't. Honestly, we have been here before,' Mark said firmly, dismissing my words and heading towards the kitchen. 'You are just tired, exhausted after the pain. Come, I can make you a cup of tea …'

'No! Mark, listen! Listen to me!' I screamed. My body was shaking. 'Listen, Mark! I lied to you! I have no physical symptoms. I lied to you because I couldn't tell you the truth. The truth is I am not in love with you anymore.'

Mark stopped, his face puzzled. He looked at me in disbelief, picked up my favourite tea cup he had bought me in Lisbon.

I came closer to him and said, 'I am in love with another guy. His name is Aron. I went to dinner with him last night. We kissed before I came home.'

Mark's face went white. He slid down to the floor, my favourite cup fell with a loud bang. The cup didn't break but Mark looked as if he was dying of heart attack. I fetched a glass of cold water and dialled emergency. Mark stopped my hand from pressing the 'Locate me' button.

'Are you okay? Drink some water.' I put my cold hand on his forehead.

He took the glass and drank down.

'Leave me alone. Go. Go away.' He pushed me away, got up and sat at the kitchen table. He stared at the wall, his face pale, his eyes blank.

I left the kitchen, the flat, the building. One half of me felt terribly guilty and wanted to hold Mark and give him more cold water and cook him some sausages and make him feel good again. The other half of me knew that I needed to hurt and offend Mark so that he hated me and let go of me. I followed that other half. *You did the right thing, Katie. You feel terrible and he feels terrible but you did the right thing. There is no gain without pain. You told him truth and that is always the right thing to do.*

Jackie drove me to a café where we drank hot chocolate and talked about Aron's biceps. She prepared the couch in her living room for my night at hers, and she even switched on some Christmas fairy lights, 'So that my friend Katie feels loved,' she said.

I couldn't remember the last time I stayed overnight at Jackie's. Probably before I met Mark. I had neglected my friendship with her and all my other female friends since I got together with him. I had neglected so many fun things. I had neglected life, really. It was time to let go of my past. To experience magic. To grow myself back into a fairy tale.

Chapter 12

Lana said I could stay at hers anytime, and I took her up on her offer after five days at Jackie's.

'Welcome to the club of free, independent women! Let's celebrate!' Lana blew up a balloon but saw that I didn't share her enthusiasm. 'Okay, you might not get to see that dog so often but one should never stay in a relationship because of kids. And definitely not because of a dog!'

I was not smiling.

'Come on, girl! You liberated yourself from Mr Boring and found Mr Charming. It's Pimm's o'clock!'

Lana didn't get that I was not smiling because of what she said but because she had prepared her double bed rather than a separate bed for me.

'Have you ever regretted that you didn't have children?' I asked as I put my bag down in the living room, hoping Lana would understand I was setting my boundaries.

'Me? Never. I don't want children. I don't need to replicate myself.'

'Do you think that if you met someone who really wanted children, you would change your mind?'

'Nope! And what a weird question to ask! I can have kids anytime. You too. Just save up some money and instead of buying a car, pay Artificial-insemination.com. Having a baby is a personal choice. They'll design the exact baby you want if you choose that. You can pick temperament and nose size.'

'Services like those make me NOT want children.'

'You must listen to the anti-baby podcast. Not having a child is the most powerful statement a woman can make against the world order. Childless women care about the environment. Reduce the footprint.'

I kept my mouth shut, thinking about how Lana's old-school thinking clashed with the latest technology we worked with in our Centre.

'Anyhow, what shall we eat? I have a frozen *tom kha kai*. Shall I defrost it? It's chicken in coconut soup.'

With nowhere else to go and nothing different to eat, I agreed.

Lana's messy flat was the opposite to Jackie's ultra-clean plastic paradise. Lana had never thrown anything away, the place was growing from the inside. On the kitchen windowsill, the beetroot had grown a grey cover. In the bathroom, empty bottles of shampoo offered an arsenal of confusing choices. The well-trodden trails of bacteria radiated from every tile, ending at the soap dish, where the small remains of bar soaps lay on top of each other. I washed my hands, returned the soap to the amorphous shape, carefully as if I was placing a stone on top of stacked rocks on top of a mountain.

Lana and I finished dinner. I hadn't eaten chicken for years and would have preferred Jackie's arugula leaves, but I thanked Lana and sent her some money for the food. I said I wanted to read before going to bed, hoping I could fall asleep on the sofa instead of in her bed. Lana brought me a pile of self-help books, all of them on narcissistic boyfriends, toxic relationships and enslaved women. I thanked her and stayed in the living room, pretending to read but thinking of Mark and Aron. *I did the right thing by leaving Mark. I left him before I cheated on him. I was not happy with Mark. I was not honest with my own feelings when I was with him. I was constantly re-bandaging our relationship, like a wound that wouldn't heal. Aron accelerated a decision I'd made before I met him. I made space for Aron, I was honest with my feelings. That must be a good thing! I didn't jump from one set of arms to another set of arms as some girls do. I did the right thing!*

'You must read this – it will change your life. It's based on Schopenhauer's tetragamy, you know, two husbands and two wives living together. But it's rewritten for modern times with a Chinese twist.'

I looked at the cover with a 3D yin-yang symbol, switching its core white-black colours as I touched it. The tagline on the cover read: From the New York Times bestselling author of *Parallel Marriages*.

'You didn't read *Parallel Marriages* either?!'

I looked up at Lana and shrugged.

Lana searched her library for another bestseller to indoctrinate me. 'It's a total page turner! The girl married her yang partner to father her children, and then she married her yin partner to have intellectual stimulation. She lived together with both. Instead of waiting and ageing, she had two marriages in parallel, yin and yang at the same time. The kids were balanced, the parents were balanced. Awesome! Read it!'

'Okay, thanks, I will. But not now. First I need to figure out what to write to Aron and Mark.'

'You write to Aron that you want to meet him again. You write to Mark that you don't want to meet him again.'

'If only it was so simple, Lana! I also need to find a new place to stay.'

'You can stay at mine for as long as you like. Do you fancy something refreshing?' Lana generously opened the fridge and poured us the only thing there – some old pineapple juice from a soaking cartoon.

How can I get myself out of this? I don't have money for hotels and I don't have enough savings for the deposit required by most landlords. I couldn't ask Aron for help, I didn't want to come across as poor and desperate in a budding relationship. I couldn't ask mum or dad, they have enough problems of their own. I could stop paying my share of the mortgage for the Lavender flat. It's located in a poor neighbourhood but it's still a lot to pay. Mark won't be able to cover the whole amount with his salary. I couldn't make him homeless.

'I can help you.' Lana interrupted my focused look at the pineapple juice. It looked orange in the blue glass.

'No, thank you. I got into this mess myself, I need to fix it myself.'

My only option was to work more to earn more money so that I could rent a place for myself. There were many offers for small jobs at the university, some extra teaching hours here and there, some extra proofreading for undergraduate theses. They were jobs that could be done in late evening hours, during the commute or at weekends.

Lana knew I was working twelve hours a day, but after I moved out of hers, she didn't know that I had made the office my home. I bought a sleeping bag and I would usually shuffle myself under the office table around midnight. I took out the cheapest gym membership to take showers there. I ate foods that could be prepared with boiling water from the kettle, instant noodles and porridge oats were the most frequent choices. I didn't plan it that way. Practical solutions happened as I filled every waking minute with a money-earning opportunity. I didn't have the time to think about a more sustainable solution, I needed money quickly and would not debase myself to the kind of job industry Jackie represented. Jackie thought that I was sleeping at Lana's, and Lana thought I was sleeping at Jackie's.

I worked hard, I slept little, I ate almost nothing. Because I worked so much, and Aron was busy too, we spent too little time together to qualify as a couple. I daydreamed about better times, about joint holidays together. Aron suggested somewhere green and wild near Tbilisi in Georgia. We talked about sex in a tent once, although we hadn't gone beyond kissing at our dates in the city park. We met infrequently and we didn't write much either. We had to change the platform two times. His ex-wife was obsessively checking up on him, or so he told me. We moved from Instagram to a fully encrypted messaging service. He said he wanted to be careful while everything got legally settled. I respected his decision and took a similar path avoiding Mark. I told him not to contact me, and I didn't see Rooster for a month. The only contact we had was a confirmation of the money transfer from our joint bank account when I paid the mortgage. Mark hadn't changed the passwords, and I saw he notified our lender about single occupancy. I also saw that he notified them of 'painting the walls and changing the kitchen wallpaper'. I didn't complain about paying half of the cost. I knew it was Mark's way of covering up our joint memories. I wanted to help him move on.

Chapter 13

Mum asked me to help her get established in her new job and I reluctantly agreed. I asked Jackie and Lana to help too, as I sensed there could be a benefit for them: Lana would spend time with Jackie, whom she adored, and Jackie would have new material for her IG story. Jackie drove, Lana and I sat in the back of Jackie's Cabriolet. Lana had her window open and teased Jackie about how dirty it was. Lana was different around Jackie – or perhaps she was just different outside the work context. She seemed kinder and more attentive to others. She searched for Aron on her phone but could not find any information about him, apart from his new Twitter profile that I had already found.

'With such a common surname, it could be any of the thousands of 'Milton A' accounts!' Lana enlarged Aron's Twitter profile photo. 'Wow, are you two shagging each other?'

'Told you! He is really hot!' Jackie shouted from the front, her contralto cutting across a karaoke version of 'Otherside'.

'Totally. He looks like he is in a high-power job. I mean, that suit?' Lana was still staring at Aron's profile photo. 'He tweets like a robot though. Look, all Tweets are automated. Does he have dyslexia?' Lana asked.

I hadn't seen that. I thought the Tweets were rather well written. I downloaded Aron's photo and Photoshopped it with my arms around his shoulder. I made it my laptop screensaver. It gave me a little kick every time I logged into work and needed motivation.

'He dominates you, doesn't he?' Jackie was circling the block of flats where mum moved to, looking for a car park. 'Did he ask for an American?'

My face blushed dark red.

'You have to be gentle with Katie, she grew up in a Puritan family,' Lana said, then winked at Jackie. 'Not a religious cult but, you know, no sex talk, ever!'

I didn't know about sexual positions. Until now, Mark had been my only sexual partner. And Lana was right: my parents never talked about sex.

'Aron and I like it classic.'

Lana's and Jackie's faces showed confusion.

'Basic. Me on top.' I added.

'She is the possessive type!' Lana giggled. 'She likes to be in control all the time!'

'Right here, to the left, you can park there, Jackie!'

Jackie squeezed her Cabriolet into a tiny space between two old Teslas.

'He looks like a man on a mission, too sexy to commit. These kinds of hero guys want just one-night stands.'

Lana's comments drove straight into my heart. Aron said he was in the middle of a divorce and that he was staying overnight at his mum's, who was sick with cancer. I trusted him on that. Our inability to spend the night together was one of the reasons I wanted to earn enough money to get a place. To get space for a bed. For a nice double bed. I had a bed in my Amazon Wishlist, together with the same brand of luxurious bedding as they had in the New York hotel. With pillows and sleeping lights and an innerspring mattress. So far I had enough to afford one of the pillows.

'He's probably hiding from his wife,' Jackie said, pouring salt on my wound. 'Or maybe he is a convicted criminal. I couldn't find him on Viral-love.com. No history of previous alliances, boyfriends or girlfriends.'

'Are you two just envious? Not everyone has their life listed online. Aron is not a social media guy. He told me that several times. We agreed not to put our pictures online.' I was cross with both Jackie and Lana. Besides, I was not interested in Aron's past – I was interested in our joint future.

'What? You're finally dating a hot guy and you are not going to share it?' Lana asked. She stopped scrolling Aron's five Tweets and slowly opened the car door, trying to not hit the Tesla next to us.

'I can't see how sharing our photos could make our relationship better,' I answered brusquely, opening the door right into the other Tesla from my side of the car. I hit the part below the window, scratching Jackie's pristine Cabriolet door. 'Jeez, I am so sorry, Jackie!' I tried wiping the scratch with a tissue.

Jackie inspected it, took a photo and smiled. 'Don't worry, it's a good Insta story, I'll tag my insurance, and they'll cover it for free.'

I tried to smile to show my relief.

'See! Photo sharing brings multiple benefits!' Lana nudged me. 'Don't you remember the lecture we had on photos at uni?'

I remembered it very well, it was part of the module on memory. The professor told us that photos were powerful. That they could set people into action. That they stayed in memory longer than words. That was partly why I did not want to post any photos of me and Aron – I did not want to hurt Mark. If he saw me with another guy, especially with such a good-looking guy, he would sulk and ache even more. Perhaps, after a year or so, his wound would heal somewhat.

'Everyone benefits from sharing! As long as it's properly acknowledged …'

'You know I am a hopeless, old-fashioned academic, Lana,' I attempted a joke. 'I prefer anonymous peer review!'

'You talk like that farting professor! Does he really think that no one knows where the smell comes from?!' Jackie tapped Share, tagged her insurance company publicly and one of her exes, the one who was a car mechanic, privately.

'Jackie knows Nicholson?' Lana asked and laughed. 'You are right. Anonymity is extinct … unless you are a total loser who has never written anything. Nicholson has forty thousand citations, but everyone in the field knows his writing style. No point in anonymising.'

I didn't argue anymore with Lana and Jackie. I was tired of them, but I was grateful that they came to mum's with me. Being around mum these days was difficult. Anything or anyone deviating from her scheme could unleash a crying episode.

'Welcome to your first Prio,' mum welcomed us in her home, handing us small tote bags. Fifteen women, me included, and one man, compressed ourselves into a tiny lounge. One woman had the tote bag on her knees, another one sat on it and Lana had it on top of her head.

'Did all your mum's friends meet on Roots-Forum.com?' Jackie whispered, activating her Siri's silent mode.

The women appeared the same age and had the same Russian accent as mum. Mum explained that to qualify as a certified Prio representative, she needed to have at least fifteen real-life measurements. We were the guinea pigs, basically, in mum's training to become an adultery detector. Mum kept on using the word 'basically', which was new and annoying to me.

'This is just a test, basically. I will not share the results with anyone. It is just for me to practise, basically,' Mum said, beaming with enthusiasm. She believed this new job would empower her, and enable her to give back something to the community. Basically.

I looked up Prio on my phone, their profile had little information. The company paid their employees based on the amount of picked-up and verified cases. The only equipment they gave their employees for free was a subscription to the Prio app. The model seemed to be more abusive than the old Uber economy. With 360 Google cameras calibrated for milliseconds, and micro-servers storing the personal data of all Westerners, the likelihood that the company would survive more than a few weeks was minimal. I wanted mum to get a well-paid job with a social safety net, but in Britain those were reserved for bankers and MI6 employees.

'Use the coaster!' I stopped Lana from placing her glass on the table. 'Mum gets upset easily these days,' I whispered, though it was difficult for the other women not to hear me in the tiny room.

Lana rolled her eyes and used the coaster but took no prisoners with her words, 'Your mum should get a psychologist.'

The woman next to Lana whispered, 'She still carries her husband's shadow. She needs to burn some sage leaves over old photos.'

Mum heard sage and began stressing about where she could get the perfect sage leaves and taking notes on for how long she should burn them, in which position, how many grams, at what time of the day.

She has always been like that, obsessed with precision and the need to fix things. There was always something to fix in our house and we needed to save up for it. We had a small, terraced house that looked just like twenty other houses on our street, but ours was always in urgent need for extra care and maintenance. Dad used to say that mum was a great driver, which was wonderful for the car but hapless for fellow passengers. I didn't understand the meaning of that sentence until today.

'Don't worry, Irena, you don't need any sage.' The man put his right hand on mum's right shoulder. He was tall and spoke in a soft voice with Macunian accent. 'History cannot be set right. If we could repair the past, we wouldn't be sitting here tonight.'

The man turned to me. 'I'm Lionel. Nice to meet you, Katie.'

I blushed. *Did mum tell him my name?* I didn't like the thought of mum talking about me to a stranger. I had hoped that mum did not tell him about my MS. Or about Mark.

'I had a daughter of your age,' Lionel added.

I turned away but there was too little space in the flat to escape intense looks.

'Are you no longer in touch because you cheated on her mother?' I looked with disdain at Lionel's hair. It was in the shape of fresh parsley.

'No, my daughter died. Bulimia … But my wife Maryl is still with us.' Lionel smiled, revealing his big white teeth and a lovely pink tongue.

'Lionel's wife has dementia and is in a care home. She doesn't recognize Lionel anymore but Lionel comes to see her every day. He let her shout at him. As if he was a stranger invading her privacy!' Mum sounded like the app company she was supposed to be representing. 'And Lionel's brother was killed in a racially motivated attack,' mum added, as if that horrible experience gave Lionel extra points.

I looked down at Lionel's hands folded on his hap. He had beautiful, almond-shaped nails.

'It's the working class. It has always been them, basically. Strong politicians can keep them under control but all the uprisings after, I don't know, is it worth it?' Mum asked Lionel, then served us blinis. Her hair, woven into an around-the-head braid, made her look like a walking advertisement of post-Balkan nostalgia. Mum and I have never been very close, but seeing her like this reminded me just how many miles were between us. She kept on talking, mostly to herself. 'Poor people are dangerous. It is scary. Are you not scared? It's your generation.' Mum looked towards me.

'Scared? Me? I'm not scared of the working class. I'm scared of who supports Wilfred. I'm scared of *why* they support him.'

'Wilfred has periodic follower dips. It leaked on Buzzfeed yesterday. He bought at least 80 per cent of his followers,' Jackie unexpectedly added to the discussion. She was standing next to the circle of women where I was sitting. The women stared at her high heels and how she was tapping her right foot up and down. All seemed to be in awe of Jackie, even though none of the ladies heard what the pretty face said.

After mum's presentation, no one waited around. 'Katie, we are leaving now,' Lana said and waved at me from the entrance. Jackie was already outside. I wanted to stay and help mum tidy up but Lionel insisted on helping too. He said he enjoyed cleaning and washing. He whistled while he was collecting the plates. Despite losing his daughter and all the trauma, there was no bitterness in his eyes. I quite liked him and wondered whether mum did too. I left when mum and him started talking about the bear dances at Izmailovo market. It was mum's favourite childhood memory but her constant vocalisation of how much she deplored the British colonial record made her looked sad. Lionel was cheering her up, I had to leave the scene.

The evening at mum's reminded me how glad I was to leave my past behind. I did not want to keep any remains, not even the dried red rose petals, that Mark had given me once for Valentine's Day. With Aron there was a fresh trail of originality, shrouded in an exciting mystery. The less I knew about him, the more I liked the gradual unfolding of his faceted identity. I was not interested in knowing who he was with before; what mattered was that he chose to be with me in this precise moment. In his presence I felt loved and cherished, I felt like an academic, like an attractive young woman, like the Katie I aspired to be.

Chapter 14

Aron didn't rush into having sex and that made me desire it even more. The image of us making love, somewhere with rays of sun coming through half-open curtains and the aroma of Nespresso coffee, hung in my mind. I kept on adding the sunlight Snapchat filter to the Photoshopped picture of Aron's Twitter profile picture and my selfie, decorated it with a double bed from Vividus and with Sakura perfume puffers. The image brightened every new boring report I worked on. Aron unleashed an unknown source of energy inside me that propelled me at work from early morning until late night.

The university rewards hard work, and at the end of the summer, I was promoted to associate professor, which meant I had enough for the flat deposit. I rented a one-bedroom flat in a leafy area close to the university in the same area that the staff recommended to Professor Mukherjee when she moved from the US. Her house looked like a cut-out from Harrogate or Tunbridge Wells, with a romantic front garden and a big front door. My basement flat was a cut-out from history books about servants' dwellings in nineteenth-century Britain. But I was over the moon to have a place on my own. I said that to Valerie when I met her at the corner shop. She complained about the lack of Molton Brown boutiques. She wanted more shopkeepers in tweed jackets and brown shoes who greeted customers by name and sprayed the latest fragrance on their wrists. I celebrated that the corner shop opened because they sold reduced chickpeas. Despite our differences, Valerie and I smiled at each other every time we met in the office corridor or on the street, as good neighbours and colleagues do.

Lana never smiled at Valerie. To keep her job, however, she had no other option than to attend the department seminars and participate in group discussions.

At the most recent meeting, Lana had to raise her virtual hand three times before Valerie let her speak.

'I have an interesting case,' Lana said, her hand still hanging on the wall where Valerie projected the slides. We were sitting in the same room but Valerie followed the hierarchy of virtual meetings.

'Fill us in!' Valerie said, pressing the 'unmute' button, totally disregarding Lana's physical presence.

'Jenny. A girl in her early twenties. She was diagnosed with MPD last January. Was referred to our Centre by Jenny's boss.' Lana began sharing her slides on the wall, Valerie's PhD students got their note-takers out. 'Jenny's boss noticed that she was arranging fake Zoom calls to appear productive. Jenny scheduled regular meetings not only during work time but also in the evenings and weekends. All meetings were only with what Jenny referred to as her 'family'. Lana paused, the PhD students adjusted the sound on their note-recorders. 'The boss sent me one of those videos. Jenny displays four personalities. A budding politician fighting for female rights; a young, romantic girl who likes to walk in nature; a nasty forty-year-old misogynist; and a three-year-old baby needing protection. I looked up Jenny's online record. She has set up mini universes for all four persona, including the toddler. The toddler is presented in YouTube videos for toys' endorsements.'

'Remarkable. What are you going to do?' I asked as I emptied three sachets of instant coffee into my mug.

'I am going to theorise the case for the *Journal of Visualities*.'

'What's the argument of your paper?'

'I want to link it to the Film Quantity hypothesis. I think Filton-Polard was the first to discuss it.' Lana looked towards the PhD students, who nodded, but I didn't know the hypothesis, so Lana explained. 'Basically it predicts that the higher quantity of films watched, the more prone subjects are for reality confusion. Filton-Polard applied it to the Corona Generation and argued that lockdowns reinforced the propensity.'

Valerie corrected Lana. 'It wasn't about fictional stories in films. Filton-Polard specifically referred to lockdowns and increases in video-conferencing with front-facing cameras. Seeing themselves on video activates the sense of a blurred identity. MPD sufferers feel as if they are someone else, so they act as someone else. It's not just a performed identity but a felt identity.'

'Important distinction!' said one of the PhD students.

'I don't think it can be limited to just videos. What about those Snapchat filters that can change one's face to look like an old grandma or a little baby? Surely they are triggers for MPDs? I mean the filters are captivating even for healthy individuals,' I was speaking with confidence, Valerie's tacit support of my ideas boosted my self-esteem.

'True! And TikTok spoofs and challenges. I have a paper about it in the *Journal of Telemarketing*. You need to add that to your paper, Lana! And use my societal theory as your guiding framework.' Valerie took over the shared screen and displayed her paper.

'I was going to use another theory.'

'No, you need to use the societal theory. You are part of this Centre and citing works of your colleagues is showing collegiality in the Centre.'

'By colleagues you mean *you*,' said Lana, and threw her empty Coke bottle in the bin right next to Valerie. 'You don't want to be the paper's co-author so that it doesn't count as self-citation. You want more citations by forcing junior colleagues to reference your papers. I know your tricks. It's pathetic!'

Valerie's jaw dropped. She looked at Lana from head to toe. I sensed a storm coming, and I wanted to avoid an argument.

'There is no need for a dichotomy here. As we know, there is something about linguistics that disempowers the bodily ...' I threw in a quote from Professor Nicholson's book hoping it would dilute the argument.

Valerie stood up and hissed towards Lana, 'Don't forget that everyone is replaceable.'

'Are you threatening me?!'

Valerie didn't answer, but she put on her khaki-coloured coat, with bits of fox fur on the top, and big round buttons. She didn't button up and loudly walked out of the room, with her PhD students immediately following her. It was the end of the tutorial, I anti-bacted the room and returned to the office.

'Are all those PhDs blind or really that incompetent?!' Lana asked, opening the office door for me.

I was trying to defend Valerie but Lana didn't stop even when I sat on my office chair and began typing.

'Do you want to co-write the paper with me? You can be the second author. It will be Dr Fidgely and Dr Kuznetsov.'

'No, thanks.'

'I have the introduction ready. I set the context for how right-wing politicians strapped teenagers of cash and stability, then a short lit review of the digital media havoc, and then Jenny as a case study.'

'I am trying to write less and ... and *do* more.'

'You chose the wrong job then! Writing *is* doing in academia. Stop being so naïve, Katie!' Lana loudly sipped another Coke. 'Our Centre is not for activists but scientists.'

I ignored Lana, opened my diary, began writing:

> Science has been stagnating in universities because of the 'publish or perish' mantra. I want to listen to our

participants more. I want to be with the MPD sufferers, have their experiences impregnate my skin and build a deeper understanding. Maybe Socrates was right in saying that writing ruins it all. Writing introduces a distance. Modern universities were much more applied, focusing on immediate problems and solutions. More business-like. I want to speak with Aron about this.

I drew a heart.

'So do you want to write the paper with me or not?'

'Honestly, Lana, I think that writing a paper won't be of any help to Jenny. Or any other MPD sufferer. They need direct support. Specific advice. Now. Not in a year's time when the paper gets approved and published.'

'You can't tell people what to do. Academia thrives on vagueness. And publishing is quicker for small-scale study. We barely have data here, it will get through the review quicker. Come on, Katie, we are in this together! Academia empowers people by giving them knowledge. That is your Mother Theresa bit.'

'Empowerment with no support is fake. We can't just inform people. We need to make people wiser,' I objected.

'You want to give practical advice? Go on then, squeeze your paper into handouts with bullet points. You get a higher impact score, Valerie will like that. But remember that for all impact work they will want you to get the Dean's permission and charge a hefty consultancy fee. Your beloved Valerie surely knows more about it. Academic consultancies are all the rage in US.'

I quietly moved away a from louder and louder Lana.

'Can you not see her strategy?' Lana opened the window above my desk. 'That bitch paints you like her protégé, then overloads you with meaningless tasks so that you don't have time to work on things that matter for *your* CV. She does it on purpose so that you can't be promoted again and threaten her position!'

'You are bullying her. And me. Stop it please.'

'Ah, come on, a bit of bullying will toughen you up. It's part of natural selection.' Lana lit an electronic cigarette, the puff went directly into my face. I opened the window more, moved to the back of the office, put the kettle on, sat down on the floor next to the mini-fridge.

'Sorry.' Lana stopped smoking, shut the window, went quietly to her desk.

Perhaps Valerie has grad students making coffee for her. Perhaps she delegates everything as Lana says. I did not know how to climb to the top. I did not know how to walk on the ground either. All I knew was that I was in love with Aron.

Chapter 15

ARON'S MOVES WERE ZIG-ZAGGING MY calendar in unpredictable ways. I simultaneously loved and hated how unpredictable he was. When I desired him most, he would go off radar and not text me for a week or two. Then he would turn up at my door. Maybe he did it on purpose to break my habit of scheduling and planning things. I got incredibly nervous and tense on the days he said he would come, counting the minutes, checking my hair and clothing millions of times, not eating all day to keep a flat stomach, and praying he would not cancel and come. I liked it best when he gave me a date in advance, then I could starve and overwork myself for a couple of days, so that when he appeared, I felt resurrected and ready to die in his arms.

He was so sharp and intelligent, I didn't want to sound like an idiot by being completely me, so I carefully prepared my lines for each rendezvous, jotting down my thoughts when I was waiting. I scribbled them in my secret little notebook, and I read them to myself before he came. I pulled out a line or two when I was stuck for words and that happened each of the four times that he visited me in my new flat. I felt I had so much to learn from him. Intellectually and bodily.

We finally had sex. Though it was far from the sun-stricken, slow love-making I dreamt of, my body had never been this excited. Aron said he had good control and I completely trusted him, so there was no need to use condoms. It was rough and yet pleasant. He did not just change my understanding of sex, he revolutionised it.

Aron was fifteen minutes later than the ETA that he texted me. I jumped when he rang my doorbell.

'You always park so far from my flat!'

'Ha-ha, just avoiding the parking charges. You look great, come here!' he grabbed me, giving me a long kiss. 'What have you been up to?'

'Just waiting for my prince charming.' I blushed as soon as I said it, remembering that I had memorized five good sentences precisely to avoid such stupid clichés. 'No, just kidding. I have been grading some students' work.' I quickly corrected myself. 'Until the blue Twitter bird blushed with a heart emoji from you.' The last sentence was from my notebook.

'Ha! Red dots are powerful!'

I wasn't sure whether he was making a reference to the Hindu tradition of married women or whether he was quoting a romantic film I that hadn't seen, but I felt committed and compelled. I drew my fingers through his hair, carefully avoiding the gel. He stayed for dinner and we made love for the fifth time, Beethoven's *Eroica* playing in the background. He waited for me to come first, moving us from movement one to movement two, from innocent to dirty stuff, without making me feel dirty. Every time I thought that he would come, he would take it to yet another key change. We made it all the way to finale and the last tones of the fourth movement.

I woke up early. Aron's loud alarm was set for 5.30 a.m. He didn't want breakfast, not even a cup of coffee. He packed his stuff as soon as he woke up. I have never seen anyone as tidy as him. He always put his clothes in a little pile, always checked twice that nothing was on the floor or kitchen counter before he left. I liked it, though I wished he left some love tokens behind. A simple note would do. Or an unfinished coffee. Or a strand of hair. Every time Aron left, I drank litres of green tea, trying to fill the emptiness in my heart. I wished we could bridge the waiting times between our meetings with some kind of virtual presence, but I respected Aron's discreetness around that. I tried to be more responsible for my irrational feelings. I gave Aron small gifts every time he visited, comforted by the thought of him carrying a little plastic heart on his keys, or eating the piece of chocolate I put into his coat pocket.

'Could you drop me off at work?' Aron agreed and I was delighted we could spend the extra minutes in the car together. I was hoping it was dark enough that he couldn't see my puffy eyes and hurried make-up. I had barely slept that night and was addicted to caffeine, but I felt totally awake in his presence. Driving with him through the morning rush hour and listening to some Moby songs made me feel the closest I have ever been to my dreams. He drove me all the way to the university gate. I quickly put a mint in my mouth and kissed him goodbye. Aron drove off, his tyres squealing with a James Bond effect. I waved at him, my tummy tucked in, breasts and buttocks, out. *Perhaps he will spot the fruit salad I left on the back seat and enjoy it for lunch.*

'Muah, muah, how sweet,' Lana mimicked. She had seen Aron and I kissing from the office window. 'Feeding each other from beak to beak. Smack, smack. You two should get a cage and stay inside!' She closed the window with a bang.

I tried to focus on work but all I saw was Aron's face: on my desktop, printed on all documents, stuck to the kettle and in the window reflection. I wanted to be with him all the time or at least call him.

Lana had classes all day, and I was supposed to work on the paper Lana had started on the Jenny case study. I had no desire to write another paper, but Valerie had 'strongly recommended' I co-write with Lana. I began typing some words but could not concentrate on the article. I was doodling in my diary, trying to compose a nice text message to Aron. I switched on the playlist that I had titled A&K's Songs, and I listened to them over and over, thanking Google for serving me romantic songs in a loop. I looked out the window, then returned to the text message. I rephrased and edited my sentences, then finally sent it at 5 p.m., assuming that was appropriate for ordinary working hours.

Aron didn't respond, and I couldn't see whether he had read it because he had the restricted messaging mode on. I texted him again the following day and the following day but got not reply. It must be one of those 'going off the radar' weeks. I was coping less well with those after we had sex.

I lost seven kilos in the two weeks Aron went silent. I was eating little and haphazardly. I only shopped at the small corner shop close to the university, it offered very few choices but it was cheaper than the big market in my neighbourhood. I needed to save some money for the exclusive chocolate range that I eyed for Aron. I wanted the chocolatier to make it personalized, the chocolate bar in the form of Aron's car. I drew the form into my notebook, it was warming me in the nights, the paper covering the top of my palms instead of the steel silence of Aron's absent hands.

The corner shop had an independent supply chain, so they needed to sell everything they had on their shelves. I could get a basketful for less than ten pounds. The vegetables were slightly stale but good enough for a broth. I trained my eyes to spot the REDUCED label – a light orange sticker – and I could see it from several metres' distance. When buying food for Aron, I would not touch anything with that label, of course. But for my food, the orange sticker was a badge of approval.

I was sorry that I could not keep the impressive two-hundred-pound top that I had splashed out to wear for one of my dates with Aron. He previously said he liked me in white. The top was pristine white with tiny, embroidered crystals. I could not afford to keep it, so I kept the tags on, hoping to return it right after the date.

'It has clearly been worn.' The shopkeeper refused to accept it. She sniffed it like a police dog.

'I just tried it on with my perfume on,' I lied.

She was adamant and I had to keep the top. I took a photo of it, stuck the photo inside my diary, then gave the top to mum for her forty-fifth birthday. I hoped she would not wear it for her meetings with Lionel.

Chapter 16

'ARON PROBABLY WENT BACK TO his wife. Maybe you made their marriage better. That's quite rewarding, isn't it?'

I didn't respond, I wasn't in a mood for Lana's cynical words. She handed me a tissue.

'Don't take romance so seriously. Just keep it flirty. A butterfly memory,' she said as she pulled her office chair away from mine, adjusting the volume on the radio. I turned the volume down, I didn't want to listen to catchy summer songs. Lana kept on singing, 'Love, love, love, a way to remember your past, past, past.'

'You don't understand. He was the love of my life, he …' I couldn't finish without bursting into tears and I didn't want to cry in front of Lana. Aron hadn't responded to any of my messages for more than a month now and I took it as a sign he had ghosted me.

'Don't be pathetic! You two barely saw each other. You don't even have any pictures together. Look on the bright side. He helped you to move on from Mark. Now you are free to date someone who deserves you!' Lana continued singing the refrain, 'Love is nothing but a memory … memory-ry-ry … prompt machinery-ry-ry… .'

I grabbed my laptop and went to the library, thinking I could work from there.

Surely this is not over. This is just Aron not being contactable for a while. Why am I so impatient? Back in days couples communicated via letters. I am just being spoilt with the immediacy of modern communication. Stupid Lana. She brought me down so easily. I don't want to date anyone else. Aron is my soul mate. But what if Lana is right and I was just a fling for him?

I devoured a package of crisps and felt even worse about myself. *What if Aron lied to me and never got divorced? What if this was his way of telling me that?* The worries planted themselves inside me, insidiously invaded my core, competing with other thoughts I wanted to grow. I didn't get any work done, staring at my phone all the time, hoping Aron would ring or text. My obsession continued the following day, and the following day and the day after. I couldn't motivate myself to do any work, to go for a walk, to ring someone, to get out of bed.

I got a bit better when my paper got published in a top tier journal. I again sent Aron several short messages, two photos of the sky, two selfies from the office, asked him what he was up to the past three weeks. No response. No digital trace on any social media. We had agreed we would not ring each other because we could disrupt an important meeting. But he hadn't replied to any of my: 'Can I ring you?' messages. The worry that he ghosted me reappeared every time I looked at my phone. After much debilitation and hesitation, I bought myself an energy drink and my favourite cookies, sat down on the sofa in my flat where he had sat five weeks ago, and I dialled his number.

The phone rang three times, then I heard a female voice. 'The number you have dialled has not been recognized.' And again. 'The number you have dialled has not been recognized.'

Had he changed his number? My heart beat faster and my hands began to sweat. I had no other way of contacting him besides that telephone number. He said he was no longer checking Twitter. I didn't know where he lived. I had no other platform, address or object to identify him. I took several long breaths, trying to calm down. I rang Jackie. Half an hour later she arrived at my flat.

I thought Jackie had come to soothe my heartache but our roles reversed as soon as she entered the kitchen. Her hair was bright blue, her eyes dark green. She sank onto the chair, showed me her phone and cried, 'Look! Look! That bastard posted a video of me kissing him while I was COMPLETELY naked!'

'Revenge porn? Oh, no. Report him, Jackie.'

'I don't have time for that. Look! 441k views and it's growing!'

I saw the numbers going up in real time, together with a torrent of comments and emojis, some heart ones, some vomiting ones.

'Jackie you have to report him!'

I stared at the responses flowing in, Jackie kept her eyes on the video.

'It's completely the wrong angle. It shows my hair extensions! And I look so fat!'

'What? My dear you're worried about that?! Anyway, look, the video's all over the Internet now, you need to report him to take it down!'

The video spawned memes, and the hashtag #FakeyJackie began trending in London's Twitter feeds. Jackie was furiously deleting all the posts she was tagged in from her timeline. 'What shall I do?! Help me!'

I put on my calm, academic-authority voice. 'As I said. Report him. To the police. And to Instagram.'

Jackie completely ignored me.

'Or you can continue the faking and say the video is not you.'

Jackie looked up from her phone with a bright smile. 'Like a deepfake? Genius!! Thanks, Katie!'

Jackie jumped to the corner of my kitchen, tossed the curtains a bit and started her piece-to-the camera, 'Hey folks, here is some info about the video Mads has just posted. It's a deepfake. Look closely and you will see it's not me but a version of me faked by Mads. He made the video in his garage. Probably while masturbating to porn. He does that a lot. So guys, if you share the video, you're supporting the porn industry. Thanks for NOT watching.' She added some filters and stickers and posted it as a 'hot update'.

I thought the saga was over, but after posting her update, Jackie collapsed again and burst into tears, 'Everyone knows now that I dated a loser!'

'It's okay. You did the right thing. People will listen to you. They won't watch it. Instagram will take it down in a few minutes, don't worry.'

'No, I don't mean the video. I mean people will know I dated Mads and he has only 1,200 followers. I can't jump to Josh now, you know he has massive fanbase. I need to work my way up from the bottom again!'

I was trying to remain rational and supportive but I found it extremely hard not to let the emotions take over my voice. 'It's gonna be all right, Jackie.'

'You have no fucking idea! You get notifications when someone mentions your boring papers. I get notifications when someone abuses me! When I am trending in a disgusting video! I feel so sick! I feel so sick! I need to vomit!' Jackie got up and threw herself on the floor.

There was no vomit. I tried to lift her up, she was lighter than a two-year-old child. I sat down on the floor with Jackie, she was fidgeting, howling.

'Shuush, shush,' I said as I patted her back, caressed her hair, pushed aside any sharp objects in her reach. She eventually calmed down and apologized. I made her hot chocolate, wrapped her up in blankets, sat next to her on my double bed. I was no longer in doubt – it was clear that she was ill. It wasn't just some kind of by-product of the sick influencer world, it was a strange mental illness taking over her.

'Thanks,' Jackie whispered, sipping the chocolate foam. 'I didn't grow up with grandparents you know. I am vulnerable. I have not experienced unconditional love.' She sounded calm again.

I caressed her head. 'Where did you read that?'

'The therapist told me. She said I need a family. Or at least a golden retriever.'

'What about a good friend?' I smiled back at her. Jackie took a long sip, looking into the void. 'I see, a nerdy friend is not popular enough.' I said, continuing to smile. 'A golden retriever in front of a fireplace would get more Likes.'

Jackie didn't smile, she stood up, her voice serious, 'You study these things. Tell me what's wrong with me. I am sick of hearing it's complex, and that I need more therapy sessions with expensive bills blah blah blah.'

'I'm not a therapist, Jackie. I'm not clinically trained. I can't give any advice.' I could not stand looking into Jackie's disappointed eyes. 'I don't know. I would perhaps …' I was going to suggest limiting social media use, but Jackie had the phone in her hand again, checking the responses to her video story.

'He responded two seconds after I posted the story! Such a loser! He was just waiting for immediate revenge!' Jackie put the unfinished chocolate on the floor, straightened herself on the mattress and started typing while still talking, 'Shit! I forgot to make myself invisible! Delete! Delete! Ufff! That was close. Now, where are you hiding you bastard? You think I can't see your fake account? I'm gonna shoot you down!'

I stared at Jackie, I stared at my empty hands. Jackie was in a flow and I knew I had lost her to the gambling design again. I let Jackie sit on my bed, shooting her messages and comments until she was completely exhausted. When she eventually stopped, she looked at me, lying there next to her. I was holding my phone, looking at old photos of Rooster and me running in the park.

'What's wrong?' Jackie asked. Her eyes veered towards my pillow, wet with tears.

'Nothing, sorry.' I moved to hide the cushion away, but Jackie stopped my hand.

'What's wrong? Seriously, tell me!'

'Nothing is wrong. Nothing is good either. There are no goodies or baddies. Life is not a battleground, Jackie.'

'Did you break up with that Agent 007?'

I nodded, then said, 'Not a break-up, he's just gone silent. It's been two months.'

'Maybe he is just ill. We all are, anyway.' Jackie got up, put a big scarf over her face and left my flat.

She sent me a basket with chocolates with the evening delivery as a surprise thank you. She had that strange way of being my Jackie, with that confusing kindness. I was not sure whether I was interpreting her behaviour correctly, I was not sure whether I was interpreting Aron's silence correctly. 'We are all ill,' Jackie had said. Maybe Aron fell ill. He was so fearless, always acting like my hero. Maybe he was unwell and disappeared inwards because he didn't want to show any sign of vulnerability in front of me. Or maybe he had the Type A personality, and that's why he was avoiding me. Type A personalities are always busy and smart, but they get very avoidant when they are in a relationship. Maybe he was so much in love with me that he needed to detach himself.

I replayed the last night we were together over and over, the kiss in the morning, blaming myself for not being dressed or having done my make-up better. Friday blurred into Saturday and Saturday into Sunday. On Sunday afternoon, 4.34 p.m., a message from an unknown sender bleeped on my phone:

Hey princess. Lost my phone. New number. How are you?

Chapter 17

I stared at the message, the words sending a lightning discharge into my dark room. He wrote to me! Aron had lost his phone, not interest in me! He is back! He loves me! Aron! My Aron!

I trembled with joy, and if I had any tears left, I would cry them and convert them to happy droplets of sun-infused rain.

I texted back, my fingers trembling: **Can we meet? I missed you.**

Aron: **Sure, what about Wednesday? Fancy a little trip?**

A trip! Aron invited me for a trip!! I had a seminar on Wednesday but I cancelled everything and spent Monday and Tuesday putting myself back together. I looked like the walking dead after all the crying and sulking. I needed at least two days of full detox, juice and cabbage purging. I needed to get rid of the dark circles under my eyes and the annoying pimple on my left cheek. I got my eyebrows done and even treated myself to the hairdresser, who tidied up my fringe. I scrubbed the floors in case we made love there before heading off. If Mark were to come to my place, I would not bother to change from my sweatpants. For Aron, two days of preparation weren't enough. 'Why did I fool myself for so long thinking I was in love with Mark? For the false hope of comfort and safety? It was Aron who opened up my heart to true love. The sort of love that happens only once in a lifetime – if one is lucky. I am lucky! Very lucky!' I was talking to myself aloud, I was laughing at the craziness of it all, letting it rock me to the euphoric extreme of madness. It felt good after the dark days of uncertainty.

Aron knocked on the door, I opened it wide. He had a new beard, accentuating his sexy cheek bones.

'Ready for a ride, miss?'

I nodded, as enthusiastic as Rooster used to be when I grabbed his lead for his afternoon walk, jumping as high as the door handle, overjoyed with anticipation.

'Remember the windows.'

Yes, of course, shut the windows! I could not think of anything mundane in that moment. I knew I was infected with the love virus. I had all the physical and mental symptoms of being madly in love, and I was proud of it. I grabbed my carefully packed bag, forgot my coat, and skipped alongside Aron towards the car. He rented a BMW especially for the trip to the Lake District. We were going to stay in a hotel where he had booked a room. I didn't need to worry about anything. Just lean back on the big seat and relax. I opened the car window and stuck my head out like a Labrador.

'Feels like I have a puppy in the car,' Aron said, laughing. He placed his hand on my thigh while steering with his other hand. I was overflowing with happiness. I wanted to hug every person we passed on the motorway but mostly Aron sitting right next to me.

I enthusiastically kissed him on his cheek, he smiled, he must have sensed it was my very first trip like this. I had told him about my childhood, how I grew up with a mother who loved planning things to the extent that there was a 'to-do list' for every day, for every member of the family. Going on a trip was part of the military family procedure: there were scheduled toilet breaks, a sandwich prepared with a calorie count written on top of the serviette, dad's count slightly higher than mine. This trip with Aron came out of the blue. I did not know exactly where we were heading or for how long. All that mattered was that we were together. I caressed Aron's hand.

Our first comfort break was a petrol station, Aron got an egg sandwich, I got a bottle of mineral water.

'You don't eat much … a car needs fuel, you need fuel if you want to be racing.'

I nodded but still refused to eat. I offered him some pomegranate seeds from my bag. I had painstakingly peeled them the day before, but they seemed to have gone off. I should have kept them in the fridge and not in the bag, I was embarrassed that I had not checked before I offered them to Aron.

'You are so caring, you will be a good mother.' He cleaned the rest of the egg from his mouth. The knot in my stomach doubled in size when he said that. Was he considering having a family with me? Would I be a good mother for *his* child?

'You didn't pack anything?' I changed the topic, hoping to sound unattainable and thus more desirable.

'Just the toothbrush.'

I looked at the toothbrush he was pointing to, it was an electric one, nonchalantly thrown on the backseat. He caught my look and the concealed raised eyebrow, he laughed, 'You are thinking of the germs, hey?'

'How did you know?!'

'It beamed through you darling, you are too transparent!'

We both laughed again.

'Well, I just think that toothbrushes should always have a cover. At least for travelling. You didn't pack any extra clothes?'

'I've got the whole wardrobe in the back. One pair of long trousers, one pair of short trousers, two T-shirts and two pairs of shoes. And a jacket.' He said 'jacket' with the 'k' at the end sounding like a musical triangle.

'That's your entire wardrobe?'

'Yup. You know me. Minimalist. Adaptable.'

I smiled. I didn't want to spoil the moment by asking whether the divorce was complete. I figured it must be if we were to stay in a hotel and he had to carry his wardrobe inside a rented car. I put my hand on the back of Aron's neck, stroking him gently while he looked towards the road. He put the music volume up. Classic FM. We passed a little wood with birch trees. The sun was shining through the birch leaves, cutting them into silver coins, falling out the sky. It dawned on me that this was the big love they sing and write about. The real love that runs through all veins from toes to the place where dreams are knitted together. I was living it, there and then.

Aron found the hotel by checking it once on the map – he had an incredible sense of orientation. It was a small but posh hotel. The room had its own kitchenette and even a washing machine and two bathrooms. Aron jumped into the shower as soon as we arrived. I knew we were staying just for one night but I loved the feeling of unpacking my clothes and placing them on the empty hotel shelves. I caressed Aron's shirts, then hung them up in the wardrobe, placed his toothbrush upright in the bathroom glass, ensuring it stood right next to my toothbrush, the heads of both toothbrushes approaching a peppermint kiss.

I arranged our shoes by the doormat, quickly cleaning the mud away with a piece of toilet tissue. Aron had taken his shoes off as soon as we entered the room. He liked to go barefoot. I had first noticed it in my flat. I was pleased when I spotted it in the hotel too, and that I recognized it was a pattern, an intimate detail I knew but Google didn't. I imagined that one day Aron and I would live together, we would share an IP address and our Google recommendations, we would become more compatible as couples living under one roof do.

Aron got out of shower with the towel around his waist. It was the first time I saw his hair without any gel. He looked so cute. His chest seemed to have been shaved and was in the middle of growing back. He moved swiftly towards the coffee machine and threw two capsules in, shedding small drops of water on the grey carpet.

'Could you wash my stuff?' He handed me the jeans, underwear and socks he had worn that day in one big ball. He began shaving his beard using the shaving cream and razor provided by the hotel, while I stood there holding his clothes, looking help-lessly at the washing machine. I was not good with old-fashioned gadgets. I hoped there would be one button to set it in gear but there were hundreds of options and settings. Aron closed the bathroom door, and I cursed the washing machine aloud, 'Can you just not think for yourself and do what you are designed for?! Wash!!' The washing machine just beeped so I had to call reception. The reception lady refused to come up to the room, but she needed to see the garments to gauge the setting she said, so I ran with the pile of clothes downstairs to show her. Her long fingernails ran through Aron's shirt that was on top of the pile.

'Go for thirty, A32,' she uttered the verdict as a command for a slave. I regretted asking her. I thought of her long nails touching other clients' hands and door keys and those germs now sitting on Aron's shirt. That shirt should have only my viruses on it. I felt an urgent need to wash the shirt on ninety degrees, getting rid of all possible contamination, including a possible distant touch of his ex-wife. Aron left the bathroom, his freshly shaved chin smelling of aftershave, his clean body ready to move in the rhythm of the washing machine drumming in the background.

'What, Full Monty?!' I grinned at Aron's naked body occu-pying the entire length of the double bed. He got into a starfish position, inviting me to join him. I had put on an expensive vintage nightdress that I bought in an online auction. My skin was soft after the oil-soaking procedure I had the previous night. I slowly lowered myself down on the bed next to Aron, tummy in, breasts out, my heart racing. I didn't feel like a starfish but Aron assimilated me into his generous position.

'Come here, babe. You and your spiny arms, we'll make a constellation!'

He vigorously moved all the duvets and coverings on top of his body and then away, pushing them to the side, making the bed look like a little nest for me to fly into. He grabbed me by my waist, pulled with full force towards him, undressed me in a second. He lifted me up, while lying on his back, then gently penetrated from below.

'Am I squashing you?'

'You are light as a feather.'

His rhythm coming in and out couldn't be more perfect.

'Sex with you is almost as good as sex with myself.' He laughed.

'Is it because we are soulmates?' I smiled, and extended my arms. Aron held them with his stretched arms.

'Four butterfly wings.'

'Entangled thoughts and bodies …'

'Flying towards a new destination …'

Chapter 18

ARON STOPPED KISSING ME, I abruptly stopped too.

'Can you give me some?'

'I … I have never done a blow job before. …'

Half-hesitantly, half-reluctantly, I slid down his chest. He guided my head, pushed it down according to his rhythm, told me to hold my tongue down, teeth away. I was good at following instructions. Aron came almost immediately.

'How was it?' he asked, wiping my chest and arms with scraps of toilet paper that he grabbed from the bathroom.

My head was banging, I had to think of the right word, completely forgot anything I had ever written in my notebook. I uttered, 'Tolerable.'

He smiled.

'I guess I need to practise a bit more.' I smiled, feeling the blush in my face.

'Happy to be your practice man,' Aron whispered, shortly after he fell asleep.

He must have been exhausted after the journey and sex and God knows what preceded it, and yet, he didn't snore. I lied next to him, looking at the ceiling, evaluating in my head what has just happened. *A starfish! Aron had new and cool ideas all the time. I loved it. I will not get bored with this man. Ever. Maybe blow jobs are what all men want, only Mark thought it was selfish and never asked for it. I would do anything for Aron.* I let my eyes caress his sleeping face, then whispered a short made-up prayer begging the universe to protect him. 'You there in the Heaven, please do not let Aron die. Please keep him healthy and safe. Please make him stay.' I finished my prayer, took extra MS medication, remembering that Miss Peake said I should take a double dose when feeling the signs of an approaching attack. I wasn't sure whether it was that or the extreme excitement that day, but I did feel losing sensation in my right leg. I would take any medication and prolong the moment of bliss.

I woke up to a loud paramedic siren.

'Argh!' Aron reached for his phone.

What a horrible ringing tone! I was still half-asleep.

Aron picked his phone up in a brusque move, put a shirt and pants on, went out of the room to the hotel corridor. He came back when he finished the call.

'Sorry,' he whispered.

Not an ideal romantic morning to wake up to, I thought. 'No worries.' I yawned.

'I have to do some work.' Aron began dressing.

I looked at the hotel alarm clock on my bedside. 'It's only 6 a.m.? Don't … don't you want to have breakfast together?'

'Not hungry. But you need to eat. Just go ahead, babe. Will be back when I am finished.' He kissed me on my forehead and disappeared. I was so sleepy and surprised at the sudden departure that I didn't ask when he would be back or anything else. I stared at the hotel door with a sinking feeling. I lied in bed running the scenario I had imagined for us. I had hoped to wake up in his arms, enjoy the hotel breakfast together, plan the day ahead. I felt so disappointed. *But who are you disappointed with Katie? Aron didn't do anything wrong, it's just that his scenario was different from mine. This is a different kind of love. I need to stop my old schemes! I need to stop disappointing myself with my own expectations.*

I got up, smiled at myself in the mirror, inspected my skin for any new blackheads, then took a long hot shower. My neck was stiff after the sex yesterday, my head was exploding with a hangover although I didn't drink any alcohol. I dressed up, spent half an hour arranging my hair and another half an hour doing my make-up. Then I went to the hotel lobby to have the breakfast on my own.

The breakfast bar was impressive considering how small the hotel was. I really fancied the full English breakfast with organic eggs and fried bread. But Aron could be back anytime, I couldn't show a bloated belly to him. I chose the grapefruit fruit salad. The sugar gave me a high, and the unpleasant banging in my head temporarily stopped.

I checked my phone. No messages from Aron. I wasn't sure what to do. I didn't want to disturb him if he had something urgent to deal with. He would be back soon, surely. Check-out was at twelve o'clock, so we still had four hours before we had to leave. I was cross with myself that I didn't bring my laptop with me. I could have done some work while waiting for him. Why did I think we would be just walking and hugging each other all the time? He had said 'trip', and it could well mean a business trip. It was my stupid expectations again, thinking it would be a romantic trip. I went upstairs to the hotel room, tidied up. I used half of Aron's mini shampoo to clean the wash basin in the bathroom. I enjoyed being useful for a while, at least the cleaner will have less to do. The room looked almost like when we checked in.

It was 10.30 a.m. and I was getting hungry and annoyed with myself that I didn't foresee it and pack a Knäckebröd from the breakfast table. I decided to leave the hotel and explore the town a bit. I wrote Aron a message, added some hearts with my lipstick, put it next to the pad by the telephone on the night table, left the room key at the reception in case he didn't ring me before returning to the hotel. I had no idea where I was. I didn't pay close attention to the road when we drove yesterday. Luckily Siri provided some sanity and told me how to get back to the hotel.

By 11.30 a.m., Aron still wasn't back. I threw my hand-written message with hearts in the bin. At 11.45 a.m. I was getting anxious. Was I supposed to check out and pay for the room? Or extend the stay by one night? I had our belongings packed by the door, I checked the room ten times that we didn't leave anything behind. At 11.50 a.m. Aron stormed into the room.

'Hi, babe, here you are Sleeping Beauty!'

I was on the bed when he arrived but I definitely wasn't asleep.

Aron came closer to the bed side, 'What am I going to do with you?' he grinned and pulled his pants down. He was standing, I was sitting on the bed. He pushed my head down, same as yesterday. I opened my mouth, tongue down, teeth away, up and down, up and down. I nervously looked up, looking for the clock with one corner of my eye. I saw Aron was holding his phone and filming me. I pulled away.

'Just keep on doing what you are doing.'

'Why are you filming me?'

'For later when we are not together. Please, baby.'

I felt very uncomfortable but continued. I saw it was 12.02 p.m. when he came and let go of my head. He went to the bathroom, put his pants back on, smiled at me. I didn't smile back.

'Ready to rock-n-roll?'

I trembled, followed a step behind him.

The pretty receptionist gave into Aron's flirting and let us go without having to pay for a late check-out. She glanced a long envious look at me. I knew Aron was extremely attractive not only to my eyes. I pulled my suitcase, followed him to the car. We drove for about ten minutes in complete silence.

'You're a bit quiet this morning,' Aron said, searching for a suitable music list on his phone.

'It's not morning anymore. It's past lunchtime now. Where have you been?'

'With a client.'

'Why didn't you tell me?'

'I didn't know. Remember the phone this morning?'

'Yes, I remember the phone. I remember what you did with your phone this morning.'

'Are you sulking?'

I turned my face towards the window.

'Can you delete the video?' I asked quietly, my head still towards the window.

'Okay. Yes, I will. I'm sorry.'

I turned my face back from the window, and Aron gave me the cutest smile I had ever seen. He placed his hand on my thigh, pushed the pedal. He turned up the volume, it was Tracy Chapman's 'Fast Car', my all-time favourite. I hummed the lyrics, caressing Aron's hand on the wheel.

There is so much for me to learn about life. Maybe men liked being loved in the way Aron was showing me. I was spoiling the journey for myself by following my old schemas. He must have had a lot of stress at work and yet he was so calm. He must think I am totally inexperienced in bed, that I must have lived like a nun before I met him. He wanted to do a bit of filming, that's what men do these days. He wanted it for himself, not like that psycho ex of Jackie, who shared it with the world. What was I sulking about? It should be me apologizing to him. I turned my head towards Aron, kissed him on the cheek.

'You must be tired. You didn't get to sleep much last night,' I said to him and stroke his arm.

'I'm an elephant. Elephants sleep two hours max.' Aron smiled.

'I'm a bat then! I need a long sleep.' I thought of how very short my nights were when I thought that Aron had left me when he went quiet. 'You never have a lie-in?'

'Never.' He looked straight into my eyes.

'Is it because it would make you feel vulnerable?'

'That's some heavy psychology for me here …'

We both laughed.

I thought of the personality type psychology lessons at uni. Aron didn't eat warm foods either. I guessed it was because warm food would make him feel sleepy and that would not fit with his Agent 007 mission of saving the world. He was driving fast, I was scared but I enjoyed it. I figured Aron would rather have an accident than slow down. Just like on our first date when he would have rather frozen to death than admit he was cold.

On the motorway, Aron accelerated the car twice the permitted speed. The tyres squeaked, I got really sacred.

'Aron, please!' I screamed, he slowed down.

'You know you don't need to prove anything to me. I love you as you are.' Aron kept a close look at the speedometer, I slowly continued. 'Inside out. I love your true colours.'

Aron turned his head towards me for so long that I had to remind him to watch the road.

'Cindy Lauper stuff?' He asked, still looking at me. I nodded. Aron commanded Siri to play the 1986 version. Lauper finished singing and we almost banged our heads with a passionate kiss, both of us longing for it right at the end of the song.

Chapter 19

'LET'S TAKE A DETOUR AND stop by Windermere, shall we?'

I nodded eagerly and Aron confirmed the car's recommendation. He parked close to the lake. Last time I was in the Lake District was when I was eleven, I didn't remember anything from the trip, only that mum and dad argued about some parking charges. We went for a walk around it, talked about our families. Aron got me to reveal my secrets to him within an hour. He asked intriguing questions at the right time, adding a bit of his own answers, now and then, but essentially making me say things in the way I wanted. Oprah's interview technique paled in comparison with Aron. I told him about my relationship with mum, dad, Jackie and her Instagram stories. I told him about Mark too, I focused on the good parts, I felt no bitterness towards Mark. I told Aron how Mark cared for me when I was unwell, how much we enjoyed having Rooster together. I finished with the clichéd, 'But he is an ex for a reason', to reassure Aron about the uniqueness of our bond.

I asked Aron about his family, and he told me that his father died in an accident when he was a teenager. I knew that would have made him mature more quickly than his peers and probably strengthened his bond with his mother. He visited her occasionally, he said. We talked about work too, it was mostly me talking and Aron listening again, but he told me that he had many professions in the past: a truck driver in Germany, then a tour guide, then an accountant, shopkeeper, now trying it in business. That flexible work history explained why he was so attractive – multiple identities, when sequenced well, make people interesting. Had Aron been juggling several jobs at once, he would be like one of those clowns swapping hats for money. But having a rich work history meant he knew how to deal with storms and how to deal with people. Closing the door in one domain meant opening the door to a new opportunity. He was resilient and there is nothing more attractive than resiliency.

As we walked around the lake, Aron recounted some world history to me.

'So essentially, the rich and powerful always live by the water. In Paris, if you take a boat tour on the Seine, they show you the French palaces. In London, on the Thames, it's the Hampton Court. In Queenstown, on the lake they show you the villas of the Chinese. It's always about water.'

I nodded, assimilating his words. I knew little about the world's order. Mark and I had only travelled the world with our fingers on Google Earth. I wished I could experience different countries as Aron had, expanding the predigested knowledge I had been receiving through books and media with the in-the-flesh experiences one can only gain when walking the land.

'The Chinese have only 7 per cent of the world's fresh water for 18 per cent of the world's population. Can you imagine? That's pretty much why there are periodic conflicts.'

Aron's knowledge was expanding and amplifying me. I wished I could follow Aron to work one day. I wished I could get a peek inside Aron's fridge and smartwatch. I wanted to know everything about him. I didn't want to come across as obsessed as I actually was, so limited myself to periodic nods. We stopped by the swans, we kissed. I wished I could know whether his heart rate went up in that moment, whether he too felt the desire to expand his body with mine. It was a beautiful moment and I didn't want to spoil it but as we stood there by the swans, I could feel a beginning spasm. I knew I couldn't, nor shouldn't, hide my MS from Aron.

I wished to tell him in a way that would neither scare him nor make him feel sorry for me. So I told him everything, including how I was misdiagnosed with MS2, how they told me my brain was infected with a virus and how that thought had terrified me but how it was proved to be a misdiagnosis and that the MS2 virus never existed.

'Brains evolve. They reorganise as they expand. Like companies.'

'True …' I waited for him to comment on anything else about MS that I had told him but he didn't. I was so relived he did not make a big deal out of it or ask for details. He continued the conversation in the relaxed way we talked before, so I did too. 'Did you know that humans think seventy thousand thoughts per day? That's why human brains need to rest regularly. To consolidate.'

'Or maybe to expand even more. Which is why, my clever Dr Princess, we are going back this way. Here! Because walking back the same path is not good for our brains!' Aron turned around and took me back to the car down a different path. I couldn't believe he knew that psychology bit too. I told him about the neurological studies showing how periodic walking on different paths expands the creativity area in the brain. That the brain needs regular cognitive stimulation to keep the regeneration juices running.

'That's why you hate going back the same way!' Aron gave me one of his gorgeous looks, I told him more about the human desire to constantly learn and expand. It was not as strongly ingrained in all people as in Aron. He struck me as someone who kept young because of his curiosity, that's why I was never bored in his company.

We stopped in a quirky café on the way back to the car. Aron got a cake and coffee, I got a matcha tea.

'You drink green tea?' Aron touched the edges of my cup with his fingers, looking surprised. 'You didn't say you were a vegan!'

'Green tea has nothing to do with veganism?' I said, laughing.

'Ah, it's the same genre.'

Aron knew how to make me laugh. And I loved how good he was at spotting details. He would be an excellent poet if he had the patience to write his thoughts down. I had no clear lines in my head even though I was drinking the 'supreme matcha for clear mind'.

'Look! A penny!' I picked up a silver-coloured penny lying by the table. I showed it to Aron. 'Pennies bring good luck!'

'That's quite a statement for a scientist.' Aron smiled and put a finger on my lips, 'But I won't tell anyone.' He got up as to go to the bathroom but I knew he would go and settle the bill. He was such a gentleman. So observant. So generous. I was bathing in my thoughts about Aron, I felt as if we had travelled the whole Earth that day, thousands of images streamed through my mind, flowing me into a whirl of Aron's face, some leaving a more permanent trace than others but all mixing in one giant web of memories.

It was getting late. The clouds were shifting colours and shapes, merging from one into another one, with no clear beginning or end.

Aron came back from the till with a plastic bag. He gave it to me fast as if it had something living inside.

'For you!'

'A teddy bear?!'

'Yeah. For memory.' Aron smiled uncomfortably.

I took the teddy out of the bag, straightened the tiny, white Windermere T-shirt on the teddy's belly. 'I'm going to call him Winder!' I removed the price tag and hugged the teddy together with Aron.

We got back to our temporary mobile home. We drove back to London, taking the expensive motorway. Aron said he didn't mind paying extra to avoid the traffic. I joked he behaved like a spy, avoiding people but not the invoices. We got back to my flat very late, it must have been 1 a.m. or 2 a.m. I headed straight to bed. Aron got his laptop out and worked while I was falling asleep next to him. I put Winder's plush body against my cheek. It was raining outside, but I thought it was snow. The gentle touch-typing of Aron's fingers on the laptop made me dream about sylph-like ballet dancers performing *The Nutcracker* en pointe.

Chapter 20

I WOKE UP WITH ONLY Winder next to me. Aron must have placed it on his pillow before he left. I stroked the teddy, threw it towards the ceiling, caught it, laughed as he fell into my arms. I got up, made coffee while humming the *Eroica* tune. I wanted to walk to the bus stop but I could feel my legs being less and less responsive. I felt light and elevated, struggling to place one foot in front of the other. I thought of the video with Christina Koch sitting on a wheelchair after she returned from the International Space Station. I felt the trickle of sweat down my spine. *Is this the beginning of another MS attack? A relapse now, when I couldn't wish more for being healthy?* I took out the metal straw from my bag, ran its cold end down my thigh, right upper body part, back. I felt the straw, I had no pain from the cold touching my skin. I had not lost sensation. *You are okay Katie, it is just the love hormones overwhelming you.* 'Please Multiple Sclerosis, please don't spoil it for me, I deserve to be happy. At least for a while. You and I are friends, okay? I feed you interferons. I respect your need for exercise. I have been a good girl all year long, please don't take this from me.' I must have said the last sentence too loud, as the lady standing at the bus stop looked at me suspiciously. I smiled at her. I had Aron, I had Winder, I was happy and could be giving kindness to others. 'The Winder Effect' I typed in nice lettering on top of my smiley selfie in the bus and sent it to Aron.

Lana was already in the office when I walked in.

'Someone had sex yesterday!' Lana turned from her screen, pulled my office chair next to hers, expecting me to sit down and recount the details.

'I literally jumped out bed this morning. I feel like everything has meaning now. Do you know the feeling? I feel …' I didn't want Lana to know all the details but there was no one else to share it with and I was just SO happy. I felt loved by the man I loved. 'I feel like … like I've been resurrected. Like he replaced the black that was inside me. Do you know what I—'

'Yeah, yeah, mad love.' Lana cut short the string of my unconnected words. 'How do you know that he actually loves you?'

'What a silly question! Do you expect some kind of checklist?'

'Did he give you that look?'

'You don't really believe in that nonsense, do you?'

'Then how do you know?'

'I feel it,' I said.

Lana was clearly waiting for more, obstructing the entrance to my desk.

'I feel it. I see it. He has that sparkle in his eyes when he looks at me. Like little stars.'

'That could be cocaine.'

'Oh my God, Lana! Would you stop?! Aron and I never argue. What about that?'

'You barely know each other – of course you never argue!'

'He gave me a teddy.'

'He treats you like a child and you like that?! He is going to force you into sadist sex next, just wait for it!'

'Lana! Stop please! How disgusting. I am in love. Stop spoiling it for me!'

Lana pulled her chair away, quietly adding, 'I just don't want you to get hurt, that's all.'

We worked silently alongside each other at our desks until 5 p.m. But I wasn't writing the annual report as Lana was, I was drafting a long text to Aron. I wanted to thank him for the weekend trip and I wanted to suggest something that would take our relationship to the next level. I wanted it to be sexual. I wanted him to desire me, to want me, to lust after me. If love is a power exchange, then it could be me dominating him sometimes, too. Would he like that? What would he like me to do?

I didn't send my flirty message. I was worried he could misinterpret it and whatever I typed sounded clumsy. I wanted to propose something concrete, maybe buy some lingerie and surprise him with it, like he surprised me with Winder. I was getting excited as I was constructing the plans in my head. In the end I just messaged him: **When can we meet again?**

He had time the following week on Friday. I put it in the calendar, blocked the whole day in a blue colour for 'Heaven' and the day before that in red for 'Starving day'. I liked how Aron's presence introduced a new colour scheme into my diary, and a new structure to my days. Time was defined by periods of *waiting* for being together and periods of *being* together. I didn't work longer than my contractual hours that day, it was still daylight when I finished work. I stopped by the supermarket before taking the bus. I didn't buy the reduced vegetables nor the slimming chocolate. I bought an expensive prawn salad that I actually liked. I sat down on the park bench to eat it, looking at the people passing by. I felt so different and yet the world was the same. I began reading iNews on my phone, there was a terrorist attack in Myanmar. I clicked on the headline: 'It is time for the community to get together'. I sent some money to the families and rescue workers. I finished eating my salad, I felt satiated. I didn't feel guilty of eating too much, I enjoyed my slightly bloated belly, caressed it and wondered whether it would look the same if I was carrying a baby.

I texted Aron with a pink heart emoji: **I see the world around me differently. That's why I love you.**

He responded back with a pink heart emoji. I was beaming and decided to walk home even though it took fifty minutes and it was drizzling rain. I found a penny on the narrow pavement towards my flat's entrance. I picked it up and tossed it towards the sky. I looked up, the clouds flew in slow motion, merging with the sky, occasionally merging into delicious shapes, one of them in the form of Winder.

I was surprised to see Jackie standing in front of my door. I hadn't checked my phone since Aron texted back. I hadn't anticipated anyone else contacting me. I checked Jackie's face, I checked Facebook. I understood. Jack had changed his status to 'Married' and posted a whole wedding album, together with a video of the first dance with his new wife. Jack was one of Jackie's closest friends, he was the only boyfriend Jackie had found outside of social media. I thought how I would feel if I saw Mark's wedding pictures. If all of our joint fifty-six friends saw him laughing with a beautiful girl in his arms. If I saw him touching and kissing her the same way he used to touch and kiss me. If I saw the fully-blown scenes in full-colour photographs, if I held the video in my hand, the same hand that held Mark some time ago, knowing that the scenes were shared and liked by our mutual friends.

Jackie must be broken to her core. I lit a candle scented with fresh orange peels and spicy cloves, moved Jackie to sit inside the kitchen. 'Breathe, don't forget to breathe.' I stroked her back. Jackie calmed down eventually. I wondered what I could do to take her attention away from the online misery.

'Let me take you to a concert,' I said, typing in the last-minute ticket booking website. 'You've never been to a classical concert before, have you? You will like it.'

Jackie reluctantly accepted and I was happy that she would be, at least for two hours, forced to focus on something different, with no phones allowed. Jackie was not happy with that restriction, without photographic evidence that she was at the concert, it was as if it didn't happen. But she accepted going into the concert hall, eventually.

'It's good for the locals, I get it,' she said.

People in the concert hall watched Jackie's every step, she was too beautiful not to be stared at. Jackie wore a dark red and black dress, the same that Julianne Moore wore to Cannes, her smile innocently calling for a hug, her badly dried tears calling for a human shield to protect her from any pain. It wasn't promiscuity; Jackie knew she was the femme fatale type, but she did not come across as adultery material – it was a strong sense of possibility that cried from her piercing eyes, and that was a universal seduction power.

'Let's have a drink in the bar,' I suggested after the concert.

Jackie was clearly not in the mood, with the phone ban applying to the entire concert hall, I worried how long she would hold together. I was anticipating a storm of angry tears, and prayed she would wait until we got home.

'It's fucking useless this place. It's the same as the football match.'

'Ha! Good comparison!' I enthusiastically started a conversation. 'You are right, I guess, the formula is the same: long security and safety controls, a bit of content on the stage, then a toilet break, longer queue for women than men. Perhaps the only difference is that the concert hall sells posh ice creams, and the football kiosk, hot dogs?'

'As if it mattered! It all ends up in the same sewage system anyway.'

I nodded, enjoying Jackie's attention on me and not her missing phone. We sat by the bar window, Jackie had a glass of white wine, I had orange juice diluted with tap water. We exchanged a few obligatory sentences but it was clear to me that Jackie was just waiting for an appropriate moment to leave and immerse herself in an online conversation.

'Maybe we could go and see a musical next time? You know, local artists need support—'

'This is creepy.'

'What is creepy?' I turned around, didn't understand what Jackie was scared about.

'This staring at each other with nothing between us.' Jackie took a sip from her glass, put it back on the table, then briefly looked into the distance as if she could summon the Likes from her online absence. She had another sip of wine, but the overall amount of wine seemed to have been unaffected by the frequent sips.

I felt so lonely in her company. It wasn't that I felt excluded by the thousands of potential friends waiting to contact Jackie from her phone. Jackie had always been popular, there was always someone else she would talk in parallel while talking with me, a boyfriend or a new female friend. Their presence always threatened the intimacy of our friendship and made me feel ambivalently attached to Jackie, on one hand rejecting her, on the other hand desiring her fervently as my closest friend. I was thinking about it and felt that Jackie's depression was dragging me down, even though I had loved the concert.

We left the bar after I finished the cocktail with some sips. I felt sorry for Jackie but I also felt sorry for myself. I had known Jackie for years, we grew up together, mum adored her, dad had whiskey with Jackie's first boyfriend. It was Jackie who was with me when I was unwell at Critten. I felt a sense of obligation to be there for her when she was struggling. But with her so openly dismissing my presence in favour of her online world, it was hard. I didn't feel much affection or joy spending time with her. I would much rather spend that time with Aron.

I found two pennies on the stone staircase near the entrance door to my flat. I picked them up. One was shiny silver and looked almost new, the other one was old and dirty. I threw the dirty one behind my back pronouncing a silent wish, and I took the clean penny inside, placed it on the kitchen windowsill, next to my basil. I watered the basil, contemplating the meaning of the two pennies. *If it is true that everything happens for a reason – and if one doesn't believe in that, then what holds them together in crises? – there must be a meaning behind the two pennies so close to my flat. Maybe I have been holding onto the wrong people for too long. Maybe it is time to decide who I want to keep in my life and who to say goodbye to. Aron is my treasure trove of ideas and joy. I should earmark all my free time just for him and the numberless gems he has been hiding. I should reserve all my resources for the riches we could be collecting together. Yes, that's what I should do. Jackie, my parents, Mark, they need to be moved to secondary characters. Aron is my hero to craft a new chapter in my life. I need to keep the story simple, and thus give it a higher chance of success. Not an academic-like story, layered with life's complexities. I need to keep it a creative writing-style story, with a simple message: everything, the good and the bed, is a reflection of love's manifestations.*

Chapter 21

I HAD ANTICIPATED THAT MARK'S revenge would be to keep Rooster for himself, but I had hoped that over time he would realize that it was best for everyone if I could take Rooster for walks sometimes. *Five months is long enough for that realization to happen.* I decided to text Mark, and I suggested we meet on Sunday in the park close to our old flat. Rooster loved it there and it wasn't far for Mark to walk to. Mark responded to my text after two days, with nothing more but the thumbs up emoji. He could have written 'OK' or 'hi' or 'Rooster has been missing you' but he chose the shortest reply possible. I tried not to overinterpret it, tried not to be offended by it, in the end what mattered was that he agreed for me to see Rooster. I knew that after our bad break-up, Mark and I were in it for a marathon, not a short run.

That Sunday I woke up with anticipation. I put on minimal make-up and took no care to look good – I didn't want Mark to feel attracted to me in any way. The meeting was supposed to be about Rooster, about handing over responsibilities, as amicably as possible. I could hear Rooster barking when I entered the park and my heart jumped with joy. He loved a good bark when fetching the ball and a long loud howl when he couldn't find it in the grass.

'Roosti, Roosti!' I didn't need to shout more, he ran full speed towards me. If he was a bigger dog he would definitely knock me over. I was wet from his saliva all over my face and blouse but I didn't mind. I was glad it hid my tears of joy. Mark scuffled to us eventually. Rooster was barking and jumping aloud and high, visibly celebrating that his pack was complete.

Mark said a barely hearable, 'Hi.' He handed me a pack of poo scoop bags and Rooster's lead.

'Thanks.' I put the poo bags into my pocket. 'When do you want him back?'

'In five months.'

I tried to catch Mark's eye, but he didn't look at me.

He got onto one knee, patted Rooster, said, 'Bye, buddy.' And walked away.

Mark's sadness was such a contrast to Rooster's elation that it forged the whole park scene into a sad stony face. I didn't want us to be like that. I didn't love Mark but I was fond of him and it pained me see him so cold towards me. It hurt me he treated me worse than a stranger and harboured hatred towards me. I wished we could remain on speaking terms, be friends. I wished we did not let recent events take over the good times we had had together. By handing me Rooster in that way, for exactly 'five months,' there was no attempt at a possible joint walk one day. Rooster would love it and we could talk about our recent news.

'Wouldn't a walk together be nice? Don't you think so, Roosti? Wouldn't that be a more adult way of handling things? Am I again the one who followed the wrong schemes to expect that?' I was talking to Rooster, his tail never stopped wagging. I put him on his lead and took a photo of him smelling grass.

I texted the photo to Aron: **My new roommate for the next five months.**

Typing the text to Aron made me realise I didn't have my landlady's permission to have a dog for so long. I didn't have any proper space or cushions for Rooster and I was not sure whether Rooster could wait for me inside the flat while I was at work. Pragmatic worries took me out of wallowing over Mark. I bought extra food and bowls and blankets on the way home. I didn't mind spending my monthly savings on arranging Rooster's space at mine. He needed to have a place to lie down and something to entertain him while waiting for me to return from work.

The first two weeks went well. Aron wrote to me he needed to visit some clients in China and I enjoyed having Rooster in the flat to fill the void. I spoilt Rooster with expensive snacks with money I had been saving for Aron's visit. I enjoyed our walks in the mornings and evenings, each of us glad to have a real being to direct our self-talk to. I talked to Rooster in the same high-pitched voice as I did to the three-year-old who wanted to pat him in the park. I leaned down and saw on Rooster's chip that Mark hadn't taken him for his annual check-up.

You forgot about the annual check-up?? The insurance bill is 50 per cent higher because you missed the appointment!

Mark didn't text back, so I wrote again. **At least we could each pay half.**

Mark texted back: **Nope, your turn, your expenses.**

I texted: **I'm already paying towards a flat where I am not living!!**

Could he be a little bit less selfish and see things in perspective? I was working my socks off to afford a roof over my head, pay for his flat and now also for Rooster. Could he think about my own happiness for a change?!

I put three angry emojis into the draft text but did not send it to Mark. Instead, in that moment, I decided to stop paying for the mortgage. On an impulse, I rang the bank, explained the situation and demanded a fair share of the payments made. 'I should be paying less or nothing since I am no longer living in the flat.' I explained as calmly as I could.

Mark and I didn't have any formal partnership certificate, which complicated our already complicated mortgage agreement. The bank insisted that they needed to speak to both of us simul-taneously and rang Mark. Mark responded on the third attempt and during the whole call dismissed the eye-contact reminders, which irritated not only me but also the mortgage advisor, who had to remind him two times that fiddling with the camera invalidates the identification process.

'When did you separate?' the mortgage advisor asked in a robotic tone. The camera view switched over to Mark.

'Yesterday,' Mark said.

'No, that is incorrect.' The camera view switched over to me. 'We separated four months ago.'

'Did we? Prove it!' Mark shouted. I was grateful the screen was separating us.

'You can either provide a lawyer's verified confirmation of a *mutually agreed* separation date or you can agree between yourselves and contact us when you are ready.' The mortgage advisor responded and disconnected the call. Mark called me back but I didn't answer.

He texted me: **If you return Rooster a month earlier, I'll push the separation date a month earlier.**

I texted him back: **Pretty low of you to use Rooster as a negotiating chip!**

I was disgusted that he had anticipated that the mortgage situation would come up and push me into the corner like that. After two weeks of furious text messages and one call full of shouting, Mark and I agreed on three months. I was going to keep Rooster for three months and that would be the frequency for us to exchange him between us. We were going to say to the bank that Mark and I separated three months ago and that I paid 'only' two months of Mark's rent. Those were the terms and conditions of my new contract with Mark. We needed to have a contract because the cornerstone of our past relationship – trust – was irreversibly gone.

Rooster, of course, didn't understand any of that. He understood, however, that there was a new man in my life and for some reason, Rooster didn't like Aron. He barked when I called him and treated him like a burglar who needed to be bitten and barked at when Aron came for a visit after his China trip. Rooster wouldn't let him enter the flat, so I had to keep him on a lead inside the living room while Aron visited. He was howling so loud that Aron and I barely heard each other and the tenants above me complained to my landlady. Aron left after some minutes. The next time he could come, Rooster made it literally impossible for Aron and I to dine at mine. Aron came after 11 p.m. and that was too late to go to a restaurant. We had two short meetings in the three months I was looking after Rooster, which was the biggest punishment for me. I knew Rooster was jealous and it was his way of protecting his territory but I was annoyed with him. I loved the dog to bits but I was counting the days to return him to Mark, so that I could have my freedom again. I had plans to travel with Aron to Buckinghamshire and go for a plant exhibition there. It was Aron's birthday in October and I wanted to take him somewhere special. I still hadn't shown Aron the sexy lingerie I had bought.

I delivered Rooster to Mark after three months of custody. I made sure I was at the flat at 4 p.m. sharp, not a minute earlier, not a minute later. Mark came down wearing a face mask even though the infection rates were very low that day. We naturally kept a distance and neither of us had even the remote desire to touch. Seeing Mark with that face mask made me think of my Critten days and life full of illnesses and problems. When I thought of Aron, I saw blinding sunlight. When I thought of Mark, I saw only some faint rays of sunshine and my body full of holes to patch up. One ray of light came through the hole on the right side of my body, left behind by MS. The other hole was in my hands, my friendship with Jackie leaked through it. There was a hole on my shoulder after my parents' divorce, there was a huge hole on my belly for the baby Mark expected me to have. Mark knew about all the holes, he partly dug some up. Aron did not know about my shadows. He and I met in light.

I was so glad that I didn't need to go up to our old flat with Mark and see the messy kitchen and Rooster's muddy pawprints everywhere. I was so glad I didn't need to cater for Mark's only form of exercise that day by opening my legs for him. I said bye to Rooster, and almost ran away from Lavender Street.

I took the fast train home, my head buzzing with thoughts. There is so little passion inside Mark. He had no big hobbies he burns for. No big job he would prioritise above everything else. No curiosity to learn new skills, or get a new certification or embark on a new course. Yes, he was the crying shoulder when I failed, but he was not the inspiration to lift me up. I put the intellectual rim around his boring life. I understand that my life-style of working hard, wouldn't work for Mark, but did he think that the secret for climbing the corporate ladder is working less each time one got a mini promotion? Aron knew how to climb ladders, he seemed to have enough money for sustaining both of us if I ever asked him for it. I would not ask, of course not, Aron liked strong, independent women, but I could if I wanted, and that thought was exciting enough.

I felt a sudden urge to hold Aron in my arms.

I typed: **A quickie at mine?**

I blushed, immediately deleted the message. Luckily Aron had no notifications activated so he won't see it. I drafted fourteen different text versions.

In the end I just sent: **Hi babe, how are you today? ;-)**

To my surprise, the phone bleeped back within seconds: **With immediate effect, stop texting this number.**

Chapter 22

I STARED AT THE MESSAGE, unsure of whether it was a bad joke or whether something bad happened to Aron. I obviously couldn't verify it by texting back if it was the latter. My heart sank, I deduced it was his ex-wife, perhaps his still-wife, who was spying on us. I had hoped the divorce was over but it seemed that there were some nasty things still happening in the background. My conflict with Mark jeopardised our meetings over the last three months and now it was Aron's past that loomed over our future meetings.

Why does life need to be so complicated?! Wait, Katie. What if Aron and his wife are still close? What if he was unsure of who to choose? What if there were children involved? No, no, he would have told me if he had children. So stop thinking and saying that to yourself. Aron and I talked openly, we talked about family. He never mentioned children. It must be that his ex is controlling. Maybe she wanted to use his phone as evidence of adultery for the court proceedings. Maybe their separation did involve an actual lawyer and was much more onerous and expensive than my split with Mark. Maybe if I told Aron about my problems with Mark he would dismiss them as a benign conflict between two students. Real divorce involves nasty stuff like stealing private communications, forcing the other to sleep in hotels or hiring the virus detection company like the one mum works for. What do I know?

My internal voices began mixing in first and second person. I knew I needed to sort them out by dealing with the anxiety and not pushing it away. I knew I needed to be patient, wait for Aron to re-emerge. I needed to show the exact opposite of the chaos, distrust and nastiness he must be experiencing at home. What options did I have in that limbo situation? Nothing but waiting.

And so I waited. And waited.

And waited. Days went by and I withered like a poorly watered garden. My eyes shrank to the Zoomed-out size as I distracted myself with work again, taking on extra teaching classes. There was a limit on how much I could teach as a university employee but only my bank knew of the extra income that I generated from external contracts. I took on guest lectures for private secondary schools, paid by posh parents, who were hoarding opportunities for their extra-talented kids. Most of them were online and I could pre-record them at night but one primary school academy insisted on a face-to-face lesson. I agreed to it since they covered my lunch too, and food was especially good at private schools. I hung around the staff room and packed some apples and bananas from the shared fruit bowl when no one was looking.

The lesson went well and the private school issued me with a temporary contract for regular afternoon lectures. It was good money. It was not good for my body or psyche but both needed to be dampened with the neutrality of financial rewards. On one of my teaching afternoons, I was walking towards the classroom when I saw a young girl in the school corridor. She must have been eleven or twelve years old. My stomach twitched, the girl sat in a wheelchair, the same type of wheelchair as the one I had used when I was in Critten Hospital. The girl commanded the wheelchair to move closer to a set of chairs by the classroom door.

'Do you want to sit on this chair?' I asked the girl, pointing to the chair next to me. I knew exactly how it felt being asked that question. People would never offer me a sitting space, everyone assumed that if I used a wheelchair I had no need to sit on other chairs.

'Do you ask because the law requires you to give your seat to disabled persons?' The girl said in a quiet but firm voice.

'No, I asked because it's common sense.'

'The government puts things into law because people don't have common sense,' the girl said with the same quiet and firm voice.

'True. Some countries institutionalise common sense to dis-empower people. To prove that the state has power to think humanely, but individual citizens don't.' It was too advanced of a topic for a pre-teen but it was exactly the kind of respect that she was hankering after. Her face softened and she leant towards me as I sat down on the chair next to her.

'Do you think it would be better if there wasn't any state, if we could all decide what we want?' Her small eyes were burning with questions.

'I don't know. What I am saying is that we need to be clearer about what the trade-offs are.' I looked into her clear blue eyes. 'I have Relapsing-Remitting Multiple Sclerosis. I have been val-uing up the trade-offs of medicine versus side effects since I was eighteen.'

The girl burst into tears. I held her hand, she opened up. She told me about how the latest lockdown had affected her. How she was alone at home, how she started having panic attacks, feeling fatigued, unable to move. She was repeating the same meticulous details over and over, I knew she had been traumatised. Her name was Amy, but she also had personalities called Amelie, Ann298 and Annabelle. When she was Amy, she used the wheelchair, but when she was Amelie, she could walk perfectly well. Amy wanted people to notice she was unwell and needed help but Amelie was strong enough to help herself. She self-harmed a lot, she showed me the scars.

There was no light coming through her voice, only more dark-ness as she recounted the abuse she experienced at home. I was appalled that Amy's psychologist induced false stories into her head in the name of narrative therapy. Without the proper tools, Amy fragmented herself into a 'healthy Amelie', detaching the new identity from herself instead of integrating it. My MPD training kicked in, I kept on repeating, 'I feel your pain. I am listening to all your voices, all your identities. I am here for you and for them. I accept you all as one family that can never be separated.' Amy kept on talking and I felt more and more helpless with her pain inside me. I was angry at everyone who ignored her until she damaged herself enough for others to notice. Amy's tears lingered on my cardigan, small shards from a broken soul I had no tools to repair.

My mind was with spinning multiple questions. How can such damage be undone, how could our politicians make such big mistakes, how could our institutions help young souls like her? I had no drugs to recommend to her, I wasn't even sure whether cognitive behavioural therapy would help. I asked Amy which class she attended and who her teacher was. But she didn't want to share anything else and left when my lesson started.

I felt awfully useless. I wanted to burn the three hundred-page-long thesis I wrote that was sitting somewhere in the university library. I wasted three years writing it instead of directly helping girls like Amy. I was fed up with teaching others about psychology theories – I wanted to make a real difference.

'Real and direct impact. Applied research, you know,' I said, explaining my frustration to Lana back in the office.

'You won't get a promotion with applied stuff. There is no money in community work.' Lana saw the big question mark on my face, she explained, 'Community work takes time to do well. And as you know, in academia we are paid for results, not time.' Lana adjusted her loose breasts under the blouse and continued, 'Unless you inherit a fortune like Valerie, you will struggle to make ends meet.'

I sighed. I sat down at my desk, opened my emails when I got a notification. I first thought it was a clever spam that made it through the university filter system but it wasn't. It was Aron, writing from an ordinary Gmail address. I knew it was him because he misspelled the word 'tommorrow'. He didn't use predictive spelling and he had dyslexia – I never told him that but that was my theory.

Hi princess. Sorry for the silence but I was not well. Do you want to meet tommorrow?

I printed the email and waved the paper in my hand. I was so happy that he got in touch. He hadn't written because he was unwell … of course that neatly matched my intuition that he had the hero syndrome, that he never showed his vulnerable side, that he always wanted to be the greatest one. I made sure I removed my long signature and that my email sounded as a short text message. That was the style Aron liked and used, the platform or format didn't matter. What mattered was whether the message was delivered with the correct set of instructions. A military writing style.

We agreed to meet at mine at 8 p.m. I made a lasagne, bought new cushions for the kitchen chairs and even a bouquet of flowers since I knew he wouldn't bring me any. The roses looked good for a romantic dinner. I was wearing my expensive lingerie, hoping Aron would stay overnight and I could surprise him after dinner.

He emailed me at 8.30 p.m.: **Sorry must take a rain check. Complicated client. Had to leave the country.**

No further explanation, no suggestion for an alternative date. I stuffed myself with the pan of lasagne. Then took a pack of green tea slimming tablets that cause immediate diarrhoea. I spent an hour on the toilet, then bleached the inside of the bowl and all bathroom tiles, took a long shower, went to bed, kicked Winder in his head towards the door, then took a sleeping pill and slowly fell asleep as if nothing happened.

Chapter 23

I woke up with a bad headache. I was late for my morning bus. No email from Aron. The insecurity and unpredictability surrounding his behaviour were driving me insane. I took the flowers to work – I decided to give them to Valerie as a thank you for citing my paper in hers. If Aron 'left the country' again, the flowers would fade by the time he was back anyway.

Valerie was not in her office. I scribbled a short note for her and left the flowers with her secretary.

'Did you know that Valerie has a PA now?'

Lana was busy preparing for her afternoon lecture, she did not raise eyes from her notes as she responded, 'Well, good morning. She has had one since she got the promotion. But good you noticed it NOW. Remember that's how it works with academic ladders. Delegate, delegate, delegate. Elitism and individualism.'

Lana's cynicism was so thick, I couldn't help continuing on with it. 'I thought it's about finding your niche and building a bubble of evidence around it,' I said.

'That's for the long run. If you want a shortcut, you need to schmooze with the influencers. Oh, and keep a simple but consistent personality, so that you are recognized as "good in X" for your lifetime achievement awards.'

I wondered what Lana's niche was. She didn't have a clear one identified, and she was clearly frustrated that she was given so much teaching. She had to repeat the same lecture at least ten times, so that all students got an equal experience of tutorial support, as specified in their terms and conditions. They demanded in-person lectures to get their money's worth and nothing was more exhausting than reciting content over and over – especially to a bunch of bored international students whose studies were sponsored by their rich families. Our university was too prestigious to have first generation students or students who wanted to study for the sake of studying. Most students were there for the degree certificate for their future jobs. That's why past generations paid for their studies.

Lana took out a stick that looked like incense from her bag. It smelt like Christian incense, the kind of frankincense that monks dispense around churches to reduce heart rates and high blood pressure in believers. Lana was using it on her students, so that they were more willing to listen, and would unquestionably absorb what she said. I thought it was weird and manipulative, but I liked that secret alchemist streak to Lana. I inhaled the incense, Lana went to teach her students. I opened the office window and sat down to process the blush of dizziness. Some building work was going on, it was noisy and dusty, I shut the window. Still no email from Aron. I took my bag and went outside to get away from Lana's frankincense. I decided to visit the local church. I wanted some authentic church incense, and I needed a quiet place to tidy up my thoughts.

No one was inside the church, so I sat down in silence with the statues and frescos. I watched two people enter, bow, dip their fingers into a container of water. I wondered what was going through their heads.

Are life's paradoxes getting bigger with each generation? How can we have tourists booking a hotel stay on Mars and at the same time have people praying on their knees to wooden statues? How is one supposed to keep any normal schemes with such polarities? I began typing:

Fragmentation happens when there is tension. Huge tensions fill our society – no wonder we are witnessing the epidemic in multiple personality disorder. People are getting fragmented. It is their way of creating a small niche for themselves. The 'me, myself and I' was the space they could hone, become expert in.

My ideas were shooting out as my fingers quietly typed them on my phone. Why did I not think of this connection before? This could be the breakthrough necessary for moving the MPD field.

People always have at least two stories going on: one they live and one they want to live. One they show to their closest relatives or friends, one version to show to acquaintances and social media. The two stories get fragmented into micro-stories because there is no standard polarity anymore. The online and offline personalities are a myth. People are a completely different version online and offline. It was never about hybridisation, that was just part of the under-theorized metaverse narrative. The two extremes of humanity are diametrically apart and that tension has fragmented the two central stories of evil and good, into multiple micro-stories. No central narrative holds the chaos together. People can no longer tailor the same story to different audiences. They have to tell a different story for different audiences. MPD sufferers are the vulnerable members of society responding to this societal pressure.

I saw graphs emerging in the words I was typing and the citation count on my publications skyrocketing. I got home and continued writing until 3 a.m. My thoughts were running at extreme speed: I was in a flow, this was powerful, this was the missing piece in the multiple personality disorder theory. I added social media as a mediator to the fragmentation cycle. I was thinking of Jackie's case: as an individual splits into an online persona, self-integrity suffers and gives in to social pressures of misrepresentation of the true self.

I was thinking of my dad: with the first lie comes the first fragmentation between the truth-telling self and lying self. With layers on top of the original lie, the self divides into the socially acceptable self, the faithful and good husband, for example, and the socially undesirable self, the secret lover and cheater. The social and personal self are in tension and that creates another point of fragmentation. I added the word 'truth' into the statistical model I was drafting.

I re-read my paper and sent it to Valerie the following morning. Valerie was impressed and suggested only a few small changes. She put herself as second author and we sent it to the highest-ranking journal covering identity disorders. We asked for an expedited review process, and the editors responded favourably. Within two months of sending the paper, it was accepted for publication. The university communication managers constructed a news brief around it and my name was mentioned in most national newspapers. I got a request for a radio interview and even spoke for two minutes on *Good Morning London*. My rise in popularity happened so rapidly and seamlessly that I didn't have the time to process or reflect on it. A new position for associate professor came up and Valerie 'strongly recommended' that I apply for it. So I did and I got the position. Other candidates were in their forties and fifties, I was the youngest candidate, with the shortest time after PhD completion. Only once before had the university seen such a rocket career rise with a male physics student. I got a permanent position in my twenties, with my own office. My salary jumped up four salary scales, I no longer needed to find the orange reduced labels in the supermarket and I no longer needed to work twelve hours a day.

My professional self was jubilating, but my private self was withering away. Is this how it works in life? The extremes of pain and gain, is that what give rise to life force? Is that why Aron's absences generate my best work performance? I tried to calm down by drawing pastel Zentangle mosaics into my MS diary:

> The only way to survive life's pendulum swings is to fall for mosaic selves. Replace two extremes with myriads of possibilities.

If I dis-integrated my days into manifold fragments, I would be less disappointed if one of them failed me. My life would be about micro-achievements, small pieces that can be celebrated or dismissed in short bursts.

I was pencilling my thoughts around the colourful patterns.

> No need for year-long commitments or big hopes. Balance resides in the short-lived micro-existence of multiple self-fragments.

Chapter 24

'MONOGAMY IS THE MOST STUPID thing ever invented. It causes more stress than anything else. A completely unnecessary, voluntary lockdown.'

I blinked at Lana in surprise, she continued.

'Monogamy eats people from within. I'm transitioning to polyamory.'

I did a quick Google search 'how to respond to polyamory status update', clicked through congratulating and sympathy card templates, got even more confused, then spontaneously asked, 'You have time to date?'

'Oh, with polyamory you save lots of time! No hiding, no prioritising, no strings attached.' Lana was browsing the stationery cupboard in the staff room. The cupboard was empty of paper-based materials, the room void of conversational agents.

How can that ever work in practice? But what do I know about the practicalities of dating? If it works for Lana and her partners, why not? There is no normal, there never has been a normal in love encounters. Dating is either individualized and authentic OR Tinder-like and algorithmic.

I returned to my marking. Half of my tutorial group needed to resit the exam because they plagiarised each other. Another 20 per cent used a ghostwriter for their essays. When I raised the issue with the Student Rep, the students complained they did not cheat but were 'inspired by each other's ideas'. It was a typical student-dispute case, generating lots of additional paperwork and overtime we were not paid for. I picked up the HR-sealed, confidential envelope from my pigeonhole and was headed to my office when Lana stopped me again.

'So you are successful now, right? People seek you out!'

'Is that the definition of success?' I opened the envelope. It was the delayed contract for my new position. 'Success is interesting … the higher you climb, the more people want to include you in their party lists. But it's a lot of work too, you know …' I looked at my watch but Lana didn't get the hint. So I continued, moving slightly towards the door, one centimetre per word. 'You wouldn't believe how many documents I have been sent in the past month to endorse. How many reference letters I was asked to write. Random people tag me on Twitter, hoping I'll retweet their latest publications. It's quite tiring when people seek you out, trust me. …' Lana was still obstructing the door. I adopted my authoritative tone of voice, looking at my watch and tapping my right foot. 'And all the daily requests like, "Dr Kuznetsov, can I pick your brain on this?" or "Can I have just two minutes of your time?" People think that their two minutes are worth the same as *MY* two minutes!'

'This is exactly why I don't want to get promoted. To talk like you. With that kind of contempt for everyone who is not in the same echelon.'

I was in no mood to argue with Lana. She was a robust woman and was clearly harassing me but there was no clear protocol to report it. My technique to kill the enemy with kindness has backfired into her believing I was interested in her.

'Sooo … what happened to Mandy, that nice girlfriend of yours?' I stepped back inside the staff room, glanced over the glass bowls with hand sanitiser sachets, remembered the oranges and bananas in the private school I was no longer teaching at.

'Mandy found out she was straight. It's all good. I am glad I helped her figure out who she is.'

'Will you be okay?'

'Me? Of course! I have trained my mind to respond positively to this kind of stuff. She found a boyfriend at the gym. They have their own company now. Check out @twofitbuddies if you want a laugh! The guy wears gym clothes everywhere he goes. I hope he wears some decent trousers to their wedding!'

'Positive mind training?'

'It's the elite sports technique. You never heard of it? It's pretty simple. When you lose, you must first cry, feel raw and sorry for yourself. Then you get angry, analyse the situation and blame everyone else. Then you pick yourself up, fill your life up with positive stuff and after that you are ready to compete again. It works for the greatest sports superstars, so it also works in relationships. I mean big relationships like when you shoot for stars. Mandy was very pretty, you know.'

I looked outside the window towards the half-full staff car park. Aron was very handsome too. He hadn't written since that unexpected rain check from the lasagne dinner. I was still in the first stage of Lana's elite sports technique, crying and feeling raw about it. I had all notifications enabled yet was checking my phone every five minutes to see if Aron sent any signs of life on any existing platform. There were just work requests everywhere, all the time. I was jumping from one task to another, from one work appearance to another. I worked closely with Valerie on her new project about micro-servers designed to counteract personality splintering. She encouraged me to develop the prototype and test it out. It required a lot of work, but it was an honour for a junior academic to be collaborating with the Faculty Dean, so I dedicated all my spare time to the prototype development.

I got into the habit of working seven days a week from 7 a.m. till 7 p.m. again. Without a meeting with Aron on the horizon, there wasn't anyone else to prioritise my time for. Mum was absorbed with her new detective role, dad with his new role of a baker's lover. Rooster was with Mark and Jackie hadn't contacted me since I 'abandoned' her at the opera bar. I could get a lot done. Valerie was giving me more advanced tasks.

She prefaced each assignment with, 'It will be good for your career, Katherina.'

So I couldn't say no. She also suggested I attended the school's evening seminars, which I found hard, as they were long evenings, but I wanted to have the attendance on my CV for another promotion. I was on the list of potential Fellows for the Identity Society, and I needed to submit a three hundred-page-long vision statement. I drafted it while sitting on the bus and while lying in bed before falling asleep. I had no time to think of other things than work and yet, the light of Aron's face and the shadow of worsening MS symptoms hung over me like sun over a guileless country.

When Valerie entered the staff room, both Lana and I jumped up in surprise. Lana stepped away from the door, almost stepping on Valerie's sari.

'Thought your PA was picking up your letters,' Lana said in a barely hearable anger-laced voice.

'Good morning, Professor Mukherjee!' I said loudly.

Valerie ignored Lana and didn't say good morning to me, but she asked me to collect more interview data for a new project on collaborative technology. More data collection implied a lot more travel, but I agreed. I wanted to be part of the primary evidence gathering, as it guaranteed co-authorship on a paper and I needed at least four strong publications per year. Valerie 'strongly suggested' Lana go to the participant interview I had planned for that day, a recommendation we knew was a thinly veiled order.

'You will spend one day on data collection with Katherina, Lana. As you have surely read in the staff newsletter, Katherina is in a higher position than you, so she will mentor you on this project.'

Lana categorically refused. Valerie adjusted her head scarf and left the room. I booked two train tickets and headed to the station together with Lana.

The train was on time. I enjoyed the quietness of the off-peak travel. People were reading, eating breakfast, listening to podcasts. Such a difference to the packed peak train I used to take. I began writing my thoughts, they were not field notes but they were research related, so I filed them under 'observations' in my private folder.

> Data collection days are the most fun part of a research job. Analysis and article writing are interesting, too, but being in the field, with real participants, documenting their lived experiences, that is what motivates me. People in the train seem motivated, too, unlike the desperate morning commuters, holding onto the bar, sleepy eyes, clutching their coffee cups and laptop bags against their chests. The women in this carriage were not desperately doing their mascara on the go. These workers could flexibly adjust their working hours and follow a career of passion and self-fulfilment. I am one of them. Smiley face. I am writing this diary and looking outside the train's small window, absorbed in the scenery. I am sitting here with the aloof Lana, she resents her position of my mentee for the day.

'Tickets, please!' said the ticket controller, a tall white man, very good-looking in his bright green uniform. He had a lovely nostalgic look that fit well with the slow milk train we were on. The train was stopping at every little station on the way to Cambridge. I smiled at the controller, showed him my ticket. He smiled back.

'Did you see that?' Lana asked.

I thought Lana was picking up on his good looks and knowingly winked, but Lana was furious.

'That fucking bastard! He is checking that boy's ticket again! Totally delegitimising, fucking spoiling his journey! Disgusting racist!'

I looked towards the young Black boy sitting close to the carriage door. He held his ticket high in his right hand, so that the date and time and type of train were clearly visible. He was entitled to be on this train, but the ticket controller made him feel he was not: the boy had to show his ticket at every stop.

I was as disgusted as Lana, and I was glad she made me aware of it. When I began my studies, I used to jump trains. I couldn't afford the expensive on-peak train tickets. I hid in toilets, pretending I was doing my make-up. I was not in the suspicious category with my light hair and cute glasses. But this boy had to be reminded that he was not to be taken for a frequent traveller, that he didn't have the privilege to lean back and watch the scenery pass by. Every station was an obstacle on the smooth journey, a reminder of how many more stops he had left on this exclusive ride.

The injustice got me up from my seat, I went to the tiny train toilet at the end of the carriage. The soap smelt like the soap we had at Lavender Street. I must have stolen some when Mark and I were short of money. I threw the rest of the tiny soap into the bin and ticked 'toilet in need of a clean' on the train evaluation app. I filled out a quick survey giving minimal points for the 'journey experience' and the quality of ticket control. I wanted to smile at the boy on my way from the toilet but he was no longer in the carriage.

'It's collective, you know, every effort needs to be collective to be meaningful,' I said to Lana when I returned to my seat. 'That's why we are working on these collective technologies with Val.' I saw how the shortening of Valerie's name annoyed Lana but at least she paid attention to what I was saying and stopped playing the annoying Egg Hunt on her phone. 'You need to have many balls in the air all the time. If you ever want to be successful in anything you need to have parallel projects going on so that if one doesn't work out, you have a back-up. Success needs to be collective. So don't ever rely only on one person.' Lana was not taking notes or returning my eye contact. I was unsure of how I was supposed to mentor someone who was so ignorant of my words. 'People will steal the ball from you if you have just one, but if you have many, you will steal the game.'

'That sounds like recipe for online polyamory to me!' Lana interpreted my mentoring speech in her own way. 'Date many to avoid disappointment. You should join the Stopes community. Great community support.'

'Stopes community?'

'Jeez, girl, you really need to catch up with life, you are totally gripped by the academic bubble! Marie Carmichael Stopes, the feminist who popularised birth control, normalised adultery marriages with lovers. Do you want to join? They have a promotion running this month. I get a bonus if you use my link for signing up.' Lana sent me the link.

'No, thank you.' It was a firm 'no,' said with authority and no possibility for negotiating. I learnt to say that kind of 'no' at the self-defence course I took after my break-up with Mark. I also learnt at that course that my evening 'nos' uttered to Mark should have been accepted and not taken as an invitation for discussion. Sadly, as was evident from the other course attendees, I was not the only one who heard that for the first time at the course. When I finished the course, I got 'No' tattooed with temporary ink on the top of my wrist. It was supposed to be a reminder to say 'no' to all the requests I was receiving and that I was unable to reject.

I wondered whether I should share my thoughts with Lana. I saw she hasn't even opened the 'Mentee success criteria folder' that I had created for her. I wrote my thoughts into my diary instead:

The process of learning to say 'no' was very beneficial for my way up the academic ladder. Those who make it to the top are those with sharpest elbows, pushing others to act on their behalf. Promotion works like a two-way traffic system: I was promoted because I worked harder than others and said 'yes' all the time, but once I was higher up, I needed to say 'no' to keep my position and go even higher.

An email popped onto my screen: **Sorry about last time. How are you princess. Want to meet?**

My blood pressure rose 100 per cent, I stared at the phone in disbelief. It had been more than four months since Aron had been in touch. I re-read the message. I put the phone away. I was not sure how to respond. I was hurt that Aron ignored me for so long and yet I was deeply touched he re-contacted me. I picked up the phone again, Aron's message still on the lock screen's notifications. 'Princess.' I am still his princess! And he wants to meet! I bathed in the glory of being desired by him. I looked outside the train window, the town we passed looked so pretty, I wanted to forget about the data collection, get off at the next stop, meet with Aron in the town's little café, dance on top of the tables there. I turned the phone camera towards my face, looked at myself. I put on lipstick, it made me feel more confident. And it stopped me snacking. It would made me look better if Aron suddenly video-called me.

Lana was nervously clicking on her laptop, trying to close a private browser window. Her computer was low on battery and the more she clicked on the browser, the longer it took until the whole page crashed. Lana swore and angrily shut the laptop down. 'Why are you staring at me? Not everyone got a promotion with a free laptop!'

'Sorry ... but, but Aron texted me!' I couldn't hold it back, the joy was flooding into my body, I had to pump it out by sharing with others.

'You guys gonna meet?'

'Yes, tomorrow!!!' I had to stand up and stretch my legs, the messages uprooted me from my seat.

'Tomorrow? You can't play it as always available. With that kind of impatient love you're just going to fuck it up, excuse my French. You are just going to crush it.'

I didn't care what Lana was saying, I didn't want to hold back. I had been draining for four months, I was turned on just by the thought of Aron touching the phone and writing to me. I looked outside the train window again, still standing. The air seemed clear, not as blurred and fuzzy as when I woke up alone in my flat. The clouds drove in the opposite direction of the train, suddenly a bird passed through, its black body crossed the rolling scene, like a quick advert in a nice film.

'It's our stop!'

Lana grabbed her bag and my hand. I was glad she travelled with me. I would have easily missed the stop and ended up in Bradford instead of Bedford. Our study participant had requested to be interviewed in a public space, so we agreed to meet in the local garden centre. The participant preferred the pronoun 'they' and said they would meet us as George but we could also speak to their other persona – Annika, Michael, Georgina and BabyX. George was the primary identity, they told us. They were diagnosed with multiple personality disorder two years ago and they volunteered to participate in our study for a £50 Amazon voucher.

George waited at the darker corner of the garden centre entrance. I gave them the consent form to sign and the voucher with a thank you card signed by Valerie. I explained that Lana would lead the interview and I would take notes as Lana's mentor. George agreed. They were wearing a big black hoodie, only partially revealing their face: paper-thin pure White skin, pin-small black eyes and feminine lips.

Lana started the audio recorder and asked, 'How long have you had therapy for?'

I sat behind her in clear sight of George, quietly taking hand-written notes.

'I stopped therapy last year. I am not acting violent. I don't need therapy. I need love. I am a victim. I have mental health issues.'

'The different personalities you mentioned in the question-naire, are they somewhat related to each other, do they ever meet inside you?'

'My fragments you mean? Annika, Michael, Georgina and BabyX? We are one family! We all live in harmony.'

'Do you use different email addresses and online platforms for each?'

'Yes.'

'Are you family or friends or both?'

'Not friends. Family. They are part of me. They will not disap-pear. They are here to stay.' All of sudden George began shouting. 'No one can stop me having them! You understand? No one can stop me. I am them, they are me. They are here to protect me. If they go, I go. FOREVER.' George revealed a huge forever tattoo on their left arm.

Lana got her pepper spray out in case George started being violent but George quickly calmed down and Lana continued the interview.

'I understand. They are your primary persona. Do you have secondary persona too?'

George nodded.

'How many?' Lana had her eyes on the interview protocol.

'Sixteen.'

'I see ... but Georgina comes out most often? What is the trigger to make her come out?'

'George, not Georgina!!!'

'Apologies, yes, George.' Lana nervously looked at me, I sent her a reassuring look. It was a difficult interview and making a mistake with names can be very destabilising for the MPD victims. Especially if the interviewer uses a nickname that the MPD person reserves for only closest family members.

'I got fucking nervous when I messed up the name!' Lana had her mentee folder open, typing into the 'Post-interview reflections' box. We were on the train home, George was probably on their way to a new therapy centre. 'When should one use nicknames? It's so tricky, they can open the familiarity door or it can totally backfire.'

'True. Nicknames used wrongly or in the wrong context seal the gate with painful embarrassment.' Lana gave me a surprised look as if she never heard me talk before.

'Now move to the case evaluation box,' I said in a lower voice. Lana finished the post-interview evaluation within ten minutes. If she is to become a good fieldworker she needs to be quick with her evaluation reports. Fieldworkers are paid by the number of completed cases, she needs to get ten cases per day if she wants fieldwork approved as a skill in her portfolio.

'Clear MPD case. Sexually abused by their father when they were little, hence Baby X persona. Their father's name is Mike, hence the protector persona Michael.'

'Did you see the videos they posted?' Lana asked me, I nodded. I saw the videos before the interview, they were part of the visual analysis necessary for a full participant profile. George posted them on their BabyX account. The videos showed an adult acting like a baby, with fairy lights all around their neck, eating small packets of fruit, listening to lullabies. Then screaming and violently throwing toys away, protecting the baby's face with their hands and shouting, 'Leave me alone!'

I was disturbed after watching it, it was clear to me that the childhood trauma was a strong contributor to George's MPD.

'It wasn't just their father, it seems. Remember how they said towards the end of the interview, what was it ...' Lana played the audio recording in her headset, 'Ah, yeah, the mother said that "The BAD George will be taken by the police if the GOOD George doesn't come back." So maybe the splintering started with the mother. I mean the identification of a good and bad persona, that kind of good girl and bad girl that would fuck up anyone's mind.'

Lana highlighted the relevant transcript line in her notes with a yellow highlighter, I ticked the box 'good observation' in her mentee's portfolio.

'Sexual abuse combined with deep insecurity of belonging to the family. We have seen that pattern in several MPD sufferers. That was the reason they created their own families, all composed of their own selves. It gave them a sense of security they did not experience as children.' I was talking while browsing other boxes that Lana needed to tick before returning the form for Valerie's signature and HR's reimbursement of our train tickets.

'George seems to have made peace with all five persona, they did say they keep a diary, remember? So they communicate with them, they are not just performing them.'

'Yeah, George was very protective of the journal. I wonder how much the journal exaggerates George's symptoms, though. You know, if George is meeting all five personalities in writing, they keep them alive and constantly create new scenarios for them.'

'There was a paper about it in the past *Identity Issue*. The team at Jearen University found that keeping journals decreased the frequency with which MPD sufferers performed their persona. So the more they write them out, the less they feel the urge to perform them.'

'Good point, which box does that go in? Ah, here, references, okay. Also, George said all five persona were primary but George was clearly the hero. The super powerful one who could block all past traumas.'

Lana completed the form, we sighed in unison. I was not sure to what extent Lana and I were united in our mission to help people like George. Perhaps she too was frustrated by the fact that upon coming to our office, George will get an ID number and will be added to the expanding database of MPD sufferers. The data will be shared with the Five Eyes countries our university had agreements with, so that researchers in the UK, US, Canada, Australia and New Zealand could further develop the MPD theory. Someone would turn the theory into an intervention programme, an app or a training programme. They will outsource the product from the university to a company that will charge a hefty consultancy fee. Would our long hours of work ever reach individuals like George? Lana and I were silent for the rest of the train journey. The day was nearing its end, the sun was shining through openings in clouds, sending spectacular beams of parti-cle-scattered light towards the green golf fields by the train track. I wished fervently that George had never been traumatised. I prayed to the sun that no human soul would ever be perforated with holes. I prayed to the clouds to let all humans shine as the bright star that they are, not spotlighting their fragments.

Chapter 25

I WAS FEELING RATHER LOW when I got home, but the prospect of seeing Aron the following day was raising me up. I was upset with him that he had not in touch for so long but I didn't have the context – I didn't know what challenges he had faced, so I couldn't really be angry with him. I was keen to talk things through, explain to him that his sudden disappearances have become a pattern that was growing larger than the beautiful relationship we had together. I was feeling nervous about confronting him but I knew I had to do it if I wanted a change. I prepared my speech by writing it down, I scribbled my words on the back of an envelope in the kitchen. I wanted to sound firm and clear and was worried that if I spoke spontaneously it would turn into an argument or worse, a tearful whine from a needy girlfriend.

Aron texted me: **ETA 6 p.m.**

I started panicking, I had not straightened my hair, and he was almost round the corner! I quickly glanced at my envelope scribbles:

> You want to be mine then don't make me whine. Do you want to be with me or shall I set you free?

My notes were far from Emily Dickinson's beautiful rhymes, I shredded them two seconds before Aron rang at the door.

I opened the door and my eyes widened, but instead of giving Aron a big hug I clasped my hands at how different Aron looked after the months I hadn't seen him. He was bigger, mostly around the waist, his face unshaved, hair longish and untidy, his hug was not as strong as usual. He had an empty look, as if he came straight from a battlefield. There was a little scar under his left eye. He told me he had pain in his shoulder. He looked like a refugee who needed to be taken home and looked after rather than my boyfriend who I was supposed to talk to about the frequency of our love messages. How could I fault him? I had no idea where he flew from, how long it took him to travel to Belsize. He might have come from a difficult meeting at work. His wife might have done something. He could have had a rough fight in the pub. Someone close to him might have died. Maybe his mother died. So selfish of me to only see my part of the story. His whole body was enacting a part of a story I knew nothing about.

'Come in, have a rest.'

Aron nodded but he didn't want to sit down, didn't want a shower, didn't want a cup of tea. He was all wet from sweat but didn't smell bad. When Mark sweated, it was unbearable, his cheap cologne evaporated after a short walk. But Aron never smelt bad, he used branded perfumes and when he was sweaty, the amber tones came out in beguiling wooden aroma. I offered Aron the tomato soup I made, he had two bowls of it. He ate up the baked potatoes and chocolate cake too. He spoke little, he wanted me to talk, so I told him about the promotion, the theory I had developed and published, the sad MPD case that Lana and I interviewed the previous day. He listened, smiled occasionally, and I was pleased I could take his thoughts to another place.

'It was the typical celebrity effect you know. When I was un-successful no one wanted to talk to me but as soon as I got some publications and awards, colleagues began to be interested in my name. Now everyone smiles at me at meetings and asks me to join this or that club. Is this called meritocracy or hypocrisy?' Aron's beautiful lips curved into a soft smile, I knew he would like the last sentence. I wrote that thought down three months ago.

Aron didn't want to eat or drink anything more, we went to the bedroom, made love, slowly, and carefully, as if we had just met. I didn't want to hurt his shoulder, he didn't want to come. I had a slow and profound orgasm, he kissed me with satisfaction, fell asleep. He slept for nine hours. I was long time awake when he finally opened his eyes.

'Good morning, some coffee?' I brought his cup to the bed. He drank it while sitting in a semi-upright position, looking blank. He got out of bed, took a shower, said sorry at least five times, then drove away, in a car I haven't seen him in before. I knew it was painful for him to be with me when he was aching and vulnerable. I had an immense desire to get that hero instinct out of his mind, to persuade him that I cared about him whether he won or lost the last battle. But his eyes were so unattainable, I felt the only connection I could make with him was to continue to play my part of a princess for the superman to save.

I texted him: **Thank you for a beautiful night. Please come again. I need you. I miss you.**

Messenger immediately offered me an array of heart emojis. They looked so simplistic in light of the web of emotions hidden in my fifteen words.

Aron came two weeks later, again late in the evening, again in a rented car. This time it was more the Aron I knew. He raised me up in his arms, his eye slightly twitched, reminding me of his shoulder pain, but I did the usual Hallelujah! to show how happy I was in my Legend's arms. Aron only had half an hour he said, he was about to go to an important meeting. I didn't want us to fall into the old pattern of intermittent meetings and long absences. I plucked up my courage and began, 'Aron, I think we need to talk …'

I pushed the bowl of hummus and carrots towards Aron and while his loud munching was breaking the tension, I continued. 'It … it hurts when you just disappear for months without me knowing where you are. And then you reappear again. Or cancel our meeting last minute. I want to be able to reach you. I want us to date like couples do. Do things together. Enjoy life. Like the trip we had.' I was so nervous, I could not remember any of the lines I had written down, I was just verbalising my immediate concerns.

'How is Winder?' Aron asked mouth half-full, getting up from the chair, ready to go.

'Do you need to go already?'

'Where are my keys? Did you see my car keys, babe?'

Our eyes crossed the second time he asked.

'I don't know where they are, maybe in your pocket?'

We spent the last ten minutes of his visit searching for his keys. I cursed the bloody keys for stealing away the precious time I had with Aron, I was angry that instead of talking about important stuff we talked about keys forgotten in the bathroom or in the bedroom.

'Can I write to you when you are away?' I asked when he sat in the car, the engine on. 'I mean write a bit longer, not just a few words. Like letters, digital letters.'

'Sure, let's do that. Love you.' And off he went.

I had the rest of the hummus the following day at work for lunch, cracking loudly while clearing my inbox from students' emails, pondering whether Aron registered anything from what I said while he ate the carrots. An email popped into my inbox and it was from him, as if he knew that I was eating his portion in that very moment.

Aron: **Use my username and password is Winder007!.**

It took me a while to decipher what he meant but then I figured it out. I gave the screen a big bright smile. We were going to use Aron's Gmail as our shared inbox. I no longer needed to be worried about sending private emails from my work account. I logged into Gmail, using Aron's email address as username and Winder007! as password. I got in immediately, no further verification steps were needed. There were no other emails in the inbox, just the ones I had sent to Aron. I looked around in the Drafts, Bin, Archive.

I saw an email come to the inbox, written by Aron to Aron, but the text was addressed to me: **Hi princess so here we are in digital space. A xxx**

I responded to the same thread, my email got highlighted as a new message but in a few seconds the message appeared as 'read' because Aron opened it at his end. It was not like messaging from two separate accounts, the other person not knowing what the other person did – we shared our actions. Deleting a message would delete both his and my words. Seeing a message in drafts meant either of us could finish it off. Customising tools were not for adjusting the display to an individual's taste but to our shared preferences. Both of us could change the background and customise the settings to surprise the other with a new wallpaper or font size.

I loved Aron's idea of this shared digital home. See Katie, you didn't need to agonise over whether Aron got anything from your badly formulated plea for better contact! It may have been roses in the twentieth century but a shared inbox was the most romantic thing lovers could have in the digital era. You complained you didn't like his unpredictability but that was part of the innovative ideas he was coming up with. You can't have it both ways, Katie! Unpredictable means that – unpredictable.

My next date with Aron was again at mine and again with hummus, this time bought by Aron. He brought two 300 gram pots, one of them with the reduced label on it. I wondered whether he had seen me buying reduced food before and wanted to please me or whether he didn't mind eating foods close to the sell-by date, but I was embarrassed to ask. We kissed a hummus kiss and we lay on the bed tickling each other and laughing.

I signed up for an online sewing class and made some outfits for Winder. Aron laughed when he saw the teddy in a sparkly T-shirt with green shorts. He said I could have him on my knees when we drive to Brighton. I sewed a safari outfit for Winder too, I dressed him up with a hat and binoculars when we drove to Longleat safari park. The safari visitors took selfies with Winder, asked what the teddy bear's name was. Aron and I took photos with our eyes, only for the private, flesh memory albums inside our heads. Those snapshots were deeper than any pixels could ever recreate, they were recorded through all six senses and stored in the red cells that make the heart pump out more blood from life.

We had several one-day trips, Aron's rented car was our temporary home on wheels. We sang random radio songs, we had a few sandwiches in the boot and we had us – which was everything. Aron was an impeccable driver, he drove without the navigation system, and he always gave way to pedestrians and birds crossing the way. He never broke abruptly, except for one time when he stopped at an empty zebra crossing. He said he had to let pass the urge to make love to me. He kissed me passionately, continued the journey, his hand on my right thigh, his eyes on the road. I put my hand on top of Aron's, begged MS to give way to such moments of unutterable happiness.

***

It was the middle of yet another pandemic lockdown, we had been prescribed a home office. Aron said he had to leave early in the morning and collect some stuff from his office. I told him I was vulnerable with MS and he promised he would be careful with social contact. Nevertheless, I developed a bad flu after that meeting. What kind of variant that was I didn't know, but I was very sick for three weeks afterwards.

You gave me a new variant of the love virus! I emailed jokingly from bed, still feverish and coughing.

His email appeared immediately in our shared inbox: **You infected me first! Now we will be just mutating the virus between us!**

It could be he had brought the virus from his travels abroad, it could be he was not careful enough when travelling locally. I refused to get tested for the origin of the infection, I didn't want Aron to get into trouble in case it was him. I needed to be completely self-isolated for twenty-one days, the local support group brought food to my doorstep and checked on me. It was supposed to be my turn with Rooster that month but when Mark heard that I was sick he agreed to switch months. He even finished his text message with **get well soon**, which was a big step in our communication.

How ridiculous that I needed to be ill for Mark to show any kind of empathy towards me! Could we not have kindness as the basis for all human communication? We all can have an illness, I had MS under control but who knows, perhaps there were other illness that I was carrying too. Mark could have diabetes or pancreatic cancer or any other serious illness. We can never fully know the viruses our bodies are wrestling, so why not always be kind to each other?

I was really looking forward to be back in the office when I was finally symptom-free. Aron wrote he might be able to pick me up from work. I spent forty minutes going through my wardrobe, trying to find a piece of clothing that I would look good in after three weeks of isolation, a garment that Aron might like and that would make him think that I was a confident woman. I knew he liked me being confident, and I wanted to be confident but I didn't know how to express it other than with the clothes I was wearing. Despite the freezing temperatures and slippery roads, I wore high heels to work that day. I appeared taller and bolder but without Aron's shoulder to support me I tripped and badly hurt my knee. *Stupid girl, now you are even more dependent! You need to invest in platform heels!*

I cursed myself while checking, for the hundredth time that day, my shared platform with Aron. Since Aron had shared his password with me, I was checking the Gmail inbox all the time. With Instagram, Twitter and iMessaging there were always other people I was messaging with or whose profiles I visited. But with our shared Gmail there was no possibility that the incoming message was from someone else. Opening that inbox felt like opening our joint flat. I checked the log-in history for the exact minute, second and IP address for when Aron had been in, I watched over messages whether he responded or deleted a spam message. I checked the drafts, I checked the bin and whether it had recently been emptied. I could not create a notification for all those micro-inspections, I needed to perform them myself. I both loved it and dreaded it, I was coping less and less well with Aron's absences and their digital confirmations.

I worked slowly on my first day back, I was still tired after the weeks of severe fever. Lana got a plaster for my knee. Valerie proudly unveiled the nameplate for my office that she arranged while I was ill. I grew three centimetres taller when I saw it.

I ploughed through the tsunami of unread emails, responded to some of them, drank three coffees. I waited for Aron until 5 p.m. *He must be very busy, it is okay, I have a lot of work to do, I can do more work while waiting for him.* The clock showed 6 p.m., then 7 p.m., then 8 p.m. I was still sitting in the office, still checking whether Aron logged into the inbox, distracting myself with arranging the books on my office shelves.

Finally Aron's email flew in: **ETA 10.30 p.m. Will you be still there?**

My heart sank. I didn't want to wait for Aron for so long in the office. Everyone went home hours ago. I was still weak, my knee was swelling and getting purple. I wanted to lie down on the couch at home for a while.

I responded: **You would need to carry me home by then.**

Aron opened and replied to my email within a millisecond: **Happy to carry you:-)**

Me: **Let's leave it for another day :-)**

I checked he had read my reply and logged myself out. I wished Aron and I would call each other, perhaps he would hear from my voice how disappointed I was and would make more effort. I tried hard to hold myself together and not check the inbox until I got home. Aron didn't write more, it could be days, weeks before he would write again. *Should I have waited for him? But what if he cancelled again? There were no buses to Belsize after midnight and a taxi would cost me a fortune.* I threw the heels into the corner. My legs were aching, I felt like I had the bad cough back. *Does Aron not miss me? Is it just me who is in love? Is it normal that I want to be with him all the time?* I needed to get those questions out. I didn't want them to grow into monsters chasing me in my weak moments. I used a light black pencil, so that my words were barely readable or sharable.

> How can one tame one's own thoughts? Work doesn't seem to be helping anymore. Should I distract myself from my worries on the digital playground?

It was the same notebook in which I had written my theory of the MPD origin and in which I took notes when studying for the Identity Society fellowship. The three-week absence put me behind schedule, and the fellowship was important for my career, so I decided to distract myself with that.

Two weeks of no new messages from Aron, I passed the Society exam with the Excellent mark. I was pleased that the long nights had paid off. As a Fellow, I could ask for a salary rise and

I could get a research assistant. I sent the request to Valerie, she authorised it the same day. There were not enough finances to open a new position but I got allocated a research assistant's help one day per week. Her name was Sally and I knew her from another project. She had the nickname 'Hypersally' because of her hypersalivation when someone explained something to her. It was irritating, I had the urge to hand her a tissue to stop the drooling but I knew she was also hyper-effective and that worked well for the project. Valerie agreed that I could work from home for the rest of the month. Two weeks into my home office work I got the email that my latest journal article was shortlisted for a prestigious award. I even received a box of chocolates with a plaque from the journal. Valerie rewarded me with another incremental salary rise. The pay rise meant that I had enough to move into a flat that was not in a basement but on the actual level of ordinary citizens. A flat with a view not towards a stone wall but towards Belsize Park. A dream flat.

I envisaged my new flat as a project that would bring me joy and make think of something other than Aron all the time. But it was impossible for me to not wonder whether Aron would like the walls in dark blue or light green or whether I should invest in king-size or double bed. I asked Aron, sent him photos of colour samples, but he had not logged into our shared inbox for the last three and a half weeks. His birthday was approaching, he told me he was born on 6 December like St Nicholas. I wanted to arrange a special party for him in my new place. I wanted to suggest that he could partially move in with me if he wanted to. Instead of staying at hotels and temporary accommodation, he could stay at mine when he is in London. I duplicated my keys and bought a cute key ring for his set.

Four weeks since our last meeting and no new log-ins into our shared inbox. I knew Aron was busy but I had hoped he would at least briefly check in, read at least the latest email of the twenty-eight unread ones that I had sent him. I wanted to get at the core of Aron's thinking, cut through with sharp questions, unpeel the layers of bravery covering his true core. Winder sat on the new armchair I had bought, staring at me with his plastic eyes.

'If only you were a smart teddy … if only you could respond to all the love I am projecting onto you. If only you could send it to Aron. Stop giving me that dull look! Sorry. I know that you are not dull. You are tough. You are always here even when I am mean to you.'

Winder was the diamond I never got from Aron, he was my cushion to cry into, a healing altar for my wounds. Can an object ever hold so many emotions? I took Winder to places where I missed Aron most. I had him in my bag when I went to a classical concert and wished Aron would sit next to me, hold my hand, listen to the concerto with closed eyes. I took Winder to my presentation for TEDx too, the biggest event our Centre ever advertised on its Facebook page.

Not every fresh graduate gets the opportunity to present at the top conference. It's a gem for your CV. Valerie's email got automatically assigned to my Urgent Inbox.

I got the TEDx invitation in my private email but Valerie insisted that I got it because of my affiliation with the lab. She requested to see the transcript of my speech and forced me to include a reference to her work in it. She presented herself as my mentor to everyone at the pre-conference party and told at least five people that I had MS. She said to me that she was proud of me because I inspire other disabled women and asked I mention the Centre's 'generous and unprecedented support to women in my position'.

I did not talk about my disability, I focused the talk on MPD and how it affects girls like Amy or Jackie. I was nervous beyond belief that day and wished Aron would tell me good luck and smile at me from the auditorium. Instead, it was Valerie who was sitting in the row reserved for family members. Focusing on Amy and Jackie during my speech made me less nervous but I still had to look at the speech cues twice, which ruined the overall impression. The YouTube comments were merciless. No one commented on what I talked about, all comments were about what I looked and talked like. The comment 'Why is she shaking so much? Does she have an Parkinson's?' was Liked 455 times.

I got home exhausted, I took Windermere to bed, cried into his belly, wishing fervently I would wake up in Aron's arms. I didn't reveal anything of this to Aron, I did not want to appear needy, I did not mention nor ask when he would come again, so that there was no pressure, so that he would appear when he needed, when he wished. Winder had no choice, he had to go where I wanted him, whenever I needed him. Winder had to absorb my pain and he had to withhold the happy squeezes when I found a penny on the pavement or got a message from Aron. Winder withstood the ambivalence that I sowed into him. He was designed to bear scars and smiles and not to give away any of them. His fake plush was more reliable than human flesh.

Chapter 26

Mark texted me at 1 a.m. on a Sunday: Rooster is unwell. Three days of fever and diarrhoea. With blood. The vet worries it could be the new strain of parvo. Mark put all words within one message. This was serious.

The media were full of devastated dog owners losing their beloved companions to the deadly new virus. There was no vaccine yet. I immediately travelled to Mark's. Rooster was lying on the kitchen tiles, shaking. Mark and I sat on the floor next to Rooster. Mark wore an old jumper that seemed too big for him, covering his hips, the pale colour reflecting the bags under his eyes.

'Not sure whether he'll make it,' Mark said, stroking Rooster, looking into his eyes, not mine.

'May I stay overnight?' I whispered, Mark nodded.

I sent Mark to bed, put a cover and duvet on the couch in the living room, lay down next to Rooster. I stroked his fury little body, putting cold cloths around his ears and feet. Rooster licked my finger occasionally, his eyes watery and absent.

'Roosti, darling, you can make it.' I stroked Rooster's little head, scared of the eerie absence in his black eyes. I could see that he was in deep pain, his small body was shivering, his tongue hung out of his mouth, he was breathing heavily and irregularly. Mark and I paid for the premium vet service but they were overwhelmed and would not answer the phone. At 2 a.m. Rooster began coughing and vomiting blood. The emergency vet was late, I was hysterical, Mark had to hold me as I was shouting into the phone. The emergency vet eventually arrived at 3.30 a.m.

but there was nothing they could do at that time. We lost our beautiful, precious Rooster that night.

Mark and I openly cried in each other's arms, both of us distressed with the look at Rooster's motionless body. We cursed the person who imported the virus to the country, we blamed the veterinary services, we blamed the government, we blamed ourselves. We looked at the photos of Rooster hanging around the flat, then cried even more. I arranged for the pet crematorium, the cremation was expensive, they were clearly taking advantage of the increased deaths in the area. Mark and I buried the ashes under the oak tree in the park where Rooster enjoyed fetching his stick. We stood by the oak for a good hour, staring intensively at its bark, letting our intertwined memories run down its branches and roots. After a quiet prayer, we began slowly walking around the park, both of us silent, missing Rooster's happy barking and flopping ears. Mark gave me a friend's hug, I wiped my tears, we continued walking.

'You want to see my new place?' I broke the silence. Mark waited a while, then nodded. We took the underground directly to Belsize Park. Mark sat on the opposite side of the underground train, so that we faced each other.

The carriage was half-empty but the journey was loud, Mark had to speak louder than usual. 'You live close to the global rich, now, hey …?' He teased me.

'Yup. All the Russian and Middle Eastern oligarchs are my neighbours.' I attempted to joke back. 'Come on, it's not Belgravia. But it's a nice neighbourhood, you will like it. Rooster would have liked it.' I picked up the free *Retro* newspaper lying next to me, skimmed the headlines, zoomed in on the new avocado bar in town. I could feel Mark's intense look at me, I looked up, our eyes met, our lips curved into grief-stricken smiles.

We got off at Belsize Park, it was the first time Mark was in the area. He took some photos, some of the Brazilian tourists, some of the mansions we passed by.

'Eating just organic quinoa now?' Mark sarcastically commented when we passed two independent bookshops, three dry cleaners, one Porsche and the Belsize French bistro that never serves a fixed menu with fixed prices. The clock hit 5 p.m. and the whole street filled up with men and women in grey-black suits, rushing out of their cages, disturbing the sunbathing pigeons. The energy of possibility was palpable in the air, the pigeons wafted in the air together with used face masks and an occasional lost glove.

'When did you move in?' Mark kept on asking questions as we were approaching my place.

'Three weeks ago. I mean I got the mortgage approved two months ago but we exchanged contracts three weeks ago. I didn't have extra to pay for the solicitor recommended by the estate agent, so they dragged their feet.'

Mark nodded knowingly, we experienced a similar procedure when buying the flat in Lavender. We didn't need to talk about the fact that the home-buying system was set up to stress out the buyers so that they pay the middle men. Mark looked around the small park by my flat, took several photos of the trees.

'You still do your morning runs?'

'Yeah, but I joined the gym too. Go figure! I want to be part of the local community, you know.' I saw Mark's raised eyebrows so quickly added, 'We get a discount as university employees. Gyms are not just for posh wives, Mark!'

Mark was still in disbelief, he knew I didn't like gyms and associated them with pretence.

'Honestly, this gym is cool. You know what happened last time,' I began laughing. 'Last time in the changing rooms there was a lady, like a really sweet lady, she looked at me as we were changing and said, "Do you want some coconut on your feet, hun?"'

Mark and I held our bellies as we laughed at my pronunciation of 'hun'. Mark knew I had very dry skin, especially on my feet and hands because of the decreased circulation. He lifted my hand, gently stroked it, then let it go, walking so close by me that he could hold it any second.

It felt good to be walking like that with Mark and sharing local stories with him, yet it also felt wrong that it was not Aron I was sharing the walk with. I felt strange wrapping my new life in an old foil. I unlocked the door, put down my jacket.

'Come in, you can leave the shoes on. My place is not so big. Hang your coat in the corridor.'

Mark took his shoes off, breathing heavily after he had to bow down, I felt guilty I didn't have a shoehorn. My flat was the size of the neighbour's bathroom but it was close to the park and much bigger than my previous place.

'So this is the bathroom, and voila, my kitchen! Isn't the small sink window cool?'

Mark examined all rooms as if he was a detective looking after a murdered love, carefully checking the rooms for any signs of roses or cards. He opened the wardrobe to 'Check the size,' he said, though he only looked at my clothes. I thought he might even inspect whether there were any missing condoms inside the pack in my night drawer. I let him perform his checks, there was no photo of Aron anywhere, in fact, apart from Winder there was nothing in the flat that had a direct connection to Aron. Aron was always very careful not to leave any traces behind. Mark seemed to take it as a sign that I was single. He didn't ask me directly, perhaps because he feared I would say that I did have a boyfriend, perhaps because he was so sure that I didn't. He was in his generous, happy mood, stayed for dinner and said he would wait for my new sofa delivery.

I booked the late-night delivery slot to save money. My new sofa was delivered by two young Poles at 11.30 p.m. Neither of them spoke English but the body language of both indicated their contempt for posh Brits who had big sofas to chill out on, while they had only small beds to resuscitate their tired limbs.

The two delivery men worked for the same company as the old delivery man who brought my kitchen table three weeks ago and who told me three times what a great buy it was and could he get another cuppa. The two Polish men had five other deliveries that evening, they quickly transported the sofa into the lounge, got me to sign the delivery papers within seconds, sneered at Mark's big belly, brusquely shut the door. They were so fast that they seemed aggressive.

Mark attempted to help me with the sofa and he did a bit, but I didn't have the correct screwdrivers. He said he would get them the following day, I told him three times not to worry, he insisted, then left at 2 a.m. I could not focus on my yoga exercises that night. Instead, I wrote a long email to Aron, told him about Rooster in detail, about the delayed emergency services, about the crematorium and ashes under the tree, about how much I missed him. I mentioned that Mark came over in one sentence. I didn't want to make a big deal out of it, I just wanted to inform Aron because I knew that if I hid it from him, it could become a big problem. Maybe it was that mention of Mark, maybe it was just Aron's mysterious algorithm, but he responded in return.

Want to meet tomorrow evening?

I typed immediately back: **Yes!**

Aron wrote back: **Can I invite you for dinner? To celebrate your birthday. BELATEDLY.**

He capitalised belatedly because I had used it for writing about celebrating his birthday. He got my hint but he no longer apologized for his absences. He understood that I got used to his bilingual presence, one speaking of profound passion, one of withdrawal and cold absenteeism. He knew that he had trained my heart to speak his language.

Chapter 27

With my flat in the rich Belsize area, I felt like a proud Londoner. I could book an evening theatre ticket and I didn't need to worry about leaving the performance before it finished because I would miss the last train home. Before I moved to Belsize and wanted to have some kind of cultural outing, I needed to pre-book all transport in advance and arrange for a late start the following morning at work. No matter how exciting the concert piece was, the magic of the show evaporated when I sat on a cold train journey back to a dark house with snoring Mark. With my new address, I could truly enjoy what London had to offer, the kind of city magic that only Londoners understood.

I cancelled on Mark and the sofa screwdrivers and went for dinner with Aron instead. It was almost Christmas, one could tell by the amount of big paper bags Londoners carried in Oxford Street. Mine was from last year, a sturdy white Body Shop bag from Jackie, I carried a small gift for Aron in it and two issues of the *Identity Journal* to keep the bag straight and look like new. Aron and I met at Trafalgar Square. He wore a thick grey-black coat, had it open, revealing a dark green Christmas jumper. He was freshly shaved, his hair up with gel, chest upright, showing he had been training. *Stop shaking, Katie, you deserve it all! Yes, the whole package! A job that fulfils you, a nice place to live, a fabulous boyfriend! You have worked hard, you have waited for long, now enjoy it!*

'Lovely to see you princess. Quite surreal!'

Surreal was exactly the way I felt. Aron's intuition was astonishing. He squeezed me tight, apologized for squashing my new white coat.

We walked among the busy shoppers, his left hand warming my right hand. It started snowing, Aron stopped under a lamppost, made me look up towards the warm yellow light illuminating the snowflakes' gentle darting. He hugged me from behind, kissed my ear. I could feel him harden as I stood with my back against him, his breath going quicker, his tongue in my ear more persistent to enter me. He slid his warm hand inside my bra, I gently stopped him. He didn't mind, and I didn't either. We teasingly grinned at each other.

'You know if you look really carefully,' Aron gently bit my ear again, 'the snowflakes are not falling down in a line but they are bouncing off each other.'

I pored over one of the snowflakes elegantly landing on my tassel bag.

'See? Every time they hit each other they fly in another direction. And with each collision, they make each other smaller.'

Perhaps it was the metaphor in his words, perhaps it was because I was hungry, perhaps it was because Aron aroused me, but I saw an angel clearly appear in front of us. It happened for a very brief moment, quicker than a second, but it sparked a revelation for me, an epiphany. It was as if in that very moment I understood that I couldn't have my life determined by the speed of random snowflakes, no matter how beautiful they might be. I understood that if I wanted to be remembered on this Earth, then I needed to follow my own trajectory, avoid the collision of other small snowflakes. I needed to be the snowflake that survives when it falls on the ground. The snowflake that attracts other snowflakes to bind to her, and forms a snowball that can turn into snowmen that makes children laugh and that lasts all the way to spring until the fields are green and the snowdrops come out.

We ate at Pollock's for dinner. I ate the same portion as Aron, I had dessert too. I did not feel guilty about it because I knew I could go on diet when he disappeared again. I savoured the tastes in my mouth, I savoured Aron's eyes on my blouse, the guitar music cutting through the city bustle. I was not thinking about what time we would need to leave the restaurant, I was not thinking about how much the dinner would cost or how many weeks I would need to eat less to make up for the extra calories. My mind was fully and exclusively focused on the moment there and then. I was fully present. Fully alive.

Aron paid the bill, drove me home but couldn't stay overnight. I thanked him for a fabulous evening, we passionately kissed, he disappeared in the night. I put on the vanilla candle I had bought for the evening, sat down at the kitchen table, began doodling in my notebook. I never doodled freely before, it came just like that, spontaneously to me. I wrote Wonder-Winter-Winder in calligraphy letters, decorated them, then fell asleep, in my tight evening dress, hugging Winder.

I sent Aron an email spontaneously at 9 a.m. the following morning: **Please spend Christmas with me.**

I didn't write more, I hoped that since I never asked for things before, Aron would deduce that it was important to me. Aron didn't respond. I waited, counted the days, checked every two hours whether he logged into the inbox. I went to the Christmas party at work with Winder in my bag, I sat and danced with half-drunken Lana. I checked the inbox every hour, Aron still didn't respond. So I spent the twenty-second with dad and the twenty-third with mum. I said to both that on the twenty-fourth and twenty-fifth I was with my boyfriend. I enjoyed seeing their respect for my self-created bubble, I liked how that distanced them from my new life.

I bought small presents for Aron, practical little things I thought he would find useful for his car, some snacks I knew he liked and then some personalized ones, like photos of Winder in different outfits in different places we visited. I wrapped them in special paper, with ribbons and small stars on top. It was obvious they were from me to him but I amused myself with writing his name on top of the stickers, using the calligraphic font I invented for Winder. On the twenty-forth, Aron didn't confirm or respond to my message but I saw he had read it and I sensed he would come, as he used to, last minute, turn up at the door with his hero smile, probably no gift but that would make it even cuter. I got us some special salmon and put on my new glittery dress that looked like fish scales. I sang carols as I was decorating my first ever little Christmas tree. I bought only white garlands and ornaments, I knew Aron associated white with me, and I associated it with angels and weddings. I heard my neighbours laughing and the warm smell of turkey coming from others' windows as I was watching the Christmas special, pretending it wasn't already 8 p.m. on the twenty-fourth and I was still on my own. Aron didn't turn up at the door, I fell asleep on the sofa with the TV on.

On the twenty-fifth at 8.24 a.m., Aron emailed me: **Merry Christmas babe.**

Nothing more. He wrote just that sentence, into the subject line, not even into the email body. I stared at the three words, the romantic light from the fairy lights disappearing under the sharp light from my phone. I looked at the gifts underneath the tree, at the salmon in the oven, at my tears sliding down the glittery fish scales on my tummy. *I can handle this, right, Winder, we can handle this?* I placed the teddy on Aron's chair, I breathed in and out in long breaths, I held it for about ten minutes, then totally broke apart. I never felt as lonely as that day. I felt very close to grabbing the kitchen knife and running it across my veins. I remembered that I had had the urge for cutting before. I looked at my right arm, at the scar I lied about to Valerie when she asked why I had it. It was embarrassing for an educated girl to say she lost her mind when she was sitting in a wheelchair at nineteen. That she thought she could end her presence with a big piece of glass. The scar seemed to have grown over the years, there was no hair growing on it. I did not open the scar that night. I deleted Aron's email, I curled myself on the floor in the living room, I pulled the table cloth over me, I didn't care about breaking the porcelain plates and spilling out the wine glasses standing on top of it. I stammered and suffocated in convulsions on the kitchen tiles in my glittery dress, thinking of dead fish on shores where no one ever walks and can throw them back to the sea.

I woke up with a sunray piercing through the window blind directly on my forehead. It was a cold crispy morning, I heard children's laughter in the park. I ate some of the salmon in the oven, put on warm clothes, got out to the park. The sun and the rest of the snow on the ground were blinding me, I walked the road I usually jog on. Out of habit, my arms and legs moved without receiving any conscious commands form my head. As I gained speed and saw the trees and crystals around me, I began feeling warmer, somewhat happier.

See how strange you are, Katie? Yesterday you thought you didn't have the will to live anymore and today you feel like it was such a small thing. Christmas is just a day, Katie! The moment of celebrating can happen anytime. You and Aron had that lovely dinner together. That was like Christmas for you. It is not like you two broke up or one of you died. In fact nothing happened. In fact Aron wished you Merry Christmas. It could all have been a misunderstanding, mis-communication. Perhaps he thought you were celebrating with mum or dad. Perhaps you were not clear enough in your email. In fact it is completely your fault. You didn't even respond to his email of Merry Christmas. You deleted it! Even from the bin! Why? You totally failed! Maybe you could still retrieve the email with a scraping technique. Maybe you could respond to it with a thanks and a nice photo of Aron's gifts waiting for him pick them up. You can fix what you messed up.

But wait a moment, isn't it normal to expect a boyfriend to want to spend the special day with his girlfriend? Isn't it normal to respond something more than just 'Merry Christmas' when your girlfriend begs you to spend Christmas with her? Isn't it normal to give each other gifts for Christmas? Should I just leave them for next Christmas? They were personalized gifts, chosen and made especially for Aron. Not socks or aftershave to pass onto another man.

Don't be pathetic, Katie! Why should we follow any traditions? Life is about disrupting them, thriving in the unexpected. You should think like Aron, show a complete disregard for any schedules, any plans or expectations. Life is easier that way.

I got home with an unbearable, splitting headache, I had to take two paracetamol, lay down. I finished the salmon, drank a strong coffee, then opened my laptop and began searching. A serious search for any information about Aron. I was as systematic about it as I would be for work. I took notes of profiles that had the same first name/surname combination but were not him, of photos that could be him but also someone else. I ranked the photos and categorised them in terms of likelihood and source of information. It was a painstakingly long search because there were so many places to check. Without one official, publicly available micro-server, his online persona lived on multiple platforms, with data sprinkled across providers and institutions. I had the right tools and I followed the secret but well-established procedure in our Centre. I didn't use the university search software but I did use the patented search techniques, so I was technically breaking my employment contract by searching for a civilian and not a patient from our database of MPD suffers.

I knew that if someone found out it could cost me my job but I also knew that finding some information on Aron could save my sanity. I was looking for a trace, an address, a work history. I found the latter. I found out that Aron worked for multiple IT companies. At least five different companies in the past four years. That explained the frequent travelling, the stress with clients he talked about. I found out that his last employer was IJ Consulting and they were based in Bristol. Aron was listed as their product advisor. The company was closed on Christmas and New Year's Day but they were open on the thirtieth and thirty-first, with shorter working hours. I checked the address again, it was three hours by train from my place.

I acted on impulse, I bought a morning train ticket for the thirty-first, put all the presents into one big box. I didn't expect Aron to be in the office but I dressed up and spent two hours on my make-up anyway. The box was too big to carry in my rucksack, so I carried it in a big plastic bag, carefully balanced so that it didn't hit other people I was passing by. Siri misguided me and I was exhausted from walking with the big heavy box on unknown Bristol streets, so I took a taxi, which cost me double because of the New Year's surcharge.

The building of IJ Consultancy was unassumingly pale grey, with big windows and a small sign on the glass door. The receptionist told me she was a temp and didn't have permission to check who was in the building or who was in the work registry. I insisted she check and ring Aron's extension number, but I saw security cameras everywhere and did not want to come across as pushy towards a clueless temp. In the end we agreed for her to keep the gift at the back of the reception area and to deliver it to Mr Aron Milton when she saw him.

On the train back I ordered a cup of tea from the train trolley, it was the usual cheap black tea in a bleached tea bag with lukewarm water and a capsule of creamer full of conservatives and sugars. I indulged in it, I needed a bad drink to celebrate my Pyrrhic victory. The train began moving, I began typing a long email to Aron, wishing him Merry Christmas and Happy New Year. I revealed that there was a gift waiting for him at work. I tried to make the text sound jovial and festive with lots of ribbon emojis around the black-and-white letters. I added: **You are very welcome to unwrap the gifts at my place if you wish. The pyjamas** are made of organic merino wool, I hope I got the size right, please wash it on a low temperature or just bring it to mine and I will wash it for you. The card is hand-made by a blind child, tactile art they call it … Btw I think that when you open it, it will be the first time you will see my handwriting. :-) They say that handwriting can reveal a person's character so have your guess about mine. :-)) Oh, and the feather inside the envelope is from a pigeon from Belsize Park, just as a reminder that love brings us closer to Heaven. Love, your Katie XX

My connecting train got cancelled so I had a long waiting time at the station, I was cold and bored with no work to distract myself with. I got off at Belsize Park at 9 p.m., the New Years' fireworks had already started. I heard only the loud noise, wrapped in lots of cowboy-like smoke. I saw no colours. I found a small penny by my flat door. I considered picking it up, but then shuffled it away with my foot for the street-cleaner to pick up in the new year.

Chapter 28

I have a Christmas present for you!

These were the words I wanted to read but they were sent from Mark, not Aron. I looked at the message, hesitated what to answer. I felt like I didn't want to have anything to do with any Christmas gifts for the rest of my life. But I thanked Mark, invited him to mine so that he can bring me his gifts. I offered him some of the gingerbread I had baked for Aron three weeks ago. It was still edible, though the fragrance has almost disappeared. Mark would not mind it.

It was kind of Mark to think of me for Christmas and I felt guilty I didn't give him anything. But I didn't want him to think that I thought of him in a romantic sense, and giving him a gift could raise false hopes. It was enough to have to comment positively on his new look. He told me that he had joined the gym and lost ten kilos. I wouldn't have noticed it if he hadn't specified that. What I did notice was that he shaved off the long beard, ending up with a short moustache that accentuated his double chin. I told him that he looked great and that I was pleased for him. He asked whether I think he should cut off the moustache completely and I didn't have the guts to tell him the truth. We were in friends' territory now, there was no need for the complete honesty expected of a girlfriend.

Aron didn't respond to my long Christmas email, I could see in the inbox that he has not read it either. I kept on logging into the inbox, but there were no sign of his log-ins. Then on 10 January I saw that he logged in and read the email. But he didn't respond. My agony grew even bigger. *Perhaps he liked the gifts and will send me something in return. Perhaps he hated it and thought my email was pathetic. Perhaps he was cross with me that I tracked him down at work.* My heart skipped a beat every time I got a notification and thought he may have written. I didn't trust the notifications, it could be his email was misclassified as spam, I needed to check the junk inbox too.

I was the only one in our department who didn't take winter holidays, Valerie texted me some ski photos from Calgary and left a desk full of work before she left. I practically ran the whole lab on my own in January. I managed quite well – on the surface. The only thing that our collaborators noticed was that I was finishing all Zoom calls half an hour early. I used to say it was because I had another meeting to go to. There were no other meetings. I just needed to sit down and quietly cry, quickly reapply my make-up before the next meeting. My MS was getting worse, it turned out that my constantly cold hands and feet were an actual symptom that needed to be treated as I could lose sensation in the extremities with so little blood circulation. One specialist said I could have MS combined with rheumatoid arthritis, which would explain the pain I had when walking. I wore sunglasses everywhere. Not like a pop star, but like someone who is willingly blind. I told colleagues it was to protect me from the light of the computer screen, which was partially true. The whole truth was that I preferred not to participate in the world. Wearing the big sunglasses was my statement of '*Je refuse.*' I refused a world where colleagues bullied each other and bad-talked behind each other's backs to get promotions, where boyfriends would not write for weeks and where the January wind found its way inside my bones, making me ache at every step.

I thought of ringing Aron in the office or sending an email to his office email address. But I didn't want to break the rules again, we agreed we would only use our shared email. And above all, I didn't want to come across as desperate. Maybe he had huge problems at work. Maybe his ex-wife was clinging to him and terrorising him. I could relate to that, I was clinging to Aron too. *Who wouldn't, he is far too perfect to let go.* I could rationalise the whole thing for one minute but the next minute the whole situation was a blur, I questioned whether I had actually met him, whether the emails in our shared inbox were not just messages sent from myself to myself. I could not picture his whole body or face, all I could remember were fragments. Winder was the only whole, permanent and concrete storage holding my memories together.

On 5 February, an email arrived: **Sorry for the radio silence. Was out of country. Want to meet tommorrow?**

The 6 February was Mark's celebration of getting his driving licence. I had promised Mark that I would throw a little party for him, with some of our old friends, I had invited mum too. But I couldn't say no to Aron, it could be another month or four or more, before he is in the country again, I was dying to see him.

Yes!! What time?

6 p.m. Just a heads up, I am a bit tense.

Him writing that he would be tense made me tense and I knew that if he saw that I was tense he could get even more tense, so that was the first conundrum I had to resolve. Then it was Mark's party that needed to be fixed. I rang Mark, I told him something else came up. He asked what was the 'something else'. I didn't want to lie. Not after that big lie we had when we broke up. I told him the truth, that I had a date with the guy I am together with. He asked why I hadn't told him before I was dating someone, I said he didn't ask directly. Mark hung up, I didn't call or text back. I rang mum, I told her something else came up and the party was cancelled. She asked if just the two of us could meet and chat like mothers and daughters do, that she had something to tell me. I said I couldn't because I had a date, and she got upset that I prioritised a date over her. I tried to be honest but I was hurting people by seeing Aron and I knew I was hurting myself too, and yet, I was so desperate to hold his body against mine that nothing else mattered.

It has been months but the anticipation of meeting Aron has turned into the same routines: I painted my nails, curled my hair, put my best clothes on, prepared the meal and candles. As the evening approached, I was getting more and more excited, sitting by the window. Aron has been sending me regular updates on his ETA and I felt like a customer waiting for a special package to be delivered at the door. Aron came on time, he wore a gorgeous suit, I never saw him so elegant before, black jacket and white shirt, even new, polished black shoes. *He made such an effort to dress up! My handsome Aron!* I could not resist giving him a long, passionate kiss.

'You look gorgeous,' Aron said, rolling my front curl between his fingers.

I gently pulled him towards me, slowly opened my mouth. I wanted to talk about something that would inspire him and distract him from feeling tense.

'Now, did you know that Mars smells like an old penny?' I tickled him and he burst into laughter.

'You and pennies! My Penny Lady! I didn't know that. But bet you didn't know that the moon smells like a burnt almond cookie?'

'I've got some cookies. I baked them myself. Come in.'

'Okay, but can only stay till 6.30 p.m.'

'That's … that's in twenty minutes?'

'Yeah, sorry …'

My heart sank, all the things I wanted to tell him about what happened in the past months couldn't be summarised in twenty minutes. I had prepared a three-course dinner, the main was in the oven, in twenty minutes he would barely touch the starter.

We went into the kitchen, I got quiet. I felt the time pressure and I never performed well under time pressure. Aron saw it, he tried to break the ice with tickling me, joking about the weird sound coming from upstairs.

'Soo … you got promoted you wrote?'

I nodded.

'A Fellow, hey? That's pretty impressive. And you wrote things were not going so well recently?' I nodded again but my tongue was paralysed. I kept on thinking that maybe he dressed up for another event and I was just a stop on the way there. I wasn't sure how to tell him that writing to him was no substitute for our physical meetings. I didn't want to write down our lives but to live them. As one thread, not separate strings of messages.

He looked at my quiet face, I looked at his black-and-white suit blended against a Monet painting on the living room wall. I saw no pretty impressionist landscapes, I saw only Picasso's sharp shapes. I pushed back the tears as hard as I could. Aron ate a cookie, we talked a bit about the ingredients and how I made it, then he had to go. *To where? To whose arms? To which dance floor? To which rhythm?*

I walked with Aron towards a white Ferrari I had not seen him drive before. I glanced inside the car, it looked completely new. *Who will he drive in the car? Will he put music on? I wanted Aron so much for myself that I was even jealous of his listening to a female singer.*

'Can I come with you?' I asked boldly. 'You don't have to take me to your party, just drive a bit. I can take the train back. I just … just want to be with you for longer.' My voice was breaking up, I bit my lip and looked down at the car's wheels.

'No, sorry babe, next time.' Aron started the engine.

'Why? What's going on? Aron, you are not being honest with me.' I could no longer hold my tears.

'Sorry, see you babe,' he mumbled and shut the driver's door. I saw the Ferrari speed up on the smooth road, then disappear round the corner. I looked in the distance, thinking whether there was something that would force him to make a U-turn and come to me. *If I told him that I had cancer and would die in a few weeks, would he then prioritise me? Or if I said I was pregnant with his baby? Or if I forced myself into his car?* I dragged myself to the front door, held the door frame, waiting for my inner earthquake to pass. I felt such a high when he came, I was so low after he left. I didn't have time to ask when we would see each other again. I forgot to offer him the soufflé I made. I forgot to ask whether he got the Christmas gifts. The unfinished evening was bothering me, like an unfinished rhyme, I knew that until I find the right words to wrap my thoughts around, I won't find peace.

Chapter 29

Dear Aron, so here I am again, sitting in our shared home at our Google address, waiting for my Prince Charming to return. I have tidied up the junk email, changed the background to brighter colours. I wish you were here with me. At least be my digital boyfriend if we can't meet physically. We have moved places, Instagram, Twitter, messaging, now this shared email for our digital thoughts.

It is getting late, the early evening goldenized into a fiery ring around the sun. All I hear are my fingers on the keyboard, as I am writing and hoping you will read what I write, accepting it is entirely your choice of when or whether. I have to grade my students' work, write a revision for an article, prepare a conference presentation but none of that is as important as writing to you. You teach me things, Aron. You teach me the meaning of 'love you and leave you', the quintessentially British ambivalence of high ideals and harsh reality. How many times did I wish you would skip the second part and just love me and stay … because every time you leave I get smaller. My heart shrinks with doubts and anxiety that I won't see you again for a long time. You know, my dear Aron, I grow taller when I am with you and I go low when you leave. You bring out a different version of me, one I didn't know existed, one that both scares and excites me.

What do you call this kind of love? The kind of love that invades my body and mind, that makes my heart rate go up, my vision blurry, my hands shaky. This kind of love is viral. It is unhealthy, it starts with a bout of flu-like symptoms that weaken the body. I don't want that kind of viral love. I want love that flows, that nurtures, that reflects the sun. Like Lake Windermere.

I know you don't have it easy and need to travel a lot and deal with multiple clients and I admire you for that. I'm busy and ambitious with my work too. Then there are illnesses and our history (past relationships) complicating our schedules. Difficulties are necessary for happiness. Without the bad and black we wouldn't see the good and white. So I realize we cannot be together all the time and if we were then we would probably not like it. I am, in a way, grateful for your absences as they bring the light.

I admire you for so many things and one of them is your ability to guide us into new territories, new places. This shared inbox is one such new place. The emails we send each other here, these strings of black lines and white spaces, they build a path for our thoughts. Our minds meet every time we let our eyes trace the path.

My dear Aron, you may have not realized it but by opening this digital space, you created a home for my thoughts. In writing to you, my memories and dreams come together, they are sheltered, they are understood, they are at home. I used to write my thoughts into various notebooks and on scraps of paper, but now I have them all in one place, for no one but you and me to see. It makes me vulnerable and it makes me happy. The anticipation that you will pick my thoughts up when you log in, and hold in your mind the small tokens of my love for you.

My first long email to Aron took me a day to write but my subsequent emails took usually an hour or two. I drew on the notes I had written for myself in moments of missing him and there were many, many notes, on back of milk cartons and serviettes, sticky notes and digital phone notes. I was excited to be sharing my deepest inner life with Aron this way, I regretted I hadn't done it earlier, holding onto my secrets as if they were reserved for someone else. I enjoyed thinking that Aron would pick my words up, reciprocate with his when he read them. The thought of him holding my secrets in his mind was enough to bring to climax my writing impulses.

I began writing more, an email per week. I drafted the words in my head, then typed them up, read and re-read, then hit the 'send' button, sending the email from me to me. I numbered the emails, thinking a number in subject line could guide Aron's digital steps towards my heart. I wrote for thirty-five weeks, there were thirty-five unread emails. I assumed it was the usual scenario of Aron going off the radar, I didn't see him anywhere online and relished in the expectation that he would have a little book to read when he returned to our digital home.

On the thirty-sixth week, on a pleasant August morning, I saw that Aron had tweeted. He tweeted about some new programme in Africa preventing children's deaths and asking for donations. I immediately liked the Tweet and logged into our shared inbox, waiting to watch Aron open my emails, one by one, retrieving my digital traces. But he didn't log into the inbox that day, nor the following day. I was confused, disappointed. *He was online and he didn't check our emails? He was two taps away from our emails, so why didn't he respond to me? Was that public Tweet more important than saying good morning to me? Is this how much he cares about me?* I sent Aron a message via Twitter. The message was delivered but I saw only one tick. *Did he block me?! Did he go offline immediately after he tweeted? Or maybe I did something and he is genuinely upset with me?* I re-read my public posts on all social media sites in the past five months. I re-read my messages to him, I couldn't find anything that could have upset him. *Come on Katie, be rational about it! You should be proud of him that he is promoting a good case. It is his hero mentality that he needs to save and serve others, there is nothing wrong with that. You are disappointed because you were not the one he was prioritising, but maybe he had time only for one Tweet and that went to an anonymous group of African children, not to one desperate girl typing from her London office.*

I opened our inbox again, asked: **I saw you online on Twitter but you are not responding here, what's going on?**

As I was typing the message, I jumped. What was this? Our previous emails began disappearing, someone was deleting them under my fingers. I panicked, I tried to stop the invisible hand, I quickly went to the Recycle bin but the deleted emails were permanently deleted. I quickly clicked on the inbox and the remaining emails, but they were being deleted in bulk, pages and pages disappeared until there was nothing but an empty inbox staring at me. I felt as if someone pulled the rug out from underneath my feet. I stared at the nothingness of the empty digital bin, my entire being sucked into it. I didn't have a back-up of any of the emails. The back-up for my carefully crafted thoughts was supposed to be Aron's mind. The digital book that I nurtured and birthed for Aron got murdered.

I checked the inbox multiple times, the emails were definitely not there. *Did he move them elsewhere? Did someone break into our account?* My initial shock descended into suspicion. I checked the history of my messages with Aron on Twitter. They had also been deleted. So it wasn't a random burglar breaking into our inbox. It was Aron deleting our digital history.

Why did Aron do this to me?! I felt deleted. I didn't feel I wanted to write anything else to anyone, ever. My memories, my secret desires, poems, photos, all tightly knit together – they disappeared, leaving no possibility of retrieval. I did not know how to cast off in the middle of such a crisis. I threw away the rest of the expensive BB cream that I used to apply for dates with Aron, I washed the little heart he painted on the bathroom mirror. Winder was no longer sitting at the kitchen table or in the gym bag, he was strangled in a bin bag shuffled behind my jumpers at the back of the wardrobe. There was no point in keeping any illusions about home. I will never be able to repay the mortgage for a London flat as an academic anyway.

I turned my flat into an extended office. The mahogany kitchen table got snowed under with printouts of academic articles, the kitchen cupboards got covered with sticky notes with missing food items and reminders of deadlines. I binned all the pretty motivational quotes and their fake promises, the fridge magnets held council and electricity bills to be paid. I was not confident to send emails without copying at least two other people in them, so that if mine got deleted, there was a copy elsewhere.

I felt I didn't own anything but the dark thoughts hurting my days with their sharp ends. Mum and dad barely spoke to each other but they were very eager to speak to me, which I was vehemently refusing. I saw on Housesale.com that the brick-terraced house, with a warm attic room that I used to call home, was now for sale. Mum and dad needed to sell fast, so that they could buy their separate flats. The place that held my memories in dolls and teenage posters would soon be converted into someone else's home. Mum put my old clothes into big bin bags for the local charity, they were all too small for me to wear. She didn't ask about my school exercise books, she recycled them together with the few books I had kept.

I felt outdated, ready to be removed from any place that held a material trace of me. My mind, alien in a grown-up body, was refusing to synchronise the recent events with any future prospects. *Do I struggle to process simply because I never experienced it before? Was Aron's deletion of our conversation some kind of modern way of breaking up?*

My thoughts seemed old. Old enough to join a club of some sort. There were many options, being single at thirty was nothing unusual, thirties was the new age for midlife crisis. I rejoined Instagram, the place where Aron and I started chatting. Or perhaps where we started dating. Who decides where the border is? I posted a selfie with the Stunning Beauty filter on and got 180 Likes. I checked every single account who liked it, scrolling up and down the street of hearts. I was still likeable. I still mattered. I still existed. I posted another post, it was not liked by so many people. I posted another selfie, with a stronger filter, counted all the Likes again. I was never that needy before. I used to post something and come back to it another day or a week later. After the email deletion I got upset when the number of Likes went down or if someone unLiked what they previously liked. I knew I needed to Like others' posts too to get them Like mine. I had no respect for what or who I Liked, leaving my heart emojis on accounts of some weird men in hope they would like my picture in return. And many did. Many men and women were as desperate as me for a sign of affection. I got into the loop of 'I like your photos, you like mine', constantly checking the feed to ensure I didn't miss someone's update and upset them with not Liking it. It didn't matter what people made with my generic, superfluous markers of affection. My most sincere, most intimate thoughts were deleted by a man I loved. My sense of self was nothing more than the shifting emojis on my face, there was no genuine emotion behind them. They could be stolen, cheaply sold, used to boost someone else's account.

Chapter 30

Local trips to Dinoland. Search!

Czechoslovakia history. Search!

I did not care about training the algorithms to my persona, I deliberately confused them with random searches, so that they sent me generic news that had nothing to do with my gender, location or age. After two months of meaningless searching, I began feeling hungry for more information. I wanted to know why Aron acted as he did. Apart from that dead Twitter account and some old webpages that I knew from A to Z from previous searches, there was no information about him. I took a trip to the building I thought was his office, the company was there but the receptionist didn't recognise the name Aron Milton, said it was not in her database. I paid a premium search for an address look-up, only to find there was no physical UK address registered for a person with the name Aron Milton. The less possible it was for me to contact Aron, the more I hoped he would contact me. I kept on checking my Instagram, Twitter, Facebook, emails and messenger apps every five minutes, just in case there was some kind of glitch with Gmail and he was chasing me on other platforms. I had all notifications on, my phone was constantly buzzing with others' messages. When there were no notifications I still checked all the platforms, refreshed the feed, just in case.

Why did he delete all the emails? Did he not like them? Did he think they could harm him? Did he share them with someone? I kept on asking those questions over and over. I was used to asking complex questions at work, big complicated questions that can go unanswered.

The kinds of philosophical questions that expand the human mind. The questions I was asking about Aron shrank the valley of possibilities into howling tunnels that demanded immediate answers. The questions blurred my mind, reshaped it from an ingrained curiosity to a girdling circle. I fervently hoped that the answer would reveal itself to me by coincidence. Or that one day, Aron would appear outside my office, apologize with a bunch of roses behind his back and give me an explanation that I couldn't come up with but that would make sense. It was not just my thoughts and their digital expressions that were hazy, I was moving across the streets aimlessly, drawn to men wearing the same coat or shirt that Aron had on last time I saw him. Once, on my way to work, I heard a car beeping, I ran to it at full speed, saw a smiling woman's face. If it had been Aron beeping, I would have jumped into his arms, cleared my diary and we would have travelled to Georgia as we had dreamt about. The woman slaughtered the dormant butterflies in my stomach, I had to sit down on the pavement, shivering with chills and stomach cramps. The woman saw me going into convulsions from her rear window. She stopped the car, drove me home.

It was not just random strangers who noticed that there was something wrong with me, Valerie noticed it too but she was accountable to the vice chancellor and her performance was evaluated on the number of products of the employees under her finger. At the last Zoom meeting, she asked me to unmute myself even though it was clear to everyone that my microphone was on. I was unable to speak and when I spoke, I repeated meaningless phrases and talked very slowly. Valerie asked me – at the meeting with twenty-three attendees – if I needed a break. I did not respond, I was terrified of working or taking a break, I was anxious of making a mistake, I was worried that whatever I said or wrote could be abused, dismissed, wiped out.

Valerie was giving me more and more work. 'I urge you' prefaced all kinds of tasks: 'I urge you to undertake this review', 'I urge you to respond within the next half an hour', and 'I urge you to participate in this seminar'. I told her about the lower garden bed in front of the council house, with completely depleted soil and the loss of investments, but she didn't get the metaphor, still planting new bushes into my dry brain, assigning me to big projects, hoping that I would miraculously bring them to fruition. She set publication targets that were difficult to meet without working overtime. She spread the word that it was she who had expanded the MPD theory, which has become received wisdom in the department and gradually in the identity sciences field too. She made herself co-author on papers she barely read before they were published. Her position in the field got stronger, yet she still perceived me as an opportunity for her to climb higher. Lana said that Valerie was toying with the idea of going into politics, I was not sure about it, Valerie seemed to perceive all young scholars as a potential threat to her current position as Dean.

'She is a bully, I told you! You need to raise a grievance issue. HR will help you.' Lana came into my office holding a half-dead orchid. 'HR will hold a grievance hearing with you, investigate it and you will present the evidence. You have more than enough evidence now!'

Lana handed me the pot, I turned it around, tested whether it needed water, put it on the windowsill, then stepped back, looked at it from three different angles, then put it on the desk, checked again whether it needed water, until Lana stopped me.

'For Christ's sake give me that plant! Your insecurity is unbearable! Worse than your mother!'

I was low that day, and Lana's remarks were dragging me lower. Valerie and I had a breakfast meeting with the collaborative technology designers. I spent days preparing for it, drawing on the contacts I had built in the past years. Valerie opened the day, chaired the discussions, I was serving coffee in the breaks and helping with the projector. I was an assistant professor yet I was treated worse than an unqualified cleaner. After the meeting,

Valerie requested I send her the full list of the collaborators I had been involved with over the years. She said it was for the lab's database, but I knew it was for her private email list, the long Bcc list that she used to send updates on her achievements.

'I'm sorry, Lana. Apologies. It's a lovely plant, thank you.'

'Stop saying "sorry" all the time. That bitch is abusing and misusing you! Can't you see how miserable you look, if you don't raise the grievance issue then I will, I'll—'

'I can't.' I interrupted Lana. 'I tried to contact the Head about the workload and Mukherjee got furious. She said I had no authority to contact anyone above me without informing her first. She called the Head afterwards and told him I had created the additional work myself.'

Lana was about to interrupt me but I quickly added, 'And she has this new article out, you know in the *MPD Journal*, I'm co-author, if they discredit her as a bully, my career will suffer too … I mean there is really no point, Lana, she is stronger, she will win this anyway.'

'That article is not worth the paper it is written on!' Lana ripped off one yellow orchid leaf and stuck it inside the soil in the little pot. 'The world needs to know that the so-called expert on collaborative technology is a bully! A fucking bully!'

I sensed that Lana was right but I was low on energy and the whole procedure seemed so paperwork-heavy that it would probably bury me.

'The system is screwed, Lana. It has always been. It's simple physics, really. Power generates energy, so the higher one goes, the more energy they have from their power position. And the procedure, the procedure is just too complicated.' I looked down, remembered how mum used to say that the British always have a procedure, and if they don't have a procedure, they will invent one.

'Procedures exist for a reason, okay? Procedures exist to protect the vulnerable. Think of the many young academics who she will abuse if you don't say anything. Silence kills!'

I agreed with Lana's last sentence but for very different reasons Lana knew nothing about. I did not exaggerate when I said that I was low on energy. The insecurity around Aron's silence deprived me of oxygen. I was trying to accept that he chose to disappear from my life, but I could not find closure in the extremeness surrounding the sudden departure. I was not a lunatic, I did understand why I felt that way, in the end I wrote an essay about the psychological price of happiness. I knew that as people we only had two choices, we could either lead a meaningful and unhappy life, or a happy life with no meaning. The two don't correlate, it is either/or. The more meaningful people's lives become, the less happy they are. Extreme events like the death of someone close fill life with more meaning and that makes people more unhappy. My life with Aron had a real purpose, and there were many extreme events filling it with meaning. The psychology law was spot on: I ended up being extremely unhappy.

'This is just disgusting!'

I thought Lana meant Valerie, or the cold coffee she served herself from my cafetière, but she meant the article that she was reading on her phone.

'Did you see it? Fucking bastards! Is it 10.30 already? Shit! Have to go and teach my class now, see you, Katie!' Lana popped her head through the door opening, 'And remember, you are not alone, together we can change the world!'

'Yeah, yeah,' I nodded, jumped as Lana loudly shut the office door, then opened the link to the article that she sent me.

Viral Love in the Form of Spies

London, 14 March 2035

The London Times has discovered that undercover police officers ('spies' hereafter) were forming sexual relationships with top-flying female academics. The allegation comes from a group of academics who have had their lives turned upside down as a result. This state-sponsored deception has been ongoing since 1968 and was a rare but known tactic deliberately employed by the police force to infiltrate political and religious groups. The spies, who operated within the Special Police Branch – a secret undercover unit, were trained to create an illusion of genuine affection to get access to the academics' intimate lives and internal intelligence. The spy who used the fake name Brayden Hudson had multiple, parallel relationships lasting several years with at least five female academics, which enabled him to gather significant intelligence for the unit. He mirrored the victims' interests and beliefs and through psychological manipulation, deceived the women into believing they had met their soulmate. With one of the victims he fathered a child, who he abandoned in 2021. This prompted the victim's years-long search for his real identity, which came to light last month when Laura (pseudonym) discovered that Brayden was an undercover police officer paid to spy on her.

The victims' accounts list seven common techniques deployed by the five spies:

- creating physical dependence by performing female-satisfaction–oriented sex
- alternating between being present and absent, establishing opportunities for the spies to passionately rekindle the romance before unexplainably disappearing
- reassuring the victim of their unique bond and the spy's unwavering affection via intermittent contact
- showering victims with gifts and affection while together

- portraying a life of a successful and busy businessman
- meeting exclusively in the victims' home to enable access to IP addresses and infiltration of all communication on the victims' devices
- portraying strong sexual attraction to the victims, who were insecure in their attractiveness and often had naïve attitudes towards romantic relationships.

The spies specifically targeted academics in stable and long-term relationships. Four of the five victims have broken up with partners of several years to accommodate the seemingly ideal relationships. This targeting was explicitly encouraged, given that women who divorced or separated from long-term partners were more likely to commit to the new relationship since there was no chance to return to their previous partners. The spy's relationships with victims typically ended abruptly, accompanied by the spy's explanation of a loss of interest and deleting evidence of long-lasting communication. Two of the victims reported that the relationship compelled them to engage in extreme behaviours, leading to mental health disorders.

The police recognised the profound damage these relationships had on the victims but highlighted that the practice is vital to accessing relevant intelligence in an undercover role. The Government Communication Bureau described the value of the classified research as proportionate to the threat it represented. They condemned the manipulative conduct of Brayden Hudson and issued a public apology to all affected. The victims opposed the motion, arguing that the value of the intelligence gathered through these relationships does not justify the practice. The trial continues.

I finished reading the article.
I fainted.

Chapter 31

I WOKE UP WITH A cold paper towel on my head, the water dripping into my eyes, I was semi-lying, semi-sitting on the floor, held by someone who looked like one of my students.

'She is okay now, you can cancel the ambulance! Cancel it, they're gonna charge premium if you don't cancel the helicopter!' the student shouted.

I sat up. I thanked her, dragged myself into my office, closed the door. I read the article again. I ran the fake news check on it, verified the name of the journalist who wrote it, checked the links to the hearings. The story was on multiple news sites, covered by several journalists. University vice chancellors issued statements. Feminist groups were up in arms. The story wasn't fabricated, there was proof. I listened to one victim's testimony. I trembled and cried because her description of the love pattern completely mirrored my experience with Aron – those infrequent but absolutely perfect visits, the secrecy around communication, the same kind of midsummer's night dream that never stays because it is too good to be true, the meetings in the 'victim's house'. Yes, victim, that's how the reporter referred to the academic. I was a victim too. A victim of the state.

As much as I wished for it, the article was not fake. The article was the truth. I was shaking so hard that my phone fell out of my hand. I sat on the floor, stared at the words, unable to accept the reality. I could not process, not accept that I could be one of the female academics who was spied on, deceived into a sexual relationship for the government to gather 'intelligence'. My mind, soul and body were denying in full force that Aron was paid to love me. That he was a human spy, instructed in love techniques to seduce 'insecure, naïve' academics like myself.

Why was I a target? I don't process any special or secret data, I was not planning a terrorist attack, I was not even a political activist. Is my devotion to work, my passion to help MPDs victims the reason I was on the list? Is my involvement in the National MPD Society and other charitable organisations the reason I was targeted? I gave Aron access to my home, to my data, to my mouth, to my vagina. Is that what they call 'intelligence gathering' in the British police force? That attractive halo that Aron had, the feeling of soulmate it gave me, was that part of the training he undertook, paid from my own taxes?

I never read crime novels, I watched half of one of the James Bond films. I knew that undercover policing existed, that they used some distasteful techniques to attack the enemy, such as the use of nerve agents or hacking into control systems. But I never knew they did things like this. This was not about infiltrating a system and destroying a sophisticated threat. This was not about locating and killing a radicalised fighter. This was about twisted sexual gratification of brainwashed men, authorised by the British state.

I re-read one victim's statement, 'heartbroken, humiliated and disrespected on all levels.' Yes, that's how I felt too. My body turned into an empty corridor for memories with Aron running on repeat. Spotify eagerly matched my dark mood, recommended dramatic songs, expanding my pain to a different dimension. When the Hero play list entered my feed, I broke my phone screen. I wrote flamingly negative reviews of all James Bond and Superman films on Authenticreview.com. I felt I wanted to take some action but felt helpless and powerless, scenes with Aron rolling in with unstoppable currents of tears. I could not believe that everything, everything I experienced with Aron was a lie.

He lied that he was impressed with my work. He lied that my hair smelt nice. He lied that he liked my cake. His serendipitous surprises were callously precalculated meetings running according to prescribed scenarios. The sudden appearance at the exhibition, that was just a tactic directly copied from the Three to Tango romcom. The coincidental suggestion for meetings when I was supposed to see friends or family, that was a targeted manipulation to appear unreliable to everyone but to him. Perhaps the pennies I found were part of the deception tactic too – perhaps Aron or a random police officer sowed the neighbourhood to make the naïve academic believe in fate so that she felt destined to fall in love with her hero Aron.

Everything fell together like a puzzle. Aron's frequent travels abroad. Aron's parking away from my flat and driving different rented cars. The change of telephone numbers, communication platforms, the idea of a shared inbox. The booking of a hotel room with a washing machine to remove all my viruses from his clothes. The 'work' he had to do while I was sleeping next to him. The teddy bear to remind me of his presence while he was away. It was all preprogrammed and I bought into it all. I hurt Mark, mum, my friends. God knows whose emails Aron read and downloaded while accessing the university servers with my password. I exposed my colleagues to threats.

I began shivering, feeling a strong pain on my left hand side. I knew I had to massage my heart, lift my hand up to avoid a heart attack. *Breathe, Katie, breathe. Breathe!* Aron's face was opposite mine, like a hawk attacking me, pulling my eyes out. *Breathe, Katie, breathe!* I saw a lot of white light, probably fainted but woke up in a few seconds, sitting on the office floor again.

I was bleeding from inside, the pieces of my broken heart running down my chest, torturing me to an unbearable degree of pain. I tried to get up from the floor. *I must go home, eat something, get some sleep*. I was awake but unable to move, the whole room seemed grey. *Katie, try to get up, walk, go. GO.* There was blood on my tongue and little blood left inside my veins. I got up halfway, half-kneeling, half-walking, held on the office chair, rolled it towards the door, clinging onto the chair back. I opened the office door, I collapsed back on the chair, crying uncontrollably. Then I heard some steps down the corridor, it was the university security guard, he was patrolling the building, my office was the last one with lights on. He asked me if I was all right, I didn't need to answer for him to call the ambulance.

The emergency nurse examined my breathing and extremely heavy heartbeat. She asked whether I had witnessed an accident, I said yes. She said I had a prolonged panic attack. I stayed for one night of observation, was released the following morning, with some Prozac that I was supposed to take every day. I took a taxi home from the hospital. I checked three times that the taxi driver was indeed a taxi driver, that he knew the address, that he knew how to drive. I walked into my flat, went through all rooms, checked all lamps, fire alarms, curtains for hidden cameras. I checked in the cupboards and underneath the bed too. I didn't find anything. I took a sharp knife, pierced Winder's belly and looked for a camera or recording device inside his wool. I didn't find anything there either. I reset the modem and changed my Wi-Fi password. I threw the bowl with collected pennies away. I deleted all my personal emails, I archived all my work emails in a separate server.

What else could I do to feel more secure? I doubt everything around me. The bird in the garden, is it fake too? Is it a drone recording me? I wanted to throw a stone at the bird, strangle it, get to his intestines and check if they were real. The fourth wall could be pulled anytime, reality could swing the other way in a flick of a second. Anyone could be leading a double life. That doctor smiling in the toothpaste ad, he could be abusing his daughter at home. That husband buying an ice cream, he could be cheating on his wife with his secretary. That beggar on the street, he could be trafficking heroin. That rain falling on my windowsill, that could be the neighbour's hose. The air smelling of plum trees that could be someone drinking Slivovitz. The spam email in my inbox, that could be a malware sent by another spy.

I looked at the destroyed teddy bear. It was no longer Winder personifying the love of my life, it was an ordinary teddy bear that had no place in my home. I threw it in the bin, took the bin outside and emptied it in the big container on the street. I felt hot in my face, I was grinding my teeth and clenching my fists. If Aron were there, in this moment, I would grab him by the neck and punch his face. I was shouting at the door, the pain inside my stomach was penetrating my voice with a hue I didn't recognise.

'Okay dear Aron, so help me get the cover story right. I want closure, you see. I want to tell you eye-to-eye what I think. My dear Mr Agent 007, you think you are helping the world when you fuck up naïve girls like me? Tell me, who was I really to you? A free prostitute, an escort, Pussy Galore? How did it feel to get sex from someone madly in love, was the payment from your boss sufficient?'

I thought of how Aron insisted we didn't need to use condoms, that he was in charge. I could have got pregnant like the other victim. Perhaps my under-eating saved me.

'You never cared about me, Aron, did you? That moment when I laughed in your arms in the white linen on a Sunday afternoon and told you I found happiness with you, that moment just got deleted from your memory like my other words I had been for-mulating for months, right?! You just removed them from your mind, as soon as you shut my flat door and drove to another woman. I wonder, dear Aron, you know, I wonder how it feels to lead such parallel lives, how do you manage to keep track of all the women you abuse? When you sit by the table and your right hand caresses mine and your left hand texts your other lover, how does it feel? Does it give you a high, a happy rush? Does it give you a hero feeling that you got us, that you are manipulating several hearts at once but yours is intact? You think it's brave, don't you, you think that you are protecting the country, right? You think you have to fulfil the difficult mission you have been tasked with, don't you? Let me tell you something dear Aron, or whatever your real name is. You are not a hero. You are a filthy coward. You have never been a hero, your mission was driven by egoistic greed, you are nothing but a puppet, a primitive soldier following wrong commands. A piece of shit!'

I was no longer shouting or talking. I was lying on the sofa, my head lying in a puddle of tears, my eyes barely recognizing the ceiling I was staring at, my body occasionally shaking from a big electric shock. 'Are you here, Aron?' I whispered to myself in the cold, dark room. 'Because if you are, I want you to know that you misled and hurt the most fragile place a human being holds. You violated my vulnerability to an extent that it cannot be repaired. You did not destroy one woman or a few women. You destroyed a generation of women. This incident will be re-membered by all women who have ever entered the job market with passion for a higher cause, who made personal sacrifices to earn their positions. Women who became the target of the state they worked for. These women and their partners and husbands, and their daughters and sons, existing or unborn, they will be perpetuating the bile you threw into their hearts, the doubt sown will tarnish any attempt at romance in their future loves. Did you not realize this would be a result of your mission? Did your bosses not realise either? In all these years, when you were driven by your perverted desire of being on the pedestal of heroism, above anyone else, did that thought not cross your mind? No, it didn't. Because you had the secret knowledge, you were higher on the pecking order, you did not need to care.' I was no longer whispering, I was shouting again, my voice breaking at each sentence. 'You are not a legend! You are not a hero! You abused your power to an irreversible degree. You left a dozen people traumatised. You taught a generation that life is brutal.'

I looked at the scar on my arm, I said to myself quietly, 'I will carry these wounds to other relationships. They can teach me anew, but I will never be able to love fully again.'

Chapter 32

I HAD NO DESIRE TO get up, the walls to climb were too tall, the dark hole I was in was better than the world beyond it. I needed to pee, I wet myself, let the sofa under me absorb my urine. I was a piece of dirt that people needed to be paid to love.

You accomplished your mission, Aron. You conquered me, you destroyed all the enemies, no other men will ever get close to me, you have me now, as your loyal wife forever. Anyone can smile at me, write to me, sleep with me. They won't get to my core as you did. All they will get is a cold body attached to a doubtful brain. You hold the key to my old self who was capable of loving with full heart, unconditionally. All other men will get only a cheap substitute, a pretend-like love to keep some kind of social bond. Are you listening, Aron? Because I am talking to you, I am adding to the 'intelligence' you gathered about me, the information needed for the secret code to my heart. You have gathered enough information. Enough to recode me into a different human being. So now you can steer me from a distance. I will be a good robot, you can trust me on that. I will eat at regular hours, select foods that are good for the body but have little taste, I will exercise to keep my legs walking but not dancing, I will sleep to regenerate but not to dream. I won't care about pain or pleasure anymore. I will complete tasks that are inhumane to manage in a day, I will give pleasure to others but not myself. Energy in, energy out. Eat, work, sleep, repeat. I'm yours, Aron, use my bones to climb higher in your undercover job.

My eyes were scanning the ceiling from left to right, my body was shaking up and down.

How could I be so naïve? Of course Aron was not interested in me. Who would ever be interested in me other than fat Mark. Who would ever genuinely think that I was pretty, thin or remotely attractive. Who would ever think that I was really intelligent or writing anything that made sense. Who would ever say 'I love you' to me without an agenda behind it, who would ever sleep with me with the only desire for me to enjoy it. Who would ever touch a defected body full of Multiple Sclerosis. How could I ever believe that such a good-looking man could fall for such an ugly fat cripple like me. Just look at you, Katie, look at you right now. With that red, pug-like face, with your legs in spasm and your eyes full of flies, you are a corpse ready to be taken to morgue, not a bride to the altar.

I could refer myself to a psychologist, I could say I had clinical depression, take something that would make me stop thinking of Aron so intensively. But I didn't need anything to make me feel numb. I felt numb already. I felt that I could give myself to any man or woman in the street. I felt like the cheapest prostitute. Or not even a prostitute. No one needed to pay me to have sex with me. Aron didn't pay me either. They paid him to have sex with me.

I could get in touch with the police, say that I was one of the victims, that I wanted compensation. I could find out whether Aron was on trial, or whether he was with his real wife leading a fake ordinary life, or whether he was sleeping with another academic right now. *I did nothing wrong, I acted out of love. He was the criminal. The law is on my side.* But I had absolutely no energy to go through questioning or evidence gathering. *And besides, when they ask for evidence, what proof do I have? A desiccated teddy bear in the bin and a destroyed human being, aka myself? And what would I gain, anyway? Even if I got some money, what would I do with the extra cash? Spend it on a nice dress? I have no desire to dance. For a better place to live? I bought my flat so that I would have a place together with Aron. I have no wish to search for a new place for me to cry on my own.* And I did not trust the police anyway. It was the police who deliberately deceived the public, I did not want any contact with them.

What if Aron did not delete our emails but copied them and shared with his employer? What if a bunch of police officers were now reading them, having a laugh at my long-winded scrapings? What if they are looking at the intimate photos I sent to Aron? Those that took me a week of dieting and a day and a half to take, those with my blushing face where I was in nothing but a bra and thought they would seduce him. Maybe they watched the video of me giving him a blow job too. Maybe he filmed more but I didn't know. Maybe he had a camera in a contact lens and was filming everything I ever said or did to him. Maybe all that 'content' is now being traded and analysed, put into categories, assigned to an intelligence folder.

I kept on googling my name, checking if there was a photo of me somewhere. I enabled all tagging on social media, and created Google alerts for my name in case someone mentioned it. I wanted to be in control of the story. Because for me, there was only one story from the beginning. One pure narrative. I fell deeply in love and I gave everything for it. *How come Aron's story never intertwined with mine? Could a person really fake affection to that degree? That passionate kiss under the lamppost, how could that be fake? Was I the villain in Aron's story? Why? Why?*

I had multiple scenarios running in my head, I was the enemy in all of them. I was the inexperienced Katie who got seduced by a hero. I stared at that enemy every morning in the mirror, played a simple game with her. The game had one simple rule – to eliminate any pleasure. Because then I would not care that I was just a cheap gatekeeper for providing access to academic files.

Then it didn't matter that Aron faked our joint interests better than Google. I was a winner every day I achieved hating myself. I slept irregularly, I couldn't take more melatonin, the overdose was making me nauseous. The shower was not helping anymore, the meditation app either. I had to exhaust myself with work, eat very little, exercise so hard I vomited. Still I couldn't sleep and woke up at 2 a.m., 3 a.m., 4 a.m. I gave up on the idea and just slept whenever I managed, often a few hours before going to work. I was desperate to have a dream, to integrate the chasing thoughts, change the narrative.

I did not read or watch things that I liked, I listened to cheap pop instead and only ate foods with grated ginger and other disgusting sauces. I could eat a whole jar of hot sauce with a dessert spoon. It was supposed to be for tacos and the chilli was supposed to break down the heavy avocados. I was breaking my heavy thoughts with it. My diarrhoea was bloody and I had haemorrhoids, making toilet visits unbearably painful. The skin on my cheeks was chafed, my lips cracked, my mouth hiding multiple ulcers inside. I kept on producing like a robot. A new paper. A new report. A new student work marked. I did well on the university performance metrics. No one cared about the journey to those products, it was the raw number that counted.

It was sheer biological perseverance that was keeping me alive, no rational volition. A breath in was worth as much as a breath out, my life was of the same value as my death, they were run by the same algorithm. My body, like a simple machine learning gadget, had learnt the algorithm from centuries-long pattern recognition. There was nothing more to it.

Chapter 33

After several months of over-performing, my health got too bad to hide it and Valerie forced me into taking a few months of medical leave. At home, my movements were reduced to a few steps from the sofa to the kitchen cupboard, toilet and bed, my thoughts tamed to only think about which pill I would have when, accompanied by which pre-packed meal, followed by which kind of diarrhoea. I was not creating anything those days. I was transacting. Like Aron did. Transferring a file from A, Katie's IP address, to B, the police force. I was transferring the potato from A, my mouth, to B, the toilet bowl. No composition necessary, no creativity required. Remaining alive was assured through sliding a bar from left to right, typing in 0 and 1, flicking the black-and-white switch on the wall.

I was not trying to get better. What for, who for? The job waiting for me at the university would continue those simple transactions. I would be writing low-quality papers that would be read by the academics who reviewed them and perhaps one or two graduate students who wanted to publish in the same journal. The articles would not report any new insights. The text would be just a rehash of old ideas in a language that was trending in academic circles. Thanks to Valerie's attendance at relevant parties, private magnates were donating money to our Centre, redirecting the tax savings to the payment of our salaries. Our novel findings will be replaced by newer findings, pages of knowledge will get rewritten, reloaded with the F5 key.

'Do you want to go shopping with me?' Mum asked enthusiastically. She was wearing her old yellow cardigan, the colour clashed with my gloomy thoughts. I sat at her kitchen table, watching how she put on the *BBC Good Morning* radio show, prepared a Twinings tea. She too was transacting, subconsciously, she was sustaining an old state with an old woman's state pension.

I did not go shopping with mum, she went with Lionel instead. Dad never went shopping with mum. Mum's adrenalized shopping style and glorification of carry bags clashed with his ritual of online deliveries. He never seemed to have noticed that mum bought food in the overcrowded supermarket at lightning speed but took hours at Harrods. She browsed their wide aisles with unique merchandise, delighted in talking to the shopping assistants in uniforms, escaping to a sparkling clean fairy land where everything was neat and abundant. Maybe after dating Mrs Baker dad had understood why mum was permanently stimulated with shopping and buying new things, however small. Maybe dad needed to date a baker to realise how important it was for women to get a whiff of a fresh goodness every morning.

Lionel did not change mum but he slowed down her hunger for perfection. He seemed to understand that it was beyond him to make mum befriend herself, but that he could be her friend for activities that required little self-investment. Lionel's and mum's yearning for a land that would grant them safety drove them to a remarkable union of different skin colours and accents. Achievements did not matter in that union, their sexless friendship was in exchange of a permanent residence in each other's lives. It was the kind of friendship I had with boys when I was a teen, before I took notice of the differences between our body parts.

Mum had no idea what I was going through. Nor did dad. Mark stopped contacting me, as did Jackie. I told them all I wanted to be left alone. My so-called friends at university cared about me only in the work context. They sent me a generic 'Get well soon' card and a basket of fruit when I began my medical leave. When Multiple Sclerosis took over my body, I was thrown headfirst into isolation but I could compare my pain with similar cases online. With Aron's betrayal I was completely on my own.

I returned to work after three months. I was told the university had space issues and I could no longer have an office on my own. My desk was moved to the dreaded shared office area, where all viruses get circulated and noises concentrated. Unlike businesses, the universities did not learn their Covid lessons, all new employees and graduate students needed to use the open-space office. Being degraded to that space was a clear act of demoralising those who didn't meet the performance indicators.

When the invitation to represent the lab's findings at the multiple personality disorder biannual conference in Moscow came, Valerie sent around a round robin email asking for volunteers to represent our lab and present her paper on her behalf. Apparently it was an 'honour' to present research to an audience that could only read our papers with Google Translate and to stay overnight in a two-star conference hotel. Valerie's email was circulated two times. I waited three days, then responded to the second invite that I would be happy to make the trip. Visas shouldn't be a problem with my parents' heritage and I didn't have any plans for that weekend anyway. Valerie copied my response to the secretary, I took it as a 'thank you'. The secretary booked the trip, selecting the cheapest 6 a.m. departure from Heathrow, which meant I would not sleep the night before and would need to take the train at 2 a.m. I needed to take the Covid21 vaccine before the trip. There were reports of additional side effects for people with autoimmune diseases, but with the state I was in, I did not care.

Mum was the only one outside the university who knew I was travelling to Russia, she sent me a long list of confectionaries I was supposed to buy on my way back. I started packing a week before, my pills, my snacks, my toiletries, my passport. The passport was not in the travel purse where I usually kept it. I always had it there. I would normally panic and question things but things were so out of place that nothing surprised me. *If something is missing, it needs to be filled in, a hole in my heart with new tissue, a missing passport with an emergency one. You don't need to analyse things anymore, Katie, you don't need to think anymore. That would be your old self. You have learnt that all originality will be taken away one day. So follow your new identity, that one who just executes whatever the circumstances push them to do.*

'Issuing a new passport for British citizens travelling to Moscow requires undertaking extra criminal record checks,' said the guy at the passport office. 'So you won't get it by Wednesday.'

'But my Covid test will expire by Wednesday,' I said more to myself to him, he had no idea that delaying my departure by two days meant that the virus test paid by the university would expire and I would need to pay for a new one myself. I insisted on getting a temporary QR code, so that I was not cut out of travelling forever. The private practice charged me £1,200 for the new test, three quarters of my monthly salary. I could not say 'no' at that stage, cancelling the trip could mean irritating Valerie to the extent that she would dismiss me. I had to rebook my flights too, I spent three hours on the phone but customer service was adamant that changes were not allowed on low-rate tickets. I bought a new ticket, a flight through St Petersburg and a local airline to Moscow, departing at 5.30 a.m. but cheaper by £500 than the direct flight. I would still make it for the scheduled presentation, which was good.

I departed in a hurry, the taxi driver was by the door when I was still in my bra. I was locking the front door when I heard a screeching sound under my feet. There were pennies on the doormat, they were stuck to my shoes. They formed some kind of Morse code, I counted at least seven. *You think you can still seduce me with your old tricks, Aron? I am no longer that naïve, you know.* I pushed all pennies aside, for a second thought I spotted Aron's eyes in the bushes, then in the taxi driver's rear window, then in the taxi driver's face. *Will Aron's shadow chase me forever? Will it accompany me to all destinations?*

The immigration officer had to double-check my new passport photo, I did look like a zombie and unlike my other photos in his database, my cheeks were grey, my hair greasy and my eyes bland blue-green. But the iris and fingerprints matched, so he let me through. The waiting lounge had no windows, vending machines or toilets. There were about fifty of us waiting, with about fifty gadgets in our hands, except for one guy intensively looking out the window. With everyone busy with some kind of technology, it was weird to see him stand like that. He didn't have the body of a yoga man but he seemed fit and had a thick, chest-length beard and long hair, precisely matched in their dark brown colour. He turned slightly away from the window, our eyes met and he dropped the kombucha tea bottle he was holding. The glass broke and the black tea splashed all over the airport carpet, filling the room with the scent of fermented raspberry. One cleaner arrived within seconds but she didn't have the equipment to clean carpets, so she just stood next to the stain, supervising, ensuring that no one stepped on it.

I looked at the man, his red face angled down, his eyes soaking up the carpet stain. The stain supervisor loudly reminded everyone, every five seconds, NOT TO STEP ON THE STAIN. The stain enlarged with each mention of 'not to step on it', drilling deeper into everyone's memory feed. The whispers between the fifty passengers were infallible in generating a sensation out of a meaningless splash. After five minutes, another cleaner came, this time a short Latino man with a short broomstick. He started sweeping the stain, tearing the fibres in the carpet and leaving bright yellow and red broomstick hairs on top. The supervisory cleaner watched, his arms crossed, together with twenty onlookers, all of them holding their smartphones and giggling.

I slept most of the journey, woke up shortly before landing. The plane hit the ground as if landing was not planned, making us jump in our seats. The foreign passengers waited till we were parked at the gate, the Russian passengers were standing, pushing each other, loudly talking on phone, the cabin crew desperately shouting through the PA that we had not arrived yet and they should remain seated.

'Whatever!' one of the Russian passengers shouted. He wore a golden cross but he didn't seem to believe in anything, the constant threat of existence reflected in his contempt for anyone trying to control his movements. The woman standing next to me had bright red lipstick on and eyebrows intensified in thick, black semicircles. She looked like a status symbol ready to be taken by a man, tossing round her synthetic blond hair, completely untouched by #MeToo. *Maybe I could be like her. Maybe my travel to Russia is a sign. Maybe I should interpret it as a country for me to live in, maybe I could find a job at the university in Moscow. Mum would like that.* The Russian lady nervously turned a Marlboro in her hand, the old kind of cigarette I had seen only in films before.

I had only thirty-five minutes to change planes in St Petersburg, and we had been delayed on arrival by ten minutes. I ran through the airport hall, my heart pounding, my eyes pulsating with every minute flashing on my watch. The airport disabled Wi-Fi to all foreign passengers and all the screens were written in Cyrillic. I spotted a woman in a black uniform, ran to her, showed her my ticket. She reluctantly looked up my gate number, said, '*Pyat.*'

Pyat, pyat, pyat, that must be five! I remembered that it meant five. The exercise books mum used to drill maths with me with before I started primary school finally became useful. I boarded the plane with the cabin crew yelling what must have been the 'last call' announcement in Russian. I dropped down on my seat bathing in sweat. Two seconds after me, the Kombucha Man boarded, this time not carrying anything. His intense blue eyes reminded me of Aron, I looked at him but he completely avoided eye contact. He dropped down on a seat three aisles behind me, his heavy breathing was immediately erased by the loud and shaky take-off.

There was no requirement for face masks on the second flight either and yet we were not served any food or drinks. I was hungry and thirsty when we landed, chewing the fifth and last piece of chewing gum I had in my travel bag. The Moscow immigration officer inspected me with suspicion, the cleaning lady took her time cleaning the one airport toilet despite my nervous hopping in front of the door. They were bitter, perhaps, because I was not Russian and therefore an enemy. Or perhaps because of their distant war memories, or perhaps because of the recent state oppression. Or perhaps simply because of our differences. I was unlike any other woman at the airport. All women wore something synthetic, T-shirt or trousers, very tight on their bodies. Baggy, natural linen clothes had not arrived in Russia, they were reserved for the privileged women in New Zealand. In Russia, the form counted more than the content. People with good clothes and posh Louis Vuitton bags got priority at the security checks. No wonder everyone was rude to me – I didn't have that gold drizzle on me.

I took the university-recommended taxi to the hotel. It could be my usual post-Aron trauma or the vaccine's side effects, or simply the jet lag of crossing time zones but I felt dizzy, not feeling or thinking anything, just following whatever was written in my diary. If someone swapped that diary with someone else's life, I would have followed that, without questioning it. I looked outside the taxi window, everything seemed so heavy to me. The coats, the girls' make-up. We passed huge shopping malls with packed car parks and an equally big church with no cars in front of it. *Religion replaced by materialism, classic story*, I thought but did not bother jotting the thought down. I checked into the hotel, was too tired to put my antivirus blanket on top of the smelly linen. I could not figure out the heating settings so just slept in the jeans and coat and winter hat that I arrived in.

I woke up starving but there was almost nothing in the hotel breakfast buffet that I would like, everything was bathing in oil and mayonnaise. I spit the creamed coffee I drank. They closed the buffet while I was having my black tea, there was no warning or information. I figured that unlike Brits, Russians do not warn, they do not explain, especially not to foreigners. Russians don't bother disguising it either: it is blatantly clear that premium service requires bribery. For getting the Wi-Fi for my room, I needed to pay the receptionist and then the cleaning lady who brought the log-in details on a piece of paper, written in giant print.

I went from the breakfast room straight to reception, asked them to order a taxi for me. She said it would take twenty minutes for the taxi to arrive. I had no intention to pay for a faster service and decided to wait in my room. I took the stairs up and almost collided with the Kombucha Man. *Is he following me or is this a string of coincidences? After Aron's secret spying am I now being followed in the old-fashioned way? Or maybe it isn't the same man?* I could not rely on my marred mind, I could not rely on the hotel's services, the taxi arrived an hour later than they said. The taxi driver had a simple pay structure: 500 roubles for a single journey with no receipt, 600 roubles with receipt. I gave him 600 roubles, he said it is 750 because he drove extra close to the conference door. I said I never asked to be driven extra, he insisted, so I gave him extra 200. He enthusiastically opened the door for me as if I was a royal, even bowed as I got out.

Quite a few female Russian presenters were at the conference, they were not very attractive. I saw two ladies who looked more like Jackie but they didn't seem to be academics, with their flowery dresses and lots of jewellery. Lana would have said that it was a clear sign that the only way to climb the social ladder is to marry a rich magnate and become a trophy wife. I missed Britain and my emancipated colleagues, I even missed Lana. Siri sent me an automatic 'memory' from New York, picking up on the keyword 'conference' on top of the sign I took photo of. I hesitated whether to forward it to Lana, then decided not to. *What for? Her Siri can generate more relevant memory prompts.*

My paper presentation was in the afternoon. There were about twenty women and two men who came to listen, a typical gender ratio for a social-cause–oriented conference. I was nervous and said half of what I was supposed to say, forgot to move the slides on two occasions. A Lithuanian PhD student came to me after the presentation, and said she liked it. She spoke in staccato English, and louder every time I asked 'Sorry?'. It turned out she was studying in Britain and saw me at the breakfast table in the hotel.

'Maybe you come to my presentation?' She suggested. *Quid pro quo*, I thought, and increased the number of her attendees from fifteen to sixteen, enough for the university metrics to judge it as a medium-sized audience.

'How do you like my paper?'

'I liked your presentation very much, you carried out an important study,' I lied without twitching an eye.

'When do you fly to London?'

'My flight back is tomorrow.'

'Me too!'

We agreed we could split the taxi costs to the airport.

'Nice meeting you, anyway, I think I'll head back to the hotel now.'

'Me too!' her copycat behaviour was disgustingly resonant of other low-ranking academics, I didn't want to spend more time with her.

'I'm going to walk.'

'Walk?! It's more than half an hour. And it's dark. This is Russia, it's not safe to walk here.'

'Don't worry, I always walk. See you tomorrow morning at 7 a.m. at the hotel reception.' I even attempted a smile for her to leave me alone.

I started walking, my legs aching, especially my knees, even though I increased the dose of pain medication. But I knew I had to force myself, I had been sitting most of the day and would be sitting on the plane the following day, I needed to keep the circulation going. I put on the navigation system, listening to the Google Map assistant in-between the news reports. It was quite a nice path, away from the main road, there were not many houses there, it looked like a park or small forest. There was not much happening in Britain it seemed from the news.

BANG.

Ouch!

BANG.

I got punched in the stomach, I fell on the pavement. Someone grabbed me by my waist, put a hand on my mouth, carried me inside the forest, threw me on the ground. I wanted to scream but they put a cloth inside my mouth, it was two people, one was wearing a mask in the shape of a cobra, one a black bandit mask. The bandit mask shouted at me in a male voice, with a Russian accent, 'You spy! You fucking bitch spy! You say me now what you spy! You say me now everything you spy for Britain!'

The cobra mask kicked me in my stomach again.

I bent in half.

'Speak!' the cobra man shouted and took out the cloth out of my mouth.

'Speak!!!' he kicked me again.

'I have nothing to say. … I am not a spy. …' I trembled, talking in hiccups, shaking vehemently. 'I am not spying on anyone. I don't know anything.'

The bandit mask said something to the cobra man in Russian. The cobra man started tearing my clothes apart, got to my knickers, took them off and threw them to the side, pulled his trousers down, saw my knickers had a menstruation pad full of black menstrual blood.

He shouted something, then threw me to the ground, half naked. I felt something cold being inserted into my vagina, my anus and my mouth. I threw up.

'You fucking British spy! You are Russian, you are our girl and you spy for British. You tell us what you steal here. You say me now!!' the bandit mask slapped my face, I was crying profusely, unable to say anything.

'Decko?' asked the cobra man. The bandit mask nodded, the cobra man disappeared for a few minutes, came back with a crying baby in his arms. The baby was barely clothed, must have been a few months old, crying in hunger and discomfort. The cobra man pushed the baby into my arms, I held it, rocked heavily, the baby continued screaming.

The cobra man was shouting directly into my ear, 'You tell us. Or we kill the baby. You understand? You tell us or we kill the baby.'

'Speak!!!' The bandit man kicked me and approached the baby with a sharp knife.

I started screaming, lied down over the baby, trying to protect it with my body. The bandit man pushed me aside, took the baby by its tiny little hand, held the baby by the hand high, the baby screaming beyond what any creature could bear to hear.

'I am not a spy!!! I am a researcher! Research! I have no in-formation! I did not come here to spy! I came for a conference! Please don't kill the baby! Please don't kill the baby! Put the knife away, please don't kill the baby! Please!!!'

The cobra man grabbed the baby. I didn't see what happened but the cry stopped.

The two men said something in Russian to each other, the cobra man ordered me to put my clothes back on, pulled me by my hair towards a car, opened the car's door, threw me on the back seat. There was another man in the car sitting by the wheel. The three men said something to each other, laughed, drank some alcohol, then the third man started the engine. We drove for about ten minutes, then the car stopped.

The driver shouted, 'Out! Get out you *kurva*!'

I was unable to move, the man cursed and shouted, then got out of his seat, pulled my legs, threw me on the ground. As he saw me lying there he knelt down and whispered into my ear, 'You tell somebody what happened and we kill them. You understand? You tell your mummy, we kill your mummy. You tell your British friend, we kill your friend. You tell and we find you and you regret forever.'

I nodded, collapsed on the ground. The three men drove away.

I must have lied on the ground for a few hours, when I opened my eyes I felt I was being carried in someone's arms, then was driven for a while, then I saw a staircase that looked familiar, then the interior of my hotel room. I looked at the man who was carrying me, it was the Kombucha Man. I could not speak, he did not speak either. He boiled the mini kettle and with a warm towel washed away the blood stains from my red arm. I saw everything blurred, I could barely hear anything, I did not hear him leave the room.

I woke up to the loud ringing telephone by my hotel bed. I let it ring, I could not move. I looked around me. The curtains were semi-opened, letting in daylight. My coat and shoes were neatly placed by the door. Aron used to place his shoes like that. I could smell his cologne in the room. I began shaking and crying, the phone kept on ringing, the regular sound piercing my ears. I began crying and shaking again, grabbed the phone, I wanted to stop it from ringing but instead I answered the call.

'It's 7.30! Where are you?! The taxi driver and I are waiting! Come!' It was the Lithuanian student.

I must have got back to the hotel, back to my room and back to my bed last night. I had no recollection of that. I saw the cobra face and the screaming baby everywhere. I looked around me, the phone rang again. 'I must take the flight home,' I whispered. I grabbed my purse, my laptop, put the coat on, ran downstairs.

'Are you all right?' the Lithuanian student asked me, looking at my badly buttoned up coat, bruised face.

'Yes, yes,' I could barely hear my own voice.

'You have no baggage? Just the laptop?' she raised her eyebrows.

'Yes, yes. Please, we must go.'

I had my passport in the purse and I had my Prozac in the coat pocket. I was on 20 mg a day, but right then I took 60 mg on an empty stomach and another 60 mg before we landed. I said goodbye to the Lithuanian student, got to the arrivals gate. Mum was waiting there for me.

'Oh my God, Katie! Jesus, my daughter, what happened to you?!' She wanted to hug me, I pulled away. She looked at my empty hands holding only the laptop and my little purse. 'Did they steal your baggage? Did someone attack you? What happened? Talk to me!'

'I can't talk. I am sorry.' I was whispering, my dry lips barely moving. 'I am sorry. Sorry mum. Sorry I don't have your confectionaries.' I broke down and began crying.

'Oh, don't be silly,' mum wanted to hug me again, I pulled away again. 'What's wrong? Where is your bag? Why are you so, so untidy?!' Mum was asking hysterically. 'Why do you have that big bruise on your face?'

My tears were running involuntarily; I was pacified by the Prozac. Mum didn't ask more, she put me in the car, drove directly to the motorway, then to her flat. She undressed me, asked why there was a penny in my bra, I said I didn't know, she washed me, put her nightgown on me, carefully avoiding the bruises and scars, then almost carried me to bed. She switched off the light, pulled the curtains, lay down next to me in complete silence. She smelt of pink peony and milk.

Chapter 34

I STAYED AT MUM'S FLAT for five months. Mum asked several times about the bruises, I told her I fell down because my legs were not responding. I told her I broke up with my boyfriend and had a MS attack, and I did not want to talk about it. The lie turned out to be close to the truth – I had a serious MS attack two days after landing. I was hospitalised for intravenous treatment for a week, then returned back to mum's.

I couldn't eat, mum forced me to get at least some liquids into my body, first with a straw, then intravenously. The needles left my arms in blue tattoo, the Russian bruises turned grey, my body could not look more sky-like. My days were measured by Prozac, my questions limited to how many grams I needed to take me to the next day. Mum often cried, she wanted to hug me, caress my face, I told her not to touch me because of allodynia. I used to get allodynia with MS attacks. It was a typical symptom when I had a relapse, my skin became untouchable, every small tap on my body would hurt. But I didn't have allodynia this time. I knew because it didn't hurt when I touched myself or when I ran a metal spoon on my thigh. This time I just couldn't bear anyone touching me. This time my skin was untouchable because of the trauma of having been touched by men I never wanted to be touched by.

'I don't need a blanket!' I didn't want mum to put the blanket over me, I didn't want any human being to come near me. But mum was a strict nurse, she shouted at me when I refused to eat. If she could, she would feed me everything in the fridge.

'You need to stay warm! And EAT!' Mum put the porridge closer to my mouth. 'I lost my house, I lost my husband, I don't want to lose my daughter!'

I tried to persuade myself I had to live for mum's sake, but other thoughts took over my psyche. Mum never loved me. Her actions of love were just actions to keep me alive so that she doesn't fail as a mother. She is trying to heal me just because she hates deviations. My illness is just another unexpected betrayal to her regulated life. She wants me to be her obedient daughter. That is her mission. Just like Aron's absurd mission. They both wanted to save lives, protect some big ideas. Just like the idea of love. Love with a capital L, the so-called force that moves humanity forward. There is no such force. The only thing propelling us forward is an inborn set of order movements. The evolution algorithm. A neutral chain.

I didn't respond well to the medication, I was getting thinner and thinner, so light that mum could carry me in her arms to the toilet and back to the sofa. Dad came and helped too, I heard him talking with mum and consoling her when she cried. Children of divorced parents sometimes fake an illness in a desperate attempt to get the parents back together. I didn't fake anything, I didn't care about anything, I was barely speaking, barely eating, barely breathing. I was a collection of bones, addicted to darkness. I shouted when dad switched on the lights in the room, when mum opened the curtains for the sun to come in. I wanted more and more destruction. My body was already destroyed with MS and the Russian attack, I wanted to destroy my thoughts next. Whenever mum wasn't looking, I watched videos of men abusing animals. I thought the horrific scenes would replace the images from the forest with the Russians. But instead, they created a prelude to them, they cut across them, amplified what happened to me into a bigger, collective scar. I listened to a podcast of genocide survivors, I felt closer to them than anyone who knew me by name. The algorithm recommended an old ISIS beheading video to me, I saw scenes of women being raped, their children killed, the women being shot or mutilated by the men. Some of the women had my face, some of the men had Aron's face. I hallucinated that I had blood on my arms and legs. I looked at the scar on my right arm, I wanted to pierce it with a fork and let the blood run. But mum wouldn't give me a fork, only plastic baby spoons.

Mum needed to rest, dad took over for a couple of days. I was desperate to get some sleep, to stop the nightmares and 'daymares', to immerse my thoughts in a place with no demands upon my memories. I had to be careful about what I googled, dad connected his mobile to mine, he checked my browsing history every day. When I confronted him about it he said it was the psychiatrist's recommendation. I didn't have such strict rules even when I was eleven. I couldn't search for the spy scandal stories because it would intrigue dad and he could ask me questions. I did get access to one story, it came as part of the generic news package. It was an update on the court hearings, another witness came forward. A social scientist in her thirties, originally from Slovakia, soft-spoken, shy, attractive. She gave a full account of dating a spy for five and a half years, who apparently stole not only her data but also that of her friends. She described the man as charming, highly attractive and intelligent, who always put her needs first when they were together. He justified his frequent absences with the unexpected death of his father and the need to look after his vulnerable mother. I shivered. Aron told me a similar story. A false narrative of vulnerability that worked well for emphatic academics. *Was that Slovakian girl dating Aron? She said the spy used her unpublished findings to fuel a smear campaign against an old professor in Racial Studies. Did Aron steal my unpublished data on MPD, will he use them to damage my reputation? Did he steal my love notes and use them for internal training purposes? Did he use my love declarations to seduce that Slovakian girl?*

I waited for mum to take over dad's supervision duty and then googled the story. It was part of national news coverage. I read that a retired senior judge was heading the inquiry. They delegated the case to a weak authority, clearly to cover up the misconduct. It was a scandal: around two hundred police officers had been spying on academic groups in Britain since the late 1990s. *Aron must have been one of the spies. And I must have been one of the academics being spied on. Aron must have followed the protocol: gather intelligence and avoid any real emotions. What to do in case the victim falls in love was not included in the protocol.* The end of the article contained fifteen names of the police officers. The judge granted lifelong anonymity to rest of them. Two of the fifteen fathered children with their victims. Those two were convicted, as they crossed the line of duty, apparently. I searched all fifteen names. A few of them had photos. One of them looked like what could have been Aron when he was in his early twenties. Vincent Cobbelt was the real name. I googled all versions of the name – Vincent Cobbelt. Vincent Aron Cobbelt, Aron Cobbelt, VA Cobbelt, Vincent A. Cobbelt. The last one brought up a LinkedIn profile with no photo but 500+ connections. I investigated all 500 connections. I worked up a connection to the IT company Aron worked for when I delivered the gift. I googled the company, it no longer existed. The guy who was listed as the CEO of the non-existent company was now leading a professional intelligence surveillance and security agency in London.

Things began making sense. Aron left the police force and got involved with a private spy agency. The Russians must have thought that I had information on Aron and that information could be useful to their secret services. Did Aron work for the agency when he dated me? Could it be that he was not one of the spies and that he did love me? That he genuinely cared about me? There are parallels with the victims' stories, but maybe I was not one of the victims. Maybe Aron did not date me because he was paid for it. Maybe he just happened to have similar behaviour and the story happened to fit the pattern. Maybe Aron never was undercover and the Russian incident had nothing to do with him. Maybe Aron was just a busy businessman going through a complicated divorce who fell for me at the wrong time in his life. Who knows the truth? Who has access to the full story?

I was unable to think clearly. I was under heavy antidepressants, and I could not talk to anyone about this. The Russians were clear they would kill anyone to whom I told the truth, I did not want to put dad into danger.

'Mark, it's Katie's mum. I am sorry to call you like this. But I think we are losing her,' mum's voice broke, she held the phone tighter to her mouth, 'I think we are losing our Katie.' She cried hysterically into the phone, dad grabbed the phone from her, said, 'We are at a loss, mate. She is not likely to survive many weeks, the doctors said. If you want to say goodbye come to 4 Clifton Street. If you want of course. It's up to you mate. We just thought we would let you know.'

Mark did come, he looked shaken when he kissed my legs and stroked my cheek. I was half-asleep, half-conscious, I said a faint, 'Mark.' He turned his face to the wall, began shaking, saw my parents' wet faces, wiped his tears, quickly left the room. Jackie came at some point too, she left some heavily scented flowers by the sofa.

'Eat! Sweetheart please, eat!' Mum was forcing a spoon of a vegetable puree inside my mouth. I couldn't see the spoon, everything was muddled around me. Aron's face was the blurred background to my thoughts, a shrieking baby resonating in my ears.

I swallowed the puree. Mum gave me more, I swallowed again.

'Piano …' I whispered.

'Piano? You want me to turn the volume up?' Mum activated the radio assistant, put the volume up. It was E flat major. *Eroica* by Beethoven. I recognized every note. I could clearly see Aron's face looking at me, he was dressed all in white, surrounded by a yellow halo. The music was full volume, mum sat next to me, stroking my hand, drying the current of tears soaking my white pink night gown. I saw Aron floating above me, extending his hand towards me. I heard his voice in-between the tones, I saw him crying, I heard him whisper, 'Sorry.'

'Sorry, my princess. I am so sorry. Katie, my love, forgive me. Please forgive me. I love you. I always did. Please never doubt that I loved you.' I extended my arms towards Aron, mum hugged me back, cried with me, calmed me down, brought back to Earth.

Chapter 35

'SHE HAS ALWAYS WANTED TO learn the piano,' mum said.

Mark held one side of a piano, dad the other side. A torrent of sweat ran down Mark's forehead, mum handed him a tissue. The piano was a white Clavinova, an electronic piano with an analogue sound. Mark plugged it in, dad ran his finger on the keyboard, do-re-mi-fa-so-la-ti-do.

'Good sound,' dad concluded.

'I will ask Lionel whether he could give her some free lessons,' mum said.

She seemed to have smiled at dad. Perhaps she had forgiven him. Perhaps Lionel was her revenge for Mrs Baker.

Dad smiled back, said to Mark, 'Lionel is at least seventy so no worries there.'

They both grinned.

Perhaps dad genuinely invited Mark for some beers to talk, not just to moisturise his bruised relationship with me. Perhaps dad genuinely liked Mark even though he was such a contrast to the masculinity dad represented. Did I fall for Mark because he was dad's opposite? And did I fall for Aron because he was Mark's opposite? Is that what Lana called 'the love shadows'?

The afternoon sun was reflecting off the shiny piano cover, I noticed the dust particles on the table in front of me. I was sitting on the sofa, I didn't want to use the wheelchair, I preferred to walk with crutches than to be pushed and pulled around. I was regaining my sense of space awareness, I was less dizzy, though still clumsy when holding a cup. I attempted a step forward. *Stepping back would be stepping back to the grave. Not stepping anywhere would be stagnation analogous to death. I need to step forward if I want to survive this. Aron, my angel guardian, will be moving my thoughts forward. I have to, I MUST believe that Aron genuinely loved me. I must, if I am to survive this.*

My first lesson with Lionel was on a sunny afternoon. He was freshly shaved, his trousers had a very strong line running down the middle of both legs. His plaid shirt was crisply ironed, he even had a handkerchief folded nicely into a pocket square. I wasn't sure what exactly the return on investment was for Lionel, but I accepted his free piano lessons. Every time he came to mum's flat, he went straight into the living room to the piano and me.

Lionel motivated me to play every day. I started with one finger, then the right hand, then both hands slowly together. I enjoyed playing my own little songs. I was amazed that my swollen fingers could produce beauty. It was as if I suddenly discovered a new pocket on a coat I have been wearing for years. Sometimes Lionel held my hand, guided it into the right position, warmed it up, stopped it from trembling. He pushed the white and black keys down with full understanding of the many melodies they could create. He taught me how to improvise and how to let my mind run for free when I composed my own piece. The Clavinova was not a grand piano but the sound was nice and the piano keys were weighted. Lionel told me I needed to think about how hard I pushed them down in each song. I pushed harder when I thought of Aron. The different depths brought new dimensions to each song.

'Would you like a glass of water?' Mum asked Lionel as he was standing in the corridor, ready to go, his long coat revealing a thin and frail body.

Lionel smiled, accentuating the determination to not look weak. 'No, thank you, dear.'

'Can I at least refill your bottle?' I asked and Lionel let me put some water into the tiny bottle he carried with him, and never finished, even if he stayed for hours. I wanted him to have a bigger bottle, to drink more, but he said he could not carry more. I wondered whether he faked the joviality, whether inside he was preparing for a second life where no water is necessary for survival. I was preparing for a return to work. I drank litres and litres of water every day. My pale skin contrasted with Lionel's dark complexion, my reluctance to live contrasted with his immense joy that reclaimed youth. I hated the contrast, but I grew fond of Lionel because he saw me only as a future pianist. He was fully present with me, when we had a lesson, it was the piano and us. Mum respected it, she worshipped Lionel, she thought it was him and the piano that brought me back to life.

After six months, the remission period of my MS started. I slowly regained sensation in my right leg and the pain in my back subsidised. My vision was better too, the black flies were gone and I could read for two hours without seeing them. I was in less pain and began eating more, meal by meal opening my shrunk stomach with foods that had a texture. Six months was the maximum medical leave the university paid for. I was determined to get back to work, I needed to replace the pill-by-pill daily structure with a schedule of meetings and writing deadlines. I needed to get paid and repay mum.

People at work were told I had a bout of depression, which was quite common at our Faculty. It was a simple narrative, colleagues knew how to act. The employee handbook had the instruction not to ask too many questions. A simple 'How are you?' could trigger a teary response – and the university didn't have the resources to support counselling on work premises anymore. The mental health crisis after Covid left all public institutions devoid of any direct support, apart from thick guidance documents. My first day back at work was thus unsurprisingly quiet and I was grateful for that. I was just about holding it together, working from home helped with avoiding looks and unwanted small conversations, I wouldn't manage working from the office.

I didn't want to live at mum's but I was too weak to live on my own. Mum's main task was to see that I stuck to my strict routines. She excelled at the task, her drill had beaten all sophisticated monitoring devices. Get up at 7 a.m. A glass of water and exercises until 7.45 a.m. Get dressed, wash, 8 a.m. Breakfast, 8.30 a.m. Log into work 9.30 a.m. Lunch break, 12.00. Log back in, 1 p.m. Log out, 4.15 p.m. Walk, 5.15 p.m. Dinner, 6 p.m. Bath, 7 p.m. A chocolate or ice cream for reward. I had an alarm clock for getting up, for having breakfast, lunch and dinner, for going to bed every day at the same hour. The only activity I was looking forward to was my piano lesson with Lionel, once a week. Mum pre-prepared all my food in boxes, there was a portion for morning, lunch and dinner. There was a forty-five-minute walk scheduled for each day too, I could meet friends or family exclusively in that slot. My routines became a habit and my body responded well to habits. I was walking without a stick after two months of strict recovery routines.

The University's Employee Assistance Service lady recommended I streamline my tasks and I decided to follow only one goal. Working on anything other than on the one specific goal per day was a distraction that was sabotaging my success and that I perceived as a threat. So I never had a coffee Zoom chat with colleagues or answered a spontaneous call from a student. My day was divided into chunks of time that included the steps necessary for finalising the one goal, the one task that day. If I relaxed, it was only with the intention to continue with the task when I stopped relaxing. No energy was wasted. When goal X was achieved, it was replaced with goal Y and the cycle repeated.

The one-goal mindset gets rewarded in top professions. Athletes and top-performing CEOs do not waste their time on small decisions and multiple tasks. They are not family people *and* career people. They are career people and they put all their eggs into one basket – their job. And it pays off. It did pay off in my case too. I got a promotion in the form of a single office space again. That motivated me to physically return to work.

Chapter 36

'I like the book cover,' Lionel turned the hardback in his hands, read the title aloud, '*Theory of Integrated Personality in the age of Fragmentation. By Dr Kuznetsov.* But don't we all have many personalities?'

'Yes, sure, we do. If we didn't, it would be quite boring. But MPD is a disorder because some people fail to integrate them,' I was talking fast, I did not want the book to take away the precious time we had for music.

'I see …' Lionel turned to the piano, played some lovely tunes, then turned to me, his left hand still playing in the lower tones, 'Do you like it? It's the same melody as the right hand. The same musical theme. Just different variations. You like it?'

I nodded.

'Me too … because it's harmonious … or what was the word you used? The psychological word?'

'Integrated. Coherent.'

'Yes, that.'

'Many stories but one overarching narrative.' I tried imitating Lionel's hand movement.

'Yeah, otherwise it's poison. Did you read *The Poisonwood Bible*? That is about one narrative but is fragmented into many stories.'

'Yes, a good book. Shows that life is a collection of recollections. Some of them integrated, some of them disputed,' I added in a louder voice, Lionel's playing was going louder too.

'Memories fight inside each person … when they get too loud, they contort a human face into a grimace,' Lionel said as he loudly pounded on the keyboard. 'A solid story does the opposite. A solid story grows into a smooth face. It flows. Eyes look at you directly.'

'Do I have such a face?'

Lionel stood up, I remained seated. He looked down at me looking up to him, he was smiling but he did not say 'Yes.' It was excruciating to me. I looked down. I had a flashback of a memory in Majorca, when Mark was on his knee asking me to marry him and I did not say 'Yes' immediately. I felt sorry for Mark, for every second of silence he had to go through in that moment. I looked back at Lionel.

'You think I have divorced personalities? You think I am broken inside?' I asked, insistent, but Lionel did not answer, he sat back down at the piano, began playing again. I did not let him finish the song, I asked louder, 'You think I have MPD, the multiple personality disorder I am researching, you think I have it?'

Lionel placed his right hand on top of my two hands clasped together. 'My girl, I have not read your book. And you are much more clever than I am. You know I am just an old bloke tinkering with the piano.'

'That's not true. You know stuff. You have been through things.'

'Yes, but the past is past. I am not the Lionel of the past. I am the Lionel of now.'

'What about the third identity they talk about? The anticipated, the future Lionel?'

'All three Lionels are in harmony.' He smiled a big, broad smile. 'Watch!'

Lionel played a song with strophic elements, I followed his fingers and how they matched the sheet music, the initial alignment of notes did not carry over into the strophes, the song was disjointed and dissonant for a while, but then, like in a jazz concert with many players, Lionel's fingers played notes that, one by one, blended together, optimised the song to a beautiful experience.

'My girl, you need to break with the past if you want to be a new person,' Lionel stopped playing and looked deeply into my eyes. 'I don't know what happened to you and I don't need to know, but dear, someone should know …'

I began shaking and he turned back to the piano and played more.

'The divorce was tough on you, I know,' he said when he stopped.

I nodded, I was glad Lionel came up with a story that fit my circumstances, not the thoughts gnawing my soul.

'And the break-up with Mark. Irena told me about it.' Lionel was placing his words carefully, looking at me from the corner of his eye. I looked straight into his eyes, I wanted to reassure him I did not mind mum telling him about Mark. I was grateful mum had introduced me to Lionel, she couldn't have known she would find me a teacher, a mentor and a friend. No one else has ever fulfilled those three roles in one for me. Not even Mark, although he once meant so much to me.

'Love is complicated, my girl. Life is complicated. Music is complicated. All you can do is to try to look for the most har-monious set, optimise it for the audience you play for.' Lionel concluded and was about to get up, but I stopped him.

'Why do people marry if most of them divorce? Like why do we bother with the illusions of wholeness if everything breaks apart eventually anyway?'

'Because we like things complicated!' Lionel laughed in his delightful haughty tone. 'It's much easier to tear apart a page than to glue it together.' Lionel laughed more, he knew I could not understand how he could play from printed sheet music, the half-torn pages looked generations old compared to the notes on my iPad's score reader. But the paper seemed to keep him focused, there were no message notifications, no colourful games distracting him from the black lines and circles. I checked my phone, more out of habit than any expectation, I had only my work email and alarm clock installed on it anyway. I had removed the meditation app too, I wanted to have a clean and tidy screen, my mind was littered with messy questions no one could respond to.

That urge to tear apart what is supposed to be held together, where does it come from? Does it start in the womb and set out with the cut of the umbilical cord? Is the child's separation from the mother the reason why humans are so obsessed with divisions, divorces and differences?

'You seem to be thinking about something very important.' Lionel distracted me from my thoughts.

'I was just thinking about what you said. You know, whether the urge to bind and separate is what makes us human … whether that is what love is all about. You know like the black-and-white keys create music. So love is created through the pulsating space between belonging and liberty.'

Lionel sat in silence for a while, then said, 'I think that's right. Pulsating space … that's a nice word. You know, things of the heart, they are uniquely human. But fate plays a part too! I think that once two people fall in love, there is no one, no other human being, who can stop them from acting on the longing they feel for each other.'

'So you think it is fate and not people who cause affairs?'

Lionel stepped back from the piano, put his right hand in his pocket.

I wanted to know the answer.

'Did you ever cheat on Maryl?'

Lionel didn't reply, I knew it meant 'yes'.

'Why? And did she forgive you?'

Lionel pinched the piano key.

'There was nothing to forgive. It is always about two sides, little girl. … It doesn't need to end up in a divorce, it is all about how you communicate about it. ... Meryl knew the lady, they became best friends.'

I couldn't imagine mum becoming best friends with that baker. But I understood that dad's secrecy around the whole thing was more hurtful than the actual affair. Lionel turned to the keyboard and played a Ludovico Einaudi song. I had heard the song before, but I had never heard this tender version. Lionel's fingers glided on the delicate keys, avoiding flats and sharps, carrying the melody in a wave of a silver veil. The veil fluttered in the gentle breeze from the half-open window. Lionel began singing, softly, in low tones.

> I used to be a dragon of three heads
> A brother, a husband, a father
> Time has cut them off
> I lost my brother, my wife, my daughter
> I used to believe in eternal youth
> An easy life for me, for us, for you
> Time has revealed the truth
> We grow when pain strikes through
> I used to think I could lie
> My words, thoughts, actions hiding what is true
> Time taught me to be me, myself and I
> Integrated in what I think, say and do

I sat up on the sofa, clapping my hands. 'You must have added "integrated" tonight!'

Lionel laughed, we both laughed.

I got tired, I lay down on mum's sofa opposite the piano. Lionel came to the sofa, held my hand. I have not been that close to anyone since my trip to Russia. He caressed my hair, asked almost whispering, 'Is it too much? I've been talking a lot ... The old chap rambling, sorry, Margaret. I mean, Katie.'

Lionel had called me Margaret before. I knew it was not just a Freudian slip, I knew he thought of me as a father thinks of his daughter, but that didn't take anything away from my deep persuasion that he was giving unconditionally, drawing from the place of genuine humanity.

'No, not at all. Tell me about Margaret.'

He got up, moved to the piano, sat down on the piano chair that suddenly seemed too small for him.

'She was in so much pain, my little girl …'

We talked a lot about life and the afterlife. We had both been close to death at various points in our lives, to a different degree, with our own bodies or through the bodies of those we loved. That shared experience brought us together.

'She is without pain now …' I placed my hand on top of Lionel's, stopped him shaking.

'And she is still with me, you know. Right here with us …' Lionel whispered, looked at me, looked towards the window.

I followed his eyes, watched the moving curtains, semi-closed my eyes. What I think, say, and what I do need to be in harmony if I want to be happy. Was I happy before I met Aron? I think that when I was with Mark I was saying very little. I was thinking a lot but I was mostly doing stuff. I have been working a lot. Was that what caused my imbalance and made me fall for the wrong man? But I need my work, I desperately need my work to structure my days and keep me healthy. Is it the production treadmill that is my therapy? Seeing small products coming from my hands, in the form of marked students essays, small written articles, emails and graphs, is that what makes up my self-esteem? My work is the soul-plaster to keep the wounds quiet while it is on. The wounds are still there, they howl as soon as I touch the plaster. Even in the short moments when I have half an hour of waiting in-between tasks, I become restless, inundated with images of the cobra-masked man holding me naked in the forest, of Aron asking me for a blow job, of the piercing baby's cry.

'Did you get therapy after your daughter died?'

'I had a good therapist, Annie. She is dead now, you know I am old! But she helped me understand Anthony's death …'

'Anthony was your brother, right? The one who got killed … so brutally and needlessly, right in front of you … that must have been horrible, Lionel. How did you make yourself strong again, how did you manage to stop asking, "Why him? Why you?"?'

Lionel swallowed, looked towards the window again, said in a barely audible soft voice, 'I never understood. Anthony was beautiful. Innocent . . . How could someone ever have the will to take him away from us …'

I felt so sorry, watching Lionel in pain. I wished he'd never had to bear witness to such a tragedy, that I could delete it from his mind, from Anthony's biography, from the world's history.

Lionel pulled himself together, said in his usual friendly voice, 'You asked about therapy. Annie helped me sort out the difficult questions. She listened and she saw me …' Lionel sipped from his little bottle, looked at the piano.

'Music is a good therapist too. … You don't have to live all the pains of the past. You can play them, let them dance around you. When it gets to you, Katie, play. Whatever melody or tune, just play. With your eyes closed if need be. But play.'

Chapter 37

After that lesson with Lionel, I began playing more piano and taking less Prozac. I got back to a reduced Prozac dose and I wanted to get off it completely.

'I don't need a pill to control how I feel. I wanted to be me!' I said to my psychologist, who strongly disagreed, but he let me make that choice. He only had the sanitized version of my past, I could not relate to him.

The only thing that I thought was useful was: 'The first three days of withdrawal will be difficult, you shouldn't work on those days.'

I took that advice to heart, closed myself in a room with candles and music and portions of food. Mum was on a four-day retreat, I didn't tell her I had planned my Prozac break when she was away. I survived those three days but I was very low afterwards. I had the typical 'Prozac poop-out' for some weeks. I could control some things, like immediately switching off the radio when they played Adele. Her lyrics and songs were so strongly associated with Aron that they threw me into a bout of uncontrollable crying. But I could not control those scenes from the forest from invading my eyes. I had short panic attacks every time it happened, the triggers were random, the body response the same, sweat running down my spine, shaking. Even when mum was back, I was waking up in the middle of the night, my eyes wide open, walking in the flat at wolf's hour, checking three times whether the door was locked and whether someone was standing outside the door. I switched on the lights, washed my face in the bathroom, looked into the mirror. I didn't see anything in my eyes but I saw everything around me clouded. Or perhaps it was clouded and there was something invisible in my eyes. I wasn't sure, I couldn't be sure. If I could replace the memory with an artificial chip, I would.

'It could be that I partially called those nightmares upon myself. Watching those horrid scenes on YouTube when I was sick certainly didn't help,' I said to my new psychologist, she was the fifth one I was paying for regular conversations, she studied homeopathy and called herself a 'naturopathic psychologist'. She was same age as me and interested in alternative healing methods for trauma.

'Have mercy on yourself. You didn't know how to deal with trauma. Your body and mind suffered, you lost your energy balance. Now you need to surround yourself with examples of positivity,' the psychologist said with her broad, permanent smile. 'You say you can't go to many places, but you can go to nice places online. I recommend my clients to create a folder of positivity. A collection of motivational quotes, beautiful photos, links to goodness projects and examples of generosity. It will fill you with positive thoughts every time you open it.'

I created the positivity folder, it didn't help much but I was grateful for every percentile of improvement. I felt my leg and vision were getting better after the MS attack, but I was unsure of whether my mind was on the mend. I was not sure who I could ask, I couldn't tell anyone about what really happened in Moscow, that I knew 100 per cent. The naturopathic psychologist said I should widen my social circle.

'You mean, I should meet new people or people who knew me before I got ill? I don't know if I have enough energy to invest in new relationships. But then, my old friendships and connections are full of past problems and issues. Maybe you are right. But frankly, I'd rather just shut the door behind them, move to a new country, find new friends, new colleagues there.'

'You need to be ready with the old ones first, otherwise the past energy will keep on chasing you in your new relationships. Of course you don't need to be friends again. You need to weigh up the amount of energy you want to invest into broken connections. But if trust was broken, you need to forgive. Forgiveness powers healthy relationships. Think of how vulnerable every human being is and how you can make them strong again. Be the positive power in their lives.'

I sighed, I knew she was right and there was a lot of repair to be done in my relationships. I began stitching my past relationships together, one by one. I started with Valerie, I needed to meet her face-to-face anyway, it was part of the protocol of my phased return to work. I dreaded the meeting, but I followed my naturopath's advice and rationalized Valerie's bullying behaviour towards me. I pictured Valerie's empty family picture frames in her posh house in New York and the fresh roses on her mahogany table brought by her secretary instead of her deceased husband. I forgave Valerie for pushing me to my health limits, she had her own issues. In a world dominated by male power, she could not play a soft female who mentors future professors. Maybe she never heard 'I love you' from her husband, maybe the jewellery box on her top shelf was the closest she ever came to feeling his affection towards her.

Lana was angry that I was on Valerie's side, but I was not on either side. I saw Valerie's bullying separately from her humanity and the same for Lana and her polyamorous promiscuity. Returning to my relationship with Jackie was harder, she had started her own YouTube channel, changed her teeth, the size of her nose and her first name. I could barely recognize that the Jacqueline in *Jacqueline's Beauty Tips* videos was the Jackie I knew from playing in our neighbourhood garden. She bought a new companion too, she went everywhere with her new macaque called Mac. She trained Mac to wave at the camera and perform in the background of her Zoom calls, which gained her even more followers. I felt sorry for the pet, the little macaque had clearly no say in being groomed to increase the halo around Jackie.

Valerie, Lana and Jackie were part of the history I wanted to clear to create a healthy new identity but Mark was oscillating somewhat between my memories and ambitions for the future. He and I were still on talking terms, we cared about each other too much to just draw the line and say a permanent goodbye. I knew that Mark would never issue an ultimatum and even though it was over between us, we still swam in the same river. We were both single and yet we both mastered the theory of relativity in love, we both understood that when time flows, a relationship cannot ever break down. The painful implication of that theory meant that I could not draw a line over Aron either, he was swimming in the same river as me, same river as me and Mark.

'You will get through this. You managed previous attacks,' Mark said and sipped the green tea we ordered for two, even though it was clearly just for me. He tried to pretend he liked it, but I knew from the little twitch in his left eye that he didn't. He had no idea I was not talking about the MS attack but another assault. It didn't matter. He invited me for a cup of tea after work, I gave him the slot reserved for a daily walk. He didn't know the deviation from my routine could cost me a possible nightmare.

We sat in silence for a while, our eyes meeting occasionally.

'Thank you for everything you have done for me, Mark,' I said slowly and looking into Mark's eyes.

Mark grinned as if I thanked him for paying the seven pounds for the teapot.

'I mean it, Mark. For when I was in Critten and for when I was at mum's. You did not give up on me. You are a fighter, not me.'

'Mark the superman!' he whistled some kind of silly tune, poured me more tea. There was silence again. He put his hand on top of mine. It was sweaty and a bit sticky, I knew he had neither washed his hands nor used the hand sanitiser when we entered the café. But I opened my hands and let him cup them in his. If we had not been in the café with the quadratic table and huge teapot between us, he would have hugged me and maybe he would have kissed me. Maybe he would later ask whether he could sleep with me and he wouldn't put the condom on, as he didn't before, hoping I wouldn't notice, and I would bring him his desired child. I pulled my hands out from his, pretended I wanted to pour him more tea and smiled. Mark smiled back, he was oblivious to my body language.

'Have you not dated anyone since? I mean I don't need the details but if you are so keen on family, Mark, you need to have children, well, kind of soon.'

'It is not about just having kids, Kitty. It is about who you have the child with.'

I agreed with what Mark said. I looked over his shoulder, for a second I thought I saw the Kombucha Man in the café. Aron could have made me pregnant and I wouldn't have minded. In fact I would have probably liked it when we dated. Why? To attach him to me with a miniature version that carries his genes?! The baby would have Aron's eyes and his beautiful lips. It would be a gorgeous baby. Smart. Talented. AND deceitful. Katie! Stop kidding yourself! Aron would be a terrible father, always on the hunt for more, spending time elsewhere but not at home, you would be never sure of whether he was sleeping with another woman and was telling you the truth the following morning. Mark would be a loving and caring father. He would give you and the baby everything. Why could you not give him that? Why were you so cruel towards him? And why were you so cruel to an unborn child? Thinking of a child as a tool to satisfy your perverse desire to be with a man who destroyed you. What's wrong with you, Katie?!

I looked into the sparkles in Mark's eyes in the badly lit café. I did not feel excitement, I did not feel detachment either. I wanted Mark as my companion for life, as a good friend, as a brother I choose because I never had one. *Is that desire conditional upon agreeing to start a family together and leave academia behind? I could not be a mother and keep my research position at the university. Not in Britain at least. The pressure to deliver results and the performance indicators were incompatible with motherhood.*

'You have such small hands,' Mark held my hand again, his sweat was blending with mine. He was sweating so heavily that the sweat from his hand on mine began dripping on the table. Mark noticed it too, took a napkin, dried it, said sorry.

'Don't be silly.'

We ordered a salad, he ordered extra hot sauce for me, he was surprised I took only two small spoons of it. He was running his old algorithm on my Likes, it was targeted but not precisely personalized. I could only blame myself for it, for deliberately hiding my history from him. He had some Brazil nuts inside his salad, took them out and gave them to me.

'I don't eat Brazil nuts anymore,' I said and put them back on his plate.

'Really? What happened?'

I wished Mark hadn't known me in the past. I wished we could start with some general, universal dating patterns that bring surprise. A painstakingly slow update of what no longer was valid and what I no longer preferred pushed me backwards, reminding me of my rotten past I wanted to keep firmly shut. It was making me sick.

'Sorry, I think there was something in the salad.'

I ran to the café toilet, vomited. Maybe it was the deviation from my routine, maybe it was the salad, maybe it was Mark's presence that made me throw up. I sprayed the bathroom with my mini Chanel perfume, washed my face, cleaned my mouth with mouthwash. I always carried those tools in my bag.

'All this tea makes you visit the toilet a lot! Just like in the old days. Kitty-Peee-Teeea!' Mark probably thought his rhyme would make me laugh but it annoyed me instead. I was not angry with him. I was enraged with my past. I resented everything I had been through. I didn't say anything and Mark didn't notice any change in my mood, he accompanied me to the bus stop, waited until the bus came, then leant in to give me a hug and I leant back and hugged him too. I had not hugged anyone for months, holding Mark's body against mine filled me with a warm feeling. Two minutes later on the bus Mark texted me. He deleted the message immediately but I could see from the notification it was a heart emoji. *Just like in the olden days. Mark did not dare say he loved me. He did not dare send a symbol expressing it either. But is that a bad thing? Aron said many times that he loved me, he sent me many heart symbols. There were no feelings attached to them. Aron's words and actions, they were just symbols. Just like the pennies Aron tossed on the pavement for me to find. The pennies were not signs from the universe, they were man-made symbols of an imagined absolute that never existed. The only reality is the one I grant space in my memory. I need to take control of the present, reset it just like I reset the time on my watch when crossing the Russian-British border.*

Chapter 38

MARK UPDATED HIS FACEBOOK STATUS to 'In a relationship'. The girl he tagged hadn't made any of her accounts private, so within seconds, I aggregated enough information for a long biography about her. I pieced together Caitlyn's work history from LinkedIn, her opinions from Twitter, the names of her nieces from Facebook. She had been posting photos of her and Mark a month before Mark updated his status. He didn't post any photos of them together. She didn't have any photos of previous boyfriends in her timeline but she followed the Facebook group 'Spot a Narcissist'. I zoomed into the photos she published of her and Mark. Mark didn't seem happy in Caitlyn's photos. His cheeks were red of the wine they drank together, his eyes were on the camera lens, not on Caitlyn's big breasts.

Congrats on your new relationship! I gave a Like to Mark's status update and two of the congratulation messages underneath it.

Mark texted me two seconds after my Like. **Thanks. How are things with you?**

I texted back. **I am well, thanks.**

I saw Mark was typing but there was no message sent for about three agonising minutes. Then he sent me a GIF with a Beagle puppy and the words 'Miss you'.

Is Mark with Caitlyn to heal his wounds of a missed family? Or is Caitlyn some kind of back-up girl in case I return to him? Either way Mark's response does not appear to be fair on Caitlyn. But who am I to judge this, what do I know about love rules?

The employee handbook recommended that my transition period should focus not only on job tasks but also on friend and family relationships. I didn't really have anyone to focus on. I was grateful to mum and I had forgiven dad, but I did not spend any more time with them than what was necessary out of politeness. I rejected Jackie's and Lana's requests to be friends on Facebook again. I didn't want any distractions. I was not stable enough to tolerate any deviations from my scheduled days and circadian rhythms. I did have one routine, though which was not work-related: a daily walk.

I scheduled the walks in my diary, I had reminders and I never cancelled the slot. I used to go to the river in the main park, watch the ducks and swans there, listen to a podcast or a song while walking. Most often I was crying. Uncontrollably. Just let the tears wash over me, my sunglasses on, even on cloudy days. The river's flow was my religion and the sand on the riverbank the words of my prayers. I knew I could come there in the middle of the night, undress myself and let the river take me. That feeling of control was giving me a sense of achievement. It was my explicit will not to take my life, my revenge against the fate that damaged me so badly.

I was desperate to understand why this had happened to me, but there were no clear explanations. I tried to educate myself on what was going on with me, what was a standard trauma response, what was linked to my experience, what was linked to my personality. I took the Myers-Briggs personality test, paid a premium to get my results interpreted by a Myers-Briggs specialist. I went to an astrologist to tell me how my date of birth fit with the stars on the sky and to a palmist to learn what my life destiny was. There were no clear answers about the past and no clear days in front of me. I was angry, I was fearful, I was constantly irritated and rarely laughed or smiled. I disliked everyone who did, including that lady on the morning train who laughed hilariously aloud for at least fifteen minutes. People giggled as the whole train was shaking with her laughter but I stood up and told her to fuck off because I was working. The girl who said the words 'fuck off' was not me. It was so in clash with me that when I sat back down on my train seat I was shaking.

I kept on telling myself that gratitude is bigger than fear but I could not bring myself to be grateful for what happened to me. I could not forgive Aron, I could not forgive the police force, I could not forgive the Russian attackers. I tried all the techniques the different psychologists recommended. There was little improvement. Out of spontaneity, I began taking selfies. A selfie a day, just for myself and instead of writing a diary. Quick ephemeral snaps. Because nothing mattered, anyone could delete me, anyone could date me.

Anyone, including that guy from work. He was from Australia but originally from Sri Lanka. He came to Britain to study engineering. I slept with him because I didn't want to be on my own in the house. I entered the relationship knowing it was just a fling, satisfying my physical need to lay next to someone and to have something different to read on my phone than work emails. He was good at sending emojis but that was linked to the language barrier between us. He must have entered the relationship with his own agenda. My needs were physical, his were intellectual. Exchange service. There was nothing more to love than that, I had learnt that lesson the hard way. After I had corrected his fourth exam paper, I broke up with him. He sent me a magnet emoji, which confirmed my decision.

I deleted our conversation but I kept the magnet image. It made me think that love is like a magnet. With three rotating magnets we can create electricity and sometimes couples need the third magnet to generate new energy. Sometimes it's a new child, sometimes a new job, a new illness, sometimes a new partner. The life magnet brought a new partner to Mark and maybe soon they will have a child. Judging by Caitlyn's daily selfies, Mark seems to be advancing his relationship with her at lightning speed. He did not avoid food temptations but Mark would not succumb to another girl just for lust. He will stick with this ugly Caitlyn. I can't be single forever, I need to find someone too.

I set up accounts on three different dating sites, using some nice portrait photos Mark took of me ten years ago. I lied about my age, hobbies, health status too: I set up dates with dozens of interested guys, then cancelled them at the last minute. I sent a photo of my bra to three of them, ghosted them after they started sending me photos of their genitals. I changed platforms, I changed my name to Ulla Kuslilianen on Instagram and edited the background on my profile to a Finnish pine forest. I deleted my old photos and started posting photos that gave the impression of a prolonged hiking holiday in the Pallas-Yllästunturi park. Instagram began suggesting new followers to me who were #NatureLovers and located in Finland. I followed them all and most followed me back, so my feed was soon flooded with photos of sunset grasses and hares in snow. I quickly developed the habit of opening my Instagram feed as soon as I woke up, filled my dark bedroom with bright photos of pristine nature. I scrolled through the Finnish landscape photos for ten minutes or so, there were always new photos to look at. I watched the landscapes changing colours as spring warmed up the country. I Liked all the photos to get more of them, enough to fill up my lone evenings too.

On some days I was okay, on some days, I was not. When I was not, I saw Aron's face everywhere, I heard his voice, felt his hands on me, smelt his cologne in the air. I saw our emails disappearing from the screen. I saw him smiling at me with glass eyes, turning into a full-size robot. I struggled to work, I struggled to communicate, I struggled to look at other men without thinking of Aron. Aron set the bar of expectations so very high. Whatever other men did, they were not high enough, not comparable enough to him. He was on the pedestal, the rest were just a cheap substitute so that I didn't ache. Did the secret services ever think about the consequences of training their spies to fake love? By abusing love to appear perfect, Aron killed my ability to move on to other men. It was impossible to unsee that pink shirt worn by another man, to unsmell Aron's cologne on the underground. Other men could try to infect me with their love virus, but my cells were locked.

'There are many kinds of love …' Lionel began unpacking the new sheets of music he brought me.

Mum was listening to Classics FM in the other room, I could hear a profound yet gentle crying of a cello.

'You can have love for Mark and love for music … or love for Mark and another man.'

'I made a mistake. A huge mistake by succumbing to Craig.' I gave Aron a false name so that he had an identity when I talked about him to Lionel. Lionel knew that I had loved Craig, and that I took it badly when we broke up, but he didn't know any other details. Yet, he seemed to know the whole story. Not the spy bit but the viral love bit. He seemed to know a lot about inexperienced girls falling for a perfect prince charming, who sweeps them off their feet, a love story that belongs to an 1980s film. I recognized the pattern too, I have read it in fairy tales when I was a little girl. Yet when it happened to me I got transfixed. I let it uproot me from my home, from my work, from the people I cherished.

'I loved him too much. I will never love with the same intensity again.' I thought the sky was bright blue for a short moment, but when I looked outside the window, I saw it return to its permanent grey.

'Don't be so harsh on yourself. There are no exams in love. So there are no mistakes either. It is all about how you play it.

Listen to this!' Lionel took a random sheet of music and played it for me. 'What do you think?'

I didn't see the connection between our conversation and the notes. 'A nice piece?' I tried.

'Yeah, a nice piece. You didn't notice I didn't play the notes. I mean I did a little bit. But I struggled with the second line, so I improvised over it. … If I believed in mistakes I would stop and go back and try again. You wouldn't say "nice" then. You would think I made a mistake and you would want me to fix it. You don't want that for your relationships. There is no right or wrong, my girl, and if you feel it was wrong, then be professional about it. Keep on playing …'

I pondered Lionel's words. I respected him, I wanted to follow his advice. I knew that I succumbed to Aron just like I did to Dr Andrew, that it was the same kind of love virus, a prolonged one-night stand, the perfect James Bond blond girl scenario, only I was not blond and he was not James Bond. I knew nothing about Dr Andrew, and with Aron I didn't even know whether he was divorced or married or what. I knew Mark would not abandon me, he would look after me. He would warm me up at night and console me when the nightmares came. He would wait for me when I came back from work and would make a morning cup of tea. That was love. Based on a mutual knowledge of each other. What Aron gave me was a corrupted service transaction. With Mark it was an interchange. We both bestowed love voluntarily, from a pure place of giving.

'But if I keep on playing, I will hurt myself again. I will hurt others. I need to make myself immune to this kind of love.'

Lionel burst into laughter, 'Good luck, girl! Don't think you can get a jab against falling in love.'

'Stop laughing, this is serious stuff!' I gently punched Lionel. I knew I could. We had had many lessons together by now, we were at ease with each other. I could ring him up anytime and we would drop straight into a deep conversation, there was no weather talk, no fluffing around the edges. 'I don't mean a jab against falling in love but some kind of vaccine against infatuation. So that I don't fall for men like Craig and instead love men who are good for me. Boring men. Men like Mark.'

'Come on, Katie, you know very well you didn't leave Mark just because of Craig. … The love was not there. If there was strong love you would not have fallen for Craig in the first place. … Don't give Craig so much agency. He had enough.'

Lionel was right. It had been the circumstances too, my childhood, my illness, my parents' divorce, my inability to connect with my friends and work. All that led to the imbalance that made me fall into Aron's trap.

'But shall I get together with Mark again?'

'I cannot give you any advice on that … but whatever you decide, you need to be honest with your choice. … Just because you can swim in that river now, it does not mean it's the right one for you.'

Lionel toyed with the keys, it sounded like a bird trilling in the woods. He had his eyes closed, I knew his mind was where Chopin's was when he composed that piece. Not in a busy city, not in a crammed flat with an ill girl. His mind was running its own algorithm, serving him images away from London, with the mellow sound reflecting dew drops falling on birds' feathers. Darkness had no power to disrupt that sequence. Lionel played and played, driving my thoughts in a carriage propelled by hundreds of notes bound together in a collective voice of our ancestors. We both had our eyes closed because it was a journey to light and its radiation was blinding us.

Chapter 39

Mum peeked her head through the door, she apologized for disturbing us, she just wanted to check whether we needed anything. She was much less neurotic when Lionel was around. He softened her, made her more loveable. I invited mum in, she sat down on the sofa, I played the leading melody from 'Für Elise' to her. Mum said she first heard that song when I was twelve, and she and dad had saved enough money for a concert at Royal Albert Hall. She cried, Lionel put his right hand on her right shoulder. Mum apologized, left the room. Lionel followed her, disappeared for ten minutes or so.

Did Lionel go and hug mum in the kitchen? For once extend his arm beyond her shoulder? Is that real love, what the two of them have between each other? Was mum blinded when she first met dad? Was it the kind of love I had for Mark or the kind of love I experienced with Aron? It had to be one or the other because it had so strongly impregnated my body. I carried the thread of my parents to my partners and from there it will continue to my children one day. That is what makes love scary – the permanence of its past patterns in our present lives.

Lionel made an exception that evening and stayed for dinner. We talked about all sorts of random stuff, Lionel entertained us, so that neither mum nor I had the time to venture back to the past. We wondered about the spider that had a special silk that could capture an air bubble. Lionel said the spider could attach it to a reed and catch flies in it. Then we talked about his friend Josie who died. 'It was such a fun funeral,' Lionel said, and after he saw mum's surprised look, he added: 'You know, Irena, light and shadow are two sides of the same coin.'

That sentence planted itself into my consciousness. It motivated me to wrestle with the black-and-white keys every day. My playing was nowhere as fluid as Lionel's, but I was getting better. The music took me to beautiful destinations, the black-and-white borders of the piano world could be crossed anytime, with no vaccine passports, no nationality checks. When I played I was in bright countries, happy lands.

I didn't want to appear as a desperate ex checking on Mark's new girlfriend, so I created a fake account and checked her Instagram stories. I thought I would do it just once but I was too curious and checked them every day. I saw her posting random quotes and extracts from the book *How* Not *to Marry a Narcissist*. Occasionally, she posted a selfie of her and Mark. Seeing Mark next to another girl made my heart miss a beat. I was screenshotting all photos featuring him and saving them on my phone by time and location, clearly showing signs of stalking. I analysed the photos according to the presence of filters and Caitlyn's attractiveness. She shared exclusively close-ups of her face, revealing a mouse-like smile and microbladed eyebrows. The photo from their trip to Paris must have been taken by a selfie stick to show the full Eiffel tower behind Mark and Caitlyn. She was larger than Mark or perhaps she got bigger and Mark got thinner. One day, I accidently used my fake account to check on Mark's story too, Caitlyn must have seen it or maybe Mark told her, but she figured out it was a stalker and not just a random bot spying on her and blocked my account. I didn't need to create a new one – the Instagram algorithm quickly understood my interests, serving me Mark's latest posts even though I unfollowed him.

A few weeks after their Paris trip, Mark hadn't posted any updates. I thought that maybe he broke up with Caitlyn, but then he posted a photo of himself in front of an IVF practice.

My stomach lurched when I saw the photo. *So he knows this girl for two months and is already trying for a baby?! Was that the only reason he was with me too? I was just there to extend his body, and any other girl can do that instead of me? He must be using all his savings to pay for the treatment. To what length is one ready to go to pursue a selfish craving?!*

I was furious, I didn't check Instagram for several weeks to avoid more news about Mark. I uninstalled the app to stop my urge to check. But the algorithms got me anyway – when browsing my Facebook feed, a photo of Mark popped up some months later, showing him thin and smiling, giving a thumbs up in front of a private fertility clinic. *So they managed to conceive. Mark will get his baby dream fulfilled and get attached to Caitlyn forever.*

I had no tears left to cry. I felt so empty and yet so full. I wanted to throw up but there was nothing to cast off. I caressed my belly, the little hill on my thin body, full of water that I drank to replenish my empty tear ducts. My eyes, nose and ears were overflowing with water too, I turned my head and wiped the tears flowing in. I kept on looking up, my knees slightly bent, my feet flat on the ground. I was floating in the clouds, submerging myself in Virginia Woolf's poems in Belsize Park.

I watched the clouds pass above me. I could decide which one of the clouds I could commit to memory and which ones I just let pass. I could enjoy them as a collective white fluffiness, I didn't need to follow the disintegration of my favourite one. Grey geese from the nearby lake honked loud, a random butterfly fluttered above my head. The geese, the butterfly, the clouds – they were my good messengers of death. I opened my arms for the butterfly to fly me to the clouds. *Don't pull me back to the ground, I want to fly away with you.* I got up, walked into the river in only my underwear. The water was cold and muddy. I shivered, walked deeper into the river. There was no one in the park. I looked up at the clouds, they whispered, 'It's your choice.' I was not under any influence of drugs or medication. If I took my life there and then, it would be entirely my volition, my agency, my decision. I made a breaststroke towards the main current. I smiled. I was in charge. Not Aron or his bosses spying on me. Not MS or its attacks paralysing me. Not Mark or his baby desires.

I made another stroke, this time towards the shore, but the river pulled me back in. I fought back. My heart was pumping so hard that I could feel the blood inside my mouth. The blood was not circulating but banging on all doors, open/close, open/close. *Come on, Katie, you are a fighter! You survived MS. You survived a false diagnosis of MS2. You survived Aron's betrayal. You survived the attack in the woods. You can survive this too!* I made another stroke but the current pulled me another direction. I had water inside my mouth, I pulled harder, with all my force. I saw Aron's angel arms, I heard his voice saying, 'Please never doubt that I loved you.' I pulled again. One, two, three. And again, full force. I made it to the shore. I collapsed on the grass, my eyes wide open towards the sky. The white cotton was mesmerizingly beautiful, the geese's call the perfect lullaby to rock one to sleep. I concentrated on the clouds, crying.

People could betray and hurt me but the clouds wouldn't wound me. Clouds appeared and disappeared and they were beautiful every time. Their absences were welcome by sun lovers, their presence by gardeners. Clouds would never make any false promises.

Chapter 40

'Big dreams are the adaptable ones. The more you specify them, the more they constrain you.' Lionel played with the shadows, drew the curtains closed.

'My dream with Craig is not transferable to another man.'

Lionel whistled a melody. I recognized the song. I liked it, I asked, 'Who wrote it? What's the name?'

'What if it had no name? What if it was just a melody?'

I realized Lionel was pushing me to abandon my controlling instinct. I thought of nearly drowning in the river the other day. I saw my thin body being taken by the river current and suddenly felt sorry for myself. I was an innocent victim, a little baby sitting in the corner, her head dizzy, her mouth unbearably dry. My hands were too small to carry the abuse, my tongue unable to unlearn the accent of neglect. I felt pity for the little girl, I stood up, began talking to her in an adult's voice. *You can love wholeheartedly again. You can change your story.*

'Whose voices are those, Katie? Why do you speak to yourself like that?' Lionel pulled my hand away from the keyboard. He took hold of my left hand too, held them both in his warm hands, his dark skin covering my translucent fingers.

'You have to forgive Craig, you have to do it for yourself. If you carry hate, you become hate. If you ever want to love again, you need to convert the hate to love.' I heard Lionel saying something, I saw his mouth moving but the sound was coming from my head.

'Who do you think I am, some kind of machine you can programme with your mindfulness classes?!'

'Go on then, channel it into other men, use the same tricks as Aron did with other women!' A male voice talked to me but it was not Lionel. I saw Lionel's face, he grabbed me tighter, he heard me saying things that didn't make sense.

'Get your revenge! Report him to police! Get pregnant with a random guy, post it for Mark to see!'

Lionel was saying something but I did not hear it. He shook me with both hands. 'Katie! Listen to me! Look at me!'

Lionel was not shouting but he spoke very loudly. He held my head and forced me to look at his face, into his eyes. I stopped shaking, I stopped hearing the voices. I heard Lionel.

'Good. Good girl. You are back. Oh, baby …'

I sobbed into his ironed shirt, Lionel put my head on his lap, caressed my hair with the back of his hand as I cried, put a string of hair behind my ear, his whole palm on my back.

'You need the trauma to wash over you, my girl. … Cry it out like a summer rain. Let the voices cleanse the river banks, let them run wild down black valleys. Not inside you.'

I had my eyes closed, I let Lionel's fingers disentangle my trauma, softly, hair by hair, without ever pulling sharply, he twisted and wringed them between his fingers, from my Russian roots up towards the Moscow trip.

'Why me, what wrong have I done?' I sobbed. 'Tell me why Aron, I mean why Craig, why Mark, why me …?' I pleaded to Lionel.

'There is no need for names. No need to give them space in your story. There is already too much to take care of in your head,' Lionel said and briefly stood up, dimmed the lights, then continued. 'You are loved. You don't need to prove anything to anyone. Breathing is enough.'

He said that, and green meadows – scented with buttercups and lady's bedstraws – began emerging behind my closed eyes. The clouds were passing by and no one analysed their shapes.

No one was counting the days to see if I was fertile, no one was listening to a podcast about the latest study, no one combined meadow walking with a prescribed step count. There was no need to fill each hour with a purpose.

Lionel got up as I was dozing off, he had an incredible intuition. Maybe he was born with it, maybe the music made him like that. I didn't need to tell him to boil the kettle, close the bedroom door where mum was sleeping, and bring me ginger tea.

I said thank you but I still had my eyes closed, walking in the meadow, stretching into far, far distances, with no mountains or hills in view. My legs didn't need to climb anywhere to advance forward. The meadow was full of laughter, children's chatter, an abundance of good food. There was no need for me to carry those children to another place, no need to say something clever to their parents, no need to feed or vaccinate them. Pennies fell from the sky, no one needed to pick them up either.

Lionel rocked me in his arms, connecting my slowing heartbeat to his internal adagio rhythm. He waited until I had some sips of the tea, then quietly left the flat. I understood why he was brought into my life. His whole being epitomised classical music, the heavenly art premised on the principle of Love.

Thanks to Lionel, I gradually turned black-and-white keys into colourful songs, and those hues slowly imbued my achromatic days. I began deviating from my strict routines to allocate more time to piano playing. The songs did not disappoint me, they returned as much affection as I dedicated to them. The more I played, the more gorgeousness I got out of the songs. It was a reciprocal process, it adjusted to my fingers, sound and rhythm preferences. It worked like an algorithm, only there was no product expectation at the end: I was under no pressure to add more advanced songs – there was no concert or exam coming up. The only person I performed for was Lionel and he had no expectation of my commitments to a particular song or to our lessons together. It was precisely that freedom that motivated me to expand my repertoire more and more.

I began tagging my days with #LifeIsJustAnExperience, I posted random photos of objects around me, bits of sky, bits of half-finished dinner plates. My selfies got brighter, I posted one publicly, then posted another one. The length of time that any of my fragments existed didn't matter. The length of time I was with Mark was relative to the time Jackie gave to her ephemeral boyfriends. She was selecting them from another repertoire but her strategy was no better than mine. Without the expectation of offspring, we were all just conduits of time fragments.

'To play fluently, you need to place your fingers before the chord comes, so that you don't have gaps in the rhythm. Don't disrupt the flow. You need to have your fingers ready, you know, not play one by one!' Lionel took a tiny sip of water, the bottle was smaller than his hand holding it. He continued in a slightly louder voice, 'When you know the song you can think in advance. You know the whole picture so you can anticipate your moves.'

I knew the song well, it was a piece by Prokofiev, with a vast, dreamy character. Prokofiev determined the melody, I was just the channel to bring it to life. I wanted it to sound fluid from my fingers, but could not bring myself to synchronise my two hands.

'It's not easy, I know!' Lionel's eyes were fixed on the notes, but his fingers moved flawlessly over the keyboard. I could not believe this man was forty years older than me with so much vitality in his hands. 'You need to blend the two hands together and at the same time keep the right hand louder … dominant I mean … right hand carries the melody. You can't carry a melody in both hands at the same time.'

'I get it. I mean I understand the theory. I know I need to prioritise. Right or left, I have just two hands. But I have never been good at prioritising, Lionel, I have always tried to do too much! Be a good academic, a good daughter, a good girlfriend.'

'Place all your five fingers at the same time. It gives you speed, see? That's it, elegance, full sound, lovely!'

I followed Lionel's instructions. First by playing the individual notes, individual fingers on the individual keys, 1–2, 3–4, 5–1. Then the disjointed, sharp sounds began harmonising, my fingers moved simultaneously, multiple thinking commands blended into an experience. I had the melody.

'Well done, girl! You see in this chord it is the same pattern, just a slight variation with the added B.' He marked it in pencil on the sheet. 'And in this part,' Lionel circled the chords with a thin oval, 'here you need to give more voice to the left hand. You see the left hand takes over in this short part. … That's what makes this piece so interesting! After that you carry the melody in your right hand until the end.'

I tried again, put more weight on the left hand, it sounded better. I didn't expect it would make such a difference to the whole piece but it did. I played, further, I varied the weights in my left and right hand, surprising both Lionel and myself with how different the song had become.

'You are a pro now! You are in charge of the melody!' Lionel tapped his finger on his thigh to the rhythm. 'One, two, three, four; one, two, three, four.'

I was in the rhythm again. I needed to keep an eye on the beginnings and ends, but I could be creative in the middle of the difficult parts.

'Now play again, from the beginning.' Lionel leant back on the piano chair, I pulled my sleeves up, took a deep breath, began playing. I recognized the pattern, I was guided by an old musical theme. I was slowly rewiring my brain, note by note.

Chapter 41

'SHE IS A MAESTRO NOW!' Lionel said to my dad as they were lifting the Clavinova onto a truck. Mum was okay with the piano being transported to my flat. She trusted I could live on my own now. She was busy establishing her new identity and welcomed that her friends' visits wouldn't clash with my lessons with Lionel. Dad never understood how Lionel and I could be chums, the age and skin colour difference was beyond his scheme of friendship definition. I wished he were more compassionate. I wished I was that myself, especially towards Aron. *Perhaps he took on the spy job because he was mistreated as a child. Perhaps he desperately needed some money. Perhaps he did not anticipate the implications. Nonsense! People always have a choice and people need to take responsibility for the choices they make. Aron was a narcissist, interested just in his own career and hero image.* One part of me was persuading myself that I needed to forgive Aron and put the memory to rest. Another part of me was telling me I needed to hate him to knock him off the pedestal. There was no in-between, it was either black or white. But with Mark it was different. I neither hated nor loved Mark. His presence in my life was stable and neutral, regardless of his current status. I was no longer checking his updates, nor was I interested in Caitlyn's photos. It was Jackie's text message that alerted me that Mark and Caitlyn had broken up. It surprised me – Mark would not break up with Caitlyn if they had a child together. I wanted to verify Jackie's primary source and rang Mark up.

'Yeah, it's true. Who told you? I thought you stopped following me.'

'Jackie did.'

'You mean Mrs Jacqueline, who trained a macaque to speak like Google Assistant?'

We both laughed.

'Remember Roosti and how we trained him to fetch the slippers?'

'Of course I do! He was so proud when he got the right for the right foot!'

We both sighed. There was a pause.

'I don't know how things are between Caitlyn and you now, but Mark, I am here if you want to talk.'

'Thanks, Kitty. I appreciate it.'

'How … how is the baby?'

'There is no baby. I mean there is. But it's not mine. She lied. I paid for all the tests. I knew there was something wrong.'

'I am so sorry, Mark.'

'What for?'

Silence.

'That it turned out this way.'

'I'm just too handsome, you know, girls get so obsessed with me that they have to cheat on me to get their self-esteem high enough. Body image stuff.'

'Mark, I … I …'

'OK, a bad joke. Don't worry, I'll get over this.'

We hung up, then both began typing a message that neither of us sent. I was disappointed with life, Mark must have felt disappointed with all women. After Caitlyn's lies, after all the investment he made into our relationship. I felt sorry for him, I felt sorry for him so much that I almost wanted to date him again. *Stop it, Katie! You are just about holding yourself together, you don't need a man to pull you apart again! You must play on your own.*

I was telling myself these lines when playing Chopin with Lionel. I wrote them again and again on the clouds I was watching, packaged them in a festive font to persuade myself I received them as a gift to live by. *The best way to avoid disappointment is not to keep hoping. The most optimal survival strategy is to be untouchable by anyone and anything. Passion is expensive, I can invest it into a process that can deliver tangible benefits. Like my work. The trick is to stop asking 'why' and just ask 'how'. The trick is to stop think and just execute tasks.*

Hang on, Katie, you are kidding yourself again. You want to invest into another data collection day, into another paper that puts Valerie higher in the international research ranking? The MPD Centre is the place that pushed you so high that when you fell down you were in pieces. Look at your office, at the empty plastic chairs around you. Are they worthy of the energy that you so painstakingly assembled to survive? You don't even have a private office anymore. You don't belong here. You no longer burn for the MPD Centre, the flame is irreversibly gone. The Katie who believed that the world was a fair place where good work gets rewarded is the Katie of the past.

I quieted the noise in my head by typing loudly but the noise kept on creeping into me. I searched the web for news, then began searching for new jobs. *But which British institution will have me with my medical history? And with a weak reference from Valerie?* I clicked on 'international' and one advert came up: Director of the National Multiple Personality Centre in Stockholm, Sweden. I recognised the name of the Head of Department, he was at a conference where I had presented. The job qualifications and application requirements seemed compatible with my CV. The Centre held a distinct attraction for me, it was well-known nationally and internationally. The deadline for application was tomorrow. I thought of the #NatureLovers photos from Finland that used to flood my Instagram feed every morning. I thought of the Scandinavian work-life balance I had read about in feminist books. I thought of the distance between Sweden and England, and between Sweden and Russia. I thought of the distance between new people and the people I would need to leave behind – Valerie, Jackie, Lana, Mark, my parents. *I must apply!* I spent the evening writing the motivational letter and pulling together a portfolio. I did not feel squeamish about my achievements, I felt I deserved the place, it would be the perfect validation of the work I had done. I submitted three minutes before the portal closed for new applications, exhausted but satisfied that I still had it. I still had the ability to deliver if I felt passionate enough about a goal.

After I clicked 'Send', I got the reply that they would contact shortlisted candidates in three months' time. *Wow, Swedes have a much slower recruitment process than Brits!* But the slowness appealed to me. I was ready for unhurried research that makes a real difference to individuals, not just to the academics carrying it out. I yearned for a slower lifestyle, I hated the fast-paced reality around me.

***

I hadn't heard from Lionel for a month, I was worried whether he was okay. After he didn't answer my fifth call, I rang at his flat door.

'Come in girl, it's so cold outside. You should not be walking alone so late in night. … This is a nasty neighbourhood.'

I pulled the hoodie away from my face, placed the keys and teargas into my purse. I knew they wouldn't protect me against a targeted attack but they gave me enough confidence to walk to Lionel's on my own.

'It's only 5 p.m., Lionel.' I showed Lionel my watch, he never wore one. He used to say that clocks were 'stressful'. His sense of rhythm was excellent, he never missed a metronome beat. He never had an alarm screaming in his ear at 5 a.m., but he could wake up at that hour if he needed to. He set his body to be on time and could manually wind it like a vintage watch.

He offered me some lasagne, the portion size was far too big for my shrunken stomach. I took half of it, Lionel wanted to freeze the rest, but there was not enough space in the freezer, he had to take out a milk cartoon to fit it in. I told him it's not worth freezing cheap groceries and I could bring him some fresh milk tomorrow, but he insisted in pushing the carton back in, mumbling that all groceries are equal in their fundamental worth.

'Did you crumble sage over the cheese?' I had to speak louder, almost shout. Lionel didn't have his hearing aid in, he was not as sensitive to the everyday sounds as before, 'Sage in the lasagne?'

I scraped my fork on the plate, Lionel didn't scrunch. I noticed brittle nails and dark age spots on his hands. 'Sage is a such a fancy herb! It caught me off guard with its peppery taste.'

Lionel didn't smile at my remark, I wondered whether he heard me. I called his name, he turned, his mouth half-open. It looked as if he was smiling but I knew it was just that he forgot to close his mouth, and his muscles were less flexible when he was tired. I looked closer at his face, he had a bogey on his left cheek. I wanted to tell him that, if he went outside with it, people would notice and avoid him. I didn't care about such evanescent flaws, yet I was unable to stop looking at the piece of snot and almost told Lionel to get a tissue. *Why does it bother me so much? Did my mind get corrupted with the algorithmic illusion that the world can be tailored to my expectations all the time? Am I so desperate for comfort and security that a piece of dried mucus prevents me from enjoying the beautiful Liszt sonata Lionel played for me?*

'Franz Liszt dedicated it to Robert Schumann,' Lionel finished playing. 'It's in h-moll. Have you memorised the scales yet?'

'Sorry, not yet. But I know there are two flats in minor!'

'Yes, my girl, but you cannot improvise if you don't know your scales. You need to learn the major scales first, then the minor ones … you can't just jump from scale to scale without knowing the sequence. Think of a story … events need to be put in a sequence to make sense … or as detectives say, events need to be put in a sequence to get to the truth.'

I looked down. 'Sorry.' I had an Excel sheet with the scale names in rows, the sharps and flats in columns, I managed to memorise some but I could not remember the whole string. Lionel took out a big A4 block, began writing the scales on a fresh sheet of paper. The rustling move of his wrist on the page reminded me of Aron's footsteps when I was waiting for him at Trafalgar Square, with the child-like impatience of Santa's arrival. Lionel's hand on the blank page with black notes was atoning for my past, darting back to the three-year-old Katie who believed in the fuzzy mystery surrounding Santa's sleigh. Lionel finished writing the scales, tore the page off, placed it in front of us on the kitchen table. He sighed with exhaustion, said he needed to do his stretching and then take a nap.

He self-designed his own workout, three times stretched the left leg, three times the right leg, twice per day, one time in the morning sunshine, one time in early evening. I watched Lionel go to his bedroom with the stretching mat, glanced at the block on the table. I saw many missing pages in the block, wondered whether Lionel ripped them off to help him remember he had finished writing on them. I packed the hand-written scales, and the half-frozen piece of lasagne. I got home feeling frustrated that I could not change time, that no one could change the natural order of events.

Lionel cancelled two of our following meetings because of doctor appointments. Then he went quiet, so I rang him. He told me that Maryl had died. We had talked so much about death, but when it happened to Maryl, Lionel became completely dis-oriented. He was not sure which day or hour it was, he wore a shirt that he had worn before, with creases and tea stains.

I went to the service with him. The funeral was fully arranged through the dementia support group, but Lionel was still stressing, what if the guests arrive too late, what if they get the date on the funeral programme wrong. He kept on talking about his memories of Maryl, over and over how they met in the small village where she was from, how she shivered when he played her the first song, how little Margaret smiled from the balcony in the first rented house they had together. He was pouring his memories over mine, as if christening a new vessel to bear witness to Maryl's life. The repetition of the best moments in their love story reinforced my memory.

'Maryl taught me that love cannot ever be exhausted. When Margaret died, when Anthony was shot, I thought there was nothing left, you know? But love is infinite. There is always an amount for anyone to take.' I held Lionel's hand as he was talking. 'You understand, my girl? So you will find love again. Big love. Because you are a human and all humans are capable of giving and receiving love. And you have so much love to give with all the music inside you now. Those who give receive, you will too.'

We were walking home from the cemetery, I was trying to ignore that he was pulling me back to Maryl's grave.

'Come, Lionel, it's cold, let me get us a taxi.'

We got to Lionel's flat, he was shivering and asked for a paracetamol and lemon. I made him a pot of hot lemon tea, wrapped him up in a blanket. 'Get better soon.' I wrote a note inside the block for him, then tore the page off, placed it next to the tea.

'Call me anytime. Anytime, okay?' I shouted, Lionel's hearing aid lay on the bedside at the height of his watery eyes. I came closer to the bed, 'Sure you don't want the tea here, in the bedroom?'

'I drank enough today.' I glanced at the travel size bottle of cough syrup next to his hearing aid. I stopped shouting, I whispered close to his ear, 'Get well soon, dear Lionel. Please. Get well soon. In your well-being lies the well-being of many.'

Lionel did not fight, he went peacefully, two weeks after Maryl's death. They said it was his diabetes, I knew it was heartache after Maryl.

I was heartbroken. Mum seemed to be too, although it was difficult to guess with her stone face. All she wrote into the sympathy card was that she 'lost a good friend'. I wrote a personal message, I didn't care who read it:

Meeting people like Lionel does not come about often
in life. He filled a void. He gave me the gift of music.
His departure took my living religion. I miss him dearly.

I looked at Lionel's peaceful face in the photograph behind the glass urn. It was almost a winning look. Aron would have fought for staying. Aron's conquering drive would have mutilated him into an ugly and sick man whom death devours with no mercy. He would have been forced to get fragile and admit defeat. Lionel departed with grace. His goodbye service was a celebration of a human being who always gave more than he had received. The fifty-five fortunate souls who sat at the service clapped and gave a standing ovation when the urn passed down the aisle. We all wished Lionel well on the reunion with his wife, daughter, brother and a long line of wise ancestors.

'I was fortunate to know Lionel for eleven and a half months. He departed at the right time. Like every good pianist, he had an ear for rhythm. His life is synchronised with eternity now. Enjoy the music, Lionel.'

At the end of my speech, I put a little angel statue on top of Lionel's urn and lit a candle. Mark sat in the audience, next to mum, two rows away from dad. It was mum who invited Mark to the service. He met Lionel once or twice, it was clear he came because of me. Mum said Mark had fixed her kitchen drawer, which sounded like anything but Mark. The candle's flame disappeared within seconds, quicker than the short poem I posted into my Instagram story.

Mark offered to walk me home, he was freshly shaved, the gentle puff of his aftershave lingered on his now well-defined cheekbones. It was the first time I saw him wear a shirt that was light green colour and that was only a size X. We walked slowly, spoke very little, mostly about the quality of the funeral services and rain forecast for the following day. Mark gave me a hug in front of my door, politely refused to come in, both of us respecting each other's boundaries. The hug felt nice. Mark's shirt was a bit sweaty on the back and embracing him felt like one big breaststroke in a warm harbour. No butterflies in my stomach pushed me to different heights, just a gentle pull towards the shore. I stood for a while on the grey pavement after he had left, it was me alone with an early autumn rain drizzle. I opened my mouth, let the drops slide down on my tongue, quenching the thirst beginning to hold on my heart.

Chapter 42

I was sitting alone in my flat by the piano when I heard Lionel's voice again. I talked to Lionel often, mostly on my daily walks, watching the swans in the Belsize park. His voice often blended with Aron's, I tried to console myself as one does a baby, talking to myself in first person as we had been recommending to MPD sufferers. I told Lionel about Aron, the whole story, I could share all the details now that Lionel was in a safe space. I felt rounder after I had told him, it was as if I flicked the sharp memories aside and continued my walk on a smooth path. I said to Lionel I wanted to tell him the truth, even though I did not know the truth. I could share only broken pieces of a story that fractured my bioline into dashes and dots.

It was the Easter holiday, half of the Centre was on leave, I received out-of-office replies for 89 per cent of the emails I sent that week. I was horrified of travelling to any country under Russian influence, or any past British colony, or any past-war territory. The safest place was the little radius around my flat. Mum suggested several times going for a walk with me, but I couldn't bear her whining about losing Lionel after losing dad and after almost losing me and after losing her homeland and one of her leather gloves the other day. She didn't seem to understand that I had holes in my soul too, and that, especially in relation to dad and Lionel, we each needed to patch them up on our own, so that we don't drag each other into the darkness. I sometimes rang dad, I was happy he was happy but I refused to know the details, I did not want to add another layer to my reasons for depression.

With my inability to connect to peers and colleagues at work, I began meeting with Aron's angel in the park. His soul had a permanence in the transient world of my other relationships. He was always there, always listening, always responding to my worries and fears with a positive suggestion. He encouraged me to increase my walk from thirty minutes to forty-five, he told me not to stress about what I did or did not write into my application, the Swedes will respond eventually. Aron's guardian spirit was the light that replaced the shadow which his physical presence had left behind. The stable light removed my need for external motivation to keep my daily routines, a reliable survival strategy. Stepping off the work hamster wheel was too risky. I could not risk another bout of depression if I wanted to keep my job and any sense of normality. The thin layer of skin on my right-hand scar was still not thick enough. It had grown a layer, but a little scratch could bleed into my hate towards Aron and the police force. I protected the thin layer as carefully as I protected the gentle, compassionate language spoken by Aron's angel in the park.

Unlike my virtual meetings with Aron, my meetings with Mark were physical. Our intimacy didn't go beyond hugs and the occasional peck on the cheek. Text messages were mostly from Mark, he kept sending me random Covid jokes and memes. I minimized the use of emojis to make it obvious I did not reciprocate his pink hearts. *If I show any sign of affection, he could misinterpret it that I am willing for us to get back together and I am not ready for that. I need to abandon any thoughts of Mark. I need to abandon thought of Aron, he was nothing but a puppet in a corrupt state organisation that was supposed to protect innocent citizens but that instead cleared undercover policeman to abuse academics. I need to remain rational, I need to programme my emotions. Robots survive, humans don't. Survival lies in predictability and systems managing the predictability.*

'It's all on the surface, dig deeper and you will see how rotten the system is!' Lana held a giant unframed canvas with Jackie's portrait.

The picture jarred with the gold Pi symbols on Lana's new office walls. 'More to the left! It should be more to the left!' Jackie instructed her.

'You mean the picture or our Centre?'

Jackie didn't have a chance to respond to my question, but Lana jumped in, 'We need more balance everywhere! But this place, it's all just facades, you know? Like paying the new Diversity Officer double our salary. How can one person fix the Centre's history? The Head of Department is a fucking misogynist, right Katie?'

I raised my eyebrows. 'Hasn't he just promoted you?'

Lana ignored me, continued with her eyes on Jackie's portrait. Jackie was busy scrolling on her phone, with a slightly perverse smile. On her most popular account, she was pretending to be single, on her other accounts she was pretending to date various men and enjoying the attention of new boyfriends and the lingering interest from her exes.

'Or like the SkinBook we must all use.' Lana continued, 'That was also an idea from Valerie's rotten brain. Thanks heavens she left! You know what she did? She thought she could force us to use her alternative social media platform. Can you imagine? The department even paid Valerie's secretary to post some random garden photos to make us feel good and part of one community. Total bullocks! We stopped using the platform the day Mukherjee got the mayor post.'

The portrait was hung up on the wall now, Jackie began filming it for her new Facebook post.

'I bet she wears her OBE medal to all the townhall meetings. She got British citizenship just to be eligible for that. Did you see her new profile photo?' Jackie and I ignored the question, it was only Lana who was following Valerie on Instagram.

'Standing in front of Big Ben in sunglasses. I mean where are we, Disneyland?!' Lana gave the photo a thumbs down using her private account.

'It's depressing, all the double standards in Britain,' I said yawning. 'That's why I applied for the job in Sweden. Swedes are more transparent, less lobbyist.'

'And good-looking! I have 46,900 followers from Sweden, look!' Jackie opened her Instagram dashboard, showed me the geographical breakdown of her fanbase. It was neatly matching the locations targeted by her paid ads, but I did not say that to her. I was ready to leave her and Lana and start new friendships in a new territory.

'If you get the job, I bet you marry a Lars Larsen and leave academia for good!' Lana pulled up her sleeve to reveal some weak biceps.

'Larsens have died off, Lana, which Swedish account do you follow?' Jackie corrected her, 'If you get the job, we'll come to visit you with Mac!' Jackie shortened the lead on her macaque, making him stand still and jump like a yo-yo.

'Has Mac completed the virus checks now?' Lana seemed to have been following Jackie's news much more closely than I was. 'The Swedes could use him to check if Sweden had the new virus variant.'

I turned away from Lana and Jackie, I was in a good mood that day, I didn't want to be reminded of all the rights abuses that begun during Covid19.

Jackie ignored Lana too, she was scrolling down her Swedish follower base. 'Just don't go for thirty-year-old singles. An age match would be a total disaster!' Jackie temporarily abandoned her phone, wound Mac's lead around her finger, deftly coordinated him to stand on his back feet.

'Totally!' Lana stared at Jackie's looping tricks, pushed herself forward to be part of Jackie's filming of Mac's automatic loops.

'Thirty is a golden age for women. You can either downgrade to a twenty-year-old who will do the dishes or a forty-year-old who can buy a proper dishwasher.'

'A shaver will look after kids but he could cheat on you. Go for a wrinkly, he'll change the light bulbs and stuff. Swedes are good at manual work.'

I did not understand the words Jackie and Lana were saying. I saw a wall between us, almost reached out with my hands to check if it was real. We are the same generation; we should have a shared vocabulary. But I experienced the Smooth Revolution lying at Critten rather than in front of Netflix. I was isolated because of Multiple Sclerosis, not a government rule. I was traumatised because I was raped and almost murdered, not because someone negatively commented on my Instagram story. I had voices in my head because the man I loved had been lying to me, not because I wanted to experience alternative realities with opiates. I was experiencing the symptoms of multiple personality disorder because my integrity was mistreated, not because of social media platforms that separate a person into categories.

Mac snatched at his leash, brought me back from my thoughts. One strand of Mac's hair fell out, Jackie put it into a 'life preservation box'. It was filled with Mac's hair and two of his baby teeth. Jackie uploaded a photo of Mac's hair to her gallery, embellished it with a jungle background and the heading Protecting Wildlife – Every Little Bit Helps.

'Katie is very clever. A young one will not catch up with her.' Lana attempted a compliment but I did not reciprocate. I was ready to leave, I impatiently looked through my podcast list and sipped from my energy drink.

'I've had my fair share of British men, I want to date someone from a different culture,' I said and picked up my coat, Jackie took a quick snap of it, added my coat to her collection of vignettes labelled Fashion Explorations.

'Don't be fooled. It's all the same, I'm telling you, I tried women and men. Same shit, different assholes.'

I didn't even put the coat on, I stormed out from Lana's office, heard her shouting after me, 'It's cold out there!'

What do you know, Lana! I have some Russian blood in me, I can cope well with harsh winters. Besides, Swedes know how to dress for cold weather. It is only the expats who wear flip-flops in Stockholm streets, the natives are dressed up like car mechanics, with waterproof overalls defeating rain and wind. I had been live-viewing the Uppsala uni campus every day. I was getting familiar with the local customs and faces. The end of the three-month waiting period was approaching and I was getting more and more anxious that I was not shortlisted. I checked my emails as soon as I left the Centre, there were no new messages.

I jogged to the bus stop, listening to the *Swedish For Beginners* podcast. I tried to focus my eyes on the road, my nose on the essence on my wrist. I was rational about how I engaged my senses. I wished I'd associated Aron with a bakery I could just avoid on my way home, or a platform that I could just quit and delete my data from. But I associated Aron with the whole country where I lived. The memories of our time together delineated a space I was trying to escape. The prospect of moving to another country was my golden ticket to freedom.

Chapter 43

My phone bleeped, an email from Uppsala University.

> Dear Dr Kuznetsov,
>
> Thank you for applying for the position of blah blah blah …

I skipped the long introduction.

> We are delighted to offer you a permanent full-time Professorial position at our Centre. Please could you read through the attached documents and confirm your acceptance by 15 June. We will be sending you information about our relocation package blah blah blah …

I got the job. I got the job!!! I got the full professorship in Sweden! I made it! I am on the top of the academic ladder now! I got the joooob!

'I got the JOB!' I screamed with joy, the guy at the bus stop turned, his fur coat stopping me from spontaneously hugging him. He was wrapped up in fur even though it was 5 degrees Celsius. I came closer to him, he stepped back, the bus stop was too small for maintaining a two-metre distance. I wanted to tell him everything about my new job, but he acted as if he was on his first post-lockdown trip outside, avoiding eye contact and any surfaces.

'I got a job in Sweden!' I screamed, smiling.

He pulled his jacket collar higher up, creating a face mask with the furry collar.

'My work is quite well-known in Sweden!' I wanted to show him the citations, but I thought of the way Jackie boasts about her follower counts and stopped myself.

'Sure, all Brits think they are big in small countries,' the man said.

His accent sounded like a posh royal, I thought the accent had gone extinct with Markle, but this cricket man proudly kept the queen adoration alive. 'Do you have children?'

I would normally spit at the insult but the happy news took over my mouth. I smiled at him and said, 'Not all women are defined by bearing a child. I write books instead.'

'I see.' The man was shivering but he spoke in a confident, classist, conservative voice. He pulled his collar even higher up, revealing only his forehead wrinkles. 'I support women. I read books, I read Plato. Oh, my bus!' He waved at the bus approaching the stop. He said in haste, 'Families are sacred! Books can ruin communities!'

'Yeah and riding bikes ruins female's organs, right?!' I shouted after him in my Pakistani French, wishing I had a bike and didn't have to board the back door of the same bus. I ignored him the whole journey to Belsize, writing down a list of things I needed to arrange before my departure. That man's rotten old mindset was exactly the reason I was leaving Britain. That generation of men went extinct in Scandinavia but still thrives on islands, they believe that hierarchies rule the world. It was that kind of people who instructed Aron to spy on me. *And Aron was part of that mindset. He was nothing but a brick of an old industrial structure, part of a metal cladding that covers up a cheap view. I am worth more than that. I have moved on in my thinking, I have risen above the filthy lawsuits and fights. I don't need to flee Britain,*

I can leave with style. I will not give them a single calorie more of my energy. I will not participate in the police inquiry, I will not sign the petition letter. I will not carry the negative energy with me, I will retaliate the wrongdoing by showing Aron and his superiors my success. I will defeat the enemy with my own weapons. I will defeat them with kindness.

I stormed off the bus, ran home. I opened my flat door, realized there was no one I could tell the news to, no one I could clink my champagne glass with. The empty silence scared me, *I cannot be hiding the second duvet in the bedroom cupboard forever, I cannot be playing the piano just for myself for the rest of my life.*

I sat on my sofa in the quiet flat for a while, then activated my old phone. I dimmed the lights, lit my favourite organic soy candle. I drank a glass of water, took Aconite 30c, breathed in, breathed out, put on Beethoven in the living room. I breathed in, breathed out again, then opened the Gmail account that Aron and I had. I could feel beads of sweat down my spine. I had not opened the inbox for years. The background was the same as on the day when all the emails disappeared. There was only one email sitting in the inbox. It was sent from me to me at 9.21 p.m. on the 14 July 2037, the day I heard *Eroica* in mum's living room and saw Aron's face.

The email had only one sentence: **Never doubt that I loved you.**

I did not remember whether I wrote it down after the angel's appearance. I did not know whether it was me or Aron who wrote that sentence. I did not need to know. I did not need to own that memory to stitch my fragmented self together.

I took a deep breath, marked the email as unread, logged out, switched off the old phone, activated my new one. I texted Mark. He texted back immediately, with a congratulation emoji, then short questions about the job, one word per text message, in his usual style.

Around 4 p.m., Mark texted: **Come over for a drink.**

I knew he would invite me to Lavender, Mark was easy to read. Aron would have offered me random alcohol, and I would have broken my schema and drunk it in a celebration euphoria. Mark offered me my favourite cup of tea, and I was realizing, with every sip, the value of the deep bond one develops over time. I felt an urge to preserve it, sitting in the old flat at our old kitchen table, I was running some quick calculations in my head, feeling as Darwin must have felt when he was unable to apply some basic maths to what he intuitively felt was so important for progress. I knew that love undergirds life but it did not need to define its turnings. I looked into Mark's eyes, I was not pulled to him by a natural force, I was drawn by the quintessentially human desire to connect, to belong.

'But would you really leave Britain? Leave behind everything you have built here for yourself?' Mark opened a beer bottle, poured half of it into a tall glass. He pulled his chair closer to mine, the afternoon sun cut through the window shade, refracted the bright blue wall back to the sky.

I poured tea into the white mug that Mark had sent to my office three weeks ago. He could have sent it to my Belsize address, but he wanted me to have it in my office. The cup had my latest article printed around it. I did not know Mark had paid for two such cups, I was not sure whether it was cheaper to order two instead of one cup, or whether he wanted to read my research every time he sipped his coffee. But sitting there at the kitchen table with him, I was sure that Mark genuinely loved me. And that was my chief criterion for an ideal partner.

'The job is perfect for me, Mark. The Scandinavian values correspond better to my own values. You know we talked about this, how much we dislike the British culture of transactions.'

Mark looked puzzled, I wanted to tell him more, but I could not tell Mark I felt betrayed by Britain because of Aron. I could not tell him I lost any admiration for heroism because of one policeman's actions, I could not tell him I felt ambivalent towards truth because of one lie that sealed my past.

'You know how the whole economy is about transactors, bankers and spies,' I swallowed when I said the last word. I did not know how to tell Mark that I didn't want to work for a country that conceived of 'intelligence' as that demonstrated by the spy scandal. I swallowed again, then said, 'Britain imprisons me. I cannot be free in the afternoons, I had to work 24/7 to keep my position. Sweden has better laws, they support women on top, I can have a LIFE outside of work. I could start some new hobbies …'

Mark was unconvinced. 'Like kayaking or what?'

'I can be a professor and start a family at the same time.'

Mark sat up at that sentence, his eyes filled with small stars. I was fully aware of the value those words carried for him, said by me. I read the magnet quote on the fridge: 'There is only bloodshed on battlefields.' Enough of fighting. I had enough of fighting my childless identity.

'The job opens the door to new possibilities. You know I can be more myself and less the Katie you don't like. The hard-working Katie who neglects couple time.'

'Don't be silly, Kitty. You got the Swedish job because they recognized your past achievements. They appointed you to a position that builds on your previous work. That's why the ladder is called a ladder!' Mark sipped from his beer. 'Had you not been working hard all those years, you would not have got the job.'

'Thanks,' I said faintly, thinking that if I haven't been through the suffering with Aron, I would not be sitting at the kitchen table with Mark in that precise moment, looking at his hands holding mine, forgiving him with my entire body for ever pushing me towards motherhood. Mark folded our hands into an animal shape, made barking dog shadows on the wall. I smiled. I thought of what Lionel told me about shadows and lights being one entity, about what my therapist said about the power of forgiveness.

'When does the job start? When do you leave?' Mark imitated an eagle with his two open palms, the shadow flew away from the wall to the dark corner.

'In three months.'

There was a pause, Mark took another sip from his glass, I took a sip from my cup. The sun was withdrawing from the wall, it shone directly on the lacquered kitchen table, reflecting the dark red cupboards in Mark's face.

'Come with me, Mark.'

The glass in Mark's hand shook. He smiled, finished his beer and wrote to his boss asking whether he could work remotely. That immediate action was very much unlike him, and it excited me.

The sun entered the whole kitchen, the rays reflected back and forth between the shiny surface of the yellowish table, red cupboards and blue walls, submerging us into a kaleidoscopic explosion. The multicolour pieces began circulating around us, they were not spiky, there was no danger of being hurt by any of the fragments. They all belonged to the mosaic of who we were, with and without, each other.